LILLA GLASS

THE UNSEEN

THE REEL OF RHYSIA
BOOK ONE

THE REEL OF RHYSIA
BOOK ONE

THE
UNSEEN

LILLA GLASS

CITY OWL
PRESS

THE UNSEEN
The Reel of Rhysia, Book 1

CITY OWL PRESS
www.cityowlpress.com

Cover Design by MiblArt. All stock photos licensed appropriately.

Edited by Tee Tate.

For information on subsidiary rights, please contact the publisher at info@cityowlpress.com.

Hardback Edition ISBN: 978-1-64898-399-3
Paperback Edition ISBN: 978-1-64898-393-1
Digital Edition ISBN: 978-1-64898-394-8

Printed in the United States of America

*To my husband and best friend, Justin,
for being a constant source of joy in this world,
even when my mind was lost in others.*

AUTHOR'S NOTE

The brightest tales weave through darkness, and The Reel of Rhysia is no exception. It is a coming-of-age story about resilience, sacrifice, and families both lost and found. As such, it contains passages and themes that might strike a dissonant chord in some readers, so I urge you to consult the following list before turning the page.

The Unseen contains depictions of: violence, childhood abuse and neglect, alcohol and substance use, strong language and sexual references, and vague allusions to sexual abuse.

THE UNSEEN

"When listless lyre and tambourine beguile you with their call,
The Faerie Reel of Rhysia may have you in its thrall."

*"Some spirits seek out peril, while others search for peace,
but adventure tends to find us when it's what we want the least."*

CHAPTER I
A QUIET, UNEVENTFUL TOWN

ELWYN

he town of Amblewick was quiet and uneventful. It was not the type of place where things happened; it was not the type of place where people went. This made it the perfect place for Elwyn, who was avoiding things and people.

Her last job had gone awry, and she was not in a business with a large margin of error. So, within the quiet, uneventful town, she walked the quiet, uneventful streets until she came upon what had to be the quietest, most uneventful inn in the history of inns. The sign above the door read *Mr. Elliot's* in a faded burgundy script.

The entryway door was ajar, and the steady rhythm of snores pulsed from beyond the threshold. Elwyn took her time opening it the rest of the way, taking note of the rusty hinges. She tiptoed into the dimly lit room, putting as little pressure as possible on the soles of her padded-leather boots.

A balding man with a Rhysien-red beard lay slumped over the bar, face pressed against the wooden counter. The innkeeper. A ring of skeleton keys hung from his trousers, but Elwyn ignored them, reaching instead for the half-empty bottle beside him.

"A little whiskey makes you glad, a little more will make you mean.
If either manner makes a mess, a little more will wipe it clean."

A simple truth from a complicated friend, but Elwyn was grateful for the reminder. She needed room and board and could ill afford to pay for it. If this man was half the drunk he seemed to be, she would have little trouble conniving her way into his good graces.

The remnants of a fire smoldered in the hearth, and Elwyn's aching limbs sighed at the warmth it offered them. Until that moment, she had not realized how cold she was. Beside the hearth, a small, striped cat lay curled up next to a saucer of cream. Elwyn scooped the saucer up with her free hand, then headed for the stairs with a smile plastered on her weary face. It was a liberating thing, to take what she would, no matter how petty the spoils.

She chose the room furthest from the hearth, as it was the least likely to be occupied. The lock was no trouble at all. They seldom were. The door opened on a musty space, lit only by the moonlight streaming in through a grated window. A soft breeze whistled through it, sending a shiver down Elwyn's spine. She clicked the door shut behind her and set the bottle and the saucer on the floor, freeing her hands to search her satchel for a tinderbox and candle. Crawling things scurried between the wooden wall planks as the space filled with a flickering yellow light.

"I've seen worse," she muttered. The room was hardly smaller than her Greyscale dormitory had been. A lumpy mattress and an overturned crate were the only furnishings. A pillow rested at the mattress head, while a single quilt, which Elwyn could only guess had once been white, was wadded into a pile at its foot. She fanned the quilt out and sat atop it, grateful to have a bed at all. The past two weeks without one had left her with a crick in her neck.

She pulled a rag and some bandages from her bag, then used some of the whiskey to wash her wounds, wincing at the sting of it. After, she ran the damp rag over her blade, restoring its inky luster. She hadn't expected bandits to waylay her on her way through the local woods. But then, those bandits hadn't expected her dagger to burst into violet light and rot their flesh at a touch, so she supposed everyone had been a bit surprised.

Well, almost everyone.

"It would have been worth a day's journey to go *around* the woods," Elwyn said, eyes narrowed to make her irritation clear. This was not the first time Luatha's advice had proven inconvenient. "Did you know we were walking into an ambush?"

A reply, soft and lilting, came instantly.

"I speak the truth, but never plainly. The war you waged, was it not won?
You asked directions, not for safety. Fret not, this was all in good fun!"

Elwyn pointedly ignored Luatha, giving *Gelah* a final inspection. The dagger was as beautiful a sight as ever, its crescent curve and intricate runes unmarred by scrape or scuff. She had named it after the Rhysien word for moon, which was fitting, given the blade's shape and, on occasion, its glow. It had seemed silly at the time, considering Elwyn had never been to Rhysia until now. But then, all Greyscale *icons* were named in Rhysien. The Father had long claimed the language was endowed with power from the Unseen. In *Gelah*'s case, it might actually have been true.

Elwyn turned the dagger over in her palm, hardly feeling the weight of it. After all this time, it was an extension of herself. More than that, it was a friend.

"Perhaps *Gelah* is my only friend," she said, still spiteful at the day's perfectly avoidable misadventure. She tucked the blade beneath her pillow, hilt on the right, as she did nightly.

"If you endured no struggle, you'd most surely go insane.
My blessings may be mixed, but you have no right to complain."

Elwyn chuckled. "That's assuming I'm not already insane."

She knocked back the remaining whiskey. It was raw, cheap, and it burned through her like a wildfire. She had never built up a tolerance for strong drink, considering it the enemy of both perception and precision, but tonight she would not need either. Tonight, she just needed rest, and that was a far more elusive thing.

She set the empty bottle on the ground beside an equally empty saucer. "I'm not the only one who needs help sleeping, I see."

No response.

Elwyn yawned, falling back to the pillow and reaching beneath it to clutch *Gelah*'s hilt. Her body ached, her eyelids drooped, and her resentment was melting away at an alarming rate.

"Goodnight, Luatha," she muttered, knowing the next day would bring a brand new misadventure.

BRANNON

The moon was full and bright. A single cloud, gray and opaque, passed in front of it, cloaking the stately mansions of Ebensburg in evanescent shadow. It was the moment Brannon had been waiting for. He leapt from his rooftop perch into the branches of a nearby elm. The leaves rustled softly, much *too* softly to alert those who guarded the Stanley Estate.

Hardly distinguishable from the night itself, the Greyscale alias *Black* suited Brannon well. He wore leather armor, dyed dark and tailored for fluidity, and he'd pulled his raven locks back into a sleek braid. His jet-black cloak stopped just below his hips, short enough to allow him a full range of movement but long enough to hide the glimmer of the weapons on his belt, *Aras Tosc*, the Serpent Fangs, his *icons*.

His treetop vantage gave a clear visual of the two guards that flanked the Widow Stanley's front door. They were more vigilant than many of the soldiers Brannon had dispatched during his time as an assassin—a residual effect of the commotion his associate had caused the week before—but he relished a challenge.

No matter how fortified noble estates were, they all shared the same weakness—vanity. Manicured shrubs, sprawling shade trees, and decorative statues all made for excellent coverage, providing Brannon a convenient, shadowy path to the front steps. Only once he reached his prey did he step out from hiding, allowing them a split-second of terror before lodging a dagger into the temple of one and stabbing his colleague through the eye. Both died instantly. *Pity*.

Brannon pressed his ear to the door and was not surprised by the silence beyond it. Any sensible person would deem it unnecessary to guard both sides of one entrance. That was why Brannon appreciated sensible people: they were usually wrong.

After working his way through two locks, he found himself in a spacious foyer, painted and tiled in soft pastels. Candlelit sconces blazed in the stairwell ahead, framing the silhouette of another guard in a golden glow. She stood stoically at the end of the hall, facing the servants' entrance with one hand perched on the hilt of her rapier.

Brannon ducked aside to avoid the stream of light, shifting from shadow to shadow like a panther. He was halfway through the hallway when the sentry turned unexpectedly. He pressed his back to the wall, a breath trapped in his lungs. The soldier gave no sign she noticed him, but her gaze lingered for an uncomfortable minute.

Brannon busied himself by reading the awards that hung across from him, tokens from the Widow's many causes: The Hapsford Missionary School, Lady Adeline's Hospice, and so on. Upon spotting a letter of gratitude from St. Aldrich's Orphanage, he nearly laughed aloud. Whatever the Widow had donated to the Father, it had obviously not been enough.

The light squeal of a heel against marble told Brannon that the guard had turned back around. He darted forward, wrapping a hand over her mouth and sliding a blade between her ribs. A thrill swarmed to life at the nape of his neck as her wide, brown eyes rolled back.

Three witless voices echoed down from the second story. Brannon lowered his victim carefully to the floor before following them up two short flights of stairs. He paused behind the corner, stowing his daggers and producing a glass orb, churning charcoal. Using his cape to cover his airways, he leapt into the hall. He hardly registered the guards' positions before the orb shattered on hardwood, cloaking them in swirling smoke.

It took only three steps to find and slay his first foe. The second wheezed loudly, choking on soot, until a swift slice put an end to it. Before Brannon could locate the third, a sharp pain pierced his side. He dropped a dagger, gripped the offending rapier in a gloved hand, and slid his fingers up to its owner's wrist. A sharp twist, and he was rewarded with a wail and a satisfying *snap*. His remaining blade found flesh. The guard fell with a gargled groan.

When the ash finally settled, it served as a funeral shroud.

The Widow's chamber was unlocked, and a soft summer breeze cleared the soot from Brannon's lungs as he entered the room. For a moment, he worried his target had escaped through the open window, but a quick glance dispelled that fear. The Widow Stanley sat upon her bed, still and stoic as granite. Her hair fell in silver ringlets behind her, lending a softness to her silhouette.

"Sorry to wake you," Brannon lied. He seldom allowed a target to sleep through their assassination. He made his way to the foot of her bed. She looked frail close up, a birch-thin frame draped in pink satin. A dainty necklace glinted above her collar, the same silver as her hair. "Aren't you going to call for help?"

"Who's left to answer?" the Widow replied, gray eyes unblinking. "I knew it was only a matter of time before a second attempt. How sad, they sent another child."

Brannon's fingers flexed around his dagger's hilt. He had never been a child.

"I don't suppose you can be reasoned with?" she asked. "That girl—"

His blade was at her throat in a blink, a red bead welling at its tip. "What do you know of her whereabouts?"

The Widow's lips began to tremble, and a smug smile crept across Brannon's face. No matter how strong his prey pretended to be, they always feared death in the end. They always feared *him*.

"Why are you doing this?" she asked, voice shaking.

"You're not really in a position to ask questions, are you?" He sat on the bed beside her, holding the blade steady against her skin. "Truth is, I neither know nor care. You probably think you don't deserve this. I'm sure you stood on your balcony daily, tossing coins to the beggars below. That doesn't mean a thing to me. I'm not a judge. I'm an executioner."

Something like resolve settled in the woman's eyes. It was irritating enough that Brannon considered gouging them out.

"I might as well speak my piece, then," she said. "You're going to kill me, regardless. The Greyscale doesn't leave loose ends."

Brannon cocked his head. Not many people knew of the syndicate that had reared him. Not many should. Luckily, the Widow would not live to spread the word.

"It seems your encounter with Slate has made you bold." He traced her jawline with the dagger. "I assure you, I am not so—"

"Was that her name?" the Widow asked. "Slate?"

Brannon clenched his teeth. Blood pooled beneath the tip of the blade. "It's not polite to *interrupt*."

Slate was not his colleague's name any more than his was Black, though Brannon far preferred his alias to his given name. But that was not the point of this conversation. In addition to cleaning up that girl's mess, he'd been tasked with returning her to the Greyscale. Given her skill set, he could use even the feeblest lead.

"You're going to tell me all you know about my colleague."

The Widow sighed—a defiant act, considering her predicament. "I know she was hardly more than a child, just like you," she said. "What kind of a monster turns children into criminals?"

"Careful," Brannon said, jaw flexing.

"Must be a sick bastard to run such an enterprise."

"*Careful...*"

The blade quivered.

"Only a horrid, perverse serpent would—"

Brannon ripped his dagger sharply to the right. A fine red mist sprayed into the air around him. He sighed, dabbing his face with his cape, and pushed the Widow's body back to her pillow.

"Don't talk about my Father that way."

"You cannot buy security, gold offers no relief,
The treasures that you hoard are merely beacons for a thief."

CHAPTER 2
THE HOUSE ON THE HILL
ELWYN

lwyn's dreams were dark, disturbing things, but she was in no rush to leave them. Her body remembered the wounds her mind had forgotten, and it was determined to cling to slumber for as long as it could. Unfortunately, that did nothing to mute the din of clattering pans and stomping feet that rose through the floorboards, dragging her into daylight.

Her rustic surroundings blinked into focus, and she jolted from the mattress with a curse on her tongue. Pinpricks of pain—souvenirs from the previous night's skirmish—skittered through her the moment her toes hit the floor. Intent though she was to ignore her wounds, she managed to brush each one as she wriggled from her shredded leather armor and slipped into her gauzy gray sanctuary frock. Though she'd always hated the impractical gown, its modest cut would hide her bruises well.

Deeming her outfit a smidge too clean, she donned her wool cloak overtop it, wincing at the pressure it placed on her aching shoulders. She tied her hair back and tucked it beneath the hood, leaving one dark lock free to cover the scar on her left cheekbone, which stretched in a crescent from her eyebrow nearly to her jaw. She had no reason to be vain but every reason to be inconspicuous, and grisly scars were among the features people tended to remember.

Having no mirror with which to judge her appearance, she asked a second opinion. "Do I look pathetic enough, or should I add a smidge of soot?"

"A fresh new day, a fresh new place, and you still look like you,

But never fear, the best of lies contain a bit of truth," sang Luatha.

"And in the best of truths, a few lies," Elwyn replied, strapping *Gelah* to her thigh. She bid Luatha to stay put before leaving the room, knowing good and well such edicts meant nothing to her friend.

Her first instinct was to tiptoe downstairs, but, for once, stealth would not suit her purposes. This in mind, she forced her feet flat and plodded down the steps, leaning against the railing as heavily as her slight frame allowed. For all her effort, not a single eye flitted her way. Not that there were many to draw.

The dining area boasted only six small tables, five of which were empty. An elderly woman sat at the one nearest the open window, watching pigeons peck at the cracks in the cobblestones until a passing carriage startled them away. Two more patrons sat at the bar—a couple, though the woman's flowing satin gown and the man's simple charcoal jacket screamed of economic disparity. Elwyn placed them in their early twenties, hardly older than herself. Based on the woman's accent, they too were from Pondrelle, though her clothing and dialect spoke to a far more privileged upbringing than Elwyn's own. The innkeeper stood in the kitchen beyond the counter, toiling above a brick stove. Somehow, he looked disgruntled even from behind.

Elwyn cleared her throat in a last attempt to draw attention but was not surprised when it failed. She was a remarkably unremarkable person. The gazes of others slid from her like water on oil, and her words passed by their ears like mist. Most days, she counted it a blessing, but at times like this it proved inconvenient.

Using her unremarkability to her advantage, she slipped across the room and into the kitchen. The innkeeper did not even raise an eyebrow when she plucked the kettle from the rack and swiped a tin of Rhysien Summer Blend from the shelf beside him.

She adopted the air of a chipper rural barmaid as she approached counter. "Refill?"

Unsurprisingly, the couple ignored her, continuing their conversation as though they were the only ones in the room.

"I simply cannot wait for the Midsummer Festival," said the woman. "After weeks of humdrum village life, it is about time that we experience true Rhysien culture."

"This *is* Rhysien culture, my dear Silva," the man replied. "The festival is more about the traditions of their ancestors than anything. They don't actually believe in the Unseen any more than you or I believe in the devils the church dribbles on about."

They should, Elwyn thought, though she doubted any of the locals had ever met someone like Luatha.

"Refill?" she asked again, louder.

Finally, she caught their attention. The man looked confused, as most were when Elwyn "suddenly" appeared. The woman literally turned her nose up as she scanned Elwyn's threadbare cloak.

"Yes," she said eventually, flicking a finger toward the tea tin. "But not of *that*. Pondrellen Petal Blend if you would."

Elwyn spun swiftly, lest they see her eye-roll, and nearly bumped right into the innkeeper. Apparently, she'd finally gotten his attention. From the way he loomed over her, burly arms crossed, he found the surprise unpleasant.

"Who the hell'r you?"

He had the thickest Rhysien accent Elwyn had ever heard—all trills and watercolor consonants. It startled her enough that she nearly forgot her plan.

"I asked you a question, gal."

"You forgot already?" Elwyn swept past him to rummage through the shelves. Though her muscles ached with every movement, she hid it for the sake of the ruse. "I'll admit it was unprofessional to wake late for my first day on the job, but as we discussed last night, my journey here was none too kind. Where do we keep the Pondrellen Petal Blend?"

"I don't remember hiring anyone." The innkeeper scratched his ruddy beard. "Least of all some mainland gal."

You probably don't remember your middle name. Elwyn perched her hands on her hips, huffing. "And to think I agreed to work for room and board."

At that, his bushy brows raised. "Now, that does sound like a deal I'd make." He squinted at her for a few awkward seconds. "Ah, what the hell. I suppose it won't hurt anything. You can stay, but only until the festival passes—I ain't running no charity!"

Rhysia's Midsummer Festival was roughly a week away, and it lasted for two. Elwyn could easily sneak enough coins to move on by then.

"Thank you," she said, dipping into a curtsy.

"Well, get to work then." The innkeeper threw a thumb toward the grimy kitchen. "I ain't not paying you to stand around!"

Elwyn was no stranger to labor, but the day's chores worked muscles she'd never worked before. Before the sun finally set behind the thatched Amblewick rooftops, each of those newfound muscles begged for rest. A strange breed of pride swelled in her chest as she glanced around the much-improved inn, admiring the polished woodwork and spotless maple countertops. Content with her efforts so far, she grabbed a bucket and sponge from beside the washbasin, resolved to check the last box off her list: scrubbing a decade worth of soot and grime from the front of the building itself.

She was approaching the front door when the cat scrambled across her path, meowing madly, patches of fur missing from its tail and ears. It leapt, claws first, into the lap of the innkeeper, Mr. Elliot, who'd fallen asleep hearth-side hours before. He shot up from his chair with a string of ale-slurred curses, slinging the cat to the floor.

"*Luatha!*" Elwyn hissed.

Her tiny friend hovered in the corner, just beyond the cat's reach, tufts of yellow fur peeking from her indigo claws. Mr. Elliot scanned the room several times without spotting her. Unsurprising. Perhaps that's why Elwyn had bonded so closely with the creature. They were both invisible to nearly everyone.

She had to force a cough before the innkeeper finally noticed her.

"Oh," he said. "I nearly forgot about you, gal."

"I get that a lot, sir."

Mr. Elliot's chest puffed out at the word "sir," and he offered a curt nod. He marched around the dining area, his back suddenly arrow-straight, and ran a finger over several surfaces. "Not bad," he said, inspecting his fingertip for grime. "For a Pondrellen, anyway. Say, what was your name again?"

The best lies contain a hint of truth... "El." It was the closest she'd come to speaking her birth name in a decade.

"Well, El." The innkeeper plucked a spare sponge from the basin. "I suppose I'll help you with the shopfront this once, as it's a big job and you got a late start. Come tomorrow, you're on your own."

Elwyn gleefully accepted the offer. Together they made quick work of the storefront... despite Luatha's best attempts to smudge the wall behind them. The task would have been wordless had Elwyn not noticed the white house on a nearby hilltop, three stories tall and fenced in wrought iron. It would have looked humble among the loftier manors of the mainland. Amidst Amblewick's thatch-roofed cottages, it glimmered like gold in a pile of pebbles.

She couldn't help asking about it.

"Belongs to the Devlins." Mr. Elliot practically growled the name. "Landlords to most of the town, and right arseholes about it. Pondrellens, of course—no offense meant." He shook his head, suddenly somber. "I suppose the revolution didn't change much in the end, for all it cost us. Were it not for their wee gal, I'd launch a revolt, but I'm not one for leaving orphans."

He tossed his sponge into the bucket, splashing Elwyn with dirty water. She took it as a sign to call it a day.

As she fell asleep that night, her thoughts drifted back to Devlin Manor. She wondered about the height of its gates and the strength of its locks. She wondered what treasures hid within its walls. Mostly, she wondered how lovely it might have been to have grown up in a place like that.

LYDIA

Lydia Devlin ought to have been reading. That is what her mother had asked of her hours before, and she was nothing if not obedient. Only it was hard to focus on letters and illustrations when her parents were fighting down the hall. Especially when they were fighting about her.

"You are being ridiculous!" her mother said, voice muted by plaster and paneled wainscoting. "Hasn't our Lydia gone through enough already?"

"That is not *our* Lydia," her father barked back. "I'm not even sure it's a little girl."

Lydia wiped a tear away before it had a chance to fall, missing the days when her father had called her darling or poppet. She would never grow accustomed to being called *it*, though she supposed anything was better than Monster, which was what most everyone had taken to calling her after Maid Katrin started the trend.

"Honestly, Tallehan," came another of her mother's shouts. "You're starting to sound like a Rhysien, for all this superstition!"

Lydia hummed a lullaby as she walked to her window, putting as much distance as possible between her ears and the argument. The sun was only a sliver on the horizon and the lamps in her room blared bright, so she saw more of herself than the outdoors. Even after all these months, her reflection was foreign, a ghostly parody of the girl she'd once been. People had once claimed she was a spitting image of her mother, blessed with the same rosy cheeks, emerald eyes, and yellow curls.

She lifted a limp lock of cream-colored hair and sighed, narrowing lavender eyes at her reflection. The doctors had dismissed her condition as a rare form of anemia. When they'd instructed her parents to keep her indoors and feed her lots of spinach, she'd thought it the worst punishment possible. She'd been wrong. Despite the treatments, she'd grown paler, frailer, and terrible nightmares had slithered into her sleep. Her father now believed her ailment reflected something insidious, and his cold regard for her had infected nearly the entire household.

Lydia jumped when the door swung suddenly open, and Maid Katrin's shrewish scowl appeared in the reflection behind her.

"Time for supper, little Monster," the maid said, stomping into the room and grabbing Lydia by the arm, sharp nails biting through lace. She released her a moment later when Lydia's mother appeared in the doorway. The women locked eyes for a tense moment before Katrin excused herself with a stiff curtsy. Only once she'd vanished from view did Lydia's mother crack a smile—sincere, despite her swollen, rheumy eyes.

"Good evening, Blossom."

Much better than Monster. Lydia returned the greeting with a tight embrace, and the aroma of her mother's gown helped to sooth her spirit.

Her mother adored lavender, so nearly anything in Devlin Manor that could smell of it did—clothing, candles, soups, perfumes... somehow, even the floorboards gave off the faintest of floral scents.

"Let's have a look at you," her mother said, tucking a pale lock behind Lydia's ear. "Much better. Now everyone will see your pretty face."

Lydia smiled, though she had not been pretty for some time. When her mother grabbed her hand and started toward the staircase, she followed without protest, though her heart sank deeper with every step. Dinnertimes were never particularly pleasant—not anymore—but business dinners were the worst of all, especially when the Devlins hosted Lady Yana.

"Now, don't be so glum," her mother said in too-chipper a voice. "The cook made your favorite, honeyed pheasant."

Lydia slowed her gait. She would not be bribed.

"We must be good hosts to all of your father's associates." Her mother chided her. "Even ..."

Even the terrifying ones, Lydia mused. In fact, "terrifying" might not have done Yana justice. The rigid woman was gaunt as a silver birch with ghost-white skin and hair to match. She had eyes like violet embers, lips like withered vines, and cheekbones that could double as knives. Her mannerisms were known by some, like Lydia's mother, as unladylike. Lydia simply called it *unpersonlike*. And all of that she could have overlooked were it not for one particularly haunting trait: Lady Yana could float.

Lydia had no evidence, of course. Yana's long, layered gowns always pooled on the floor around her, and she never had reason to show her feet. Still, even when walking on marble or hardwood, Lady Yana lacked something important—footsteps. No one else seemed to notice or care, not even when Lydia pointed it out. Which she had. Several times.

Lydia covered her nose with her sleeve, inhaling deeply. The lavender scent was fainter on her own dress than her mother's, but it still helped a little.

Noticing the gesture, her mother tensed. "You will not have one of your fits tonight," she whispered.

Lydia hoped that was true. If only she had a say in the matter.

The hearth dining room blazed bright, and the smell of firewood mingled with those of honey and spice, driving the lavender from Lydia's nostrils and causing her stomach to rumble. *Perhaps I can be bribed, after all...*

Trays of Rhysien appetizers spanned the length of the table, which had been cloaked with the family's finest crimson runner and set with candlelit centerpieces. Honeyed breads slathered in berry jam intermingled with plates of bacon-browned cabbage and potatoes stuffed with cheese and garden greens. Lydia's parents preferred Pondrellen dishes, but they often catered to the tastes of guests. It was the one aspect of hosting suppers Lydia appreciated.

"Riona," her father said, as his wife and daughter approached the table. He sat at the end, as per Pondrellen tradition, scribbling hastily in a ledger.

Lydia's mother returned his greeting as warmly as ever, taking the seat at his right. Lydia would not have believed they'd just been arguing, had she not heard it herself.

As the only, and therefore oldest, child of the Devlin family, Lydia ought to have sat to her father's left. It was one tradition he'd recently decided to eschew. She sat beside her mother instead, folding her hands over her empty stomach and staring longingly at the food. She would not be permitted a single bite before Yana arrived.

Lydia flinched at a knock on the door, and again when Maid Katrin appeared, escorting the evening's guest. Lady Yana looked intimidating as ever. Her snowy locks were braided into a tight, spiraled crown, and strings of obsidian dripped from her ears and neck like pitch. Her fog-gray gown was equal parts matronly and fashionable, buttoned with pearls from chin to waist, where it flared out like a fountain. Conveniently cloaking her toes.

When Katrin tried to help lift her trailing skirt, Yana swatted her away. "If I could not manage walking in a gown, I would make the switch to trousers," she snapped, her voice thin as wind whistling between branches.

Katrin mumbled an apology, face flushing bright as her pumpkin hair. As she escorted Lady Yana to her seat, her heels *clackity-clacked* against the tiles. Lady Yana's did not.

"Welcome back to the Devlin Estate." Lydia's father rose and bowed to his guest. "I trust your journey was kind."

"Tal," Yana replied simply. Though it was an uncomfortably informal address—even Lydia's mother called him Tallehan—there was no warmth in it.

If Lydia's mother was offended, she hid it well, rising to curtsy with a cordial smile. "Greetings, Lady Yana."

"You look well, Riona." Lady Yana took the seat to Tallehan's left. Lydia's seat. Before Lydia could wipe the scowl from her face, the woman's eerie violet eyes turned her way. "You've grown."

Lydia nodded, uncertain whether the statement warranted a verbal response.

"Not the eloquence I would expect, given your birth." Lady Yana looked to Lydia's father. "Has no one been attending her studies?"

His answer was a grimace. Lydia had frightened off more than a few tutors in recent months. If her ghastly appearance was not enough to disturb them, her tantrums usually did the trick. It was becoming increasingly difficult to find a local who didn't look on her with fear or disdain, let alone a local with adequate teaching experience.

"Well then, I suppose my arrival is serendipitous." Yana clasped her hands on the table, ignoring the food entirely. "With one arrangement ending, it is fitting we should strike up another."

Tallehan's face reddened. "I have given you more than enough."

"Indeed. I always get what I am owed." A wry smile slithered across Yana's lips. "I am not suggesting another business contract, but a guardianship. I've stumbled upon many a charming institution in my travels. One, in particular, would suit young Lydia perfectly."

Lydia looked to her mother for help, finding Riona's face had paled to match her own. "Our daughter's not ready for—"

"Actually," Tallehan interrupted, "I've recently been considering just that."

Lydia fiddled with her hair, lacking the words to voice her concerns. Her father had always derided parents who sent their children off before age thirteen, and she was still a few weeks from turning ten. *His mind changed when I did.*

The realization had consequences beyond the predictable heartache. For the first time in weeks, she heard the whispers. They were too soft and slurred to understand, but they still sent a shiver through her.

She brought her sleeve to her nose, desperate to silence them.

Breathe in...two...three...

"We appreciate the offer, but no," Riona said. "There's still much to discuss."

"The time for discussion has passed, Riona," Tallehan replied.

The scent of lavender did nothing to dispel the whispers, nor did it help to dull the lilac haze now playing in Lydia's periphery. The fog seeped slowly through the room, growing denser as the whispers rose. She knew no one else could see it. They never did.

Breathe out...two...three...

"I understand it is short notice," Lady Yana said, "but this offer will not last forever. If you agree tonight, it will give you a few days to pre—"

"I'm not going anywhere with you!" Lydia shouted, leaping to her feet through no choice of her own. "And you can stop talking about me like I'm not even here!"

Her anger spread to everything in reach. Gravy spattered, porcelain cracked, candlelight caught to the crimson runner. She could see her father ranting and raving, but the whispers drowned his demands, not that she'd have heeded them. Her skin had turned to ice and her vision to violet flame.

All the lavender in the world could not have calmed her.

"Some shelters offer solace as darkness offers sleep,
But those places make promises they don't intend to keep."

CHAPTER 3

SANCTUARIES

ELWYN

fter a week in Amblewick, Elwyn had settled into a daily routine—less dangerous than her former one, but no less arduous. She'd traded her combat training for common chores, her treacherous associates for entitled patrons, and her perilous missions for the most mundane of errands. Oddly enough, she found she actually enjoyed the errands, especially when they brought her to the Tamond family butchery.

"Can you take care of that cobweb in the corner?" Elwyn asked Luatha, scanning the inn one final time before heading out. "You must have overlooked it earlier."

Her friend obliged. Reluctantly.

"My kindred make most mortals cower, but you are such a bore,
You would use my ancient power to assist with tiresome chores."

"Precisely." Elwyn locked the door behind them and hung Mr. Elliott's, *I'll be back when I feel like it*, sign from the knob. "And when we return, you can use your ancient power to help prepare dinner."

Luatha grumbled indiscernibly, crossing spindly arms. Elwyn fought a laugh. When she was younger, she'd been terrified of angering Luatha, having read that the Unseen were shadowy tricksters with malevolent intentions. In the decade since, she'd come to believe the rumors were highly exaggerated. Luatha was shadowy, and she was most certainly a trickster. But malevolent?

"I'd wager we could wreck the inn and leave a ruin behind,
And that man would return so drunk he wouldn't even mind."

Elwyn shook her head. *Maybe a little malevolent.*

Over the past week, the town had become far less quiet and uneventful as the townsfolk buzzed with excitement over the looming Midsummer Festival. Most of the villagers had wreathed their homes in floral garlands, strung paper lanterns from their eaves, and hung tiny satchels of candied fruit in the trees, all to honor and appease the Unseen. Luatha paid little mind to the flowers and lanterns, though she made quick work of a few satchels.

While Elwyn had come to resent the rigid religion enforced by the Pondrellen Church, having long been subjected to the worst of its hypocrisy, she found the Rhysien folk-faith quite charming. Technically, the Pondrellens and Rhysiens worshipped the same Creator, but the Pondrellens had long ago dismissed tales of otherworldly watchers as regressive superstition. The Rhysiens no longer put much faith in the old stories either, but they at least kept up a pretense. Luatha, for her part, didn't seem to care about intentions, so long as the results were caramelized, glazed, or rolled in sugar.

As the scenery transformed, so did the faces. Merchants from the mainland had already begun to arrive, hoping to set their carts up near the town square before the rush. While it was unlikely that a Greyscale agent had slipped in among them, Elwyn pulled her hood up and made herself small. One could never be too cautious.

Much like Mr. Elliot's Inn, Tamond's butchery had managed to avoid the festival fervor. The garlands and streamers that adorned the surrounding buildings made its weathered siding and patchwork roofing look that much sadder. Flies buzzed around the string of sausage links draped around door in lieu of a sign. Were it a true sign, it would have probably read something like, "Eat at your own risk."

The shop's interior looked just as unappealing as the outside, with one notable exception. Davin Tamond was a few years Elwyn's senior, and the local girls fawned openly over his broad shoulders and shamrock eyes. Though Elwyn hardly noticed those features, he seemed amiable enough.

He was also the first boy she'd ever met who would not literally stab her in the back, given a chance, and that held a certain appeal.

She lowered her hood as the door clicked shut behind her, checking to make certain her scar was covered before greeting the butcher boy with a simple, "Good day, Davin."

He jumped, scattering the coins he'd been counting across the counter. "Oh! I din't hear you enter, um..." He scratched his head, mussing short, copper locks. "Sorry. Have we met?"

Elwyn deflated. This was the fourth time she had introduced herself in as many days. "It's El, remember? From the inn."

He blinked his glassy eyes.

"Never mind." Elwyn sighed, pulling a few copper pias from her pocket. "I'd like to purchase whatever's cheapest."

Apparently, that one took. Davin added Elwyn's coins to those he'd been counting and scooped them into his apron pocket before vanishing into the back room.

Luatha quirked her head, alighting on Elwyn's shoulder.

"It seems a curse that mortal-kind puts so much stock in sight.
The guilty hide in shadows while the shadows long for light."

"It's more my forgettability than his forgetfulness," Elwyn muttered, shrugging it off. "Besides, it's not like we'll be staying here much longer. No need to form attachments."

Davin returned seconds later, handing her a bloody canvas sack that he claimed was filled with chicken scraps. "Have a nice day...um..."

"El!" she snapped. *How hard is it to remember one syllable?*

She was contemplating tying the dolt's bootstrings together when she noticed Luatha doing that very thing. She smiled, making a mental note to pilfer a treat for her friend before returning to the inn, and turned to leave. Before she could open the door, it swung open, and in came the Pondrellen couple from the inn—Silva and Rayen, as Elwyn had come to learn.

"Fancy seeing you here, El!" Silva said, only noticing Elwyn after bumping into her.

"And to think, I'd wanted to pass this shop by!"

Elwyn stifled a scowl. The noblewoman was easily the most loquacious person she'd ever had the displeasure of meeting, and, for lack of more fashionable options, she'd begun to think of Elwyn as suitable company. Elwyn disagreed.

"Rayen and I finally decided to explore the town," Silva explained, releasing Elwyn's arm in favor of her husband's. "Would you care to join us for what remains? I've been meaning to visit the quaint little tailor shop over by the local sanctuary. Perhaps you can find something there that isn't so...drab."

Even if sanctuaries didn't chill Elwyn to the marrow, she'd have declined the offer. She had little interest in clothing, least of all the kinds of clothing that Silva wore. Surely, there was a specific subset of madness associated with marching around rural villages in ball gowns, silk gloves, and capelets.

No one else seemed to question Silva's wardrobe, least of all Davin Tamond. Despite Rayen's presence, the butcher boy's eyes widened on the pretty Pondrellen socialite, and his jaw went predictably lax.

"C-can I help you with anything, miss?" he asked, scrambling forward. His knotted laces caused him to stumble, but he managed to catch himself on the counter. Everyone present burst into laughter, save for Elwyn, who was a bit too bitter to appreciate the fumble. She instead slipped her hand into Davin's apron pocket, stealing her coins back, with interest, before slinking out into the street.

Unfortunately, Silva followed after her.

"You fancy him, don't you?" The noblewoman whispered, falling into step beside Elwyn.

"You've got a vivid imagination."

"I believe you," Silva said in a tone that told Elwyn she didn't. "At any rate, it is refreshing to see you out and about. I was beginning to think you were some kind of phantom, cursed to haunt that dingy old inn for eternity."

"Careful," Elwyn said. "That kind of superstition might get you confused with a native Rhysien."

"We intend to make a home here." Silva shrugged. "Might as well adopt the culture. Speaking of, have you tried much Rhysien cuisine? Rayen and I intend to stop for lunch soon. Surely, you'll partake?"

"Busy." Elwyn held up the bag of (probably) chicken as evidence, then melted into the passing crowd before Silva could argue further.

Elwyn had expected to return to an empty inn, given she'd locked the place down, which is why she was startled to find a stranger sitting at the bar, a full pint of amber in hand. The moment she saw him, she dropped the bloody bag she'd been holding and reached reflexively for *Gelah*. Somehow, she stopped herself from drawing the dagger. There was no reason to reveal it quite yet.

"Can I help you?" she asked, kicking the door shut behind her.

He tipped his wide-brimmed, crimson hat—a gesture that put Elwyn on edge, despite the man's innocuous appearance. His polished black shoes dangled feet above the floorboards, and he was comically wide for his height. The buttons and tails of his mottled ruby suit might have been fashionable, in a different place at a different time.

"Can I help you?" Elwyn repeated, fingers twitching above her dagger's hilt.

"Actually, I think you can," he replied, a twinkle in his summer green eyes, "*Slate.*"

A blink, and *Gelah's* curve was pressed to his throat.

"Should've chosen my words with more caution." He raised an open palm, slowly extending it. "Name's Blithely. Blithely Fox."

Elwyn narrowed her eyes. "No. It isn't."

The man took a gulp of ale, showing a sudden, alarming disinterest in the dagger. "It's a great name, though, ain't it? Came up with it m'self."

Her grip on the dagger tightened, but Luatha advised caution.

"Mince words before you mince his flesh. Impatience just won't do.
If this odd stranger dies too soon, his secrets will die too."

Elwyn did not want to kill anyone, but she would do what she needed to survive. It would not have been the first time. "Are you working with the Greyscale?" she asked.

Blithely shook his head—carefully, so as not to slit his own throat—and sighed as though he expected better. His breath smelled of carrion.

"I'm a friend," he said. "That is, if you're willing to gamble."

Elwyn wasn't. She put pressure on the blade, not enough to draw blood, but enough to make a point.

"You got me all wrong, lass!" Blithely chuckled, setting his drink aside. "You think you know stuff that you don't, and you know a great deal you haven't learned yet."

"What the hell is that supposed to mean?"

"It means I'm not here to hurt you." His smile spread like molasses. "I'm here to hire you."

BRANNON

Saint Aldrich's Sanctuary was a mountainous mass of mortar, wrought iron, and stained glass that twisted skyward in a forest of arches and steeples. Gargoyles perched along the upper reaches, membranous wings outstretched, having been sculpted ages back as superstitious means of warding off devils. In Brannon's estimation, they were shit at their job. They'd done nothing to keep *him* away.

Though he was far from religious, he'd always admired the sanctuary itself. The grim artistry of the exterior served to remind rebel souls of the fate that awaited them in the afterlife, should they disregard the wise words of Father Beaus. Fear was easily the most potent method for manipulating the masses. The garish gallery of murals and stained glass that wound throughout the interior served as a second manipulation, the promise of respite for the faithful, once they'd freed their final, pitiful breath. Should a sound beating fail to tame an unruly child, the promise of a reward would surely suffice.

Brannon slipped through chambers both bleak and beautiful until he reached the inner sanctum, where he slipped into the back-most pew. No one seemed to notice his arrival. Having traded his dark leather for the drab linens of the working class, he was just another derelict wandering in late from a hard morning's work.

Father Beaus stood serenely in the sanctum alcove, clad in the stark white robes and gilded hood of his calling. Candlelight twinkled across precious stones as he raised his gilded shepherd's crook to commence the closing prayer. The parishioners bowed their heads, but Brannon kept alert, watching as a mousy boy toted a collection box from pew to pew. To the unwitting, he was just another of Saint Aldrich's many orphans. Brannon knew him as Ghost, the Greyscale's youngest agent.

The Father's voice cut across the room like a dagger through flesh.

"May His divine hand raise the worthy and smite the wicked,
Lest an unpruned vine bear withered fruit.

May His divine eyes turn away from our sin and linger on our righteousness.
Lest we reap the full of what we've sown.
May His divine ears hear our prayers and ignore our curses.
Lest the evil we wish others revisit us tenfold.
May His divine heart make room for each of us.
That we may hope beyond the moment."

The parishioners foolishly believed each word, but Brannon was not alone in his cynicism. The Father himself, though regarded far and wide as an exemplary cleric of the Holy Pondrellen Church, preferred to practice more ancient rites in private. And not the benign ones, either. Brannon had no idea how Father Beaus had first been drawn to the darker aspects of the Rhysien folk-faith, but he had to admit, curses and hexes sounded a lot more interesting than prayers and supplications, if no more effective.

The prayer ended right as the collection box reached Brannon, already brimming with copper pias. He dropped the Widow Stanley's silver chain into the cache, signaling to the father that he had finished his job.

Part of it, anyway.

The assassination had been simple as ever, but he'd failed to catch even a whiff of Slate's whereabouts. He could only hope his feats overshadowed his flaws. Dreading the alternative, he glanced back at the two hulking figures beside the sanctum entrance, men the congregation knew as Divines Carmine and Alder. To Brannon, they were Granite and Coal. The Greyscale enforcers were not lithe enough to be thieves, deft enough to be assassins, or subtle enough to be spies, but they were more than cruel enough to take on the syndicate's more brutish business, such as collecting overdue payments, interrogating unwilling informants, and correcting undisciplined agents.

When Granite returned the stare with a wink, Brannon shuddered, knowing he now counted among the undisciplined. He sunk into the pew, fixing his eyes forward, and spent the remainder of the service scripting excuses that would not help him any.

Granite and Coal flanked Brannon as he waited outside Father Beaus' study. They'd dropped their pious facades the moment they stepped into the catacombs beneath the sanctuary, and they'd since been doing their best to forecast the future. For the last five minutes, Granite had been droning on about his latest innovation, which involved live mealworms and dissonant music. His counterpart took a more subtle approach, standing silently, save for the occasional crack of his knuckles.

There was little Brannon hated more than feeling helpless, which is what he was. While he could easily have bested both burly associates in a fair fight, the consequences of winning would have proven far worse than losing. The Father did not look kindly upon any who challenged his order.

Soon enough, the door swung open, and a man in a dapper suit stepped into the hall. He paused to tip his top hat at the agents, avoiding eye-contact.

"Thank you, again, for your generous donation," Father Beaus called after him, "*Governor* Copland."

The man grinned over his shoulder. "When I claim my new station, I will remember who put me there."

"I was only performing my civic duty." Beaus chuckled softly. "Can you imagine a woman running a district as important as Ebensburg, and a widow no less?"

So, that's my most recent sponsor. A hollow opened in Brannon's gut as he watched the man stroll away, a half-hearted spring in his step. Agents weren't usually permitted to glimpse their patrons. Things ran smoother that way. Brannon hoped the exception had been made in light of his loyalty, but he doubted it.

When Beaus bid his children enter, the enforcers grabbed Brannon by the shoulders and marched him into the study—a misnomer, in many ways. While the overstuffed bookshelves, jarred organs, and framed maps lent the space an academic air, the bloodstained altar mounted sideways on the far wall detracted heavily from the scholarly atmosphere.

Brannon half-expected the enforcers to shackle him to the stone slab straightaway, and he was only mildly relieved when they sat him across from the Father. Unwilling to meet his mentor's gaze, he stared down at the whorls in the oaken desk.

"My son," Father Beaus said. "Why are you frightened of me? Am I not a good shepherd to my flock?"

Brannon took a deep breath and forced his gaze upward. The Father's soft smile brought him no comfort. "You are, Father."

"I am glad to hear it. It is a blessing to be held in high esteem by one's flock, especially the exceptional among them." Beaus reached into the pocket of his robe, producing the widow's silver chain and offering it to Brannon. "It took you less than a week to clean up Slate's mess, and half that time was lost to travel. Hard work deserves a reward."

Brannon dipped his head, folding his hands in his lap. "I couldn't possibly."

"Pity." Beaus tucked the necklace away, his smile vanishing. "The promise of a reward is one of two excellent motivators."

Brannon's jaw flexed. "I do not lack for motivation."

"Which brings us to the other matter..."

The enforcers grabbed a shoulder apiece, yanking Brannon back to his feet. He smothered the instinct to break free and slay them both. For the moment, he was but a mouse wrapped in a falcon's talons. Prey.

What hope did he have, but to grovel?

"Father, please. I—"

Beaus held up a palm, and Brannon fell silent. He used his staff as a walking cane to rise and hobble around the desk. "Sorry though you may well be, it is important to accept responsibility for one's shortcomings," he said, settling before Brannon. "I am not exempt. Clearly, I made a mistake in sending a thief to do an assassin's job. I thought I saw something in Slate, the potential for branching out, for becoming ... more." He shook his head, sighing. "Perhaps I made a second mistake in sending you to retrieve her."

"I can fix this," Brannon growled, his throat gin-dry. "Give me another chance."

"You've always been one of my favorites, Black." The Father caressed Brannon's cheek with the cold crook of his staff. "Because of that, I must hold you to a higher standard. Any vine that produces withered fruit must be pruned..."

He raised his staff level with Brannon's temple and swung.

"The next time you are spellbound, keep one small thing in mind,
One can be both enchanting and exceedingly unkind."

CHARMED, I'M SURE

ELWYN

 mblewick was silent after sunset, with one exception: the Spriggan.

The pub was known for low stakes gambling and cheap, watery ale. A carnival of sensory distractions, it was the perfect place to hold a clandestine meeting, provided one could navigate the throng without drawing scrutiny.

Elwyn approached her destination with *Gelah* strapped to her thigh, coins hidden in her boots, and Luatha fluttering at her side. She did not know what to expect from this Blithely fellow, but she was prepared for anything. The moment she crossed the threshold, she was smothered by a cloud of tobacco smoke, raucous laughter, and the warring odors of fried food and piss. She searched the haze for only a moment before Blithely's voice cut through the din.

"There you are, Slate!" he called from a back booth. "I was starting to worry."

Elwyn slid onto the bench opposite his, scanning their surroundings for possible eavesdroppers. "Don't call me that," she whispered.

"Phooey!" Blithely spat. "Ain't no one here gonna know the name."

He was wearing the same stupid hat, stupid suit, and stupid grin as he had been when they met that morning, and the pint glass beside him was already empty, save a few flecks of foam.

"Well?" Elwyn asked, eager to get the conversation over with. "You asked me to meet you here. Mind explaining why?"

"Not a patient person, are you?" Blithely raised a bushy brow. "Business is best discussed over drinks. I s'pose that's something the ol' syndicate wouldn't teach you."

A barmaid appeared as though summoned, her Rhysien-red ringlets covering more skin than her tunic. She set a platter with a pint of ale, a cup of coffee, and a boat of cream on the table between Elwyn and Blithely.

"Thank you kindly, love." Blithely pulled a gold mór from his pocket and handed it to the woman, who smiled and touched his shoulder before walking away.

"I think she likes me." Blithely slid the coffee mug across the table to Elwyn, then set the cream to her left, conveniently close to where Luatha had landed.

Elwyn's pulse quickened. *Can he…?*

"Figured I'd set it out of the way," he explained. "In case you're not a cream person."

Elwyn exhaled, her shoulders relaxing. She had grown used to the fact that no one else could see Luatha and had no clue how she'd react were that to suddenly change.

"I'm not a coffee person, either." Elwyn shoved the mug back toward Blithely, splashing a bit of the beverage onto the already-sticky tabletop. "And I don't care whether business is best discussed over drinks. I find that it is best discussed when it is actually discussed. You have five minutes."

Blithely smiled his tight-lipped smile. "Impatience ain't a promising attribute in an employee."

"Three."

"Fine!" Blithely threw his hands up. "At least you're focused, which *is* a promising attribute." He beckoned for Elwyn to lean in closer. She held her breath and obliged. "You know the house on the hill?" he whispered. "The big, snooty one, surrounded by hedges and other frilly shit?"

"Devlin Manor." Elwyn's curiosity piqued. "What about it?"

Blithely leaned back against the bench, much to Elwyn's relief, and downed his entire drink. "The Devlins have something what's rightly mine," he said, wiping the foam from his lips. "Or it will be, in roundabout two weeks. Thing is, I need to get ahold of it a little early, and they aren't likely to hand it over willingly, so—"

"So, you want me to steal it for you."

"In so many words."

Elwyn smiled reflexively. She'd been tempted to pay Devlin Manor a visit on her own volition. If she could get paid for it, all the better.

"Anyone can start anew in word, in works, in wit.
Your past can't truly follow you unless you follow it."

A compelling counterpoint.

"What exactly is it you're after?" Elwyn asked.

Blithely's grin stretched so thin that his beard swallowed it. "Now, if I told you before you agree to the job, what's to keep you from taking it for yourself?"

He was smarter than he appeared. Which frankly wasn't difficult.

"A general idea, then." Elwyn straightened, crossing her arms. "I'm not about to accept only to find you expect me to pluck a man's gold tooth out while he sleeps."

"You could do it, I'd wager."

"Yes. But I don't want to."

Blithely laughed, and Elwyn stifled a gag. "You wouldn't believe me if I told you."

"Try me."

This time, when Blithely leaned forward, Elwyn refused to follow suit. She couldn't stand much more of the man's breath, and nothing quite weakened a person's stance in a negotiation like fainting.

"You're familiar with the Unseen, right?" he asked. "More specifically, the Unseelie?"

Luatha startled at the word, her shadow wings furling.

"Unseelie bring the Shadows to drown the Seelie light,
While Solitaries, much like me, hide safely from the fight."

"Dark fae." Elwyn kept her voice flat despite being utterly intrigued. "The evil counterpart to the Seelie Court."

"An over-simple, dualistic answer, but sure." Blithely shrugged. "Anyhow, let's just call my target an Unseelie charm."

Of all the thieves he could have sought out, Elwyn was most likely to get tangled in that particular yarn. Somehow, he must have known as much.

"Why the rush?" she asked, eyes narrowed. "If you had to wait a week or so more for this ... *trinket*, would it really hurt you?"

"Not your business."

"It quite literally is."

"Knowing is my business. Doing is yours." He produced another gold mór and slid it to the center of the table. "So, whatcha' say? You in?"

Elwyn was compelled in part by the mystery and in part by the coin and the promise of more. However, a third, more cautious part of her had snagged on Luatha's rhyme. *My past can't follow me unless I follow it ...*

Stealing from one of the only affluent families in Rhysia was sure to draw attention, and not from the Rhysiens alone. There wasn't an offer in the world tempting enough to make Elwyn risk revealing her location to the Greyscale. For whatever reason, she was not quite ready to leave Amblewick behind.

She folded her hands in her lap, conveniently close to *Gelah*. "I'm afraid you've come to the wrong person."

"Disappointing." Blithely smiled—not the jovial, tight-lipped grin he'd been wearing throughout the evening, but a threatening sneer that flashed rows of jagged yellow fangs.

Then he vanished.

Elwyn lurched to her feet, nearly knocking over a passerby, not that they noticed or cared. Heart pounding in her throat, she scanned the tobacco haze, trying to convince herself she hadn't seen what she'd just seen. Unable to locate Blithely's red hat among the patrons, she glanced again at the coin he'd left behind. It had disappeared, as well. In its place, sat a biscuit.

When the barmaid sauntered past, Elwyn grabbed her by the sleeve. "Did you see where that man went?" she asked, frantic.

The woman ripped her arm free, fixing her with a bewildered scowl. "What are you yammering about?"

"The man in the red hat." Elwyn waved toward the empty booth. "He was right there only a moment ago."

The barmaid blinked. "I'm...I'm sorry," she said, shaking her head like she'd just woken up. "Has anyone helped seat you yet?"

LYDIA

Meals in the Devlin manor were few and far between, at least for Lydia. She'd been sequestered in her room ever since the previous week's disastrous dinner, and she'd only been granted a few bowls of oats in that time. She wasn't certain if starvation was part of her punishment or if the maids had simply forgotten to feed her. Either way, the rumbling in her stomach had grown louder than the little voice in her head that told her to stay put. Inevitably, it coaxed her from her room.

She paused as her bedroom door closed behind her, both to listen for footsteps and to decide upon a destination. The kitchen was always bustling with staff, any one of whom would tattle in a heartbeat. Thankfully, it was not Lydia's only option for securing a snack.

If her father were home, she'd have never risked entering his study, but his carriage had jostled away hours before, and it had yet to return. She'd be safe so long as she was swift.

She opened the study door to immediate disappointment. Of all the rooms in Devlin Manor, it had long been her favorite, and the evenings she'd spent there—reading hearthside while her father balanced his ledgers—made for warm and cozy memories. This room was a ghost of that one, cold and dark and reeking of stale tobacco. The sight gave her pause for only a second before her belly growled, reminding her of the mission.

As always, a tin of chocolates sat upon her father's desk, though it was now flanked by an empty glass and a bottle of something dark. Short for her years, Lydia had to climb onto his high-backed chair to reach it. The lid popped off as easily as ever, revealing a treasure trove of chocolate turtles and nonpareils. Lydia filled her pockets swiftly, eager to scurry back to her room, but the books stacked on the desk caught her attention.

The tomes bore little resemblance to the almanacs and histories her father horded. These were older and of a different make, and the names on the spines struck a dissonant chord. *The Daoine Maithe and other Seelie*, *The Unseen*, *Rhysien Reels*... all references to local legend and rural superstitions. Such findings would not have been odd, considering the village they lived in, except Lydia's father had always loathed Rhysien culture. To hear him tell it, he would have stayed in Pondrelle, were it not for his business with Lady Yana.

Lydia pulled a book at random from the stack and began leafing backward through its pages. The writing was comprised of strange markings—old Rhysien letters, most likely—and the chapter titles were curious: *Sylph, Sprite, Sluagh, Selkie, Pooka, Piskie, Nixie, Marrow, Lenanshee, Kelpie...*

Even more compelling were the illustrations of strange beings, rendered in watercolor and charcoal. Many were lovely, like the *Glaistig*—a milk-pale woman with ruby eyes and hair. She was dancing in a starlit glade, and hooves peeked from the hem of her flowing green gown. Others were haunting, like the *Korrid*—a sliver-thin creature with glassy eyes and talons. It was surrounded by a legion of headless soldiers, each mounted on a coal-black horse. None looked like the pretty piskies that flitted about Lydia's folk story collections.

One page, entitled *Irli*, had been marked with a red ribbon. It featured an infantile creature with glowing red eyes and jagged fangs, and a wall of dense text. Her father's handwriting translated several underlined words: *harvest, shadow, iron,* and *cleanse.*

He'd scribbled a full paragraph in the margin.

"The swap happens shortly after birth and requires the consent of at least one parent, though few agree knowingly. While the age of manifestation varies, the transformation is marked by changes in appearance, behavior, and temperament."

On the next page, the word *glamour* had been circled. Another note was scrawled beneath it: *"No Pondrellen equivalent. According to Elias Hanrick's Almanac of the Arcane: any kind of magic which alters the refractive quality of light, so as to distort or conceal ..."*

Heavy bootsteps approached from down the hall.

Lydia slammed the book shut and leapt to the floor, trailing chocolates. As she reached for the door, it burst open, and her father's rage-red face glared down at her.

"What are you doing in here?"

Before Lydia could answer, he grabbed her hair and hurled her into the nearest bookshelf. Encyclopedias rained down around her, but her fear numbed much of the pain and stole the sound from her scream.

As her father lumbered toward her, she found her voice. "Father, please. I—"

A slap across the face sent her sprawling.

Lydia had read about creatures that played dead, and she'd always thought them terribly clever. Now, with her limbs frozen despite her racing pulse, she wondered whether they had any say in the matter. As she lay there, helpless, a familiar violet haze crept into her vision. Whispers rose in the back of her mind, writhing like nightcrawlers in morning mist.

Her father's brown boots stomped into view. "Don't you ever snoop through my things!" His voice cut through the clamor. "You hear me, Monster?"

"Tallehan?" A blur of yellow and lilac appeared in the doorway behind him. "W-what are you doing?"

"What needs to be done."

His arms wrapped around Lydia's waist, lifting her from the floor. Her limbs sprung suddenly back to life, panic fueling a flurry of kicks and scratches. Her feet swung fecklessly through the air, and her flimsy nails cracked on starched fabric. She bit down, hard, leaving a crimson crescent on his crisp, white sleeve.

Her father swore, dropping her to the floor. Her vision flared violet. The whispers swelled to the storm. At last, she could discern the words, though she had no clue what they meant.

"*Aetri en Sca,*" they hissed, over and over. They called to something deep inside her. Something dreadful.

"She's a monster, Riona!" Her father barked. "I can prove it!"

Something metallic scraped against bricks. Fingers twined in Lydia's hair, yanking her to her knees. A fire-stoke pressed against her collarbone.

Cold iron should not have burned her, but it did. Badly. A white-hot pain welled beneath the metal, rippling through her in searing waves. Empty acid climbed her throat, stifling her screams.

The agony was strong enough to eclipse all thoughts but one: "*Aetri en Sca.*"

The pain grew deeper. The whispers grew louder. The haze grew brighter,

Then it all gave way to silence...

To darkness...

To peace.

Moonlight streamed through the open window as a soft summer breeze turned the curtains to dancing ghosts. Fear and pain were distant memories. Now, Lydia felt

nothing at all, and it was a profound relief.

She could not have explained why, if asked, she felt the need to slip out from beneath her covers, to wander from her bedroom. Something about the silence beyond the threshold called to her, and she could not imagine it meant her any harm.

The halls were as empty as they sounded, lit only by whatever glow managed to seep between the curtains. Lydia paid no mind to the yellow eyes that blinked out from the darkness. They had always been there, hadn't they? Yes, Lydia was certain shadows were best known for blinking, for breathing, for inching slowly forward as she passed them by.

The staircase spiraled downward far longer than she remembered, and the carpet that climbed the steps was warmer, wetter. If she squinted, she could see some manner of mess strewn about the foyer below, she could not discern its nature for the distance and the darkness. Only once her slippered soles touched marble did the corpses come into focus. They were twisted and torn, mangled and marred, but their faces had been preserved, frozen in perfect terror. Maid Katrin. Chef Kyrell. Ren, the stable boy. Lydia felt nothing for them. Even when she stumbled over her father's broken body, the only emotion she could conjure was relief.

Then, she saw her, draped atop a morbid heap of limbs, her white lace gown and golden curls cascading down the gore. Broken ribs jutted from her chest like the trunks of barren trees, hedging a hollow void.

"Mother?"

Something pulsed between Lydia's fingers, veiny and slick. She glanced down at the throbbing heart, stumbled back, and—

—jolted upright, casting her blankets aside.

Pain skittered across her collarbone, stirred by her sudden movement. She pressed her palm to her chest, and the rough scratch of bandages reminded her what true terror was. She took a deep, lavender breath and listened to the cricket chorus that chirped beyond her windowsill. Soon, she'd relaxed enough to ease against her pillows. When she rolled to one side, removing pressure from her wound, a glimmer caught her eye.

A tiny, silver box had been placed atop her nightstand. A note stuck out from beneath it, penned on fragrant floral stationary.

My little Blossom,

I know things have been hard lately. I wish I had the power to make them easier. Though you will be leaving with Yana soon, you will always be here in my heart, and I hope I've secured a place in yours. I know this isn't much, but I pray it brings a smile to your beautiful face.

Love eternally,
Your Mother

Her mother had gone daft if she believed some silly present would make up for all that had happened. Lydia nearly threw the box in a fit of rage, but the part of her that was still a child could not resist opening it.

A knotted medallion, glinting with gemstones, winked at her from a nest of lilac velvet. Her mother had purchased it at a Midsummer Festival the year before, and Lydia had always admired it. Just glimpsing it reminded her of the joy she'd felt, sitting on her mother's shoulders as she danced in the village square. The glow from the torches and paper lanterns had caught the jewels from all angles, refracting shards of color through the air around them that twinkled and flickered like Faerie light.

Lydia darted to the window and held the medallion to the moonlight. Shards of red, amber, and violet burst to life around it, sparkling softly against the gloom.

In her mind, Lydia knew it was only a trick of light. But her heart could still believe that it was magic.

*"Just tell yourself that you've gone off in search of better things,
A puppet never thinks to ask who really pulls the strings."*

CHAPTER 5
MORBID MARIONETTES
ELWYN

lwyn had always considered boredom as a blessing, treasuring the rare moments of peace and stillness in her otherwise chaotic life. Now, she was learning what it meant to be *truly* bored, and she did not care for it.

"Tulips are hardly fit for a garland," Silva said, pouting. "Surely you have orchids hidden somewhere."

"I've told you ten times, you daft woman!" the Widow Morgan snapped. "The orchids sold out weeks back. Now buy something or leave me be!"

After days of ceaseless begging, Silva had not only convinced Mr. Elliot to let her decorate the inn for the Midsummer Festival, but that she required an assistant and Elwyn was perfect for the job. Elwyn hadn't put up much of a fight, assuming the task would be simple and swift. She'd never been so wrong.

There was only one florist in Amblewick, and they'd been at her shop for nearly an hour, but Silva had yet to approve of a single damned flower. Apparently, daisies, primroses, and cornflowers were all too subtle for festival décor. She wasn't going to let up until some orchids or frillroses magically materialized.

"Whatcha think about asters?" the Widow offered.

"Asters?" Silva scoffed. "Surely, you can't be serious! What will your next suggestion be? Dandelions? Buttercups? Shall we eschew the definition of 'flower' altogether and scrape together some brambles?"

The widow's wares had been pretty well picked through, but Elwyn busied herself with perusing what remained, all the while wishing she was in a weapon shop. She'd never seen the appeal of flowers and was absolutely flummoxed by the idea that a bundle of smelly leaves could sell at the same price as a decent pair of dirks. Near absently, she plucked up a pot of dark purple blossoms, their stems bristling with long red needles.

"Careful not to prick yourself!" the Widow shouted her way. "Plumpetals are right poisonous. Farmers plant them to keep vermin away."

"And they're hideous," Silva added, threading her arms across her bust. "Unlike orchids."

"You're a loon," the Widow said, and they were at it again.

Elwyn set the pot back where she'd found it, and one of the blossoms leapt suddenly from the stem, whirring toward her face. She startled back, stifling a gasp. Luatha burst into chittering laughter, looping through the air on wings that mimicked the flower's hue.

"I suppose that's what I get for letting my guard down." Elwyn laughed along, a sense of nostalgia sweeping over her. Luatha had played that same exact prank when they'd first met.

"Did I miss something funny?" Silva asked, hefting a coil of garish mauve blossoms over to Elwyn.

"I was just remembering a joke," Elwyn said.

"Do tell."

"It's more of an inside joke."

"Ah, so you do have other friends. You'll simply have to introduce me."

"Other...friends?"

Luatha had not missed it either. She grumbled jealously, though she had no cause for worry. Elwyn still wasn't certain what she thought of Silva, but *friend* did not seem like the correct term. Perhaps *friendly acquaintance*. Granted, Elwyn probably couldn't have identified a mortal friend if she made one. The ever-unsettling Dove was the only other girl who had survived long in the Greyscale, and Elwyn had learned early on that her male counterparts were not to be trusted.

As they left the shop, Silva transferred the flowers to Elwyn's arms. They were surprisingly heavy.

"I thought she was out of orchids..."

"She was, but I convinced her to sell me the garland from her own eave." Silva ran slender fingers over the plants like she was petting them. "One rope won't be nearly enough, I'm afraid, but we can always make more. I spotted wild primroses out past Lester's Mill a day back."

"I thought you said that primroses were too subtle for festival décor."

"Yes," Silva said, "but that was when I wanted orchids. Now that I have them, I want primroses."

Elwyn shook her head, bewildered. "You're unbelievable."

"I know." Silva wrapped an arm around Elwyn's. "I'm also uncanny, unforgettable, and a great many other 'un' words that I cannot recall at the moment but are certain to reveal themselves over the course of our friendship."

"Unstable?" Elwyn asked, and they both laughed.

Luatha did not.

Strangers stared in the direction of the women as they walked back toward the inn. Elwyn found the attention incredibly unwelcome, though it was not meant for her. Silva was not only the kind of person who drew admiration, she fed off it. Her chin jutted a little higher with every "G'day, miss," and "Don't you look lovely?" tossed her way. Elwyn half-feared that the woman's head would float right off her shoulders, but she somehow made it home in one piece.

As Elwyn reached to open the door, Davin Tamond burst through it. His eyes immediately flitted to Silva, and he greeted her with a tip of his cap, his cheeks flushing bright beneath a smattering of freckles.

"Just dropped off an extra order of beef," he explained, throwing a thumb toward the kitchen. "Seems Mr. Elliot's caught the Midsummer spirit."

"That probably concerns El more than it does me," Silva said. "She's the one who cooks."

"Who?"

Elwyn rolled her eyes and shoved into the inn, pushing Davin into the street. Silva followed after, shutting the door in the butcher boy's face.

"I knew it!" she whispered, giggling. "You *do* fancy him!"

"Less each day."

BRANNON

Brannon held his pocket watch gingerly between bruised fingers, watching the hands tick—one steady, one staggering. Aside from his clothing, it was all the Enforcers had left with him when they'd tossed him into the cell. Though practically useless for keeping time, that arrhythmic ticking had lulled him to sleep for years. Today, it couldn't even accomplish that.

The skin where Brannon's fingernails used to be stung bitterly as he tucked the watch back into his pocket. It was a lost cause, anyway. Even if he could discern the hour, he had no idea the length of his sentence. More than one agent had withered away in the Greyscale dungeons, their offenses forgotten, but never forgiven.

Bereft of options, Brannon inhaled deeply, closed his eyes, and slammed his knuckles into the wall. He repeated the process until both the bricks and his knuckles were red, all the while screaming a deluge of profanity. He was midway through a particularly artful phrase when a feather-soft melody drifted down the hall.

"Madam Madelina, mad as she can be,
You can find her swinging from a hollow tree,
All the pretty piskies, on the count of three,
You can take the rest but save the best for me."

Dove, the Greyscale's most peculiar agent by far, twirled into view like a cherry blossom.

"Lord Len Laeretty letched himself at me,
Took it on myself to sweeten up his tea.
Used a special sugar, and us girls were free,
All the ladies ask me for my recipe."

She came to a stop in front of Brannon's cell, the pink frills of her dress settling against her thighs and her cedar ringlets, wound with rose ribbons, still springing. The candlelight cast by the lantern she carried caught on the sliver-thin decanter she wore around her neck—a bauble she called *Cuileann*. Brannon had always thought it bold of her to wear her *icon* so openly, even if poison was a coward's weapon.

She curtsied, seafoam eyes glittering. "Look, Madam Madelina!" she said to no one in particular. "Lady Pumpernickel has arrived."

Brannon grabbed the bars with bloodied hands. "This is no time to play, Dove," he hissed. "I need you to do something for me."

Dove pouted, crossing her arms and huffing like a child. She twirled once more, then began to drift away.

Fuck. "Wait!" Brannon pled. "I'll play later."

"Really?" Dove whirled back around, pressing her face to the bars.

Brannon shied back as subtly as possible, so as not to offend her. Dove had a way of disarming most everyone. Though Brannon had always been an exception to the rule, he could appreciate her talent.

"Yes, really," he lied. "But first, I need your help."

"With finishing your sailor song?"

"What? That wasn't a—it doesn't matter. I need you to convince the Father to let me out of here."

"No can do." Dove fluttered her eyelashes.

"Why not?" Brannon balled his fists, resisting the urge to reach through the bars and wring Dove's pretty little neck. He leaned in close and whispered, "What would it cost?"

"No, silly!" Dove kissed the tip of his nose, then jumped back, giggling in an altogether upsetting manner. "I can't convince someone of something they're already convinced of. It wouldn't be sporting. He asked me to call you to the study." She pulled a key from her collar and slid it into the lock. Then, mocking the Father's voice, she added, "No dallying!"

Brannon trudged through the catacombs as though weights had been chained to his ankles, slowing him and sapping his strength. As he climbed the last of many staircases, a rat scurried from the shadows. He brought his boot down hard, and the creature squealed its last. Brannon felt chains snapping, a heavy weight fleeing him.

It was so much better to be the predator than the prey.

He paused before the study door, jarred by the agonized wails that spilled across the threshold. *Busy week for the enforcers...*

With effort, he shrugged off his worries. If Granite and Coal's latest project was still capable of screaming, they had plenty of work ahead of them. Brannon would be spared for at least that long.

He knocked on the door five times, pausing between the last two, as he'd been taught.

"You may enter," came Father Beaus' command.

Brannon obeyed without hesitation, snicking the door closed behind him. His eyes darted to the altar, where a young thief called Sable had been shackled by his wrists and ankles, his bare skin mottled blue and plum. Blood dripped from his toes onto a chalk map that had been scrawled across the concrete floor.

The enforcers stood casually to either side of the altar, the tools of their trade in hand. Father Beaus idled further back, thumbing through a tome as though business was usual. Which perhaps it was.

"Ah, Black, you arrived just in time." The priest tucked his tome back into the shelf, grabbing the gilded cane that had been leaning beside him. "This is something I'd like for you to see."

Brannon fought a flinch as Granite's flail lashed across Sable's chest, slicing open a series of crimson gashes. The *cracks* cut through the room like thunder. Red trickled from the thief's lips as he cried out.

Father Beaus drifted toward the altar, carefully skirting the chalk sketch. The drawing was detailed, for something so ephemeral, spanning from the mountains of Muldrain to the islands that littered the Western Sea.

"Much like you, Sable was among my favorites," the priest explained. "I have given him more than he could have possibly wanted—a warm bed, three meals a day, an apprenticeship in a highly selective field. How unfortunate, that he's chosen to repay my kindness with treachery. Is that not so, Sable?"

The boy whimpered pitifully.

"That is not an answer." The Father nodded to Coal, who pulled a cudgel from the rack behind him.

Sable's rheumy eyes widened. "I b-bet-betrayed you."

"Yes, you did. As a Greyscale thief, you were tasked with procuring that which society denied you, but those things were not yours to keep. Were they?"

"I-I'm sorry Fa—"

"You are, but that does not answer my question." The Father slammed his staff into Sable's fingers. The *snaps* were so loud they eclipsed the boy's screams. "This grieves me, you must know." He slid the crook down Sable's cheek and used it to lift his chin. "I saw you as my own child, and I treated you as such."

"I-I'm so sorry. L-let me f-f-fix things."

"Perhaps that would have been possible, had this meeting gone better. But I have little use for a thief with broken fingers." He glanced behind him. "Ghost!"

Brannon nearly jumped from his skin when the little agent appeared beside him, holding a twisted dagger. *Where the fuck did he come from?*

Sable blanched. "No! P-p-please release me. I'll do anything."

The Father smiled warmly, taking the knife from Ghost. "Of course I will release you, my child."

A slash, and blood and viscera spilled to the floor. Sable lurched against the stone, still lucid, his lips gaping around a silent scream.

As the Father passed the knife back to Ghost, his attention returned to Brannon. "I cannot hold you fully responsible for Slate's absence," he said, eerily calm. "She has a gift for going unnoticed that only a scrying spell can truly subvert. Ideally, this will aid you in your final attempt to locate her."

Bile pooled on Brannon's tongue. *Final?*

Father Beaus held his staff toward the intestines, muttering something Brannon couldn't understand, and they began to convulse. They unfurled slowly, much to the horror of the agent to whom they were still attached, smearing chalk as they slithered across the concrete. They detached with a sickening *snap*, and Sable breathed his last.

The intestines outlived their host by only a few seconds, just long enough to curl around a corner of the map. Brannon held his breath, inching forward to read the results. In the center of the bloody circle lay the island nation of Rhysia.

"There's value in a vision, but be careful what you spend,
A wish tossed in a well can never be fished out again."

CHAPTER 6
CHANGING FORTUNES
LYDIA

ydia held her necklace out the window for perhaps the hundredth time, stretching to catch the sun's final rays. Flecks of green and gold glittered in the air around her, filling her heart with a whimsy she'd thought long dead. The colors changed as the skies darkened, and new lights flickered to life in the distance—paper lanterns, strung through town in preparation for Midsummer.

Having lived in Rhysia her whole life, Lydia had never missed a festival. It filled her with sorrow to know she'd be missing this one. She stared listlessly out at the village, lost in memories of fiddles and fried food, until a creak in the hallway sent her scurrying back to bed.

She pulled the covers up, intent on pretending she'd just woken, and the wound beneath the bandages flared bright. Ever since the iron incident, Lydia's mother had been delivering meals herself in an effort to keep the maids from mistreating her. She would have scolded Lydia for ambling about when she was meant to be resting.

The door groaned open, but it was not her mother who entered. Lydia almost didn't recognize Katrin in the dark. The maid had traded her uniform for common clothes and allowed her pumpkin locks to fall loose to her waist, but there was no mistaking that scowl.

"You shouldn't be here," Lydia whispered. "Mother will be upset."

Katrin smiled, closing the door behind her a little too carefully. Lydia's pulse thrummed an alarm. The maid wasn't there to read her a bedtime story.

Before she could cry out, Katrin lunged. One calloused hand wrapped over Lydia's mouth, the other gripped her injured shoulder, squeezing tight. A muffled cry rose in Lydia's throat. The maid grabbed hold of her necklace and twisted, cutting it short.

"The Master had the right idea with the iron," Katrin hissed. "He just didn't have the guts to finish the job."

Though Lydia clawed and squirmed and struggled, the chain only twisted more tightly. Soon, her lungs began to burn, and the strength leeched from her limbs. She slumped, wide-eyed, against her pillow, as the pain morphed into a melancholy chill. Katrin continued taunting her, but Lydia could not hear it. The whispers in her mind left no room for other voices.

Aetri en Sca.

The room dimmed, blurred, drowned beneath a violet fog.

Aetri en Sca.

A flash of brilliance filled the room. When it faded, Lydia saw the world with a new, twisted clarity. Her walls cracked and peeled, bleeding like chapped skin. Yellow eyes, gleaming with hunger, blinked out from the fissures. The ceiling had vanished altogether, replaced by a charcoal tumult. Her blankets were now a bed of rotting leaves.

Katrin, too, had shed her skin, morphing into a withered demon. Her gown cascaded in crimson, dripping down her legs to paint the leaves a striking scarlet. Lydia met her gaze, and her milky eyes flexed wide. She gasped, clasping the necklace in both hands and twisting one final time.

It did not bother Lydia. Her lungs no longer needed air. She smiled up at the demon Katrin, savoring the fear in her cold, dead eyes.

"*Aetri en Sca!*"

A hundred voices writhed from Lydia's throat at once, and she pushed Katrin away with all the tremendous strength she possessed.

Lydia sipped her tepid tea, wishing she had something more to say. Detective Mannon seemed like a pleasant person. His mustache curled at the ends in a way that would normally have made her smile, and he'd brought her a blanket and drink after introducing himself—kind gestures, albeit unhelpful. Even with the warm ceramic trembling in her palms, she could hardly feel her fingertips.

"I'm s-sorry." Lydia forced the words through chattering teeth. "My mind is fuzzy."

The detective grinned, his mustache twisting into tight spirals. "That's likely for the best," he said. "Amnesia's not uncommon in cases like these. Children your age aren't supposed to witness this sort of thing."

Lydia nodded, though she wasn't sure what sort of thing she'd supposedly witnessed. Even her current location was a mystery, though the musty air and the stiff cot she sat upon implied that she'd been moved to one of the servant's quarters.

"Try one last time for me," the detective said. "Can you recall anything at all from this evening?"

Lydia shook her head. "Nothing from when I was awake."

"Now, what do you mean by that?"

"I had a nightmare." Lydia couldn't recall the exact details, but she had woken with that *nightmare* feeling—the kind that churns in a person's gut from the moment they wake until the sun's first rays. "I think there was a monster in it."

"I bet there was." Detective Mannon's voice was grave despite his sympathetic smile. He smoothed out his fancy blue jacket before turning to an officer in a slightly less fancy jacket, whom he introduced as *Lieutenant*. "Get her some fresh tea, will you? She's hardly touched that cup, and it's already cooled."

Lieutenant was a glum man, older than Detective Mannon and palpably resentful of that fact. He snatched the teacup from Lydia's hands with a snort and followed his superior into the hall, attempting to slam the door behind him. The force made it bounce back from the frame.

Lydia waited for the footsteps to fade before sliding to the floor. The ease of the motion surprised her. She was no longer in any pain. Cold, yes. Frightened, absolutely. But not hurting.

Curious, she unbuttoned her collar and peeled back her bandages. The skin beneath the gauze was scarred, gray and icy to the touch, but it no longer ached when she prodded it. In fact, she felt nothing at all—not the pressure of her fingertips, not the thrum of her heart beneath them.

"...your report is consistent, I suppose." Her father's voice drifted into the room. "She truly said nothing of Katrin?"

The maid's name brought Lydia's nightmare feeling back in full. Curious, she tiptoed as far into the hall as she could without risking detection.

"It's not uncommon for a child of her years to block out traumatic events," Detective Mannon replied. "She probably couldn't remember Katrin's face if she tried."

Lydia did remember Katrin's face now that he'd mentioned it. Not the freckled mask she'd known her whole life—the details of *that* Katrin had smeared like fingerpaints—but the frightful truth long buried beneath it, complete with milky eyes and needle fangs.

"You're certain it was suicide?" her father asked.

"Well, it's not often people accidentally stumble from third-story windows, least of all closed ones."

"Precisely. Why didn't she open the window? It's not logical."

"Mr. Devlin," the detective said, half-sighing, "I don't know how many suicides you've had the misfortune of inspecting, but in my experience, they have nothing to do with logic. Maybe she was going through a bad break. Maybe she was a hysteric. Maybe she was dying and wanted to speed things up. Regardless her reasoning, I'm certain of my findings."

"And what about the other servants?" asked a third voice, Lydia's mother.

"Alibis check out. Besides, you said yourself that it was just your daughter you found in the room. You'd have to be daft to think that little girl tossed a grown woman like that..."

Memories flooded Lydia—the bitter bite of a golden chain, her consciousness fading beneath a storm of whispers and eerie violet light, darkness thick as pudding. The next thing she remembered was waking to her mother's scream. She'd blinked the black away to find herself peering over her windowsill, Maid Katrin's body mangled on the ground below.

"It might behoove you to send her away for a bit." The detective's words lured Lydia back to the present. "This place might be a bit haunted for a while."

"Not to worry," Lydia's father replied. "We were going to send her off in a week anyway. With all that's happened, I've arranged for her to leave tomorrow."

BRANNON

Brannon snuck away from the tall ship without drawing the suspicion of a single sailor. He'd posed as the newest crewmember, a man named Redrick, for the entire journey without giving himself away. Doubtless, the remains of the true Redrick had been discovered by now, but the crew would be none the wiser until they docked back in Pondrelle. By then, Brannon would be long gone.

Alensburry was one of many Rhysien port towns, located nearer to the mainland than the others. Surely, Slate had passed through at some point. The locals likely wouldn't remember her, assuming they'd noticed her to begin with, but it never hurt to ask around. At the very least, he would get an idea of the paths most travelled by visitors and the places they led to.

He strolled down one of several identical cobblestone streets, grateful for the feeling of solid ground beneath his boots. The three days he'd spent afloat had been peaceful, by sailing standards, but it had taken all of his scant charisma to feign he possessed sea legs. Even now, the waves rolled in his stomach, but it was nothing a little ale couldn't cure.

Comprised almost entirely of thatched cottages and cheery flowerbeds, Alensburry stood in stark contrast to Pondrelle's ports, where gambling houses, dream dens, and brothels were so prevalent one hardly needed roll over to slip from one vice to the next. While Brannon found none of those activities particularly compelling, Alensburry still seemed dull by comparison.

A few minutes of wandering brought him to a combination inn and pub with the simple name *The Alensburry Inn*. He took it as a sign he was unlikely to find another place to rest. The building was surprisingly empty, especially given the Rhysiens' reputation for midday drinking. A small group of sailors played cards at a corner table and a man in a ragged suit sat slumped against the bar, his garish red hat tipped sideways.

A slight barmaid with cropped copper hair greeted Brannon as he pulled out the stool next to the drunk's, then laughed when he caught the man's spoiled-meat scent and relocated to the far end of the counter.

"Not sure what that one's after," she said, running a tartan rag inside a pint-glass. "Been here for hours, and asleep for half that. What about you? Looking for food, drink, or board?"

"I'm looking for a girl."

The barmaid raised an eyebrow.

"Not like that. She's...a sister. I suspect she passed through a few weeks back."

"Lots of folks have been passing through Alensburry lately." The barmaid shrugged, her freckled shoulders peeking from a wide collar. "That Midsummer Festival in Amblewick's a pretty famous fête. I'd attend myself if I could make the time. What's your sister look like?"

The question was more difficult than it should have been. Brannon knew Slate when he saw her, but she'd always been bizarrely nondescript, like a drink with no aftertaste.

"She has a scar running down one cheek." He could not forget that much. "It's faded, but deep. Looks a bit like a moon. The only trait we share is dark hair."

"That's not much to go on."

No, it wasn't. But it was all he had.

"She's unremarkable," Brannon tried. "Almost remarkably so."

The drunk shot suddenly upright, a string of his drool clinging to the counter. "Remarkably unremarkable," he mumbled. "A clean slate."

The word *slate* captured Brannon's attention. It was probably the random rambling of a sot, but he was not one to leave a stone unturned, however grimy.

"Rough night?" he pried.

"The worstestest." The drunk scooted awkwardly across the barstools until he sat beside Brannon, still reeking of rot. "But then, fortunes change. Name's Blithely Fox."

"Sure it is," Brannon said, declining to introduce himself. "What's that you mentioned about a clean slate?"

A tight-lipped grin sliced across Blithely's face. "Now that depends on who's asking, and why."

Brannon was not a patient person on a good day, and this day was middling at best. How lucky for Blithely, that there were so many witnesses, and that Brannon was too exhausted to slay them all. "For a moment, I thought you might be interesting." He rose to his feet, turning to leave. "It's not surprising I was wrong."

"Wait!" Blithely grabbed his arm. "What if I was to tell you Amblewick got itself a new resident a few weeks back, before the festivalgoers started filtering in?"

Brannon sighed through clenched teeth.

"You've got ten seconds."

"The whole lot of you are impatient as rot." Blithely released Brannon's arm. "Anyhow, I recently crossed paths with a lass who proved—how'd you put it?—*unremarkable*. She had dark hair and little else of note, save the vicious scar she'd tucked away beneath it."

Fortunes change indeed. "Get this man a drink," Brannon said to the barmaid.

For the next few minutes, he interrogated the drunken stranger, who had little to offer, beyond the name of the inn Slate supposedly worked at. Brannon could work with that.

When the barmaid returned with Blithely's drink, she set a second before Brannon. "On the house," she said, winking.

Brannon accepted the ale, ignoring the wink.

Blithely drained his glass in a single, impressive gulp. "Happy to have helped you find your sister, assuming all goes well." He hopped from his stool. With his feet on the ground, the tip of his hat hardly reached the countertop. "Now, if you'll excuse me, a gent in the back owes me for an earlier gamble."

Brannon waved the man off and started on his drink, content to rest a moment more before continuing his search. Even if he found Slate swiftly, bringing her back to the mainland was bound to be a pain. Might as well enjoy a moment of ease.

The barmaid shrieked. Glass shattered. Brannon whirled on his stool. One of the corner gamblers lay sprawled on the floor, cards lilting through the air above him. Blood leaked from his ears, eyes, and mouth, snaking through weathered floorboards. His companions stared in bewildered terror, faces blanched.

Blithely was nowhere to be seen.

"There are spaces between the worlds where faulty borders blur
And certain times that beg a breach, when might and magic stir."

CHAPTER 7
THE MIDSUMMER FESTIVAL
ELWYN

*nock-knock-knock.*

Elwyn raised her dagger instinctively, roused to a pitch-dark world. The sun had not yet risen, no roosters had crowed, and not a single damned bird chirped outside her window, yet someone had the audacity to knock on her door.

Knock-knock-knock-knock-knock.

"Who is it?" she grumbled, sitting upright.

"Someone entirely unrivaled and apparently unexpected."

"Damn it, Silva!"

Elwyn tucked *Gelah* back beneath the pillow and lit her bedside candle before trudging to the door. An obnoxiously chipper woman tapped her toes outside it, having clearly been awake for hours. She'd clad herself in a shimmering shamrock dress trimmed in pastel filigree and draped with a golden capelet to match her gloves, and her hair was woven into countless interlocking braids, each adorned with a single emerald and twisted into a low chignon. As though her ensemble was not garish enough, she carried a basket brimming with even gaudier garments.

"How are you so awake?" Elwyn asked, her voice dripping exhaustion. "And more importantly, why?"

"You can't truly have forgotten." Silva shouldered past her, into the room. "The festival begins today!"

"You are correct." Elwyn watched helplessly as Silva set the basket down and began pawing through it. "The festival begins today. Which means we'll be busy. Which means I'll work hard. Which means I need sleep."

Silva pulled something floral and bright and awful from the basket, held it to Elwyn's cheek, then grimaced, tossing it aside. She repeated the process three more times before settling on a sleek garment, the hue of mulled wine.

"This is the one," she said, grinning. "The color suits your complexion splendidly. Next, we'll choose accessories, but first, we'll need better lighting." She tossed the dress over Elwyn's shoulder and flitted from the room, promising—or perhaps threatening—to return swiftly.

Elwyn stood dazed for a moment longer before shrugging. "It'll be easier to just humor her," she said to Luatha, slipping from her gray frock.

"It's just as I expected; you twist to fit the mold,"

I wonder how much longer you'll simply do as told."

"Well, you know how I feel about going with the grain." Elwyn stepped into Silva's gown and pulled it up around her. The fabric was soft, nearly soapy, against her skin, but the steel-ribbed bodice was another story. "Speaking of obedience, I'll need your help lacing this thing up."

Surprisingly, Luatha did not object. It took her only seconds to lace the ribbon through the two dozen eyelets that ran up the back of the gown, pulling tight enough to make Elwyn's ribs ache.

"Don't suppose you can loosen it at all," Elwyn wheezed, unsure whether Luatha's intentions were stylish or spiteful.

Before Luatha could respond, Silva returned with a lantern in one hand and a wicker tote in the other. Rayen followed on her heels, setting a tall, oaken mirror against Elwyn's wall. He grumbled something that might have been a greeting, then shuffled back in the direction he came from without so much as opening his eyes.

"Do you have him under a spell?" Elwyn asked.

"More or less." Silva cleared off the bedside crate and motioned for Elwyn to take a seat. "I could teach you to enchant one of your own if you'd like. Judging from how you laced that bodice, you might not be as helpless as I thought."

Elwyn wasn't so sure.

Silva insisted on braiding Elwyn's hair back in a complicated style like her own, giving her ample time to ramble about cultivating mystique and securing courtships. Elwyn barely listened, certain she'd never need the information. Soon enough, she was nodding off. If she'd been paying more attention, she'd have stopped Silva from brushing her bangs aside.

Seeing Elwyn's scar, Silva gasped, letting her hair fall back into place. "I suppose we can let that stay there," she said, feigning indifference. "We'll call it a nod to Muldrainian fashion. Though, if you don't mind my asking..."

Elwyn always minded, but her exhaustion made her more open than usual. Or more pliable, at the very least. "It's from a fight I got into. A long time ago."

"How exciting!" Silva pulled a jar of rouge from her tote. "If I'd ever gotten into a fight, my father would have locked me away for life."

"Mine encouraged them."

"Lucky."

Not exactly.

By the time Silva finished painting and powdering, Elwyn's face felt unusually heavy. She imagined she looked something like Dove did, whenever she dressed up for a shift in Branwood or Wiltshire. Thankfully, Elwyn had been deemed far too plain for that particular line of work.

"What do you think of my handiwork?" the noblewoman asked, dragging Elwyn over to the mirror. "Unbelievable, no?"

That was the exact word. The gown clung and flared in a way that feigned curves, and the burgundy fabric complimented Elwyn's pale skin. Between that and the cosmetics, she now appeared more porcelain than sickly. She might even have passed for a noble, provided she kept to dim lighting.

She didn't hate it as much as she thought she would.

"I suppose it's tolerable," she said. "For a day, anyway."

"Some people don't appreciate miracles." Silva huffed. "You'll rake in ten times your normal tips today. I'd bet twenty gold mórs on it."

"I don't have twenty gold mórs."

"You will by noon. That's my point."

Elwyn shook her head, shooing Silva out into the hall. The moment the door closed, she pulled *Gelah* from beneath her pillow and strapped it to her thigh. After donning her tall boots and leather gloves, she felt more like herself.

Luatha didn't see it.

"The realm's most useless armor—you couldn't fight at all,
Though, if I catch the hem just right, I bet I'll make you fall."

"Don't you dare," Elwyn whispered, making her way downstairs. "Besides, now I know your plans. Wouldn't it be more exciting to embarrass someone who doesn't expect it?"

Luatha tapped a claw against her chin, a mischievous grin materializing.

"It isn't very often that you think of something fun.
Why limit my attention when I could vex everyone?"

"Everyone except me, right?"

Luatha didn't answer.

They arrived in the kitchen to find Silva standing behind the counter, trying her damndest to dice carrots. "Do you know where knives are stored?" she asked. "This one's dreadfully dull."

"I'm not sure I'd trust you with a sharp one." Elwyn chuckled. "You're obviously some kind of bogey who's kidnapped and replaced the real Silva."

"I've always been a hard worker!" Silva huffed. "Just look how much effort I put into your outfit."

Elwyn pulled two knives from the block, passing one to Silva. "That's not what I—"

"And if I'm such a snob, why did I marry Rayen, hmm?"

Elwyn had wondered about the lopsided union, as any passing person might have, but she was not so curious as to inquire.

"I was actually engaged to another," Silva said, butchering another carrot. "Lord Regand Edrin, a burly old chap with an estate the size of a city and a temper to match. Rayen was my tailor for the event, if you can believe it. Over the course of several alterations, I wound up falling for him. Of course, my parents would never have approved. Hence..." She waved around the inn, nearly hitting Elwyn with the knife. "My mother has probably told the family I was eaten by wolves. Less a tragedy, in her opinion."

Elwyn smiled despite herself. Impractical though it was, she'd always been a bit of a romantic at heart. Moreover, Silva's little act of rebellion impressed her. "That was a bit mischievous of you," she said. "Noble in a distinctly ignoble way."

Silva beamed. "Does that make you like me more?"

"I suppose. A little bit."

"Good," Silva said, eyes flitting toward the door as the knob rattled. "Because you're about to hate me again."

"What do you—"

Silva sprinted away as Davin stepped into the inn. He'd dressed himself up, by village standards, having traded his rustic brown linens for sleek summer plaids.

"If you're looking for Silva, she's ..." Elwyn glanced around, uncertain which way the noblewoman had scurried off to. "Well, she's married, for one thing."

"I'm not looking for Silva," Davin replied, approaching the counter.

"Oh...Well, breakfast won't be ready for another hour. Anything else I can help you with?"

"I hope so." He looked Elwyn over, unpinning the red frillrose from his lapel. "If no one's asked you to join them for dancing, I'd like to offer my evening."

Elwyn's cheeks warmed, and she silently cursed Silva. She'd never had reason to reject a man before and had no idea how to do so kindly. She spent an uncomfortable moment crafting the perfect excuse, only to have the words, "That would be lovely," spill out instead.

"I'll be waiting in the town square after the parade." Davin set the flower on the counter before starting toward the street. "See you then, Em."

Close enough.

Mr. Elliot's Inn was not a popular eatery, so the sheer size of the half-drunken breakfast crowd caught Elwyn by surprise. By noon, her patience had worn thinner than the scant remains of the shepherd's pie she'd baked for the occasion.

"That's the last of it, I'm afraid," she said, handing a plate to a surly customer who'd ordered two.

"Well, make some more, then!" he spat.

Stifling the urge to stab, Elwyn explained, for the dozenth time, that she was not so gifted a cook as to conjure food from air. The customer responded with an uncreative bevy of threats.

"Aw, feck it," said Mr. Elliot, who had surprised Elwyn by helping to take orders. "We've made more than enough coin for one day. The rest of you bloody lot can starve!"

Curses cut through the air like leaves in a windstorm as the innkeeper drove the grumbling horde into the street. Once he'd shooed the last straggler away, he hung his sign from the handle and locked the door.

"For Creator's sake," he said, wiping his brow with his sleeve, "I swear the revolution was less work."

Elwyn was too exhausted to offer even an obligatory chuckle. Eager to forge through her daily tasks, she reached straight for the nearest bucket and rag.

"You know, I loved this damned festival when I was your age." Mr. Elliot watched through a grated window as crowds gathered alongside the cobbled streets. "Granted, that was back when Pondrelle ran our nation, so something as simple as a party felt revolutionary, at the time." He offered Elwyn a wistful smile that didn't quite fit his face. "Tell you what, ain't no more customers coming in, and your work will wait. Why don't you head out early?"

"I'm not in a rush," Elwyn lied.

"That so?" The innkeeper raised a bushy brow. "And here I assumed you'd want time to pat that flour from your sleeves before you met with your suitor."

Elwyn cursed Silva again, certain she'd tattled, then sprinted off to the washroom to hide her embarrassment and deal with the aforementioned flour. When she next emerged, Mr. Elliot was still waiting by the door. He tossed her a small sack that jingled when she caught it.

"Your portion of today's profits."

The gesture was kind enough Elwyn nearly felt guilty for the coins she'd been slipping into her bodice and boots all morning. "What's put you in such a good mood?" she asked, eyes narrowed.

"Should I take it back then?"

"Never mind!" Elwyn darted upstairs before he could make good on the threat. She hid the coins beneath her pillow, lest she spend them unwisely on festival goods. If she wanted something badly enough, money would not enter the equation, anyway.

"You've been stocking up on silver for when you run away,
But it's starting to seem like you are hesitant to stray..."

It was the first time Luatha had chimed in for hours. Elwyn ignored her, frightened by the truth of the assessment. From her window, she could see the beginnings of the parade winding down the distant hillside. She'd told Silva and Rayen she'd watch it with them, if able, and there was still enough time to make good on her promise.

Festivals were not uncommon on the mainland, but Elwyn had always viewed them as job opportunities. She'd spent so much time picking pockets and casing empty houses that she'd never paused to enjoy the spectacle. There was something infectious about the colors and music, the sweet scents of pastries and the bright sound of laughter. Elwyn did not belong to Amblewick any more than she'd belonged to her mother or the Greyscale, but she wanted to belong there, if only for the day.

The throng was dense and loud, but Silva was easy as ever to spot. She and Rayen had staked out a decent corner, not far from the inn.

"What's with the crown?" Elwyn asked as she approached them, pointing to a braid of pink blossoms that now wreathed Silva's hair. The petals clashed uncharacteristically with the rest of the noblewoman's ensemble.

"Oh, this?" Silva traced the circlet with a slender finger. "It's nothing really. The townsfolk saw fit to crown me their festival queen, is all. True, it's a bit tacky, but I must give my subjects what they want."

Elwyn forwent an eyeroll and offered congratulations instead. She would never understand why such frivolity made Silva happy, but she could respect that it did. Silva responded with an unexpected, entirely unwelcome embrace and a promise that, "You'll be a shoo-in for next year, if I take a bit more time preparing you."

Elwyn nodded absently, the words *next year* churning in her gut.

The crowd cheered as a float passed by—a colorful arrangement of potatoes and cabbage that was probably intended to be some sort of...cow? Perhaps a horse.

Silva and Rayen were unimpressed.

"That's the tenth produce display," Silva said, pouting.

"Produce is the nation's chief export." Rayen shrugged. "Give them a break, love."

Elwyn's stomach reacted before her mind could. She'd spent the whole morning working with food but had forgotten to eat any. "I hope they cook them after the parade. I could do with a decent bowl of stew."

Luatha's wings whirred, a sign of irritation.

"You have morsels to choose from, friend, so don't make such a fuss.
Keep nine-tenths of the crops you tend; the firsts belong to us."

"Sorry," Elwyn whispered.

Much like the Rhysiens themselves, she'd gotten so caught up in the pomp she'd forgotten its purpose. Amblewick might have been the only town left where widows left saucers of cream on their stoops in hopes of securing a piskie boon, but even they cared more for entertaining themselves than pleasing otherworldly guardians who, for all they knew, didn't truly exist.

"Now *that's* a float." Silva pointed toward a flowery cart pulled by two snowy stallions. Four figures stood among the blossoms, waving at the audience, dressed head-to-toe in plum silk.

"The elected leaders of the Rhysien districts," Rayen explained.

"I don't care who they are. I want their outfits!"

"You would," Elwyn said. "They are completely impractical."

Silva glared and grinned at the same time.

"I mean...um...un-practical?"

"Now you're catching on." Silva patted her shoulder. "Don't worry. I'm unabashedly uninclined to hold that unmitigated blunder against you."

"This is too much work."

"Only to the *un*sophisticated."

"I un-like you."

The roar of the crowd ended the conversation as the final float passed by. Two men in opulent robes held the reins of a majestic stag, which pulled a platform that was rigged to spin as the wheels turned. Atop it stood two sculptures, locked in endless dance. The man had been carved of pale cedar, with eyes bright as emeralds. A cape of tangled ivy draped between his shoulders, and a chrysanthemum crown wreathed his copper hair. His partner was carved from ebony, and a bramble circlet sat atop her winter-white locks. Silver glitter twinkled across her navy gown, like frost.

"Who are those supposed to be?" Silva asked.

"Some king and queen of old, perhaps," Rayen guessed. "Was Rhysia ever a monarchy?"

"Not on this side of the Veil," Elwyn answered, happy to finally contribute to the conversation. "I think those are supposed to be the rulers of the Unseen: the King of the Seelie and Queen of the Unseelie."

"Seelie and Unseelie?" Rayen's brow wrinkled.

"The Light and Dark Courts."

"You must mean Faeries!" Silva squealed, clasping her fingers together. "The cute little things that grant wishes and turn little girls into princesses!"

Tiny claws bit into Elwyn's shoulder. "They don't do any of those things," she said, wincing. "And they hate to be called that."

Rayen chuckled. "Why so troubled, El? You don't seriously believe in Faeries?"

Luatha drew blood.

Elwyn shook her friend from her shoulder, prompting peculiar looks from the Pondrellen couple. "Faerie is a place, not a person," she explained, recovering. "It's like...a different world layered overtop ours."

"Well, in any case, they're pretty." Silva nodded toward the float. "Are they lovers?"

"Enemies," Elwyn corrected, "but the stories claim those are two sides of a coin."

With the final float having passed, a troupe of young dancers trickled out into the street. They wore shimmering gauze wings and flowing tulle dresses, and iridescent ribbons wafted through the air behind them. Most likely, they meant to emulate piskies, though they looked nothing like the real thing. Even so, Luatha fluttered out among them, her own violet trail outshining theirs like the moon amidst stars. She returned to Elwyn's shoulder seconds later, furling her wings and pulling her chitinous knees to her chest.

"The Unseen are a fervent folk, though there is much we lack,
And if I had to choose one world, I'd never more go back.
But if I must return to dust, I'll hold one woe within,
What I would give to sing and dance in Faerie once again."

Elwyn hadn't ever seen her friend so glum. "Are you alright?"

"Um, yes." Rayen cocked his head. "Why do you ask?"

"I ..." Elwyn scrambled for an excuse. "I figured they would offer Silva a float, seeing as they've crowned her queen."

"It's only a title," Silva said, happily allowing the attention to shift her way. "My reward is a free drink from The Spriggan, though I don't care for ale, and I doubt they offer decent wine. Have you been?"

Elwyn shook her head. She'd been trying to forget her encounter with Blithely, and she certainly didn't want to talk about it.

"I figured as much. You really should get out more, El."

"Speaking of..." Rayen elbowed Elwyn in the ribs, and she nearly grabbed *Gelah* on instinct. "Isn't it about time you met a certain someone at the square?"

"I'll head that way soon," Elwyn said, though much of the throng was already en route. "Why don't you two run ahead?"

"Very well," Silva said, grabbing Rayen's arm. "We shall claim my free drink and, no doubt, numerous un-free ones. I fully expect to see you within the hour."

Elwyn offered a parting smile as the couple slipped away. She lingered in place a moment more, partly to avoid the rush, partly to parse her own jumbled musings.

Dancing. Drinking. Courting. She had never spared those frivolities a thought. Yet, there she was, about to juggle all three at once. Thinking back on Davin's invitation made her stomach churn and her pulse quicken. Had she not always associated those symptoms with impending danger, she might have noticed the feeling was not wholly unpleasant.

*"You've many more mistakes to make, fresh chaos you could sow,
Life's much too short to only dance with devils that you know."*

CHAPTER 8
A DANCE WITH THE DEVIL
ELWYN

lwyn visited each vendor on her way to the square but didn't buy or steal a thing from any of them. She told herself she was taking in the festival, which was partly true. The colors, scents, and corner performances all proved worthwhile diversions, but the real reason she was taking her time was that she'd promised it to someone else for the evening, and she'd never had to share it before.

She plucked a silk scarf from a cart and tried it on, checking her reflection in the merchant's mirror. The dress and powders she'd thought too opulent that morning now seemed drab compared to the flowing gowns and glittering jewels worn by the other women in attendance. It would take a lot more than a swatch of silk and a puff of powder to make someone like Elwyn stand apart from the crowd.

Now I'm both uncomfortable and *unremarkable,* she thought, putting the scarf back where she'd found it. Somewhere between that cart and the next, she convinced herself that, while losing Davin's attention would be a temporary disappointment, keeping it would be more of a headache than it was worth.

"You're the only company I really need," she said to Luatha.

The piskie smiled appreciatively, then predictably leveraged her affection for food.

"To earn the love of one like me is not an easy feat.
In return for my favor, I believe I'm owed a treat."

"Does your appetite have no end?" Elwyn chuckled. "You're lucky I'm hungry, too."

She followed the cloying aroma of mixed spices to a pastry cart that sold everything from potato rolls to lemon cake. Those standing in line did not notice her passing them by, and the baker didn't so much as scoff when she plucked an apple turnover from the cooling rack.

Much to Luatha's chagrin, she devoured over half the pastry before remembering to share. As she handed off the leftovers, she wondered— perhaps for the hundredth time—what manner of code the Unseen lived by. Luatha could easily have snatched food from the hands of unwitting passersby, but Elwyn had never seen her take a crumb that wasn't offered her. Whenever she asked about it, Luatha replied with a silly rhyme about how games are less fun when everyone knows the rules.

Despite her dallying, Elwyn arrived at the square right as a band of bards struck up the first reel of the evening. Townsfolk and travelers flocked from the side streets, twirling even as their feet hit the cobbles. Within seconds there were more faces in the square than Elwyn could have counted in an hour.

She skirted lithely around the dancers, wishing she and Davin had discussed a more specific meeting spot. After ten minutes of searching to no avail, she decided to visit The Spriggan. If Silva and Rayen were still there, there was a chance Davin had joined them. If he hadn't, she would at least have company to distract her.

Raucous laughter poured from The Spriggan like water from a fountain, and the tobacco fog was thick as pea soup. A swift stroll through the smoke confirmed that Silva and Rayen had moved on, assuming they'd dared enter the pub in the first place.

"I really shouldn't be getting attached anyway," Elwyn whispered.

Luatha nuzzled against her cheek, cooing sympathetically.

Elwyn didn't need sympathy, so much as solitude. She had just resolved to return to the inn when someone tapped her shoulder. Her hand leapt to *Gelah's* hilt, and she whirled to see a familiar barmaid proffering a wine glass.

"Oh, hello again," Elwyn said, thoroughly confused.

The barmaid's expression asked *do I know you?* but her mouth said, "A handsome young man sent this your way, for whatever reason." She thrust the drink into Elwyn's hand. "He's already wandered off, but I'm sure he'll find you if you stick close."

She must have been speaking of Davin. No man—handsome or otherwise—would have noticed Elwyn without Silva's meddling. Convinced the evening could be salvaged, she marched back out into the square to find the sky was swiftly darkening. Hundreds of little paper lanterns flared bright against the twilight, their glow rivaling that of her piskie friend.

After a bit of searching, Elwyn spotted Silva, whose gown alone took up a bench between the florist's shop and the cobbler's. Not too far off, Rayen and Davin were chatting over pints. Well, *Rayen* was chatting; Davin appeared to be nodding off.

Assailed by a sudden storm of nerves, Elwyn downed her drink and set her glass aside, composing herself as best she could before heading over. Naturally, Davin didn't notice her approaching. She tapped his shoulder, and he startled, spilling what remained of his ale. *Off to a brilliant start...*

"At least I'm awake now, I suppose." Davin tried to pat his sleeve dry. "Hope this doesn't stain."

Elwyn winced, looking to Silva for guidance. *"Dance with him,"* the noblewoman mouthed.

Sound enough advice. At the very least, it would limit Elwyn's capacity for social blunders. "Would you like to dance?" she asked.

Davin shrugged. "It's what I asked you here for, isn't it?"

Disheartening though his tone was, Elwyn's pulse still thrummed when he took her arm and led her into the square. It was silly, getting flustered over so small a thing. She was a thief, for Creator's sake, not some damsel to be wooed, but the novelty of it all was enough to roil her stomach.

Thankfully, dancing came easier than flirting. After a few measures spent mirroring the other women in the crowd, she fell into the simple rhythm. When Davin stepped back, so did she. When he raised his arm, she twirled beneath it. When he swung to one side, she swung to the opposite. So long as she kept her eyes on Luatha—who looped around them in a dizzying dance of her own—she forgot to be flustered at all.

Apparently, the tactic was less than subtle. As the bards swept from one song into the next, Davin paused. "You know you're allowed to look at me, right?"

Elwyn forced herself to do just that, anxiously tucking her hair behind her ear. Davin grimaced, and she realized her mistake. By the time she covered her scar again, his gaze had wandered to Silva, who danced with Rayen yards away, looking giddy and gorgeous as ever.

Elwyn wasn't angry so much as disappointed, and much of that disappointment was aimed inward. She hadn't even been all that interested in Davin, but she'd let herself believe he was interested in *her*. That someone, anyone, might find her remarkable.

Of all the frivolous notions to humor ...

The next number was a rigid waltz, and the fluid steps and sudden stops provided ample distraction. Elwyn's spirits were well on their way to lifting when her heels began to drag. A weight like sorrow tugged on her limbs and eyelids, and her vision began to blur. Soon enough, her thoughts were blurry, too.

"Something the matter?" Davin asked, propping her upright by the shoulders. Elwyn hadn't even realized she'd slumped against him.

"I'm fine." She attempted to giggle. "Told you I've never danced before."

"Actually, you didn't tell me that."

Elwyn barely heard the reply. Whatever was happening could not be blamed on wine or nerves. Frantic, she scanned the watercolor crowd for a familiar streak of violet. Luatha burst into view a moment later, little more than a misty glimmer.

"Slink back into the shadows! Seek refuge in the night!
If you don't take this chance to flee, you're going to have to fight!"

Before the piskie's meaning could settle, Elwyn was torn from Davin's grasp and swept through the crowd. For a moment, she was weightless—a leaf tossed about by a zealous gale. She jarred to a stop only when the music ebbed, and a familiar face oozed into focus. *Black.*

The assassin pressed a blade to her throat, dipping her close to the cobbles.

"Mind if I cut in?"

"The winds of change are welcome, though often sorely brisk,
When all you've known is luxury, you learn to treasure risk."

CHAPTER 9
EVERYDAY ENCHANTMENT
AEDYN

uilt harmoniously along the spiral branches of Talune, the First Tree, the Palace Samhria was a breathtaking sight. This was never more true than on Midsummer, when all twenty-three of its gilded stories were wreathed in garlands of sugared fruit, brilliant blossoms, and delicate oraithvine filigree. The Great Hall had been converted into a lavish ballroom, and fae from all four of the Seelie Realms gathered inside to celebrate.

The topmost row of doors and windows had been opened to a crisp, floral breeze, allowing sunbeams to rain down upon a rich ocean of color and culture. Light caught in gemstones and spilled across satin as dancers twirled to the bidding of lute and lyre. Above them, sprites and piskies of every hue ebbed and flowed to the music's sway, forming constellations of living color. This might easily have been the most resplendent Midsummer Ball in Seelie history, capturing in full the magic, the mirth, and the inimitable opulence of Faerie.

Aedyn had never been so bored.

He would have happily vanished into the revel, but his father had insisted he sit with the High Judges on the mezzanine, probably as punishment for some misdeed he'd already forgotten. The actual leaders had been conversing for some time without acknowledging his presence. He sat with an elbow on the table, head propped on his fist, twirling a golden dagger on a patch of oraithvine that wove through an emerald runner. *I should stab someone*, he thought idly, watching his reflection pass by again and again. *Myself? No. But who?*

"These fountaincrests would be perfect for the wedding." The chipper voice startled him from his trance, and his dagger clattered on the table. He spared a glance to Eloana, his *Betrothed*. The word tasted bitter as blackthorn berries, even in his mind.

She looked beautiful as ever in a citrine gown that complimented her grass-green eyes and pearly smile. A few of her golden ringlets had been braided into a crown and bedecked with lilies and lapis flakes, but the rest fell free to brush the floor. Chains of white-gold and peridot wound around her neck and wrists, gleaming bright against her sun-kissed skin.

Aedyn could have easily done worse. In fact, he had done worse on numerous occasions. But Eloana, like the vast majority of things he'd known his whole life, bored him half to death.

"I know we've discussed a cobalt and yellow theme." She plucked a sprig of bell-shaped flowers from a centerpiece and ran a delicate finger over the stem, causing silver pollen to rain from the petals. "This periwinkle hue could easily serve as an accent, though you look best in green, so leafier florals might be a better choice." She sighed childishly. "It hardly matters. You'd look perfect in any setting."

Aedyn offered an obligatory smile. Apparently satisfied, Eloana shifted the conversation to her handmaiden, who feigned a keener interest in flowers and color schemes. Those details would never matter if Aedyn had his way. It wasn't that he sought to break the engagement—such scandals were more than frowned upon, especially for an heir—only he would not be required to marry until he took the throne, and as far as he was willing to consider, his father would live forever.

"What are your thoughts on the matter, Aedyn?"

Aedyn fought a reflexive wince, shifting to face his father. King Aryn of the Daoine Maithe looked as regal as ever in his oraithvine plate and emerald suit, a matching cape stretched out behind him like a mossy lea. His golden eyes were rife with suspicion, peering out from beneath a crown of gilt antlers. Aedyn's own circlet had been modeled after that very piece, though it boasted only stag spikes, and he wore it with less than half his father's decorum.

"Aedyn?" the king repeated.

The other High Judges leaned forward to see whether Aedyn had actually been listening. Which, of course, he hadn't been.

"Should we not wait and see how it plays out?" Aedyn tried. The safest answer to any question was usually another question.

Mearalas crossed her seafoam arms, her permanent scowl deepening. That ugly expression was her only imperfection, personality notwithstanding. "A cautious answer from the famously impetuous prince," she hissed through clenched teeth. "Am I the only one among us who would take action?"

Creagor burst into riotous laughter, nearly impaling her with the obsidian shards that sprouted from his shoulders. "You worry too much, my fishy friend." The Sidhe Chieftain slapped the Undine Queen's back, nearly knocking the drink from her hand. "Is only rumors. No need to beat war drums over mere talk."

Mearalas straightened her coral crown and squared her shoulders, silently regaining every ounce of poise lost, right as the Sylph Speaker-Elect flitted back to the table. Aedyn hadn't even noticed Soen was missing, though he should have guessed from the somber atmosphere. She was no less serious than the other Seelie rulers, but she was wise enough not to wear her worries plainly.

"You all look so glum," she noted, dismissing her ethereal wings to take her seat. "Did I miss something important?"

"It is too soon to tell," Aryn replied. "Some solitary allies returned from the Shifting Wilds this morning with tales of a strange being. Apparently, its powers rival the Korrid Queen, and it has been amassing some manner of army."

"Shadow Goblins," Creagor clarified. "Weak, squishy things. But, still, is concerning."

"We're certain this is a bad development?" Soen twirled a lock of her silver-white hair. "The Korrids not to be trusted. A threat to their power might play to our favor."

"The foolish ramblings of a naïve mind." Mearalas scoffed. "A familiar foe is always preferable to the unknown, especially when we've maintained diplomatic relations with that foe for well over a century." She returned her attention to Aryn, waving the other two judges off like pollen sprites. "I could send a troop of Seaglass Scouts into the Mirrormurk without fear of detection. Their reports will be far more reliable than those of court-less Solitaries."

"I cannot condone such a risk." King Aryn folded his hands on the table. "We would be breaching the Treaty of Dusk."

"The treaty specifies we are not to *set foot* on Unseelie territories," Mearalas argued. "My soldiers are swimmers, just in case you've forgotten."

Aryn's jaw flexed. "Our honor is tied to the spirit of the law, not merely the word of it. We cannot cast aside our ideals for—"

"This talk of the Unseelie is dreadful." Eloana laid her head on Aedyn's shoulder, and he nearly jumped from his skin. He'd already forgotten about her. That happened a lot. "Do you not find it all terribly frightening?"

"You know what helps with fear?" Aedyn asked, stifling a sigh. "Alcohol. Copious amounts of it. I'll go pour a couple glasses."

He shrugged her away, rising before she could object or, worse, suggest sending her handmaiden to retrieve refreshments. Such logic was the enemy of whimsy. Taking advantage of his father's diverted attention, he descended toward the dance floor with a spring in his step, feeling that the simple act of stretching his legs was in itself a kind of freedom.

Seelie fae of all variety swirled across the tiles like spring-water eddies, trailing silk, velvet, and even militant dobhriste. A few Solitaries could also be spotted in the mix, though their kind tended to avoid such bustling spaces. Using the crowd as cover, Aedyn sculpted the light around him with *glamour*. He emerged from the throng as a whole new person, having exchanged his copper complexion for a pastel pallor, his mussy bronze locks for sleek white, and his mahogany eyes for piercing blue. He'd kept his tall stature and lithe frame, but he'd traded his royal green garb for an indigo suit embellished with silver. Though exceedingly ornate, the garments betrayed no hint of his station.

Common fae had all the fun, after all.

He hadn't been lying about pouring drinks, but he hadn't specified he'd return with them, either. Intent on stalling for as long as possible, he made his way to the feasting area, where five colorful fountains of sparkling wine sprouted up from a bounty of glazed treats and candied fruits. The crimson had been procured for the enjoyment of their Glaistig guests (which is not to say that Aedyn had never tried it.) That left lavender, gold, crystal-clear, and burgundy—all equally droll.

He did not choose the lavender fountain for its heady, floral aroma, but for the dainty Sylph woman idling beside it. She plucked petals from a butterbreeze bouquet, absently nibbling on them as she watched the dancing with curious cornflower eyes.

"Enjoying yourself?" Aedyn sidled up beside her. Before she could even answer, he added, "Of course you are. Who wouldn't enjoy you?"

His fingers pressed ever-so-slightly through her ethereal hand when he took it, and his lips did the same when he kissed the back of it. A tingling sensation, like static, lingered on his skin for seconds after. *Intriguing.*

"I have not visited Samhria before," she said, smiling politely. "It is stunning."

Her hand slid through his on its way to her side. More static. "More so for your presence."

If she recognized his advances for what they were, she gave no hint. "You are familiar with the palace?"

Aedyn chuckled. Innocence fit the girl like a tailored gown, complementing her slight frame, her soft complexion, and the wispy, white locks that curled in the air around her like tendrils of fog. Much like her actual gown, he was confident it could be removed with a little effort on his part.

"I'm *very* familiar with the palace," he said. "If you'd like, I can show you around. There's a lovely solarium not far from here—peaceful, well-furnished, discreet..."

"No, thank you," the Sylph replied plainly. "I am enjoying the ball."

This might take more effort than I thought. Aedyn smiled at the thought of an actual challenge. He plucked a charmblossom and handed it to the Sylph, buying time to craft a decent compliment. She thanked him, biting into it.

"I have not tried this flavor," she said. "It is sweet."

"Not half as sweet as you."

The Sylph jumped back, feathered wings sprouting from her shoulders. "Sylphs are not for eating! You are not a Glaistig, are you? Far Darrag?"

"No! Wait, I—"

"I promise you, I am not sweet!" She flitted away, a half-eaten flower falling to the floor behind her. Aedyn stooped to pick it up, wondering exactly what he'd said to scare her off.

The sound of slow clapping drew his attention to a nearby table, where his best friend, Amatha, was doubled over, laughing uncontrollably. Several seconds passed before she regained her composure, wiping an amused tear from her eye. "Hands down, best part of the ball."

Aedyn tried and failed to glare. His friend's smile was an infectious thing, even when it came at his expense. With the snap of his fingers, his glamour slid away like silk, and he was his usual, burnished-gold self again.

"How did you know?" he asked, plucking up a wine glass and running it under a burgundy fountain. It wouldn't be shocking for another Maithe illusionist to see through his glamour, but a Sidhe stonemelder?

"You are kidding, yes?" Amatha arched an eyebrow, and a dozen gemstones winked brightly against her dark skin, their hue matching the amethyst shards that sprouted from her scalp and shoulders. "We have known each other since before we could walk. Speaking of, it is the walk that gives you away. You are like a tree, in that a poorly placed stick holds you up too straight."

Aedyn couldn't help laughing. He lifted his glass in a brusque cheer then tipped it back. Subtle notes of frostfruit wove through a bolder spriteberry flavor, lending the wine a saccharine tang. It wasn't awful, but he would have preferred something more novel. Like the mortal drinks the ball had boasted in years past.

"The offerings are scant this year, aren't they?" He perched on the table beside her and gestured lazily toward another, nearest the far wall. An array of food was heaped atop it—mostly cabbage, carrots, and raw potatoes—but the spread was insignificant compared to the bounty they'd received years before. "If we keep our distance from the mortals much longer, that table will be empty in a matter of Midsummers."

"No, no." Amatha wagged her finger. "That is not what we are going to talk about." She grabbed Aedyn by the shoulders and turned him toward the mezzanine, where Eloana still sat, listlessly searching the crowd. "She cares for you, Aedyn, and you are vowed to her."

"And?"

"And hers is the only skirt in the Light Realms you refuse to chase, not counting mine."

"Don't be crass, Amatha." Aedyn grimaced. "You're like a brother to me."

Amatha chuckled. "If I am your brother, I will offer some brotherly advice—tend the pretty girl you have and save some for the rest of us."

"Weren't you courting your father's attendant? Fedan, or Ferad, something to that effect?"

Amatha shrugged, and Aedyn let the topic slide. She would talk more about it if she wanted to. Besides, if he wasn't invited, he didn't much care who others chose to bed.

"I know you're coming from a place of concern, but you needn't worry. I've vowed to wed Eloana should I ever take the throne. That is the only promise I've made to her, and it is the only one I'm obligated to keep."

"For now," Amatha said.

"For now," Aedyn echoed, downing the remainder of his wine.

"Here." Amatha offered Aedyn a flask and a sympathetic smile. "You look like you need this."

He accepted gladly, taking a swig without inquiring about the contents. He recognized the burn instantly. Whiskey. The good kind. The kind you could not get in Faerie. After another, longer drink, he passed the flask back to Amatha, letting out a contented laugh. He tipped his head back as the warmth spread through to his toes.

"Now, how did you come across that?"

Amatha grinned, tucking the flask back into her dobhriste breastplate. She tapped her finger against her scalp shards. "I am smart."

"That I've never doubted, particularly in matters of war and weapon-craft, but I'm fairly certain that your knowledge does not extend to the smuggling of contraband."

Amatha crossed burly arms. "I am smart enough to make the right type of friend."

Aedyn's smile spread from ear to ear. "Deilin is here?"

Amatha nodded.

Now *that* was interesting.

"Be cautious with the bottle despite the calm it holds,
More oft than not, the price of wine is steeper than pure gold."

CHAPTER 10
STRONG DRINK
ELWYN

lwyn's arms and legs had gone completely limp. Her lungs labored for shallow breaths, and her lips could not shape a cry for help. Her hopes rested in the most unlikely of scenarios—that someone would notice Black forcing her through the Midsummer crowd. As usual, her hopes were in vain. Even Luatha had lost her in the tumult.

This time, the cost of her unremarkability would be steep.

The assassin twirled her as though their dance was the most natural in the world until he slipped into an alley, where he hefted her like a sack of flour. The scenery churned as he wove through the side streets, but she tried her best to track familiar landmarks—the moldy musk of the abandoned storehouse, the sepia cobbles behind the tannery, the saccharine scent of blackberries fermenting in Thompson's Distillery. She did not give up easily, no matter how dire the circumstances. On the off chance an escape presented itself, she would need to have kept her bearings.

Once the festival din had faded to a hum, Black dropped Elwyn with an unceremonious *thud*. Her head smacked hard against the cobblestones, and her vision burst with splotches of red and purple. Before the colors had a chance to fade, Black propped her back against a brick wall, pinning her in place by the shoulder. He brought his face too close to hers, looming like a storm cloud.

"You've grown careless, Slate. Accepting drinks from strange men." He clucked his tongue. "What would Father think?"

Elwyn's mind yet lagged, but the pieces were clicking together. She forced a question to her heavy tongue. "W-what did you do to me?"

"It's just a little something I swiped off of Dove back at the sanctuary," he said. "Unfortunately, it isn't going to kill you. It will simply render you helpless for about, oh ... ten more minutes or so. Speaking of which..."

Black swept his hands over Elwyn's shoulders, hips, and waist. When his fingers brushed too close to her chest, she mustered enough strength to spit. The phlegm flew past his shoulder, prompting a cold chuckle.

"I'm only being thorough." He slid a hand up her leg, stopping mid-thigh. "There we are," he said, drawing *Gelah* from its sheath. "I can't have you turning this on me once you're back on your feet, now can I?"

Infuriating though it was to see her dagger in his hands, Elwyn was nearly relieved. *Once you're back on your feet...*

He intended to let her live.

Of course, knowing how the Father dealt with derelicts, that might have been the worst of two options.

Black turned *Gelah* over in his hand, admiring its shape and sheen, then slid it into his belt to mingle with lesser weapons. "Now, what to do with you?" he asked, brushing her hair aside to caress the scar he'd given her.

A white-hot rage seared through Elwyn's veins, tingling in her fingertips and toes. Between that small sign of strength recovered and the violet blur that burst into her periphery, her hopes began to grow.

Her eyes lilted toward her tiny friend. "L-Lua—"

"Pardon?" Black asked, leaning closer.

"Luatha ... help."

The piskie needed no such instruction. She dove at Black like a hawk at hunt, clawing at his collarbone and sinking needle-teeth into his neck.

"Fuck!" He flailed blindly, striking Luatha by luck alone. The piskie hit a wall and fell limp to the cobbles. Elwyn's heart jolted, far more panicked for her friend than she had been for herself.

"I don't know how you did that," Black balled a fist, "but I know it was you."

The punch hurt, more so for the impact of her skull against the bricks. When Elwyn opened her eyes, the world had snapped back into place, though her headache had grown tenfold.

"I dunnowha..." She started, a trickle of blood slurring her words.

Black tilted his head, bringing his lips close to her ear. "You'll have to *enun*ciate."

Elwyn gritted her teeth. "I don't...know what...you're talking about."

"No, of course you don't." His voice was deceptively soft, like the hiss of a serpent, like the growl of a wildcat, like that of Father Beaus. "You've never been the sharpest knife, have you? You probably can't explain why you failed your last mission, either, or why you failed to return to the Sanctuary, or how you ended up in this shithole of a town on this shithole of an island. Can you?"

Elwyn pursed her lips. No answer would satisfy him, just as no answer would satisfy the Father or his enforcers. They were going to pry them out anyway, using every tool in their morbid cache. If Elwyn had to sing, she'd save her refrain for a proper audience,

"Some chances are worth taking, some others better missed,
I know it hurts, but rest assured, we will get out of this!"

Luatha rose on trembling legs, her shadow wings unfurling like fiddleheads in a sunbeam. Relief flooded Elwyn, and her fingertips flexed reflexively. The poison was ebbing, resolve welling in its wake.

"Did you really think you were going to be able to disappear into some droll, humble village life?" Black asked, unaware of the change. "You ought to be ashamed of yourself, Slate."

"I-I..." Elwyn stuttered, spitting blood. "I am."

Black's smirk stretched into a grin. Elwyn had never seen him show his teeth, and she was surprised to find they weren't fangs. Most monsters look startlingly human.

"You are *what?*" he asked, cupping his ear in jest. "You'll need to be more specific."

"Ashamed of myself."

The way Black breathed those words in, one might have thought they were his favorite scent. "Yes, of course you are," he said. "You were utterly unremarkable, and the Father tried to include you in something grand. It's no surprise you proved lacking."

"That's why I came here," Elwyn lied, a scheme forming even as she spoke. "I needed to make it up to him. To all of you."

Black chuckled, shaking his head. "At least wait for the drugs to wear off before you try to talk your way out of this one."

"The Father collects relics, doesn't he?" she asked, hoping the rumors held truth. She'd never been called to the study, nor had she cared to sneak a peek. "Druidic emblems and occult items, if I recall correctly…"

"What difference would that make?"

"There's something like that here in Amblewick. Something powerful enough to redeem even me."

"I highly doubt that," his brow furrowed, "but I'll bite. Tell me about this supposed relic."

Elwyn searched her hazy memories for the exact term Blithely had used when offering her the job—a trinket? A token?

"A charm." The word found her tongue. "An Unseelie charm."

Black let out a single, curt laugh. "You came here chasing a Faerie story? That's pathetic, even for you."

"It's real," Elwyn assured him, trying to muster conviction. "I was offered a hefty sum to retrieve it, but I thought Father Beaus would make better use of it than some stranger in a ridiculous red hat."

Black's smile faded, and the color drained from his face. "What did this man call himself?"

AEDYN

Aedyn wore the uniform of a palace guard—along with her face and dusky hair—but he let those illusions drop the moment he deemed it safe. Glamour had no weight, but he had always found it terribly heavy. A problem of privilege, he supposed. He could be anyone, at least for a time, but he much preferred to be himself.

Samhrai was a realm in its own right, its floors littered with grand gardens, arcane armories, prim parlors, and labyrinthine libraries. Navigating the palace was a chore, even for those who lived within its gilded halls. Lucky for him, Deilin was a creature of habit.

After climbing several spiral staircases, Aedyn stepped out into one of Samhria's largest and most extravagant courtyards. He paused just beyond the garden gates, tilting his head back and letting the sunlight soak into his veins. The rays fed something intrinsic, restoring the luster he'd lost to his illusions.

Refreshed, he leaned over the oraithvine fence to better scan his surroundings. Splendid topiaries of fae and fauna loomed over beds of frillroses. Glistening pools of azure, amethyst, and amber littered the soil— steppingstones gifted to the Maithe by the Sidhe. Piskies and sprites darted to and fro, mere dots of iridescence in the distance.

Everything looked tediously normal with the exception of one trail. Roughly half of the plants around it had withered, their stocks dried yellow and their petals furled. The rest had flourished to the point of overgrowing the path, their branches entwining and their fruit dropping prematurely to the dirt.

Aedyn hopped the fence and followed the signs, skirting piles of rotting leaves and ducking beneath mossy tangles. They led him to the garden's center, where he found his friend balanced precariously on the rim of a crystal fountain.

Deilin was a tall, improbably thin man with the sunken features and long, knotted locks of a vagrant. He wore his usual attire, a ratty patchwork suit covered in pockets and a simple black bowler cap. As he rounded the fountain, placing one foot carefully in front of the other, he sprinkled the contents of a velvet sack into the water. Colorful fish bobbed up to the surface, eagerly devouring the offering. Some grew twice their size in a blink; others turned belly up just as fast.

Poor things. They hadn't even known they were gambling.

"Aedyn, my friend," Deilin said without looking up. "Should I pretend to be surprised?"

"It would certainly make me feel better." Aedyn sat on the rim, purposely obstructing Deilin's path. "I would hate to seem predictable."

"Everyone is predictable to some extent." Deilin hopped to the ground and bowed to Aedyn, who waved the gesture off.

"You've no need for such formalities."

"I realize this," Deilin replied. "But such things are expected."

"You do love to make a point, don't you?" Aedyn leaned back, closing his eyes and breathing in the sunlight deeply. "Beautiful day, not that

Talunasa's ever seen an ugly one. I can see why you always choose this place over the ballroom."

"You are mistaken, my friend." Deilin sat beside Aedyn and scooped a dead fish from the water, then took a large bite from the creature's belly. "I do not care much for sunlight or gardens, as well you should know by now. It's only that I hate crowds and music all the more."

Fish guts dangled from his mouth as he spoke, but Aedyn maintained eye contact. His friend had an unsettling way about him, but he was not the sort of person anyone wanted to offend.

"You're here on business, I assume?"

Deilin had a smile like crepe paper. "Always."

Aedyn reached into his coat pocket, and grabbed his purse, which was lighter than he'd hoped it would be. "What can this get me?" he asked, tossing it to Deilin.

Deilin gave the bag a quick jingle and laughed a sandpaper laugh. He rummaged through a few of his pockets before producing a tiny vial. "Love spell?" he asked, offering it to Aedyn. "Add it to the drink of your intended, and you'll have no need of luck."

"I'm plenty lucky without it," Aedyn replied, winking.

"Fine, fine." Deilin tucked the vial away. "Are you in need of more shadowroot, then? Perhaps some essence of fire sprite?"

Aedyn rested his head in his hand, sighing dramatically.

"You are a picky customer." Deilin's sunken eyes narrowed. "Perhaps before I offer a cure, you should tell me of the symptoms."

"Oh, you know, the usual. The colors have faded, the music has dulled, the food has gone stale, and the drink has soured. The trysts are fleeting and the shadowroot, weak. The dancing is droll and the job ... well, the job is just boring as hell."

"It sounds like you have a serious case of *the discontent*, my friend," Deilin replied. "Not to worry, such things tend to shape the spirit rather than kill it. Perhaps you should just call these coins a gift and ride it out, eh?"

"Never a missed opportunity with you, is there, Deilin?"

Aedyn's friend chuckled, taking another bite from the fish that had begun to rot in his grasp. "A daytrip then?" he asked, spoiled guts dripping from his teeth. "There is nothing like a little distance from your blessings, if you seek to appreciate them."

Aedyn's smile lit up. "I'm listening."

"The Spring Isles are especially lovely right now, and there's always the Red Realm, if you're feeling adventurous."

"Intriguing enough, but I've been to both; I'm looking for something new."

"Aren't you always?" Deilin stroked his chin with a skeletal hand. "There is one other option," he said at last, "but I'm afraid it comes with great risk."

"I'm fine with risks if you are," Aedyn said, his interest piquing.

"Of course, it will cost you a bit more than what you've already given."

Aedyn pulled his golden dagger from its sheath, offering it to his friend.

"You may yet need that," Deilin warned.

"Not to worry." Aedyn lifted his coat to reveal an ornate oraithvine rapier. "I have this."

Deilin accepted the dagger and it slipped into a pocket far too small to hold it. He then pulled a tin cup from another such pocket, and a flask from a third, even smaller. As he poured the contents of the flask into the cup, Aedyn caught a saccharine scent.

"More spriteberry?" He groaned. "Really?"

"You know what they say about beggars?"

"That they smell bad, and they drink bland wine?"

Deilin produced a strange copper coin from who-knows-where, dropped it into the drink with a dull *plunk*, then passed the cup to Aedyn. "Drink up."

Aedyn raised an eyebrow. "I think I'll require a preview."

"Do you not trust me, my friend?"

"Did *he?*" Aedyn nodded to the fish remains Deilin had tossed to the soil.

"Fair point." Deilin licked his finger and dipped it into the drink, stirring slowly. "What do you wish to see?"

Aedyn pondered the question for a moment. As much as he loved the idea of traveling blindly, he didn't want to wind up in the middle of a battlefield or, worse, a wall. He supposed he could ask to see the prettiest woman in the mystery realm, or the most exciting menagerie, or whatever poor prick best deserved a good pranking, but those options all felt a little too small, too rigid.

"Show me something entirely new," he said instead. "Something peculiar and important that has never happened anywhere before. Something remarkable."

Deilin cocked his head and gave the tincture one final swirl. Colors danced in the wine eddy, settling as the surface stilled. The hues deepened, melting into a portrait of starlight and silhouettes. Aedyn peered through the Aether Window as two figures, mortals from the looks of them, scaled a wrought iron fence. The moment they landed, they crouched beneath the foliage, a sure sign they were not welcome wherever they were headed.

Aedyn shivered even as he smirked. He had not wanted to guess his destination, but mortals rarely ventured through the Veil. *Risky indeed.*

"You had better be right about this," one figure whispered. The voice belonged to a man, and it did not sound happy.

"I already told you," said the other, a woman. "Blithely swore there is an Unseelie charm somewhere in that mansion. Do you want to bring it to the Father or not?"

Curious. Perhaps Aedyn's guess had been off. Neither Seelie or Unseelie had been permitted into the Mortal Realm since they signed the Treaty of Dusk. Only Solitaries had maintained that right, as they had no interest in using it for conquest.

Intrigued, he continued watching as the figures slunk through the shadows, weaving their way toward a silent white house on a hill.

"What lies beyond the threshold is anybody's guess;
It's a dangerous business, but it's business nonetheless."

CHAPTER II

THE OTHER SIDE OF THE DOOR

ELWYN

evlin Manor had looked peaceful from afar, but a sense of dread gripped Elwyn as she stepped into its shadow, slowing her gait even more than the dregs of poison still seeping through her veins. The peaked eaves and ivy-laden towers looked nearly sinister in the dark of night, and the stifling silence which hung over the grounds chilled her very soul. She had never believed in ghosts, but if they existed anywhere, it was there.

It did not improve her mood any that a Greyscale assassin was hovering behind her, his twin daggers leveled at her back and a third—her own *icon*—tucked beneath his cape. That Black had agreed to visit the manor at all was a miracle. He hadn't bought a word of her tale until she mentioned Blithely Fox. Elwyn wondered what connection the assassin could possibly have to the man in red, but she did not intend to stick around long enough figure it out.

"I know you have your reasons to see the job is done,

But once you have your balance back, we really ought to run," Luatha sang, flitting ahead to light a path for Elwyn.

Elwyn nodded subtly. She did not relish the idea of leaving *Gelah* with

Black, but no knife, no matter how magical, was worth her life. She would slip away at the first opportunity, dagger or no dagger.

Knowing now was most certainly not the time, she slunk toward the servants' entrance like a dutiful little ne're-do-well.

"No." Black growled. "That's exactly where they'd expect thieves to enter."

"In Pondrelle, you'd be right," Elwyn argued. "Here, they don't expect thieves at all."

"If they catch us, it's your head. Theirs' too, for that matter."

Elwyn didn't pay the threat much mind. She didn't doubt Black would have relished killing her, but he'd already mentioned returning her to the Greyscale. He was a loyal hound if nothing else. She would have to push him pretty far before he'd disobey the Father.

She should have been elated at the silence beyond the servants' door—the fewer people who crossed their path, the fewer corpses Black would leave in his wake—but something about it felt wrong. Even if most of the staff had been released to attend the festival, a few should have lingered behind to attend the evening's chores.

Perhaps they were all upstairs.

Black twisted a dagger against Elwyn's spine. "Need I make a stronger point?"

Grimacing, Elwyn opened the door. Moonlight poured into a cramped washroom, illuminating a morbid mess. There were no full bodies, just bits of them—splintered bones floating in washbasins, eyes peeking out from linen baskets, a mangled arm tossed haphazardly atop a shelf. Red snaked between the floorboards and spattered the walls, still glossy and fresh enough to reek.

Bile rose in Elwyn's throat. She covered her mouth and turned to retreat, but her captor blocked her path, pressing a blade above her heart.

"Going somewhere?" Black peered past her, his eyes narrowed. "It seems you were right, for once. This mansion holds something of interest, and we're clearly not the only interested party."

"You must be joking," Elwyn said. "The charm has probably already been found, and whatever found it might still be here."

"Perfect," Black grinned, entirely unfazed. "Blithely didn't give you specifics, right? I was going to torture the residents until they coughed up the details, amongst other things, but it will save us a lot of time to steal the charm from another brigand."

"You think a *person* did this?"

"Of course it was a person." The assassin backed her into the washroom. "You don't believe in monsters, do you, Slate?"

I'm looking at one. Elwyn swallowed the thought. She fixed her eyes on Luatha and ascended the staircase at knifepoint. With careful footing, she could nearly ignore the entrails that wound down the steps like a waterfall.

The piskie sang all the while, but her lyrics were not soothing.

"We're marching toward the gallows, toward the belly of the beast,

But, one way or another, you just might earn your release."

Elwyn stepped into a sprawling kitchen and gagged at the stench of burning flesh. A corpse lay slumped against one of several smoldering stoves, half his face melted to the iron.

"That's a fire hazard." Black clucked his tongue. "Fix it, won't you?"

As though Elwyn had a choice.

She looked away as she tore the man free, but the *riiipping* sound made her stomach flip. Letting the body drop to the tiles, she straightened for a better look at the room. Three doorways, not counting the one they'd entered through.

"We should split up to cover more ground," she suggested.

Black's blade bit through satin. Blood trickled down her spine.

"Fine then," she said. "Can I at least search the drawers for the charm?"

"For a weapon, you mean?" Black chuckled. "No one's going to hide something supernatural in a knife drawer. I suggest you stop trying my patience."

Elwyn probably couldn't have fought Black off, anyway. He had bested her in battle before, and her scar was evidence.

At his bidding, they tiptoed through several more lavish rooms, but found nothing of interest in any of the shelves or drawers they rifled through. Thankfully, they found *nobody* of interest, either. At least, not anyone living.

The dead, by contrast, were plentiful. By the time they reached the foyer, they'd probably stumbled upon a dozen corpses. The exact number was impossible to discern, given their scattered states. The body that lay in the entryway was more intact than the others, missing only its head. Its three-piece suit was a perfect match for one worn by a man in the portrait beside the door, which also featured a woman and little girl with sunshine-yellow curls.

As Elwyn followed Luatha to another staircase, she found the missing head. It had been mounted on the spiked top of a balustrade, its eyes rolled back. Blood caked its mustache—much, *much* too fresh.

"Every one of these kills is recent," she whispered, deciding the Greyscale was no longer a worst-case scenario. "We can't risk lingering any longer. I'll take whatever punishment I owe, just please—"

Someone knocked on the door. Black whirled toward the sound, weapons at the ready. It was as good an opening as Elwyn could hope for. She bounded up the staircase, which spiraled on for much too long, but her newfound freedom died swiftly. The moment she reached the upper landing, the assassin threw her to the floor, his knee pinning her in place.

"Get off me, you—"

"Shh!" Black wrapped a hand over her mouth, grazing her cheek with the blade it held.

Hinges groaned as the door below swung open.

"I've returned, as promised." The voice was inhuman—dozens of whispers woven into one. "You should know it's impolite to keep a guest waiting."

Black held a finger to his lips, then rolled off Elwyn. When he crept over to the railing, she followed against her better judgement, peering down into the foyer.

The waning light of a predawn moon spilled across the floor, stretching the shadow of a ghastly woman into a jagged spire. She was pale as death, and her hair and gown seemed to flutter against the wind. Her eyes burned with the same violet light that trailed behind Luatha and sparked in *Gelah's* cryptic runes.

She drifted forward to loom over the body, her steps eerily silent. "You should have agreed when first I asked," she said, almost pensive. "Pity, you chose the more painful path."

At the snap of her fingers, the door slammed shut, and every candle in the foyer flared to life. The newborn flames danced in a sourceless breeze, turning her slender shadow into twenty. Elwyn trapped a breath as those shadows began to writhe, clawing at the floor with night-black talons. They stretched and strained and snapped free of their host, blinking sallow eyes into being.

"You know what I seek," the woman said. "Be swift about it."

The shadow creatures skulked obediently through the room, probing flowerpots and overturning bins. Elwyn's pulse thundered as the largest made its way toward the stairs, sniffing at the air. Its yellow eyes widened, snapping toward the woman in white.

"I...smeeell...warrrm...blooooooood."

Elwyn rolled away from the railing, springing to her feet. A chorus of feral growls broke out below, and carpet tore beneath a flurry of talons.

"Find an open window, or we're going to find our doom,

If we don't make our exit, this house will be our tomb!" Luatha latched onto Elwyn's shoulder, her claws piercing skin.

Black caught up swiftly, testing the handle of each door they passed.

Locked.

Locked.

Locked.

Lock—a knob turned.

The assassin wrenched the door open and pulled Elwyn through it. He snicked it shut behind them with a surprising amount of discretion, then placed his back to it, chest heaving.

"What the fuck is happening?" he rasped.

Elwyn was more concerned about what might happen next. The room they found themselves in seemed to belong to a little girl, with floral walls and dainty furnishings. Dolls enough for a nursery crowded the plush covers of a canopy bed, and more peered out from a toy bin in the corner. More importantly, a pair of lavender drapes rustled around an open window large enough to crawl through.

Before Elwyn could act, Luatha flitted in front of her.

"Before you let your logic drown beneath a wave of fear,

Take care enough to realize we're not alone in here."

Elwyn hadn't heard the sniffling over the thrum of her own heart, and she had no clue where it was coming from. The assassin's eyes were dry as ever, though his jaw was clenched so tightly it looked like it might break.

With no help from her captor, Elwyn shoved the toy bin in front of the door and started through the room, ears strained. The sniffles led her to a trembling pile of blankets in the corner.

Elwyn hated looking to Black for help, but he had the weapons. She motioned him closer before pulling back the blankets. Beneath them, a little girl cowered, clinging to a corpse of a yellow-haired woman with a gaping hole in her chest.

The girl shrieked, and Elwyn grabbed hold of her, covering her mouth. Too late.

"I hear you, child." Voices slithered like a viper nest, drawing closer. "Reveal yourself, dear girl. Let me bring an end to your woes."

Tepid tears trickled over Elwyn's fingers. Elwyn shushed the child, pointing to the window. The moment Elwyn released her, the girl shrunk back to the corpse she'd been cradling.

"I know you're in there," the voices sang. Something heavy slammed against the door. The wood began to splinter, violet light seeping through the cracks.

"Leave the brat!" Black hissed, eyes wide.

He was right. They could not afford an extra burden. Still, Elwyn pulled the child over to the window, and was grateful to see lattice stretching toward the garden below.

"Start climbing," she whispered, hoisting the girl over the sill.

Another *crash*. Another *crack*. Claws wriggled through crevices, rending oak like flesh.

"Out of my way!" Black pushed past Elwyn, nearly knocking the child loose as he scrambled down the lattice. He broke into a sprint the second his boots hit soil, headed for the nearest woods with Elwyn's *icon* still glinting at his side.

Bastard.

The door shattered down the center. A writhing mass of claws and teeth spilled into the room. Elwyn threw herself over the sill, her fingers and toes barely grazing the lattice on the way down. The creatures crawled out the window behind her, descending face-first like hunting spiders. Their silhouettes twisted in the wind like smoke, swallowing the nascent light of dawn.

Elwyn dropped to the ground beside the child and started off in the direction of the wood.

"P-please!" The girl called, stumbling after her. "Wait for me!"

Those sobs would drown Elwyn, if she let them, but she'd fought for too long and hard to make a martyr of herself.

I've helped more than I had to—a coward's justification, and one she'd fallen back on countless times. She'd said it when leaving initiates in the thick of their own botched burglaries. She'd whispered it as less fortunate Greyscale girls suffered at the hands and hungers of their male counterparts. She'd even uttered it at age ten, when she'd left her ailing mother to die in a brothel bed.

Cruel or not, the philosophy had kept her alive.

Elwyn was gaining on Black, who had nearly reached the bordering woods, when a violet light zipped past her.

"It's not easy to think clearly when your life is at stake,
But now might be your only chance to make a clean escape."

An excellent point.

Elwyn veered toward the nearest road, hoping it would lead her back to the village square, and thanked Luatha under her breath. Troublesome though the piskie could be, she had always been a loyal friend—comforting, cheering, and protecting Elwyn ever since she was a little...

Shit!

Something cracked. It might have been Elwyn's resolve. It might have been her mind. It might have been her heart. Whatever it was, it brought her flight to an end. She glanced back to find the shadow hordes were gaining on the little girl as she stumbled through the garden. Their banshee of a leader drifted above them, arms outstretched toward her helpless target.

Elwyn took a deep breath, cursing her conscience, and darted toward the horde. Adrenaline sped her weary feet, and she scooped the child up in a matter of seconds. A claw caught her skirt as she pivoted, tearing silk. The creatures growled, shrieked, and hissed, smacking salivating tongues against their lips. Their humid breath gusted Elwyn's legs as she ran. With every frantic step, the girl grew heavier, and the monsters grew closer. Elwyn's hopes guttered.

They weren't going to make it to the forest. Not together.

"Run!" Elwyn said, flinging the child toward the tree line. She spared Luatha—just a speck against green—a parting glance, then lifted her eyes to the sunrise. The colors looked brighter than ever before, and far more beautiful.

As far as final sights went, it wasn't awful.

A terrible weight sent her sprawling. Growls filled her ears, claws raked her skin, and gritty tongues lapped at her blood. The world turned to agony, to darkness and screeching.

To think, she hadn't even really *lived*.

Preserving the sunrise behind her eyelids, Elwyn forced her thoughts to the things that mattered. Morning dew melted against her cheek, cold and fresh and sweetly scented. A warm breeze wafted past, rousing the sting of fresh wounds. The tittering melody of a robin lilted above the snarling din. Soon, the pain and terror drowned beneath those pleasant things.

The void was not empty, as she'd feared.

Just when Elwyn had resigned herself to slumber, a familiar voice cut through the darkness, dispelling it.

"Wake the fuck up, Slate."

*"Their natures will stay hidden unless you give them cause,
Not all angels have halos, and not all demons have claws."*

CHAPTER 12
MONSTER
BRANNON

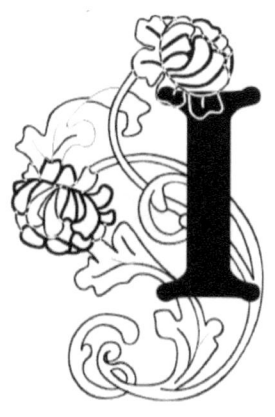 t had been a hell of a night—a literal one, in Brannon's estimation. To think, he'd never even believed in Hell. He hadn't believed in anything, really, aside from breath and the lack of it.

"Oh, good. You're awake," he said as Slate's eyes fluttered open.

"What...what happened?"

Good question. Brannon was still struggling with the existence of those horrid creatures and the ghastly woman who'd summoned them, not to mention their sudden disappearance. The moment sunlight touched them, they faded away like wisps of smoke, leaving Brannon with an unconscious thief, a deathly pale child, and nightmares behind his eyelids.

"You can stand, can't you?" He leveled his *Aras Tosc* at the thief, whose wounds looked largely superficial. "I know you're weak, but you're not helpless."

Slate shot a defiant glare his way, but rose, nonetheless. The little imp she'd stupidly deigned to save scurried to her side, mumbling a nearly inaudible, "Thank you."

Brannon turned a dagger on the girl. "Speaking of helpless..."

"There's no reason to harm her!" Slate dove in the way, splaying her arms as the world's feeblest shield.

Perhaps the child had value after all. For those burdened by sentiment, emotional tethers could be sturdier than actual chains. "Fine," Brannon relented. "We'll take her to Saint Aldrich's."

"Are you insane?" The thief's gray eyes flexed wide. "Clearly, there are more important matters at—"

"Nothing is as important as the mission!" Brannon prodded Slate's sternum with his dagger, eliciting a wince. "You decided to interfere with her fate. Now, Father can decide both of yours."

The thief's eyes flicked to where he'd stowed her dagger. No doubt, she wanted to stab him as much as he wanted to stab her. "We should at least discuss what happened," she breathed. "It could easily happen again."

Brannon was tempted to take up the offer. He could not reason away what he'd witnessed, and it would've helped to commiserate with someone, even a wayward agent. He shrugged the temptation away, swallowing his questions. He absolutely hated sharing. Even experiences. Even if they hurt. Even if it helped.

"Let's get moving." He waved an *Aras Tosc* toward the nearest road. "The nearest port town's days away, and we're sure as hell not passing through Amblewick to get there."

His threats hardly fazed Slate, which was annoying. They set the child to trembling, which was even worse. They would never reach the mainland if she cowered at his every glare. "What is your name, girl?" he asked, stepping closer.

She whimpered, shrinking behind Slate.

Brannon's knuckles blanched around steel hilts. "I asked—"

Slate held up a hand, shaking her head. That insolence would have been rewarded with a swift slice, but her simple act of kneeling by the child seemed to have a calming effect on her.

"How about we exchange them?" she asked, clasping the girl's hand. "I'm Slate, and he goes by Black."

Lavender eyes darted to Brannon and back. "We're going by nicknames?" she asked, gaze dropping to her slippers. "Then you can call me Monster."

Brannon gritted his teeth. "That's not—"

"Monster *Devlin*?" Slate asked.

The girl nodded.

Apparently, there was more than one way to get information. The child was lucky to have spit it up, too. As a member of the Devlin family, she probably knew something about the supposed charm, which added to her value. Upon returning to Saint Aldrich's, Brannon would pry the information from beneath her little fingernails, then leave her to the mercy of the syndicate.

Surely, Father Beaus would be pleased with his offerings.

"On your way then, Monster." He urged his captives toward the road. "We've a long walk ahead of us."

TAWNY

Dappled sunlight danced across the grass, filtering through branches rustled by a floral breeze. Tawny did her best to avoid the rays, but the task was nearly impossible. The Spring Isles were nothing like the Shifting Wilds, where the sun was a fixed sliver on the horizon, ever obscured by a blanket of fog.

When she'd made her very first component run, she'd returned home red as a sugar beet. Luckily for her, Mother was able to whip up a salve that leeched the sting from her skin in a heartbeat. Still, it was best to avoid the issue altogether.

She picked at a sprig of yellow flowers and was startled when it picked back, chittering madly as it scurried off into the underbrush.

"Sorry!" she called after the Hazel-Witch.

She'd always had such trouble distinguishing them from witch hazel.

After rifling about a bit longer, Tawny found the blossoms she'd been looking for. She plucked a couple tonic's worth of sprigs, tossing them into her basket, then settled cross legged in the shade to inventory her findings.

"Let's see...spriteberries and thistles. Butterbreeze and witch hazel. Lavender, cherry blossom, burn-leaf, licorice root. That about does it."

Except for the golden apples. Those were always such a bother to collect. Unlike the literally hundreds of varieties of apples that grew in the Spring Isles, the golden ones never fell from their tethers and, naturally, they grew only on the upper branches of the tallest trees. Thankfully,

Tawny was an expert climber. Of all the treats the Seelie lands offered, the apples were Mother's favorite.

The temporal difference between the Realms of Light and Shadow was difficult to track, so Tawny assumed she was running short on time. She hopped to her feet and started her search, hoping to have the kettle brewing by the time Mother returned from her journey. After only a few minutes, she spotted a glimmer of gold among the green.

The tree was probably thirty feet tall, but it was also the thick, gnarled type—brimming with natural footholds. Undaunted, Tawny hid her basket in a spriteberry bush, dusted her palms with chalk, and began her ascent.

The higher she climbed, the thinner the branches grew, and the more space stretched between them. Soon, she had to tilt to her tiptoes to keep a decent grip. Patches of sunlight brushed her skin, warm and gentle like the aura of a hearth fire. It always felt pleasant at first. Then came the burning and the blisters. She willed herself upward despite the risks, focusing instead on the brilliant landscape.

She traveled to the Spring Isles far more often than Talunasa or the Red Realm, but they never failed to awe her. Wildflowers and verdant glens blanketed the grassy hills that rolled like emerald waves to each horizon. Flocks of brilliant birds and cliques of glimmering sprites flitted between branches coated in chartreuse leaves or cherry blossoms. Sylph temples, simplistic and serene, stood sentry on cliffsides overlooking the Parting Seas. In the near distance, another island hovered above the waves, bridged to the waters below by dozens of slender, crystalline waterfalls.

Before Tawny knew it, she'd reached the canopy. When she grasped for the apple, it bounced off her fingertips, bobbing from its wooden tether. She gripped the overhead branch tightly, lifted one leg to lean forward, stretched as far as she could, and...*Got it!*

The branch beneath her bowed, cracked, and snapped.

Wind rushed through Tawny's yellow curls. Branches snapped against her limbs. She closed her eyes, praying to the Shadows that the fall would be swift and the landing soft.

The impact knocked the breath from Tawny's lungs and sent pain skittering from head to toe. She furled forward, cradling her aching head and blinking her eyes open. The tree was staring back at her, eyes keen beneath mossy, hooded lids. Thoroughly embarrassed, Tawny used nearby branches to hoist herself upright, belatedly realizing they were fingers.

"Sorry for climbing you without asking." She dusted off her tattered dress and fumbled into a curtsy. "Then again, you should expect that sort of treatment if you go around acting like trees all the time."

The tree warped in a way that made it look supremely puzzled. It tilted, letting out a wooden groan.

"Hmm...I'm afraid I'm not familiar with that dialect. I don't suppose you speak the common tongue. Perhaps a smattering of Umbral?"

It shook, raining leaves on Tawny.

"I'll take that as a no." She plucked a sprig from her curls. "What I'd give for an interpreter."

"It wrecks my entertainment, but I suppose that you did *ask.*
My friend is quite soft-spoken, so I'll speak on his behalf."

Startled, Tawny glanced around for the source of the voice until something tapped the toe of her boot. An apple-green figure—not quite five inches tall—stood before her feet. Its thorny skin reminded her of rose stems, and its wings looked like serrated leaves.

"You're a piskie!" Tawny squealed, kneeling for a better look. Though court-less, their kind rarely visited the Shadow Realms, where darker, more bitey types roamed.

The creature bowed.

"You recognize my splendor, and for that I am well pleased.
Now tell me, little human, just what is it that you seek?"

Tawny grinned. The rot-fae that fluttered around her cottage were roughly the same size and shape as piskies, but they couldn't speak, and their insectile bodies and decaying wings were not particularly cute.

"I was going to get an apple," Tawny said, shrugging. "This turn of events is far more interesting. I've never conversed with anything so adorable!"

The piskie's ink-drop eyes narrowed.

"Adorable? You call me that and think you can survive?
Just who are you? Some nosy child? What makes you qualified?"

It was more a rant than a question, but Tawny answered anyway. "I'm a visitor from the Shifting Wilds," she explained. "And I don't *think* I'm a child, though I have misplaced my fair share of days. Years, maybe."

The piskie tapped its little chin, then turned to face the tree. It chittered in another tongue—a series of squeaks and trills that somehow managed to rhyme—and it did not sound particularly happy.

"Did I somehow offend you?" Tawny asked. "Or do you just not like the Shadow Realms?"

The piskie grinned over its spindly shoulder.

A moment later, Tawny landed in a nearby bush, a bevy of apples pelting her. Always one to look on the bright side, she scooped up the fruit, happy to spot a few gold ones in the bunch. Once she'd filled her basket and sidled out of firing range, she waved at the tree-creature and shouted her thanks.

Mother was going to love this story.

The Spring Isles spun around Tawny like a whirlwind, brilliant blue and green smears melting into streaks of crimson and charcoal. They churned for some time before snapping into place, jolting her into misty autumnal woods. She fell to her hands and knees, dropping her basket and nearly spilling its contents. There, she waited for the tastes of bile and chalky potion to flee her tongue.

As exhilarating as the destinations could be, Tawny detested the *travel* part of traveling.

She'd landed in a toadstool ring; the same she'd left from hours before. At least, it had been hours *to her*, though a week might well have passed in the Wilds. Toadstool rings were among the few fixed points in the ever-changing landscape of her homeland. Once, Tawny had attempted to travel by potion alone, believing her cottage would remain where she left it. It had traveled several miles in her absence, and she'd gotten tangled in a giant spiderweb that had appeared in its place. Ever since, she'd been diligent about departing from rings.

Stomach settled, she scooped up her basket and headed toward home. The Wilds shifted around her as she walked, soil churning, roots writhing, trails rerouting in all directions. It was hardly a wonder visitors—fae and mortal alike—got lost in the woods so often. Tawny didn't have that problem. She'd lived there long enough to read the tilt of the soil, the scent of the wind, and the pattern of the dull stars that twinkled in the lilac sky above.

The forest had a percussive cadence to it. As she pressed through the ever-present fog, amber leaves rustled beneath the roots of wandering trees. Acorns fell, and rot-fae chittered. Brooks babbled, and brittle twigs *cracked* beneath her feet. She had just caught a whiff of the ginger wind that would lead her home when she heard a loud *snap* that didn't quite fit the rhythm. She ducked into the mists, dropping her basket and scrounging for a branch. Her fingers wrapped around one with a decent heft to it, and she waited.

Snap! It came from her left this time, followed by a *crunch-crunch-crunch* from behind. Tawny readied herself, following the noises with her makeshift staff. *Crash!* A hoof shot out from the foliage, aimed right at her face. She used the branch to deflect it, spinning to the side. She leapt, anticipating a second hoof, aimed at her ankles, then landed in a crouch. A pair of horns burst through the fog. She dodged them, sweeping her assailant's legs and sending them toppling into a pile of leaves.

The leaves shook with laughter, and a familiar face poked out from them. "I almost got you!"

"Thank the Shadows you didn't!" Tawny sighed with relief. "For the last time, Daulle. My kind doesn't bounce back as easily as yours."

Daulle shook his entire body, spraying leaves in all directions, but a few stranglers clung to his furry haunches. Tawny laughed, plucking a twig out from behind one of his stubby horns, then set to work retrieving the components that had spilled in the scuffle, when her basket tipped.

"Didya' bring me a present?" Her friend's hooves *clopped* loudly as he trotted to her side. Before she could answer, he snatched up a handful of berries and shoved them into his mouth.

"These are spell components!" Tawny swatted him half-heartedly. "Not souvenirs!"

Even so, she plucked a pair of apples—the red and green type with little metaphysical value—from the basket and tossed them his way. He caught the fruit with near-human hands and began to juggle as he and Tawny marched toward the cottage. Throughout the hike, Tawny told him about the living tree and its tiny friend.

"Can I go with next time?" Daulle asked, though Unseelie were miserable in direct sunlight. He tossed one apple high and bit into the other without pausing. "I alwaysh wondered wha' Pishkiee tashtes like."

"Eww!" Tawny's nose wrinkled. "If you don't start swallowing your food before speaking, Mother will never have you over for dinner again!"

"Meh," Daulle shoved the rest of the apple into his mouth, core and all. "She'sh kinda' a bisssch anyway."

Tawny punched his shoulder, prompting a flippant apology. "Mother is good to me," she said. "I've seen how others treat their wards."

Only one other mortal lived within several miles of Tawny's cottage. He was about her age—sixteen, give or take—and he belonged to a coven of marsh hags. They treated him as most Unseelie treated their mortals, using him to run their Light Realm errands and tormenting him in the off-hours. In the four years since his arrival in the Wilds, Tawny had never seen him without fresh bruises.

"How is Flint, anyway?" she asked.

Daulle shrugged, kicking a pebble from the path with a careless hoof. It rolled southwest despite the eastern tilt of the earth. "We're almost at your place," he said.

"Are you avoiding the question?"

Daulle sighed, running his fingers through his course hair, the color of rust. "Why do you care about that guy anyway? He's always been an ass to you. If I hadn't stepped in last week, he'd have probably choked you to death."

To Tawny, it had only been a little over a day. The skin around her neck still stung. She rubbed it absently.

"Mother says people act the way they're treated. He hasn't known much kindness. Who will he learn it from, if not us?"

"*Mother says mehmehmemeh...*" Daulle mocked.

Tawny tried to punch him again, but he dodged the swing. "You've no room to talk. Didn't you just try to beat me to a pulp?"

"That's different! I need to practice for my—"

"For your eventual battle with Mailair, the Prince-often Princess-Sometimes Both-and-On at Least One Occasion-Neither of the Shifting Wilds. I know, I know."

Daulle stopped, donning a serious scowl. "They killed my Father, Tawny. That was my right, and they stole it." Quick as it had come, the scowl vanished. "So, want to practice again tomorrow?"

Tawny shook her head. Emotions never stuck to Daulle. He had been that way ever since they were both little girls. "You know if you kill me, that's it, right?" she reminded him. "I don't just get a million chances like you fae."

Daulle shrugged. He'd never really grasped the differences between Augusky and mortals, despite Tawny's obvious lack of hooves and horns. Once, he'd even asked if she planned on becoming a boy at any point. She'd been considering it before Mother explained the obstacles.

"We don't know for sure your death will be permanent," Daulle mused, an opine ear flicking. "That's just what *Mother says.*"

At last, the woods opened around the cottage. Tawny was surprised by how much it had grown since she left; she might not have recognized it were it not for the waterwheel she'd helped Mother fix countless times, and the ginger wind that wafted ceaselessly around it. Once a quaint, rustic shelter, it had morphed into seven stories of jutting, asymmetrical rooms, each crafted in clashing hues and textures. Mother's Shadow Goblins were efficient workers, but they were not the most aesthetically-minded.

They were about to climb the front staircase when Daulle froze, ears twitching and hackles raised. Tawny heard it a second later—a chorus of tortured shrieks and moans, weaving through the woods. Branches rattled, tossing amber leaves to the ground, and every chittering creature in the canopy fell silent.

The Wailing Wind.

"Well, see you tomorrow maybe!" Daulle leapt forward, shifting into a true goat mid-bound, and sprang off into the mists.

Tawny scrambled up the staircase, heart pounding. The Wind was yet a ways off, but the yellow eyes blinking out from between the steps didn't help matters. By the time she climbed all seven flights, her calves ached bitterly. Soon, she'd need to graft a toadstool ring at the top just to make the journey bearable.

The door was slightly ajar, and yellow light flickered through the crack.

Damn it to daylight! So much for making it home before Mother.

A savory scent greeted Tawny upon entering the cottage, and Mother's cat, Solstice, rubbed against her leg, insubstantial as mist. She scratched him behind the spectral ear as best she could, and he purred contentedly.

The only sounds coming from the kitchen were that of a bubbling cauldron and a scraping spoon. No hushed conversations. No stomping feet or clopping hooves.

Thank the Shadows.

Mother had been receiving lots of visitors of late, and their talk of treaties and treason made the cottage feel less homey. Tawny was grateful that, at least for the evening, it would only be the two of them.

"Just in time for dinner," Mother said as Tawny stepped into the kitchen. She dropped her stirring spoon, and it ringed the cauldron rim, threatening to fall in.

Tawny set her basket down to curtsy, as she'd been taught, then dropped all pretense of civility and ran forward. Though Mother was always cold, her embrace was warm and pleasant. Tawny had never understood why others, like Daulle, were so intimidated by her. A wealth of kindness lurked beneath her stern disposition, and there was a peculiar beauty to her pallid hair and skin, her gaunt frame and flowing gowns.

"I've brought you presents!" Tawny said, nodding to her basket.

Mother thanked her, promising to sort through the spoils later that evening. "I've brought you something as well."

She raked a sharp nail through the air, slicing a gash in the Aether. Darkness wisped from the tear like smoke, twisting in tendrils. Reaching her hand in, Mother retrieved three gowns, each a different hue and size.

"I couldn't be sure what your measurements would be when I returned," Mother mused, holding the garments up to Tawny in rapid succession. "Oh, good. The green one will fit. The color is a near match for your eyes, and the contrast with your hair is stunning."

Tawny had never cared much about fashion, but she returned the gesture with a grateful smile and excused herself to hang the gown in her chamber. By the time she returned, supper was on the table, barley soup. Tawny grinned. As much as she loved the Shifting Wilds, its cuisine contained too many slugs and slimes for her tastes. Thankfully, Mother had acquired a few mortal recipes on her travels.

The Wailing Wind circled the cottage as Tawny supped and Mother went through the motions, but the conversation was a sufficient distraction. When Tawny shared the story of the tree and its piskie, Mother found it as amusing as she'd hoped.

"That explains the bruises." She pretended to sip from an empty spoon. "Here, I thought I needed to have a word with those friends of yours."

Tawny assured her that would not be necessary. The last time Mother had a "word" with Flint, he'd coughed up spiders for a week.

"Enough about me." Tawny slurped up the last bit of her soup. "How was your trip?"

"It didn't go very well, I'm afraid." Mother tapped her fingers against the tabletop in an uncharacteristically nervous way. "I didn't obtain what I needed, but I suppose I shouldn't fret. I will have a few more opportunities, and I intend to make the most of them."

Mother didn't always have a say in when she traveled or for how long. Tawny's heart ached at the thought of being alone with the goblins again, but she pushed her worries aside. "I'm glad you're home for the moment," she said.

"There is no such place as home for me," Mother replied with a sad smile. "Not yet."

The talk turned to lighter subjects as the two cleared the dishes and scrubbed the kitchen, then Mother taught Tawny how to make a broth for healing bruises.

"Use Spriggan blood for the base, if you can manage it," she said, pouring a bottle of indigo liquid into the mix. "Rot fae will suffice in a pinch, but it's half as effective. And, whatever you do, don't forget the witch hazel."

Tawny tossed a handful of yellow petals into the cauldron. The brew bubbled, devouring them swiftly. "Mother..."

"What is it?"

"I...just...thank you. I'm really, truly grateful."

"No need for all that, dear." Mother chuckled, stirring the potion. "These are the kinds of things every young woman should learn."

"It's not just that," Tawny said. "Most mortals are nothing but servants here, but you ...well, you treat me like your own child."

The stirring spoon fell still, and Mother's gaze traveled somewhere distant, unknowable. "No dear," she said, staring right through Tawny. "I would never do that to you."

"If you think your eyes deceive you, you just might be correct,
Illusion is a power that wrecks worlds when left unchecked."

CHAPTER 13

ALL THAT GLITTERS

ELWYN

he Rhysien countryside had little to offer in terms of scenery. After a few hours of ceaseless walking, the dirt roads, wheatfields, and wind-battered farmhouses all began to look the same. Trapped and listless, Elwyn allowed herself to do something unusual—daydream.

In her imagination, the previous night had played out differently, and not only in that she hadn't been captured. She dreamt that Davin had turned out to be a better person, and they'd danced together until the music died. That she'd spent the evening chatting with Silva and Rayen—much to Mr. Elliot's exaggerated chagrin—and that they'd accompanied her and Davin to the next day's events. Somewhere in the mix of it all, she'd even gotten her first kiss.

She hadn't realized how much she'd wanted to belong in Amblewick until the possibility was torn from her. There was no returning, not even if Black died. The Greyscale would continue their search—leaving no stone unturned, no bystander uninterrogated—and she could not allow her friendly acquaintances to suffer for her stubbornness. Elwyn had never allowed herself to miss someone, not even her own mother. Now, she missed several. She'd hardly gotten to know them, granted, but "hardly" was better than she knew most people.

Dainty fingers wrapped around her own, tugging her back to the present. Monster hadn't spoken once throughout the trek, and she'd fixed her sullen eyes straight ahead. Elwyn recognized that expression, having worn it often throughout her own childhood—if a childhood it could be called. It was the look of someone who'd lost everything they'd ever known, someone frightened of what lie in wait, someone determined to press forward anyway.

"How old are you, anyway?" Elwyn asked.

The slightest smile flickered on the girl's lips before guttering out. "Nine years, eleven months, and twenty-two days."

"And you might live to nine years, eleven months, and twenty-three days if you keep quiet," Black growled behind them.

"He's grumpy," Monster mouthed.

Elwyn squeezed her hand. "Being in Black's company is like standing in a sewer," she whispered. "It's a shitty time that will leave you feeling nauseous for weeks."

Monster giggled, but Black's glare bored a hole in the nape of Elwyn's neck. She resolved to quit pushing her luck for a bit. The assassin had vowed to bring her back to the Father alive, but he'd said nothing about bringing her back intact. That threat counted double for Monster.

That poor child was in for a rough future. Elwyn was about her age when she took to the streets, and she still couldn't escape the life she'd fallen into that very night. Frail as she was, Monster wouldn't last a week in the Greyscale.

All the more reason to escape before reaching the mainland. It wasn't going to be easy. Black had keen eyes and fast hands, and he would gut them both before letting them slip away. But then, Pondrelle was a long ways off. If Elwyn could not find an escape route in that time, Luatha surely could.

The piskie had been uncharacteristically quiet all day, curled up on Elwyn's shoulder. Elwyn could not tell whether she was depressed, focused, or simply jealous of the child. Evening was approaching when her silence finally ended.

"This journey is a bother; it's downright untoward.
You're clearly getting tired, and, worse, I'm getting bored."

Minor problems, considering the bigger picture, but she was not alone in her exhaustion. Elwyn's feet had begun to throb, the sun beat down with zealous intensity, and dust coated her throat, robbing it of moisture. The child's gait was becoming progressively more sluggish with each step.

Elwyn was contemplating how she might convince Black to let them rest when something rustled to their right. She glanced over but found only a single scarecrow staked at the center of a field. *Peculiar.* She'd been tracking unusual landmarks but had failed to notice that one. Then again, it had been an exceptionally trying day.

They were cresting a particularly daunting hill when Monster's legs gave out, and she fell to the dirt, barely lucid. Black growled profanities, landing a kick on the girl's back before Elwyn pulled him away.

"Know your place!" He hissed, brandishing his blades.

"She's exhausted." Elwyn raised her palms. "She hasn't lived as we have. Honestly, I'm impressed she'd made it so far without complaining."

"You would be." Black sighed through clenched teeth. "I suppose neither of you is any good to me if you can't walk. Carry her that way, and you can have a few minutes reprieve." He waved a blade in the direction of some nearby elms. "This is for my own convenience, I assure you. Do not mistake it for kindness."

"I wouldn't dream of it."

Monster mumbled an apology as Elwyn scooped her up. Thankfully, it was a short walk to the trees. Relief flooded Elwyn when she set the girl down and sank to the grass, potent enough she feared fainting.

"At last, we've found some foliage; the rolling fields have passed.
I worried that, forevermore, I'd see nothing but grass."

"Because the setting is our chief concern," Elwyn mumbled, though the piskie had a point. The shade cast by the leaves and moss laden branches was a welcome comfort, and the songbird twittering somewhere nearby lifted her spirits by a surprising degree. Monster's too, from the look of things.

The girl plucked a fluffy white dandelion from the grass and blew, scattering seeds. Elwyn followed the little white glimmers through the air, wondering whether wishes held any weight. They vanished swiftly, leaving her to blink at the greener trees not half a mile off. Dense and dark, those woods would make for excellent cover. If only Black would look away for a few damned seconds.

The assassin was slumped against a trunk, rifling through his satchel by feel alone. "Here." He tossed a lump of bread to Elwyn. "That's all you'll be getting for a while."

He lobbed Monster a piece of her own, then treated himself to an apple. Elwyn had never envied Black before, despite his success in the syndicate, but the crisp sound of that fruit made her green with envy. Her own meal had the coloring and consistency of marble. She cursed herself for having eaten only a single pastry the night before.

Monster nibbled at her bread like a mouse with an acorn, perhaps stalling on purpose. Every little bite bought them time to recover. Elwyn cracked her ration in two, handing the larger piece to the girl and setting the other down for Luatha. The piskie sniffed at the offering, then crossed her spindly arms and turned up her nose.

"Better eat that," Monster said between nibbles. "There might not be much else for a while."

Elwyn's eyes widened. *She's probably talking to me. But what if...?*

"Hello, there!"

The woman seemed to have appeared out of nowhere, manifesting dangerously close to Black. She was dressed the way every milkmaid in history might have dressed, provided their uniforms were all designed by the same pubescent boy. Her green tartan skirt brushed just past her thighs, and her blouse's plunging neckline vanished beneath her vest. She even carried the obligatory empty pail.

She dipped into a curtsy, giving Black a deliberate view of her blouse's ample contents. The poor girl was fishing with the wrong bait. If she really wanted Black's attention, she'd need to let him break one of those legs she was so intent on flaunting. Maybe both.

"I'm sorry to have startled you." She tossed a strawberry braid over her shoulder. "Do you know the way to the nearest hamlet? I'm afraid I've gotten myself a teensy bit lost."

That was the wrong thing to say. Lost people made for easy targets; anything might happen to them. Elwyn did not miss Black's fleeting smile.

"Amblewick's a day's walk," Elwyn interrupted, tossing a thumb over her shoulder. "You'll want to go that way. Quickly."

The woman raised an eyebrow. "I was talking to the handsome gentleman," she said, pale eyes fixed on Black. "Not to be too forward, but would you care to guide me, even partway?"

Seeing Black tense, Elwyn covered Monster's eyes. She was not the only one to predict an attack. With the precision of a trained soldier, the woman dodged the dagger. She grabbed the assassin's arm and twisted sharply, kneeing him between the legs and sending him sprawling to the ground.

"Well?" She asked, looking at Elwyn. Her voice had lost its airy quality, and now sounded a little bit masculine. "Are you waiting for a carriage?"

Elwyn had a million questions and no time to ask them. She pulled Monster to her feet and dragged her toward the woods with all the speed her weary legs could muster. Before forging past the tree line, she glanced back to find that the milkmaid had vanished.

"Get back here!" The assassin shouted, struggling to his feet. "I'm warning you!"

Elwyn ignored the warning, continuing through the woods. There were no true trails in the underbrush—only thin gashes carved by wild game and patches of clay too dry to support greenery—but Luatha scouted ahead. She zipped between branches, brambles, and briars, circling back with rushed rhymes of the swiftest paths with the surest footing.

Monster proved a predictable burden. More than once, she tripped over a raised root or tangle of vines, and with each stumble, the sounds of stomping boots and snapping twigs grew closer. A few more, and the assassin would overtake them.

Elwyn jarred to a stop, releasing Monster's hand. "Run," she whispered. "And don't stop until you reach a town."

She whirled around right as Black burst into view, daggers flashing, then sprinted in the direction opposite monster. As she started through a willow glade, Luatha looped frantically around her, waving tiny hands.

"You are not thinking clearly; it's been a stressful day,
If you still seek to save yourself, you're headed the wrong way!"

It wasn't herself Elwyn wanted to save. She raced through curtain after curtain of weeping boughs, stopping just shy of a red-clay cliff that stretched at least fifteen feet skyward. The willow whips rustled once more, parting around a livid assassin.

"I had hoped to bring you back to the Father in one piece." He sneered, knuckles blanching around the hilts of his *icons*. "But you're forced my hand."

Elwyn winced, bracing for the attack. A golden sliver of a rapier swept into view, and metal rang against metal.

Black's jaw went lax. "What the fuck?"

The rapier twisted, forcing the assassin back. Elwyn ducked beneath it, scrambling into the foliage. Curiosity and cowardice played tug of war with her mind as she sprinted away. Eventually, the former won out. She pressed her back to an oak trunk and peered around it. One glance at her rescuer, and she rubbed her eyes, certain they were playing tricks on her.

The stranger looked exactly like Elwyn, with the exception of her demeanor. She carried herself with a high chin, a straight spine, and the most arrogant smirk imaginable. It was the expression of someone who was having *fun*.

The imposter's confidence was well-merited. She sidestepped Black's every slash, pivoting and parrying as needed. The assassin's every attack was more fevered than the last, and also more futile. The rapier's length gave the imposter an obvious advantage, though she seemed hesitant to use it. Elwyn watched, perplexed, as her double dodged and ducked, feinted and blocked, twisted and turned, passing up countless opportunities to skewer her foe through the gut.

What she never passed up was a chance to embarrass her opponent. More than once, she feigned frailty, only to pivot so he slammed into a tree. At least twice, she swept his ankles, sending him sprawling, but instead of ending the fight, she burst into musical laughter that sounded nothing like Elwyn's own and waited for the assassin to find his footing. She didn't seem to notice when Black's jaw set, when his shoulders squared, when a serpentine resolve darkened his eyes.

But Elwyn did, and so did Luatha.

"You've two obvious choices, so hurry and pick one.
Either intervene on her behalf, or better, turn and run."

Apparently, Elwyn had officially broken her running habit. She had no clue how to help her double, but she had to do something. If only because it would have been traumatizing to watch herself die. Swallowing her fears, she tiptoed closer.

Black circled the imposter, studying her with predatory patience. He had never been one for tomes or scrolls, but he could read a person's stance like a prophecy. This time, when the false Elwyn feinted to one side, he called her bluff. He ducked beneath her rapier and shouldered her into the cliffside with such force she sank into the clay. Black dropped one blade to pin her rapier over her head, then leveled the other at her heart.

"Whatever you are, you're dead!"

Catching *Gelah's* glimmer in the assassin's belt, Elwyn took her chance. The dagger ripped free and slid across her forearm, its runes igniting at the touch of her blood. She slashed forward too late, a blink after the assassin. With a metallic *plink,* his blade stopped cold against the stranger's skin. Elwyn's dagger sliced far deeper, imbedding in the assassin's shoulder and sending him, screaming, to his knees.

"I wasn't expecting that," the stranger said. At the snap of the reflection's fingers, shards of light wilted away like rose petals. Soon, Elwyn was standing face to face with a beautiful boy in gleaming golden armor.

"Sometimes a first impression is more honest than the last,
The selfsame fire that warms you might burn you just as fast."

CHAPTER 14
UNEXPECTED WARMTH

ELWYN

 ounds left by *Gelah* never bled for long. Not if the runes were glowing when it struck. They rotted, festered, blackened, and oozed, but they did not bleed. Elwyn's dagger was exceptionally selective. Hers was the only blood it thirsted for.

The stranger pressed Black's cape to the wound for nearly a minute before realizing the effort was wasted. Rot was spreading through the assassin's shoulder at an alarming rate, turning his skin white and his veins dark. Elwyn didn't understand why anyone would want to help Black, especially after he'd just tried to kill them. Then again, everything about the stranger was...well, *strange*.

Now that he was no longer disguised as Elwyn, he was her exact opposite. His skin was the color of copper, and light glittered in his eyes even when his back faced the sun. A circlet sat askew atop his mussy bronze locks, and his golden armor shifted with his every move, soundless and sleek. His emerald cape was the only break in his otherwise monochrome palette, and even that was trimmed in gold.

"I know I'm stunning, but we can discuss that later," he said. "Right now, a little help would be nice."

Elwyn had been staring, but not for that reason. "I'm not helping him," she said, face warming. "He's dangerous."

"As are you, it seems." He prodded the skin around the wound, and Black screamed so loudly that flocks of birds burst from the canopy. "You can't just let everyone who's dangerous die. Imagine how boring life would become."

Black whimpered like a wounded pup, trembling as the rot crept toward his neck. Elwyn absently traced the crescent on her cheekbone, feeling vindicated by his suffering.

"Cúl." With that odd utterance, the stranger's armor began to shift. Each strand of golden filigree folded inward, retreating into the slender bands that wreathed his wrists, his waist, the cuffs of his boots. The suit beneath it was the same green as his cape, vivid enough to make Elwyn blink. He pulled a lump of something dark from his pocket and ripped it in two, sighing as he crushed one half in his fist.

"I had been hoping to save this for a dull moment," he said to Black. "This will only hurt briefly."

He pressed the dark powder into the gash. Black wailed like a banshee. The stranger popped the rest of the lump into the assassin's mouth, then used both hands to hold his jaw shut. Charcoal spittle trickled from the assassin's lips as he fought to free himself. He fell still in a matter of seconds, save for the languid heave of his chest.

"Enjoy." The stranger released Black, letting him *thud* to the soil.

The darkness in the assassin's veins had stopped spreading, but a shadow had consumed the whites of his eyes, turning them black as ink.

"What have you done to him?" Elwyn asked, stomach clenching.

"I could ask you the same thing," the stranger replied. "Shall we trade answers?"

"I have no answer to trade. *Gelah* just does that."

The stranger arched an eyebrow. "Ah, yes. The thing so many blades do, where they begin to glow and rot the flesh of the living. *That* perfectly ordinary thing."

Elwyn shrugged, taking a moment to scan their surroundings. She'd sent Luatha after Monster nearly ten minutes prior. The piskie should have returned with news by now.

"Your kind is known for messing with things they don't understand, not that I have room to talk." The stranger held out his hand. "Hand it over."

Elwyn glared, gripping *Gelah* close to her chest. "No."

He blinked like he'd never heard the word and flinched like it had burned him.

"It's nothing personal," Elwyn said. "I'm grateful that you saved me, but I don't know who the hell you are."

"I *did* save you, didn't I?" His smile could've blinded someone. "That might be an actual first! It's been a long time since I last experienced one of those." He sprung to his feet, sweeping into a bow and extending his hand anew. "Aedyn of the Daoine Maithe."

Elwyn reached out, expecting a handshake, and was shocked when Aedyn brought her hand to his lips. His warmth, like sunlight, was nearly as startling as the gesture itself.

She wrenched her hand away, wringing the odd sensation from it. "Slate."

Aedyn looked her over. "Fitting."

Elwyn wasn't sure what that meant, but it had the timbre of an insult.

"Well?" Aedyn proffered his palm. "Now that you know 'who the hell' I am, it's time to hand over the dagger. We practically had a deal."

Elwyn might have smiled if her lips weren't busy scowling. "That was clever, but not a chance."

"At least let me *see* it." Aedyn paced around her at a dizzying speed.

"Only if you stop acting like a vulture."

"What's a vulture?" he asked, coming to a stop.

Elwyn gestured for him to step back, then again, when he didn't step back far enough. She held *Gelah* up, blade sideways so the runes were clear. Aedyn smirked, shimmered, and vanished right as a hand reached over her shoulder, snatching the blade.

She whirled to see Aedyn—the *real* Aedyn—standing behind her. "Interesting," he said, running a finger over the runes.

Elwyn grabbed Black's fallen daggers and leveled them at Aedyn. Greyscale agents were forbidden from wielding another's icons, but what was one more broken rule?

"Give it back," she hissed, glaring.

"Do you own any other facial expressions?" Aedyn sighed, tossing the dagger at her feet. "It's definitely fae-forged, though I can't guess the age or origin, and that doesn't explain its more ... *unusual* qualities."

"All of that trouble, and you learned nothing?"

"You'd be surprised how often I hear that."

"I don't think I would be." Elwyn stowed Brannon's daggers in favor of her own, grateful to find the blade was not just another illusion. As she flipped it in her hand, comforted by the familiar weight, Luatha burst through the willow whips. She looped through the air a few times before landing on Elwyn's shoulder, and Monster's pale face peeked out from the forest.

Relieved though Elwyn was, she was even more startled. "I hadn't expected you to follow," she said. "That means...Can you actually *see* Luatha?"

Aedyn grimaced. "You call that pest by name?" he asked, incredulous. "I don't suppose your kind keep pet leeches, too? Maybe flocks of fleas? I swear, mortals ..."

They can both see her. Elwyn's head felt suddenly light.

"What are mortals?" Monster ventured out into the clearing, eyes fixed on the newcomer.

Aedyn chuckled. "It's what you are, silly."

"But not you?" Monster didn't seem disturbed in the slightest. "If you're not a mortal, are you one of the Unseen?"

"Hardly." Aedyn gave his cape an ostentatious flourish and tipped his head toward Elwyn. "That one's more likely to go unseen. I *am* from Faerie, though, if that's what you're asking."

Monster broke into a wide smile that didn't quite fit her sullen face. "I can't believe I've met two in one day!"

"Oh, the parasite hardly counts." Aedyn waved haphazardly toward Luatha. The piskie growled, flitting from Elwyn's shoulder and sticking out her tiny lavender tongue. "I am Aedyn of the Daoine Maithe."

The girl pursed her lips. "Is that a nickname?"

"Why, of course not. It would be silly to go about calling oneself something like ... oh, I don't know...*Slate*, or something. Aedyn is my name, the second bit is more of a title." He tapped his circlet as though they ought to recognize it. "And what is your name? Something completely, drearily normal that sounds nothing like *Monster*, I trust."

The girl giggled, dipping into a trained curtsy. "Lydia Devlin."

A twinge of jealousy tugged at Elwyn. She had saved the child's life multiple times now, and all it had earned her was a nickname. *But this man swoops in out of nowhere, and she's completely honest with him!* Granted, he'd been honest with her first. Elwyn did not have that luxury. Once the Greyscale got ahold of her birth name, it would be lost to her forever. They'd already taken so much.

"We must be on our way." She offered Lydia her hand, eager to put miles between herself and the unconscious assassin. When the girl didn't budge, she sighed, looking to Aedyn. "How long before that...*whatever* wears off?"

"The shadowroot?" He glanced down at the unconscious assassin. "Fifteen more minutes, tops. Depends on your lover's constitution."

Lydia giggled; Elwyn glared.

"He's not my—How could you even think that? He tried to kill me!"

"For all I know, you started it." Aedyn shrugged. "Besides, he pursued you across an ocean. Don't women like to be pursued?"

"Not like that! And how do you know how far he's chased me, anyway? We've only just met."

"It doesn't matter *who* was spying on *whom* through *what beverage*, what matters is...Oh, look—he's waking early."

Elwyn jumped between Black and Lydia, *Gelah* raised at the ready.

"You mortals greet each other in the strangest ways." Aedyn started toward the stirring assassin and immediately tumbled, having failed to notice his knotted bootlaces.

Luatha laughed for a full five minutes.

"They flit in uninvited, a sign that doom is near,
None offer Balm of Gilead or wine to calm the fear."

CHAPTER 15

HARBINGERS

ARYN

wenty minutes had crawled by since Aryn's son excused himself for refreshments, and the boy had not returned. While this behavior was far from unusual, it still set Aryn's nerves on edge. Aedyn could scarcely go a minute unsupervised without causing some kind of trouble; by now, he might well have caused twenty kinds.

Though he was speaking with a fellow judge, he caught a peripheral glimpse of Eloana departing with her handmaiden. Ever emblematic of her station, she kept a high chin and a straight spine, but there was no light to her smile. Aryn could not help pitying her. She was a fool, but a sweet one, and better than Aedyn deserved.

Aryn was not ignorant of his son's dalliances, nor was he keen to breach the subject. He'd been young once, too, after all. More accurately, he'd been young dozens of times, though his most recent youth was centuries gone— a mere ripple in the tumultuous sea of his legacy. Granted, he had always found Tearan quickly and devoted himself to her until their days ended to start anew.

Creagor and Soen were mingling amongst the guests, leaving Aryn alone with Mearalas—the one High Judge most likely to disparage his parenting, though she had no children of her own. While all Undine were a piscine in nature, their queen had always been a shark. Luckily, she'd been too distracted to scent blood in the water.

"The trials are approaching," she mused, tapping webbed fingers on her wine glass. "The docket is sizable this year, enough for two days of proceedings, unless we rush the verdicts."

"Ever focused on matters of Law," Aryn noted.

Mearalas' devotion to her ideal was a thing of wonder. More fae had been exiled at her command than angels had fallen in the Battle that Split the Sky in Two. One might even say the Law was her religion…if one wanted her to try them for blasphemy.

"Elgard Springbristle's case is significant." She stabbed her brazed kelp with a fork. "It has been decades since a member of the Seelie Court breached the Treaty of Dusk, and never over something so foolish as a tryst with a Korrid. Let us hope it does not set precedent."

Aryn clenched his jaw, riled by the accusation in her voice. Mearalas had long asserted that his son's mischief would escalate to lawlessness, but he seldom took the bait. Aedyn was childish and irresponsible, but he was no criminal.

"I fail to see the intrigue," he said, affecting an air of indifference. "There is only one possible verdict for such an act."

Mearalas's midnight eyes narrowed to slits, but the conversation ended when a member of Aryn's gilded brigade approached the table with a nervous bow. The soldier was hardly more than a child, younger than his son by several decades, and he reeked of insecurity. Aryn bid him speak swiftly, hoping to spare him Mearalas' scorn.

"An emissary has arrived," the soldier said, straightening. "She is being held by the palace gates."

"I appreciate your diligence," Aryn replied, "but we do not accept messengers in times of festivity. Send them my regards and extend an invitation to the ball. If their matter is important, I will grant them audience after the closing ceremonies."

If oraithvine armor was capable of clattering, the boy would have sounded like tin cans in a windstorm. "All respect, Your Majesty." He gulped, opening his side satchel and producing a sealed scroll. "I believe it is a matter of some urgency."

Aryn accepted the offering, shivering reflexively. The parchment was winter-cold to the touch. He cracked the ever-ice seal without glimpsing the sigil. Only one person would have penned such a message.

Dearest Aryn,

By now, you have doubtless heard of the unrest in the Shifting Wilds. I have more information in regard to this matter, but I dare not trust it to pen and parchment, so I have sent my most loyal ward to deliver the news by tongue. Do not turn her away without hearing her words. For this I swear to you, my downfall will be yours.

With no regrets,
Queen Fuara of the Korrid Sidhe

Strong though Aryn's heart was, it faltered at her words. A cryptic message sealed with a threat; had he been expecting anything more?

"Burn it," he said, handing the scroll back to the soldier. "Find Soen and inform her Mearalas and I have been called away. She'll know how to proceed. Then, gather a small troop to escort the emissary to Talune's Heart. And do be subtle."

"I smell a trap," Mearalas muttered as the soldier scurried off. "You have always put too much faith in that woman."

Yes, he had.

"The lies of an enemy can be as telling as their truths," Aryn argued, pretending to focus on his plate of roast rabbit. "Head to the throne room. I will meet you there in roughly ten minutes."

Several soldiers followed Aryn as he descended the steps to Talune's Heart, the spacious hollow at the First Tree's center that had served as his throne room for twenty-three reigns. Mearalas was waiting beside the door, as directed, flanked by two retainers from her Seaglass Guard. Her proximity to full-blooded Undine made the Queen's paler skin and sharper contours all the more obvious. She would have loathed to know how obvious her heritage was.

"I still think this is a foolish endeavor," she said, crossing seafoam arms.

"Perhaps you should have called on the company of a more pliable witness. Creator knows Soen agrees with your every whim, and Creagor can't be bothered with matters of diplomacy."

In truth, the Sidhe Chieftain's commitment to Justice seldom ran counter to peace accords, and the Sylph Speaker-elect was twice as clever as she let on; that was half the cleverness of it. Still, Aryn was sure of his decision.

"Your skepticism is an asset," he said. "The Korrid Queen is equal parts enemy and ally. It is important that, in all our dealings, we present a balanced front."

Mearalas lifted her chin, either proud of the assessment or resentful of it. Both monarchs tarried in silence as the light singers who guarded the throne room stepped forward, hands on their diaphragms. One sang the lilting melody of a sunrise; the other, the thrumming harmony of its set. Tangled locks of oraithvine unfurled in time with their duet, allowing the doors to swing inward.

"If anyone learns I was here, I'll see you tried for insurrection," Mearalas snapped at her attendants before leaving them in the hall.

Aryn marched into the throne room beside the Undine Queen. Though Talunasa was under his reign, and his alone, they regarded one another as equals. Were Aryn a guest in Chorial, he could have expected the same treatment. No one High House operated well without the other three, just as the Four Ideals—Honor, Justice, Love, and Law—balanced and perfected one another. It made no sense to laud one ruler over the next, even in their respective kingdoms.

Two guards rushed ahead, setting oraithvine chairs on the emerald carpet just before the throne dais. Mearalas audibly scoffed, but Aryn paid her no mind. He would never allow another to sit on Tearan's throne, though it had been nearly two centuries since she'd fallen to the Unseelie. Each time he glimpsed the gilded circlet that held her place, he could practically see her sitting there, her mischievous smile and glittering mahogany eyes goading him onto one adventure or another.

In all their many lives, had he ever loved her more?

"I assume the supposed 'emissary' is on its way," Mearalas whispered, taking her seat. "What do you expect will come of this?"

Aryn tore his eyes from the specter of his fallen wife. "Nothing, perhaps," he said, sitting beside the Undine, "but we must keep a civil relationship with the Korrids, for the good of both the Light and Shadow Realms and all who inhabit them."

"I do nothing for the *good* of the Shadow Realms," Mearalas hissed, having opposed the treaty since first it was drafted. "It is cowardice that stays Fuara's hands, not mercy. Still, if balance is the best we can achieve, I suppose we must humor her."

A herald's trumpet sounded, and the young brigadier from before rushed in, trailed by a troop of his peers. He stopped the requisite ten feet from where the monarchs sat and sank to a knee, timidly announcing their guest. "Introducing, on behalf of Queen Fuara of the Korrid Sidhe, her ward and emissary, Tidings."

The troop parted around a shivering shell of a woman, clothed in tattered rags. Fae-folk were famous—or, in most circles, *infamous*—for stealing away only the most lovely creatures into their service, but if this woman had ever been beautiful, all trace of that allure had fled long ago. What remained was little more than a skeleton, with craters for cheeks and matted wisps for hair. Her fingers and lips had gone blue from frostbite, and the tip of her nose was missing—a likely victim of that same malady.

An ever-ice collar glistened around her neck, its form unwavering despite the humid atmosphere. An ethereal chain attached at the nape, stretching into the air a few feet behind her before fading from view. Such tethers were bound only to the word of their host, but a sturdier anchor had never existed.

"Welcome, Tidings," Aryn said, swallowing his pity. "You may speak."

The woman lifted her face to the king, and he found it difficult to hold her gaze. A million nightmares, clawing and frigid, stared back at him in those pinprick pupils. "I-I b-b-bring w-word frrrom F-Fuara...F-f-from Fuara, th-th-th-"

"Fuara, Queen of the Korrid Sidhe. We know," Mearalas hissed, leaning back and crossing her legs. "Do get on with it."

"T-t-there, t-here has been w-w-word of-of a f-f...Th-there h-has b-b-b-"

Tidings' neck snapped sharply to the right, and she fell to the floor, motionless. Several brigadiers rushed forward, but Aryn raised a palm, bidding them still. A moment later, Tidings stretched to her feet in a single, viscous motion, rolling each vertebra. Her head slumped unnaturally against her shoulder until she took it in her hands, cracking once to each side.

When her speech resumed, the voice was not her own. "Sorry for the spectacle, dear Aryn." Her glassy eyes slid to the Undine, growing somehow colder. "Mearalas."

Mearalas's webbed fingers tensed around her armrests. "Fuara."

"These mortals simply aren't made the way they used to be." The woman lifted one limp hand with the other, releasing it to swing lifelessly at her side. "Why, this one hardly lasted half a century. I'm sure this must seem like a slight, given your compassion for these feeble creatures, but I would never have enthralled the woman had I believed she could complete her mission with even a modicum of dignity."

A lump formed in Aryn's throat, but he spoke over it. "Do not take me for a fool," he said. "You did this all to send a message. Now, speak your piece."

"Oh, it *is* of peace that I intend to speak." Laughter lilted softly beneath her words, tempered by spiteful pride. "As my ward was trying so desperately to say, a force is rising in the heart of the Shifting Wilds. A malicious presence stirs beneath the blanket of amber and umber, and I fear it means ill tidings for us all."

It sounded a lot like the report Creagor had just received, only this source was a lot more suspect. "Let me guess—this has something to do with your rival, Mailair?"

"Mailair is ruler only of chaos and misfortune, and they will fall to that nature, given time." Fuara sighed. "No, I would not consider them a threat on their best day. What I speak of is something new. Something...unpredictable."

"There is nothing new, Fuara," Aryn asserted. "You and I both know this from lifetimes of experience."

The woman smiled, cracking chapped lips too dead to bleed. "You've always relied too heavily on past patterns, dearest," she cooed. "Given infinite time and resources, anything is possible, and the problem will plague you whether you acknowledge it or not. My sources claim this new power is a Sluagh, and mine is not the only throne it seeks."

"I knew this was a trick." Mearalas shook her head. "How foolish do you think us, Fuara? *A* Sluagh? The Sluagh are many—a legion of souls too vile for Hell itself to swallow. They exist only as part of a miserable, screeching whole. There has never been *a* Sluagh."

"That is why it is new," Fuara explained with a lopsided shrug. "I cannot tell you how it came to be. I can only say that it is. And I assure you, dear allies, *it is*."

"If what you say is true, I fail to understand the urgency," Aryn replied. "The Sluagh are not fully fae, and they ceased being human long ago."

"They have been cursed to wend between the worlds, belonging to neither," Mearalas added. "How could anyone hope to conquer a realm they cannot root themselves in?"

The collar around Tiding's neck began to glisten, her puppet-smile drooping. "You speak the Law so easily," Fuara said from a world away. "Yet, you never taste the loopholes on your tongue."

With a rasping sigh, Tidings collapsed, her collar shattering into countless crystalline shards. The ever-ice melted instantly. The body followed soon after.

TAWNY

The scents of cinnamon and licorice root wafted into Tawny's chamber, stirring her from a pleasant slumber. Mother had made her favorite tea.

She's still here. Tawny slid from her bed and donned the dress Mother had gifted her. The cut was more mature than she was used to, with a squared collar and flowing sleeves. The fabric would tangle and tear all too easily.

Though her mother swore by mortal trends, Tawny had only one simple rule when it came to fashion—if she couldn't climb a tree in it, it was more a cage than clothing. Granted, if she had her way, she would run around in the nude like most of her neighbors. Apparently, mortals were not supposed to do that.

She had to lift her skirts to avoid tripping as she descended the staircase, and she could swear she heard the Shadow Goblins huddled beneath it snickering. *Creepy little things.* No matter how many minions Mother made, Tawny would never get used to them.

"Good morning, Mother," she chirped as she stepped into the dining room, belatedly realizing Mother was not present.

The two Augusky who stood at the table turned unsettling oval eyes her way, sneers stretching their already-thin lips. Tawny recognized the larger one by her curved horns and calico braids. Sasta was Mailair's beta—the most powerful of her kind, next to the Prince-Often Princess-Sometimes Both-and on at Least One Occasion-Neither themself. A necklace beaded with teeth and ears draped between her breasts, and glistening red patterns swirled across her skin. Rumor held that she never allowed them to dry.

The other Augusky was clearly younger than Sasta, with short, sandy hair and nubs for horns. A coarse goatee bristled on their chin, though their body curved like a woman's. This was not particularly unusual for the Augusky, who did not have to choose if they didn't want to.

"A mortal?" Sasta asked, nostrils flared. "Who are you, and why are you here?"

Tawny shied back, her voice trapped in her throat.

"Tawny is my ward," Mother said, floating into view with a platter balanced on her forearm. Apparently, the morning meal was raw meat, sliced into strips. "She usually has better manners."

"Oh!" Tawny stumbled into a curtsy. "Pardon."

The smaller Augusky chuckled. "I think it's frightened of us."

"It should be," Sasta said, her voice gruff. "It looks good enough to eat."

"She will be looking after things while I'm away," Mother said, setting the meat between her guests before arching a brow at Tawny. "Join us at the table, dear. It is time you get to know our allies."

They are just bigger versions of Daulle, Tawny reasoned, taking her seat. *There's no cause for cowering.*

Mother poured her a cup of tea, and the familiar aroma helped her nerves.

"Care for a bite?" Sasta asked, nudging the platter her way.

Tawny's stomach did a somersault. "No, thank you."

"More for me." Sasta grabbed a handful of meat and shoved it into her mouth, chewing loudly with open lips.

That kind of behavior would have earned Tawny a stern lecture, but acclaim came with freedom. Still, her eyes lilted to Mother, expecting some measure of distaste. Though the woman's face was calm, her form had begun to fade. Tawny could see through her neck to her chair's backrest.

She would be leaving soon.

"I must apologize for the slim spread," Mother waved a translucent hand toward the tray. "I was preparing for my next trip, and I was not expecting visitors. I assume you are here with a message from Mailair."

"More like a warning," the lesser Augusky said. "The mortal festival began days ago, and you've yet to—"

"Silence, Eigent," Sasta snapped, offering Mother an apologetic grimace. "Forgive my lesser. They are too young to recall a time before the treaty and have no notion of how slowly mortal time ekes by." Her gaze hardened. "That said, Mailair is aware of your failures so far. They are disappointed."

"I have not failed," Mother hissed. Her voice had begun to split, as it did whenever she was angry. Or when she was about to fade. "Do not forget, it is I who have opened communications with the Shadows. They will not accept any other offerings, and they will not accept an offering from anyone else. Mailair would be unwise to break our alliance."

Sasta's ears twitched. Her eyes flicked to Tawny and back.

"Have you considered a substitution?"

"I will not suffer the thought," Mother's eyes flared bright. "As I have already stated, I have not failed, nor will I."

"Good to hear it," Sasta replied. "We will take you at your word, for now. Only remember, the Midsummer stars are moving." She grabbed another handful of meat. "We will take this to Mailair as an offering."

"May it remind them of freer times," Mother said, "and herald a brighter future. The realms will soon be theirs to ravage, provided they remember whose palace they ought never raze."

Sasta snorted, shooting Tawny a parting glare as she and her lesser trotted from the cottage.

"We'll be back...*soon*." She stamped a hoof, then kicked the door shut behind her.

"Both are oft familiar despite how fresh they seem,
There isn't much difference between memories and dreams."

CHAPTER 16
ECHOES FROM THE PAST
BRANNON

rannon lobbed the stick with all his strength, hoping it would buy him a moment's peace. No matter how far he tossed the damned thing, the mutt returned a moment later. Couldn't it tell Brannon wanted to be alone? That's exactly what he would have been, were it not for the mangy pup.

Completely. Utterly. Alone.

Sure enough, the stray returned seconds later, dropping the same damned stick in Brannon's path. Brannon hurled it over a fence, then picked up his pace once the mutt scampered off. Already, the clouds were flushed pink, and he did not want to miss curfew again. His bruises from last time hadn't yet faded.

Half a minute later, the mutt returned, dropping the stick just long enough to bark.

"Go away!" Brannon growled.

He decided to ignore the pup from that point on, which worked. For a moment. Then, sharp fangs pierced his ankle. The damned thing had bitten him! Brannon pivoted, kicking the stray's side. It cowered back, whimpering. A few kicks more, and the whimpering stopped.

Brannon's vision blurred; he wasn't sure why. He didn't feel guilty over what he'd *just done, though he knew he should have. Embarrassed by the show of weakness, he wiped his eyes dry and continued on his way.*

The stench of rotting carcasses hung like fog over the property. No one had tended the farm in months, and the results were predictably nauseating. He held his breath as he approached the door, which burst open when he was still a yard off.

Rage seared through Brannon like fire, subsiding just as fast. The woman leaving his house had tangled auburn hair, rather than raven, and she wore only a loose shift, unbuttoned to her belly. All she had in common with his mother were the bruises.

"I feel bad for you." She shoved past Brannon with the grace of a wounded hog.

He spat at her, but either she didn't notice or didn't care. Brannon didn't care either. Not really. It wasn't her he hated.

He didn't blame his ma for leaving—he'd been begging her to escape for years— but he sure as hell blamed her for leaving him behind. She had always promised to keep him safe, but when things were at their worst, she took what she needed and fled. Apparently, he hadn't made the list.

Months had passed, but Brannon still hoped she'd return. He'd stopped missing her long ago, but he needed her to know what she'd left him to. He needed her to know how much he hated her for it. Without her, he was Pa's only target. Well, him and the whores. But they got to leave.

Brannon had hoped to sneak quietly to his room, but Pa was waiting in the hallway, his foot tapping impatiently. The man had always been big as a mountain, but he somehow seemed bigger when he reeked of gin. Or maybe Brannon just felt smaller.

Pa's pocket watch clicked open. "You're late," he said, exhaling a liquor fog. "Know what time it is?"

Brannon pursed his lips. No matter what the hands read, it was always the same time.

"It's time to toughen up."

He braced himself ...

Once the damage was done, Brannon paused to take inventory. His side ached bitterly, his lip and eyebrow had split, and his left wrist was swollen, tender. Thankfully, nothing had broken. Kids like him didn't last long once parts stopped working.

Pa had fallen asleep on the living room floor, as was his habit. Brannon was tempted to do the same, but it would have only made things worse. Only lazy louts slept before sundown, or so Pa said. Not that it applied to him. Those with power could make all the rules they liked without having to follow them.

Goaded by a growling stomach, Brannon forced himself to weary legs and trudged out to the barn. There, the sickly-sweet scent of rotting flesh was strongest. The odor made him retch, the retching made his ribs ache, and the ache made him furious that he was still too small to have prevented any of this.

At least they still had the chickens. Brannon hadn't been able to save the goats or hogs, but he prided himself on keeping those little birds alive. Each morning, he rose with the sun to toss them dried corn, and they rewarded him daily with eggs enough to live on. It was the kind of relationship Brannon could depend on. The only kind.

His heart dropped as he neared the coop, finding it in disarray. A hole had been torn in the mesh fencing, they hay beyond it scattered and strewn with bloody feathers.

"Shit." Brannon hobbled forward. Sure enough, his chickens lay mangled amidst the mess, their wings torn and their necks snapped. The fox hadn't eaten a single one of them. It had only been playing.

Furious though he was, he couldn't bring himself to hate the creature. In fact, he envied it. Of all the predators that roamed the woods, foxes were among the most feeble. When one saw an opportunity to show its strength, he made the most of it.

The whole thing gave Brannon an idea.

The mesh cut into his fingers as he pulled it from the fence, but he hardly noticed the sting. He was glad to see blood dripping from his fingers; it meant the wire was sharp enough.

Purpose strengthened his steps as he marched to the house—a new, thrilling sensation. He tiptoed into the living room, hoping Pa was still asleep. The bastard hadn't even rolled over.

Now more than ever, he wished the man had a smaller frame. It took a lot of effort to straddle his barrel chest without touching. Brannon stretched the length of wire between his hands, angling it just so. It stung his palms as he leveled it with Pa's neck, but the pain was a whisper compared to the thrum of his pulse.

The drunken heaves of Pa's chest set the meter. Brannon counted backward from five, steeling himself.

Five—the bastard deserves this.

Four—keep your hands steady.

Three—this is no different than the mutt.

Two—wouldn't Ma be proud?

One...

Brannon did not pause out of mercy. A breath away from murder, and not a single doubt had wormed into his mind. Had he killed his father in that moment, he would not have regretted it, but he would have missed the very point of the act. Power. What use was it if no one knew how much he wielded?

Tugging the wire taught, Brannon tapped his father's side with his boot. No reaction. He did it again, and the man's eyes fluttered open.

"Wha——?" he asked, anger stirring in his eyes as they focused on Brannon. "What do you want, you little——"

"Fuck you," Brannon pushed down with all his might.

That spray of blood was the most beautiful thing he had ever seen.

Brannon nearly toppled over, not from the ache of his wounds——he could hardly remember those——but from the sheer, dizzying breadth of his joy. For the first time ever, he wasn't scared. He wasn't weak. He wasn't prey.

Brannon was a predator.

He wiped the blood from his face and stepped aside, uncertain where his trembling legs would take him. Wherever he wound up, it would be a hell of a lot better than this place. Before leaving, Brannon spat on his pa's face and nabbed that damned watch from his pocket.

It was time to toughen up.

"You mortals greet each other in the strangest ways." A strangely melodic voice, like the warm echo of a bell tower, chased the memory from behind Brannon's eyelids, forcing them open. Light spilled into his retinas, and stark black gave way to blinding green.

Where am I?

A weight crashed into Brannon's back, flailing, and he struggled to pull himself out from under it. His right arm refused to cooperate. He couldn't even feel it.

A cold, bitter fear slithered through his chest, coiling around his lungs and squeezing tight. Brannon would never be able to replicate the string of swears that he released at that moment, but those who witnessed it would forever regard it as a feat of singular creativity.

The weight rolled away, apologizing profusely, and Brannon propped himself up with his working elbow. "What the infernal fuck is happening?"

His eyes landed first on Slate, who stood feet away with her *icon* brandished. The sickly child, Monster, peeked out from behind her, more curious than frightened. Brannon glowered, wracking his brain to separate dream from memory. The pieces snapped into place all at once, and he leapt to his feet.

"There were two of you!" he shouted, pointing at Slate with his left hand. "I don't know how, but there were. And then ... and then ... What the fuck did you do to me?"

"The shadowroot?" someone asked.

Brannon turned to see a man, perhaps a bit older than himself, clad in a ridiculous green suit and a garish, golden crown.

"I didn't relish using it on you," the stranger said. "But trust me, you needed the rest. Plus, it has that nifty little side effect of allowing you to relive the happiest hours of your life. You're welcome."

"You slipped me a hallucinogen?"

"Pretty much." The man smiled. "What was it you relived? Wild party? First kiss? First..." his eyes flicked to the child, and he cupped a hand over his mouth, lowering his voice, "...more than a kiss?" His volume rose again as he added, "My own vision changes each time, but I just take that to mean that the best is yet to come."

Brannon clenched his jaw, failing to make sense of the stranger's words. "What does it matter?" He cradled his limp arm with his good one, glaring at Slate and her wretched dagger. "You did this, didn't you?"

The thief smiled, giving her *icon* a twirl. "And I'd have no qualms about taking the other arm too."

"Creator's sake," the stranger said, gesturing toward Monster. "There is a child present." His brazen eyes flickered nervously skyward. "I couldn't help noticing that your sun is moving, and your sky seems to be darkening behind it. I assume that means we should seek some kind of shelter..."

Of all the ridiculous observations.

"Who the hell are you, anyway?" Brannon demanded.

The man sighed dramatically, slumping into a rushed, obligatory bow. "Aedyn of the Daoine Maithe. For the last time, that is 'who the hell' I am. And you're Black, though I doubt that's your real name any more than Slate is hers." He nodded toward the thief. "And no, to answer your next question, I'm not mortal, though I really wish your kind would call us something more reverent than *Unseen*. Honestly, it's just insulting. Now, can we please find someplace covered and well-lit?"

Brannon blinked several times before bursting into laughter. What else could he have done? Several impossibilities—the red-hatted trickster, the living shadows, the extra Slate, an *actual* fucking faerie—crashed together in his mind, and it did not withstand the impact. He dropped to his knees and began rocking back and forth, unable to stop himself.

What did it matter? What did any of it matter? Everything he'd accomplished and endured had been in service to the Father, and he'd failed. Images of Sable strung to an altar—his hand crushed, his skin torn, intestines dripping to stone—writhed through Brannon's skull.

I have little use for a thief with broken fingers, the Father had said.

He would have even less use for a one-armed assassin.

"Is he alright?" the little girl asked.

"It doesn't matter," Slate answered. "Leave him to the ghosts he's created. We need to get as far away as possible before they send another after me."

My replacement. The thought hit Brannon like a winter wind, slowing his pulse and strangling his laughter. A bizarre warmth, like firelight, bled through his good shoulder, and he glanced over to find a hand wrapped around it.

"Back the fuck off!" Brannon wrenched his shoulder free.

Aedyn shrunk back, only a little. "I can find help, if you'll allow it."

"And just how do you intend to do that?" Brannon rose to his feet, dusting the grass from his trousers. "I've seen what Slate's *icon* can do. I know its bite never heals. Do you intend to drop me off at a hospice or some commune that welcomes bastards and broken men? Or perhaps you plan on keeping me drugged until death mercifully claims me..."

"You're right that we won't find a remedy here," Aedyn said, voice soft. "But the Sylphs of my world don't simply heal things, they *renew* them. If anyone can return you to prime stabbing condition, it's them."

Even if that were somehow true, it still didn't make sense. "Why would you help me?"

"Well, this is a little bit my fault." Aedyn kicked the grass. "Mostly Slate's, but a little bit mine."

"I'll take the full blame for it if you'd like." Slate grabbed Monster's hand "This has been...interesting, but we'll be going our own way. You two have fun fluttering off to worlds unknown."

Brannon no longer cared if she escaped. Returning her to the Father would not redeem him, in this state. The child, however, dug her heels into the soil, her strange purple eyes fixed on Aedyn.

"Are you really taking him to Faerie?" she asked.

Aedyn nodded. "It's not going to be easy, mind you. I'm not...exactly, totally, completely supposed to be here, so smuggling a mortal back to my realm is a bit of a risk." His smile lit up. "Then again, a life without risk isn't much of a life at all, is it?"

The child pondered this for a second. "Take me with you."

Slate startled. "Lydia, what—"

"There's nothing for me here," the girl said, lifting watery eyes to the thief. "Why don't you want to come with? If people are really after you, I bet they can't follow you to Faerie."

"Wait. Just. A. Second," Aedyn interrupted. "Bringing one mortal home will be trouble enough. Smuggling three of you in might be impossible." He tapped his chin. "Then again, I'm not the only one who broke the treaty. You came across some Shadow Goblins, right? Dark, bity things?"

Brannon blinked. "How do you know about—"

"Doesn't matter. Tired of talking about it. The point is, while low fae like goblins aren't held to the same standards as the rest of us, they wouldn't have come here alone. If you can present evidence that one of the Unseelie visited the Mortal Realms, you can claim you found your own way through the Veil to deliver the news, and I can feign ignorance of the whole thing."

"If someone wasn't such a sorry excuse for a thief, we might have an Unseelie charm to present as evidence," Brannon said.

Slate crossed her arms, scowling. "We didn't even know what it looked like, and that manor was huge!"

"My home?" Lydia asked. "I've lived there my whole life, if there was a charm hidden somewhere, I'd have seen it. Thing is...what's a charm?"

"They can look like anything, really," Aedyn explained. "A charm is an item imbued with latent magic. Some have static effects, like curses or boons. Others are activated with incantations or rites."

Brannon glowered. "So, we never stood a chance of finding it?"

"You stood a small chance." Aedyn shrugged. "I stand a better one. You can tell when something's been charmed because it will be just a little bit *off*. It might be the wrong color, or the wrong dimensions. It might catch the light from the wrong angle or cast shadows in the wrong directions. Usually, it's something small, like a thimble, a tooth, a locket, a—"

"A medallion?" Lydia asked, pulling a necklace from the collar of her nightgown. The sun's fading rays caught in the pendant, bursting into glimmers of flickering light.

Aedyn's eyes flicked from the girl to the medallion and back. "Interesting."

Brannon nearly burst into another bout of mad laughter. He'd kept that little burden alive through the day when he could've just killed her and pried the charm from her cold little neck. Still, an ember of hope flickered. If his arm could truly be restored, the Father would welcome him back without question. At least, if he returned with the missing thief *and* a magical charm.

"I'm not giving you the necklace, but I'll show it to whoever you want if you let me come with." Lydia tucked the medallion back into her collar. "And Slate, too."

The thief grimaced, shifting uncomfortably.

"That's up to you," Aedyn said, eyes shifting to Slate. "You can choose to stay here and be hunted down for the rest of your short, unremarkable life, or you could follow me to somewhere new. To something different."

Slate narrowed her eyes. "If we change our minds, will we be free to return?"

"I won't try to stop you." Aedyn shrugged. "That's the best I can promise."

She pursed her lips, toe tapping as she mulled it over. "Fine," she said eventually, placing a protective hand on Lydia's shoulder.

"Alright," Brannon said, eager to return to his mission. "That's everyone, so what are you waiting for? Fly us off to Faerie."

Aedyn grimaced. "As it happens, I didn't exactly plan on traveling here, and, well," he kicked at the ground, "I'm afraid I only paid a one-way fare."

"What does that mean?" Brannon asked.

"It means we'll be taking the long way back."

"You may not even notice as their spirits are refined,
Both people and perspectives change one heartbeat at a time."

CHAPTER 17

A LITTLE BIT BAD

LYDIA

ydia was elated to see an arrow-shaped sign that read *Gilash*, though it didn't specify the miles. Just knowing an actual town existed somewhere in the Rhysien countryside was a comfort. She had never walked so long in her entire life, and on so little food.

Just a day before, she'd thought herself the strangest of people, if only because that's how she was treated. That opinion had changed upon meeting her current company.

Slate was probably the most normal of the bunch, almost abnormally so. She hardly spoke to anyone, even the piskie who sat on her shoulder, but she didn't ignore them either. Her eyes were constantly flitting between the others in the group. In fact, her eyes were always flitting *everywhere*, as though a monster lurked behind each blade of grass.

Black was just as quiet as Slate, but he was much less kind. Lydia pitied him more than she feared him. He reminded her of a stray hound, the kind mother had always warned her away from. *They've been hurt too often, too deeply*, she'd claimed. *They will lash out at just about anyone.*

Aedyn seemed friendly enough, though he seemed a bit distractable. He was constantly asking questions about commonplace things like silos, cattle, and squirrels. Every few seconds he would glance up at the sky and mutter something about how dark it was getting, and the sun hadn't even fully set yet.

At last, a tiny town appeared on the horizon, wrapped in a lumber wall.

"Thank goodness," Slate breathed, audibly exhausted.

"This stop is completely unnecessary." Black snorted. "We should get to that Sylph thing as soon as possible."

"Aedyn said we'll need to pass through a *Rath*," Slate said, recounting a conversation they'd had along the way. "Do you know where a Rath is?"

"Slate, I don't even know *what* a Rath is."

"Enough flirting, you two," Aedyn said. "We need directions, we need supplies, we need rest, and *I* need a chance to mingle amongst the locals before I'm forced to return to normalcy."

Lydia wondered what Aedyn's idea of normalcy was. "Aren't you already mingling with locals?"

Aedyn laughed. "Creator help me if you lot reflect the general population."

As he started toward the town gates, Black grabbed him by the frilly sleeve. "You aren't seriously going in there looking like that?"

"Beautiful, you mean?" Aedyn glanced around the group and grimaced. "I suppose it wouldn't be polite to outshine you all by this much, would it?" He flourished his emerald cape. When the fabric settled, he was dressed exactly like Black, blood spatter and all. He glanced down at himself and smiled. "Looks better on me."

Lydia gasped. She wondered whether Aedyn could dress her up, too. Maybe he could add color to her skin and hair, make her look more like the girl she'd once been. She decided not to ask. They had spared enough attention for her already.

"Maybe lose the bloodstains." Slate chuckled. "At least one of us should probably look mildly respectable."

Aedyn sighed, running a hand over his sleeve. The red splotches faded to crisp white. "I'm leaving the tear down the front," he asserted. "Perfection gets dreary after a while."

Slate rolled her eyes. "And the crown?"

"What about it?"

"It stands out." She flicked his circlet. "So does the rapier. Wearing all that gold openly will make you a target for people like me."

Aedyn laughed derisively. "Like a mere mortal could pull one over on—"

Before he could finish his sentence, Slate was pointing his own rapier at his exposed chest. "You were saying?"

Aedyn begrudgingly rolled his sleeve up and looped his circlet around his wrist. He muttered something strange, and the crown melted into his golden cuff, becoming just another filigree whorl. With a snap of his fingers, the fancy golden rapier in Slate's hands turned to a plain steel foil. "Happy?"

Slate handed the sword back without a word. Lydia somehow doubted she had ever been happy.

They walked past a town crier on their way through the town gates. "Tragedy in Amblewick!" the boy shouted, ringing a shrill bell. "Midsummer festivities interrupted by gruesome family massacre!"

A sob wiggled from Lydia's throat.

Slate squeezed her hand. "Just focus on what's ahead."

The advice was probably metaphorical, but Lydia applied it literally. She fixed her eyes on the town ahead of her, scarcely blinking until the dusty air dried her looming tears. Gilash, it turned out, was a filthy place. Many of the weathered buildings had begun to slant, and the alleys reeked of chamber-sludge, drawing swarms of flies. Lydia was so focused, she bumped into Black, unaware the group had stopped.

"Watch it!" He pushed her away.

"Watch yourself," Slate hissed, stepping between them.

"This should suit our purposes." Aedyn pointed to the nearest building, oblivious to the animosity. Raucous laughter spilled out from the boarded windows, cutting through a discordant din that was probably meant to be music. A man with a swollen eye sat slumped beside the entrance, vomit matting his beard. A dense crowd shuffled about in the dim candlelight beyond the open door. The words *The Wild Boar* had been painted on the siding.

"That's not the best place for a child," Slate said, though Aedyn was already crossing the threshold.

"Stop coddling the damned thing," Black grumbled, following after. "She's clearly seen worse."

That was undoubtedly true. "I'll be fine," Lydia said.

Slate sighed, gripping her by the shoulders and guiding her through the door. Her protective behavior was strange, seeing as they'd only just met, but it wasn't unwelcome. It had been a long time since anyone had tried to protect Lydia; not even her own ...

Lydia pushed the thought away before another sob could escape her lips. There were distractions aplenty with which to occupy her mind, unpleasant though they were. The Wild Boar smelled of sweat and bile, and most of its patrons were either recovering from a fistfight or fervently seeking one out. Two men in the far corner were still trading blows.

Slate steered Lydia across a bustling dancefloor, around a trio of chittering barmaids, and past tables packed with rowdy men playing cards and arm-wrestling before finding an empty booth near the back. Somehow, they took their seats a moment before Aedyn and Black appeared, a testament to just how nimble Slate was.

"This place is a shithole," Black muttered, sliding into the booth across from Lydia.

"This place is amazing!" Aedyn scooted in beside him. "Now, who wants to buy me dinner?"

"You're joking, right?" Slate said. "What makes you think we have coin? You're the one dripping gold."

"I am not trading my armor for ale," Aedyn said. "If you hand me even a few copper coins, I can feed us all, trust me."

"When someone says, 'trust me' as often as you do, it's usually a good sign not to."

Lydia's stomach rumbled loudly enough that the others all turned to look at her, and she shrunk into her seat.

Slate sighed, pulling a few pias from her boot and tossing them on the table. "This is all I've got on me."

"That's hardly enough for a pint," Black scowled. "Like hell am I going to share."

"A little money can always make more, if you play it right." Aedyn smirked. "We'll start by ordering biscuits."

The others grumbled, but biscuits sounded like a royal feast to Lydia. "Please do," she whispered.

"I suppose they'll at least keep for a few days, if we ration them wisely," Slate conceded. "I'll try to get a server's attention."

"Highly improbable," Aedyn said, chuckling under his breath. "You aren't the type to get anyone's attention."

Lydia was surprised Slate didn't look offended. Then again, Aedyn had a point. Slate wasn't unsightly or unconfident, there was simply nothing about her that stood out. Had their paths crossed under different circumstances, Lydia probably wouldn't have noticed her.

Aedyn leapt atop the table and whistled, drawing the eyes of everyone in the room. Lydia wondered whether any suspected his true nature. Even dressed in tattered rags, his hair falling loose over his pointed ears, he hardly looked human.

A pretty waitress which thick red curls flitted over as Aedyn hopped back into his seat. She leaned in close to him, ignoring the others entirely.

"Haven't seen you here before," she noted, lashes aflutter. "Anything I can help you with?"

"A great many things, I'm sure," Aedyn replied with a wink. "But a plate of biscuits will do for now."

He placed all but one of the coins in her hand and curled her fingers around them. She bit her lip, blushing, and vowed to return in half a heartbeat.

Lydia felt like the conversation had fluttered right overhead. Then again, most of the things Aedyn said sounded, from tone alone, like they could mean something entirely different.

It was frustrating, being out of the loop.

The waitress could not truly return in half a heartbeat, but she nearly managed it. The platter of biscuits slid onto the table before the others could utter a single word.

"Excellent service." Aedyn flipped her the final pia. She whispered something in his ear before vanishing into the crowd, and he beamed in response. "I think I like this world."

Slate audibly gagged.

"Jealousy?" Aedyn asked her.

"Just bile."

Aedyn waved a hand over the plate of biscuits, and they turned to a heap of copper coins. Lydia gasped reflexively. Black raised an eyebrow. Slate didn't look the least bit surprised. She plucked a biscuit-pia from the plate and turned it over, examining it. "Can you all do that?"

"*We all*, as in ..."

"Fae."

Aedyn shrugged. "Just the types with an affinity for light. Maithe, Leprechauns, and so on. Why do you ask?"

"It's nothing," Slate said in a tone that definitely implied it was something.

Lydia might have pointed as much out, but there were more urgent matters at hand. "Can I still eat them?" she asked, eying the pia. They may have looked like copper, but they smelled like butter and brown sugar.

"One or two." Aedyn whispered. "Just don't let anyone see."

Oh, thank the Creator. She scooped a few coins into her lap, checked to make sure no one was looking, and snuck one into her mouth. It still tasted exactly like a biscuit. *Neat.*

When Aedyn called the barmaid back over, it only took her only a second to materialize. "A rack of lamb to split, four whiskeys—"

"We'll have water, actually." Slate placed a hand on Lydia's shoulder.

"What's the matter, Slate?" Black asked, a wry grin creeping across his face. "Bad drinking experience?"

"So be it." Aedyn waved her off "Four whiskeys and two waters. And a room for the three of them."

"The three of us?" Lydia asked. "Won't you be joining?"

Aedyn chuckled, winking at the barmaid again. "Different plans."

The woman's cheeks turned rose red, and she scurried off to fetch their food. After a few minutes of awkward silence, she returned with a tray set with meat and drinks, and the key to room six, sliding it all on the table.

Black grabbed the key and one of the drinks. "I've had about as much socializing as I can withstand," he said.

"You're not hungry?" Lydia asked.

Rather than answer, Black shouldered Aedyn from the booth and stomped away.

Aedyn shot him a puzzled glance, then returned his attention to the barmaid. "Seeing as I'm now on my feet, now's as good a time as any to ask you to dance." Before she could even reply, he downed two of his three drinks, took her in his arms, and swept her into the crowd.

Lydia shrugged, deciding to focus on something she understood: food. As she plucked a strip of meat from the platter, she noticed Slate's eyes following Black up the staircase.

"He's not gonna leave, if that's what you're worried about," Lydia said. "He wants his arm back. People stick around when they want something."

"You seem smarter than the average ten-year-old." Slate's pupils shifted over Lydia like she was reading a book. "Tell me, what is it that *you* want?"

Lydia chewed on both a bite of lamb and the question. "Sometimes people stick around when they don't know what they want, too," she said after swallowing. "That's why you're still here, isn't it?"

A sad smile tugged on Slate's lips. "You're pretty observant, you know that?"

Lydia nodded. It was one of the few things she actually *did* know about herself. Interacting with others had never come easily, but it was simple to observe them.

"Alright then," Slate said, nodding toward the dance floor. "What do you think of this Aedyn fellow?"

Lydia glanced over to where Aedyn and the barmaid were dancing. Even in the smoke and chaos, he stood out like a peacock in a henhouse. His laughter was much more musical than the accordion or tambourines, his smile vastly outshone the candlelight, and his movements were far more fluid than anyone else's, including those of his dance partner. He didn't seem to care that she was struggling to keep up. He didn't even seem to notice.

"He's probably not a fully good person," Lydia concluded. "But aren't we all a little bit bad?"

"Some of us, more than others." Slate snatched a false coin from Lydia's lap and wove it nimbly between her knuckles before closing her hand around it. "The Unseen are beguiling beings, but they always have their own interests in mind, and it is almost never something we could guess at."

She opened her hand, and the pia had vanished. Lydia blinked up at her, puzzled, and she stuck out her tongue. The coin sat at its center, dissolving like the biscuit it truly was. They both burst into laughter.

"How did you do that?" Lydia asked once she recovered.

"If I told you, it would ruin the fun," Slate said, sipping her water. "That's probably what Aedyn's thinking, too. Only we have no idea what sort of trick he's playing."

Lydia wasn't sure Aedyn could think that far ahead. "You don't trust people easily, do you?" she asked. "I would think you'd show more faith in the Unseen, considering you're so close to one."

Slate shrunk back, and the piskie on her shoulder perked up. It fluttered down, alighting on the table and blinking up at Lydia with ink-drop eyes.

"Mortals cannot see me unless I bid them to.

My blessing was not given, so tell me, what are you?"

Lydia tucked her chin, glaring at the blue veins that peeked through her pallid hands. There was that question again—*what* are you?

Never who.

Lydia Devlin. That was her usual answer, but what did that even mean now that her whole family was gone?

"You're a girl of many secrets, I see," Slate said. "Feel free to keep them. You and I are similar that way."

"I suppose so. Only you actually know what your secrets are."

"Give it time," Slate said. "I certainly didn't have it all figured out at your age, and I like to think there's still more to me than even I know."

The words were probably meant to be encouraging, but they fell short. Lydia attempted a smile, but her face was too heavy, and she wound up yawning instead. Now that her hunger had been sated, her exhaustion was poised to take over.

"You should get some sleep," Slate said, urging her from the bench. "We have an early start tomorrow."

Lydia let Slate lead her to room six. Finding that the door was locked, Slate cursed Black under her breath, pulling two pins from her braid and jamming them into the keyhole.

A few quick twists, and the door popped open.

"Can you teach me to do that?" Lydia asked, awestruck.

"To pick locks?"

"It seems like something I'll need to learn eventually."

Slate searched her with sad eyes. "Maybe another time."

TAWNY

Tawny set her freshly brewed travel potions on the counter to cool—three green tinctures for Talunasa, and three lilac for the Spring Isles. She didn't plan on heading out anytime soon, but she liked to be prepared. That accomplished, she made her way through the chore list Mother had left for her, sweeping the floors, touching up the cottage wards, and feeding the Shadow Goblins...from a comfortable distance.

She was replacing the satchel of rot-fae repellent above the front door when she noticed something glimmering below. Curious, she traced over the lock-sigil and tiptoed down the winding steps until she got a better look. A sapphire the size of her fist glinted out from the rotting leaves.

Not suspicious at all...

Tawny fished a branch from the ground without leaving the stairs, then used it to nudge the gemstone. Nothing happened. Still skeptical, Tawny touched one toe to the earth, stretching forward to slam the branch into the ground. Twigs snapped, and a pit yawned open around the sapphire, swallowing it.

"Seriously, Daulle?" Tawny shouted in no particular direction. "What did I say about trying to kill me?"

A young goat leapt from its hiding spot in the misty forest. With a stretch and a yawn, it morphed into the neighbor boy.

"*Don't*, or something along those lines?"

"And what is this an attempt at?" Tawny perched her hands on her hips.

"Not kill." Daulle raised a finger. "*Trap*. You said nothing about not trying to trap you."

"Add it to the list."

"Oh, it was a harmless prank." He huffed, trotting around the pit. "I didn't even put any spikes in the bottom of it."

Tawny edged closer to the trap and was relieved to see only dirt at the bottom. Perhaps Daulle was finally starting to comprehend mortality. *Or perhaps...*

She pivoted sharply, narrowly dodging Daulle's horns. He leapt effortlessly over the pit, then smirked over his shoulder.

"Are you kidding me?" Tawny said, teeth clenched.

"Well, I *am* a kid. In more ways than one."

"So you're planning on tricking Mailair, now, is that it?" she asked, eager to leave bygones behind. Mother had been gone for nearly a week, and her Shadow Goblins made for poor company. "What happened to your dreams of an epic battle to the death?"

"It *will* be an epic battle!" Daulle replied. "They simply won't know about it until it's over. They are much, much bigger than me, and they have a lot of followers. A head-on fight would be foolish."

"Perhaps that means you should hold off until you're older," Tawny reasoned. "You know, serve the dish cold."

"People who say revenge is best served cold usually think meat is best served warm. Clichés seldom account for taste."

Tawny kicked some leaves into the pit. "You know you're going to help me fill this in now, right?" she asked. "Mother would hate to come home to this."

Daulle's ears drooped. "Can't we just wait for the soil to shift and fill itself?"

"Not a chance."

Despite Daulle's incessant complaining, the job took less than thirty minutes.

"Good as new." Tawny patted the soil flat with her shovel. "Now, what have we learned today?"

"Not to use you as murder practice," Daulle replied, adding, under his breath, "the same way twice."

Tawny attempted a withering glare, which only made Daulle snicker. She was going to have to have Mother teach her that spider-coughing curse.

"Now what?" Daulle asked, pawing the ground with an impatient hoof. "You've been holing yourself away, which has made my life more dull."

He was not alone in that sentiment. Life was certainly less dull with friends. Preferably, more than one of them. "We should go on a hike," Tawny suggested.

"Good idea!"

"And we should invite Flint."

"Bad idea!"

"I'm worried about him," Tawny confessed. "He knew I was headed for the Spring Isles when last our paths crossed. Normally, he'd have stopped by for a few spriteberries by now. I think something bad has happened."

"So what if it has?" Daulle's ears flicked. "He's the worst, and you've got enough on your plate without taking on his troubles." He raised a ruddy eyebrow. "Is it true that Mailair's whores have been trotting around this place?"

"How do you know about that?"

"You know I keep an eye on the royal harem. Someday, they'll help me discover Mailair's weakness. You, on the other hoof, should be careful. I know I'm a beacon of goodwill and all, but most Augusky are dangerous."

Tawny's eyes flicked to the pit they'd just filled. Already, the churning soil had covered it with leaves. "*All* Augusky are dangerous," she corrected, eager to test a theory she'd been forming. "But, if you're keeping watch on Mailair's harem, you'll want to know what they were talking to Mother about..."

"They actually let you in on the conversation?"

"It wasn't all that important." Tawny shrugged, feigning nonchalance. "They were only asking Mother about a mortal corpse they'd found in the Wilds the other day."

Daulle snorted, crossing his arms. "Why would they care about something so trivial?"

"Because of the Procession of Autumn," Tawny lied. The Unseelie festival was yet a long way off, but it was as good an excuse as any. "You know they've grown bored of hunting Goblins and Pookas. Mailair always gets first pick of the mortal wards, and now they feel like someone's stolen one of their options. They're not the type to let that slide."

Daulle's oval eyes narrowed. "What did your mother say?" he asked.

"She didn't know anything. Sasta wasn't happy. She said something about investigating the scene for herself. Tomorrow morning, if I recall correctly."

Mischief flashed in Daulle's eyes, and Tawny fought a grin. He'd swallowed the bait much more easily than anticipated.

Let's see what you've been hiding.

"Some injuries are deeply felt and others, deeply heard,
Those who place their faith in blades forget the pow'r of words."

CHAPTER 18

RIDDLE ME THIS

AEDYN

edyn woke before the sunrise and crept quietly from the room, so as not to wake...*her*—if she'd given him her name, he'd already forgotten it. Not that it mattered. Aedyn knew from not-inconsiderable experience that she wouldn't miss him either.

He knocked on the door to room six, hoping he'd at least remembered that correctly, and was thankful when it cracked open on the plainest woman he'd ever met.

"You look even more exhausted than yesterday," he said, though it was hard to tell for sure. He couldn't blink without forgetting what she looked like. "I didn't sleep much either. For different reasons, I'm gue—"

"Shh!" Slate held a finger to her lips. "You'll wake Lydia."

"I intend to wake all of you." The door scraped the floorboards as he pressed through it. "Now that we're all theoretically rested up, it's time to start on our way."

The girl's parasite flitted from her shoulder, buzzing around him.

"Of all you could have chosen, you've picked the harshest path,
Stir piskie-kind from slumber and prepare to feel our wrath."

"I'm terrified," Aedyn replied, glancing around the room. Black was still sprawled across the bed, snoring softly, and the pile of blankets at the center of the floor likely hid Lydia. One solitary sheet, thin as tissue, lay crumpled against the wall where Slate had probably slept—or rather, *not* slept—through the night.

"Do you really intend to watch over that child for the whole journey?" he asked, wondering why anyone would willingly take on such responsibility.

Slate ignored him, kneeling beside the blankets and giving them a gentle nudge. They shifted, and a mess of pale hair poked out, stretching into a yawn.

"Good morning," Lydia mumbled, not bothering to brush the hair from her face.

Slate took care of it for her.

Aedyn threw open the shutters, allowing daylight to flood the room. The mortal sun was duller than that of Talunasa, but it invigorated him all the same.

Still, Black did not stir.

Aedyn shot the girls a quick wink, then stood at the foot of the bed with outstretched hands, gathering the light between his fingers. A few artful flourishes, and he molded it into a massive wolf, poised over the assassin with widespread paws. Another twitch, and the wolf bared its fangs, foam dripping from its maw.

"Care to do the honors, Lydia?" he whispered.

The little girl tiptoed to his side, bracing herself with the frame. She took a deep breath, then let out her fiercest growl—which sounded more or less like a kitten's hiss.

Aedyn stifled a laugh, beckoning for Slate to give it a try.

"If it moves things along," she relented. She cleared her throat, squared her shoulders, then broke into the most frightful, realistic imitation of a growl Aedyn had ever heard. Black's eyes shot open, and he reached for his weapon, forgetting he had none. He flailed wildly and toppled from the bed. Aedyn burst into laughter, allowing the illusion to fade, and both Slate and Lydia joined in.

"Fuck all of you!" Black spat.

"Oh, it was all in good fun." Aedyn offered Black a helping hand.

The assassin snarled, grabbing an end table and pulling himself upright. He shot them each a parting glare before stomping from the room, slamming the door behind him.

"We'd best follow," Slate said, wiping an amused tear from her eye. Smiling suited her. "Otherwise, he might burn the place down in a tizzy fit."

"Surely he can take a joke better than that," Aedyn said.

"You don't know Black."

"And you must know him all too well, seeing as you're—"

"Don't say it."

"Lovers."

Slate punched Aedyn in the arm, but the gesture seemed more playful than angry.

"I've heard this conversation already," Lydia complained. "Can we please get some food before you bore me back to sleep?"

"A girl after my own heart," Aedyn said. "Granted, most of them are."

Slate groaned, shaking her head. "Come on, Lydia." She took the child's hand and started for the door. "If we hurry, we can steal a few bites and be gone before the maid wakes."

Good point, Aedyn thought, keen on avoiding an awkward conversation.

The trio descended the stairs and nearly bumped into Black, who had frozen on the bottom step.

"Are you alright?" Aedyn followed his gaze toward the bar and was shocked to find corpses sprawled across the floor. There were three in total, all burley men with gruff faces. Their skin had blanched, and blood trickled from their lips, eyes, and ears, pooling between the floorboards. Wet footprints trailed between them, leading behind the bar, where a plump fellow with a tight-lipped smile sat drumming his fingers on the counter. Red dripped from the brim of his scarlet hat, streaking down his face and into his copper beard.

His envy-green eyes landed on Aedyn, and he broke into a wide grin. Several rows of jagged fangs peeked from behind his lips. "Now, I hadn't factored *you* into the equation..."

Aedyn bristled. "What are you doing here, Far Darrag?" he asked, though Solitaries were free to roam the worlds as they wished. *He*, on the other hand...

"I could ask the same, Princey," the creature replied. "And I prefer the name Blithely. Blithely Fox."

Black and Slate exchanged frightened glances, and a shiver scurried over Aedyn's skin. He had hoped he and the piskie were the only fae the mortals had met. What dealings, or worse, *deals* had they entertained with this monster?

"Relax, Princey. I'm always happy to add new pieces to the gameboard." Blithely pat the counter. "Please, take a seat. I'll explain it all as clear as I can."

Aedyn had never met one of the Far Darrag before, but the tales about them had one consistent moral—never, ever, ever, under any circumstances entertain one of their games.

Naturally, Aedyn sat across from the creature. *Better a novel pain than a familiar pleasure.*

Only when the mortals took the stools to either side of his did he question the decision. He was comfortable gambling with his own life, but his alone. Still, he painted on a confident smile, fixing his eyes forward.

"So, Blithely," he said, ignoring the scents of carrion and copper, "I'm going to take a wild guess and say you're not here to serve us breakfast."

"It would cost you," Blithely replied.

"I'm sure."

"What is it you want from us?" Black asked, clenching his working fist. "Clearly, you've been following us for some reason."

"I only want what's owed me," the creature replied. "Not to worry, lad, You weren't fully in the know, so I can't blame you for withholding. *Slate*, on the other hand..."

She didn't... Aedyn's eyes flicked to the thief.

"You knew exactly what you were nicking," Blithely leaned toward her. "Didn't you?"

Slate crossed her arms, jaw flexing. "You never even told me what you were after," she said, "and I never accepted the offer."

Oh, thank the Creator.

"You accepted information, albeit vague, then went and nabbed the charm for yourself." Blithely wagged a stubby finger in her face. "If I'm honest, which is rare, I'm pleased with the outcome. I was banking on you being cleverer than you thought yourself and less clever than me. As usual, the gamble paid off."

Aedyn knew he should let things be. If Slate had angered a Far Darrag, the consequences—however deadly—were on her. Still, he felt a peculiar impulse to intervene, and he never could withstand an impulse.

"You aren't telling the whole truth," he interrupted. "We fae always get what we're owed, be it for our good or ill. If you had any claim to the charm, it would be in your possession by now."

"I don't owe you any answers, Princey," Blithely spat. "But I've got time to kill if nothing else. About a decade back, I made a deal with a wench called Yana." The name made Lydia gasp. "The charm was part of that deal, but I recently caught wind she wants to offer it to another the night before it comes due. Obviously, I can't allow for such nonsense. It wouldn't suit my reputation."

"That's just good business." Aedyn nodded. "Granted, so is word of mouth. Corpses can't give you that."

"I don't have to make any more than I already have. Just be good little pawns and hand the charm over. I'll have to destroy it, of course, but such is the cost of consistency. We'll all be sorry if it falls into the wrong hands. Trust me."

Aedyn absolutely didn't. "What do you intend to give us in exchange for the charm?"

"Your lives, of course."

"You've come all this way to offer what we already have?" Aedyn *tsked*. "I expected better from the most notorious trickster in all of Faerie."

"Careful, Princey." Blithely grimaced. "That nearly sounded like a challenge."

"Well, the cards are in our favor," Aedyn said, grinning. "In fact, there's only one card worth playing, and it happens to be up my sleeve." He folded his hands on the counter. "Tell you what: let us walk free, and the girl will hand over the medallion."

"No!" shouted both Black and Lydia.

The child's concern didn't shock Aedyn—he'd assumed the necklace meant something to her—but the assassin's was unexpected. Granted, he didn't love the idea of giving up their evidence against the Unseelie either, but it was a better fate than exsanguination.

"What do you say, Blithely?" he asked. "Do we have a deal?"

Blithely laughed, pelting Aedyn with carrion breath. "That's priceless!" he said, shaking his head. "Or, rather, it isn't. You really believe I went through all this trouble over some tacky carnival prize?"

Aedyn's chest tightened. He'd been harboring a horrid suspicion, but he'd desperately hoped he was wrong.

"I'm not after the trinket," Blithely said, eyes sliding to Lydia. "I'm after the lass who's wearing it."

Slate leapt to her feet, pulling the child from the stool and her dagger from her thigh. Already, blood dripped from both the blade and her wrist. Violet light burst from the weapon's runes.

"Over my dead body," she growled.

"Careful with your words, lass." Blithely snapped his fingers, and Slate dropped to her knees. Blood welled in her eyes, spilled from her ears, dripped from her lips like vomit. Her pet parasite sprung at the Far Darrag only to be swatted to the floor. Lydia knelt, trembling. Her own eyes began to glow purple as she wiped the blood from Slate's.

One threat at a time, Aedyn reminded himself. The thief's desperate gasps made his stomach churn, but he could not afford to lose focus. One wrong syllable could doom them all.

"You have no claim to the child," he said, feigning calm. "She belongs to me."

"Excuse me?" Blithely chuckled. "From rumors, it's possible you've made one or two, but that's definitely not one of them."

"Not *her*, exactly. I agreed to escort her to Faerie, which was sure to take a couple of days. That time is mine to barter with, and I will not see it cut short without good reason. I'm willing to negotiate, but not while you're harming my companions."

"Are you serious?" Black hissed, grabbing Aedyn's wrist. "Just let them die!"

"I'm serious."

Blithely sighed but snapped his fingers. Slate fell silent, slumping against the floorboards and blinking the blood from her eyes.

"Better," Aedyn said. "To receive the charm, you will leave this place without harming anyone, and you will never come within one fetid breath of any of us again. Deal?"

"I'm almost disappointed, Princey." Blithely smiled his sharp, rotten smile. "Given your reputation, I was expecting some trick of syntax."

"Understandable." Aedyn shrugged. "Wordplay *is* my third favorite kind of play. Now, about those terms..."

Blithely raised his palm in oath. "By the Shadows what birthed me."

"Perfect." Aedyn hopped atop the counter and knelt beside Blithely, taking his hand. "My, you look dashing today." He held his breath and kissed the creature's wrist. "It that a new hat?"

"What's happening?" Blithely asked, scowling.

"You asked for 'charm,' did you not? It's not my fault you're immune to mine."

Blithely's face turned redder than his hat, and he vanished without another word.

"Your folded fists mean little, so long as your lips are loose,
With every word, another knot is tied into your noose."

CHAPTER 19
ONE LAST DEAL
TAWNY

awny crouched low in the foliage, timing her steps with the Wilds' rhythm so the crunch of crisp leaves wouldn't give her away. Blissfully ignorant, Daulle led her down slithering trails, up treacherous hills, and over streams of silvery water. Eventually, he arrived at a circle of standing stones.

Much like toadstool rings, the stones served as fixed points in the natural tumult. They were powerful places, altars built in honor of the Shadows. Mother had spoken of them often, but she'd never mentioned there was one so close to home.

Hoping to spy on Mailair's beta, Daulle hunkered down a few feet from the stones. His horns poked from the ferns like shiny black beacons. For a second, Tawny was glad Sasta would not truly be investigating the scene, as she would most certainly have found and killed her friend. Then, she realized that she felt like killing him herself.

The sickly-sweet stench of rotting flesh filled the air, accompanied by the manic din of flies and rot-fae. Those signs all but confirmed the fate of the only other mortal she'd really known.

"You monster!" Tawny shouted, barreling toward the murderer.

Daulle's ears perked, and he whirled around. "Tawny, I—"

She hit him at full force, slamming him into the trunk of an oak. He pushed back, too weakly to make a difference. "You've always hated Flint!" she shouted, punching him over and over, wishing her strikes were stronger. "You've always seen mortals as toys! You'd kill us all if it suited your mood!"

"It wasn't me!" Daulle ducked away, nearly tripping on his own hooves. He scrambled around the tree, peeking out from behind it. "You have to believe me!"

"How'd you know where the body was, then?" She plucked a pinecone from the undergrowth and lobbed it at him, missing. "You killed him, and I *hate* you for it!"

"No! I swear, Tawny, *I* didn't kill him. But..." His shoulders slumped, "but I know who did."

From what Tawny had read, fae could not lie. Apparently, that was a lie too.

"I'm so tired of your tricks, Daulle," she said. "I wish Mother had taught me curses. It's not right that you get to walk away with a boil-free hide."

"Tawny—"

"Who did it, then?" Tawny asked, rounding the tree. "Who, but you, would do such a thing?"

"Your mother!"

Tawny froze, fists falling to her sides.

"She doesn't know I know," Daulle said. "If she did, she would probably kill me too."

"No..."

"I'm so sorry." He kicked at the leaves. "I didn't want to tell you. There aren't many things in the Wilds that love each other. She really does seem to love you, and I know you love her, I didn't...I didn't want to ruin that."

"You're lying."

"You know I can't." His ears drooped. "It happened during your last trip to the Spring Isles. You were gone a long time, so I sought her out to see if she knew when you'd return. That's when I saw her carrying him, bound and gagged, to that altar." He tipped his head toward the stones. "She apologized to him and said she needed his help getting out some kind of contract. When she placed him on that altar, I ran away as fast as I could. I came back later, and found..." His gaze dropped to his hooves. "Honestly, you don't want to know."

Yes, she did.

Tawny marched into the stone circle, swatting flies and rot fae from her path as she approached the altar at its center. Two granite bowls sat atop it —one filled with clean white bone, and the other with viscera, plum-red and rotting.

"A scrying spell," Tawny muttered through dread-numbed lips. "Mother would never dabble in magic this dark. She isn't... she's not a..." A sob cut her off.

Daulle placed a calloused hand on her shoulder. "How well do you really know her, Tawny?"

YANA

Lavender, rose thorn, tiger's eye, bay leaves. Calliwyn Yana had found everything she needed. Now, to return to her cabin before the mob caught up. She raced through the underbrush on bare feet, spry and nimble as a doe. Hounds bayed in the woods behind her, muddled by the shouts of angry men.

Calli ducked beneath a fallen tree and slid into the stream. Her condition made swimming difficult, but she fought the current with all her might, only emerging onto the opposite bank when she was certain the hounds had lost her scent.

Her waterlogged clothing added about ten pounds, but she did not allow herself to rest. Her cabin was not far off. With her components and a decent chunk of time, she could ensure her foes never found it. She pressed through brambles and rose hedges, through thistle and nettles, through ivy and splinterwood, anything to shorten the trek. Before long, she burst through her cabin door.

The locks, though numerous, would not be enough. Calli shoved a chair beneath the handle, praying to the Unseen—Dark and Light alike—that she'd bought enough time. Praying that the townsfolk were slow of step and mind. Praying that Billy Brown had been neither wise nor foolish enough to tell them where she lived.

Solstice, oblivious to her panic, rubbed against her leg with a contented purr.

"Not now, dear." Calli tossed a few logs into the furnace, uttering just the right syllables to set them ablaze.

The cat hopped onto the counter, watching with curious amber eyes as Calli set a pot atop the furnace and pulled robin eggs from her cupboard, cracking them open on the floor. She hated to be wasteful, but prudence was a luxury. She wiped the shells dry with her sleeve before tossing them into a granite bowl. A minute under the pestle reduced them to a blue-green powder.

In blatant defiance of common advice, Calli watched the pot come to a boil, knotting her strawberry locks in case she had to run again. Hopefully, it wouldn't come to that. Rhysia was a tiny nation, and she had no friends left to harbor her.

"This might be the end of us," she said, scratching Solstice behind his ear. The cat purred sympathetically, nuzzling against her. Perhaps he was aware of the situation, after all.

Calli rubbed her swollen belly with her free hand, not out of affection so much as habit. She resented the thing growing inside of her more than words could say. It was supposed to pull her from her station, considering who had sired it, but it had only spelled her doom.

Mayor Brown had gone through with his wedding even after Calli told him the news. Of the myriad mistakes that man had made in his pathetic life, that was the worst one. Now, he would never make another. Perhaps Calli wouldn't either.

The water bubbled, capturing her attention and hope alike. She sprinkled the eggshell powder into the pot, followed by the contents of her satchel, and prayed the protection spell would take hold swiftly.

Baying. Shouting. A cloying wave of torch-fire and sweat.

"The mob approaches."

Solstice leapt from counter, crouching like the tiny predator he was, gray tail twitching and claws extended.

"Good cat." Calli plucked the pot from the stovetop and set it atop her cracked kitchen door. "I suppose we must do this the old-fashioned way."

Hopeful that her front door's barricade would slow them, Calli hastened toward the back. It burst open as she reached for the handle.

"Hello, witchy."

Torchlight glinted off Rob Brown's pitchfork and he and his friends pressed into her cabin. Calli grabbed a mop, thrusting it like a lance, and hurriedly whispered a song of the ancients. Her lyrics lilted through the air, past the threshold, breathing life into the brambles beyond. They obediently ensnared the intruders, lifting them from the ground. With a scream and a wet rip, red rained to the ground.

"Serves him right." Calli dropped her broom and made for her bedroom. A window was as good as a door, in a pinch. The kitchen door jarred open, and she jumped aside, narrowly avoiding a splash of boiling water. It seared the first

intruder's skin, sending him to his knees with a shriek, but did nothing to slow his companions.

Solstice latched onto a man's ankle as Calli continued her flight. A pitchfork pierced flesh with a nauseating squelch, and Calli's heart stuttered at the sound of a dying mewl.

Someone was going to pay for that.

As Calli tossed open her bedroom door, a strong arm gripped her own, pulling her back. She swiped a fork from the counter and lodged it in her assailant's hand, but several others had already grabbed hold. They twisted her ankles and squeezed her swollen belly as they worked together to lift her from the floor. She screamed and gnashed but was in no state to fight them off. The child had taken half the energy she'd needed to save them both. *Selfish little bastard.*

"Thought you'd get away with killing my brother, eh, Witchy?" Rob barked, having somehow escaped his bramble shackles.

He was waiting just beyond the door with a crowd of at least twenty, carrying one end of an oaken pillory. Calli's captors shoved her neck and wrists into the grooves, and the trap clicked shut.

The march to Gilash was short, but daunting. Calli might have fallen from exhaustion, were it not for the cruel hands that shoved her along. The peasants had lined up within the town walls, eager for one final Midsummer spectacle. The youngest among them threw pebbles; the older threw curses.

Calli's curses would have been much more effective. She tried to laugh in defiance, but a sharp pain rippled through her abdomen, forcing a cry from her lips. She had felt the same ache days before, but it had proven a false omen. This time, she was not so lucky.

"Quiet, witch!" Rob slapped her, and a second pang tore through her, strong enough to send her to her knees.

So much for dying with dignity.

The pain pulsed stronger, sharper, deeper, as rough hands thrust her toward the central well, where Father Eldon waited patiently. Calli barely registered the priest's smile as she jostled past him. When her belly slammed into the well, a rush of liquid spilled down her thigh. *Too little. Too late.* Torchlight danced on the dark water, conjuring visions of the town in flame. *Not a terrible idea.*

"Calliwyn Yana!" Father Eldon called out with a theatrical voice meant more for the crowd than her. "You stand accused of witchcraft, consorting with devils unto conception, cursing those faithful to the Holy Pondrellen Church, and, in a singularly *heinous act, murdering the good Mayor Billy Brown and his bride on the night of their holy union. What do you say in your defense?"*

Another pain, stronger than the others, surged through Calli from nether to ribs. She wailed, and a murmur spread through the crowd.

"The demons are cursing us through her!" someone cried.

"Kill the witch afore she vanishes!" shouted another.

"Don't give her a chance to repent!" Rob Brown screamed above the clamor. He had more reason than anyone to see her killed swiftly. When the baby was born a person, not the imp the villagers anticipated, it would earn Calli's freedom at the expense of his brother's good name.

She was by no means innocent, granted. She'd earned the mayor's affection with charms, crafted a potion to ensure the union took, and then diced him and his little whore to bits before they could consummate, but she refused to take all the blame. Coerced or not, Billy had given his word. When he'd broken it, she'd broken him.

The ache grew deeper, and Calli's screams grew louder. The priest demanded silence, leaning in close. The feigned compassion on his face riled more fury than the hatred in his eyes. "It is time for last words, my child," he said. "Your body is forfeit —the cost of your crimes. Will you repent for the salvation of your soul?"

Yana clenched her teeth, fighting to conjure voice enough to breathe one final curse. One that would take the whole damned world to Hell with her.

"You think yourselves innocent. You—" she gasped, "you are just as wicked as I am, you rats! Kill me now and the beast in my belly will rise up in vengeance. It will shred you all to pieces and burn your steeples to ash!"

The priest set his jaw. "So be it."

At his signal, Calli's captors plunged her head beneath the water, holding her there while she thrashed and struggled, nails splitting against the pillory, splinters digging beneath them. She trapped her breath as long as she could, well aware she was only prolonging her suffering. Her agony rose in a rhythm until she was finally forced to gasp.

Flame and water faded to black.

The labor pain ceased. Actually, all pain ceased, even that of the weight around her neck. She rose from the water without so much as a splash, suddenly free of her bindings. The midnight breeze ought to have frozen her solid, but she felt nothing at all. Until something soft brushed against her leg.

"Solstice?" Glancing down at her faithful cat, Calli nearly let herself believe she'd somehow survived the attack. The strange green light in his eyes and the bloodless wounds in his side confirmed that she had not. Neither of them had.

Calli took a deep breath she clearly didn't need, then scanned her peculiar surroundings. The world looked as though it had been split along a seam. To her left, the townsfolk celebrated her demise, raising their torches and pitchforks with surreal slowness.

To her right a watercolor forest writhed and twisted, bleeding amber and gray. Eyes blinked out from the foggy undergrowth, but not a single creature scurried forward to greet her.

"Well, Solstice. What do you make of this?"

A storm of howls swelled in the distance—a chilling, desperate din that caused Calli to shudder. She hadn't realized spirits could do that. She slunk cautiously toward the sound, to find that a short man, dressed in all red, shared the space between worlds. One moment, it seemed he was yards away; the next, he stood directly before her.

"Evening, lass," he said, tipping his cap. It smelled of salt and copper and left red smudges on his fingertips. "Welcome to the Veil. Name's Blithely Fox"

"Is the afterlife?" Calli asked.

"It is for you."

Calli laughed, sparing the watercolor townsfolk a glance. "And they thought I'd go straight to Hell."

"They weren't wrong, actually," Blithely said. "It's just you bounced right back. See, even they *have standards."*

"So, this is ...?"

"I already told you it's the Veil. Hell doesn't want you, and Heaven's not even close to an option. Faerie can't cycle mortal souls, and the Mortal Realm asks that you stick to inside your meat sack. I'm afraid you're stuck here for the time being." The wails returned, louder than before. "Least 'til they come for you."

"What are they" Calli asked. "And who are you?"

Blithely laughed, lips parting around rows of jagged fangs. "Who'd you think you've been dealing with all these years? Piskies?"

"So, you're a demon?"

"Hell no!" Blithely scoffed. "And Heaven no, too, for that matter. I wasn't of a mind to pick sides back then, and I ain't of a mind for it now."

The wailing drew closer. Much closer. Close enough Calli could hear its intricacies—subtle variations in volume, pitch, and rhythm. They painted a terrible picture, that chorus of agonized moans, each competing to drown the next.

"You hear that?" Blithely asked. "That's the Sluagh, the Host, the Wailing Wind. All rejected by Hell, much like you. Now, they roam the Veil twixt the Mortal and

Faerie realms, feeding off one another's agony for eternity and, on special occasions, hopping the fence to visit that agony upon something else. You'll be part of it soon, just one drop in a sea of madness and misery. Lucky lass."

If Calli still had a heart—hell, if she'd ever had one—it would have turned to ice at those words.

"I don't think so."

She ran toward her body, delving into the mortal world only to find herself passing through the misty forest and back into the Veil. She tried again with the same result, and again. Soon, she found herself kneeling before Blithely in tears.

"How could you do this to someone?"

"You know all too well why." He flashed another fanged grin. "'Cause it plays to my benefit. Can't you relate?"

The Sluagh writhed into view behind him, a hazy green mist of souls entwined, their teeth gnashing, their screams like claws on glass.

"I suppose this was the cost of it all." Callie had no regrets. Only fear.

"Doesn't have to be," Blithely said.

A scroll unfurled in his right hand, and a needle-tipped quill appeared in his left. "You up for one last deal?"

Yana only ever dreamed when passing through the Veil, and that dream was always the same—a memory, an omen, a *reminder*.

Her time was almost up.

Nearly ten years had passed. Ten years traversing the realms between the Infernal and Celestial. Ten years walking among their peoples, separate but seen. Ten years spent searching for a loophole in the contract.

Finally, she'd found it. It was a small thing, seemingly insignificant. Her eyes had passed over it thousands of times until, exhausted and desperate, they came to rest on a phrase she could exploit.

"Missstressss...Yaaana...Weee...arrre...heeere..."

Her minion's rasping voice jarred her back to the present, the only time that truly mattered. She stood in the center of a circle of ancient stone structures carved with the prayers of people long dead. Their wishes had not come true, but Yana's would. She'd made sure of it.

"It looks just like the one in the Shifting Wilds," she muttered, as though her conjured companions would care.

She sliced a gash in the Aether and pulled her components—briars, beads, blood, bone—from the Veil. Her wish would join the others, painted, etched, and wept into stone, but she had to first prepare the altar. According to the vision that Flint boy's insides had bought her, things were going to happen swiftly.

"Shaaall...weee...seeek...herrrrrr?" a Shadow Goblin asked.

"No," Yana replied soberly. "For now, we need only set the stage. Do not worry, I have read the future in the curve of mortal bones, I have felt it in the fading warmth of mortal flesh, and I have tasted it in the salty-sweet of mortal blood. We will obtain what we seek." She paused, pursing her withered lips. "Provided we use the proper bait."

"If life's a competition, and death the sole reward,
Take comfort in the moments when you control the board."

CHAPTER 20

A GAME WITHIN A GAME

ELWYN

"Y ou're not asleep," Aedyn said, tapping Elwyn's shoulder. "You never fall asleep before the rest of us. I'm, frankly, not certain you sleep at all."

Elwyn cracked opened an eyelid. "What do you want, Aedyn?"

This was the fifth inn that the group stayed at in as many nights, and it was easily the safest and most spacious of those lodgings. Elwyn had not been sleeping, but she'd intended to get there once the others were out cold.

"I can't sleep either," Aedyn said. "Play with me?"

Elwyn's other eye shot open. She wasn't certain what Aedyn's definition of "play" was, but based on his interactions with the other young women the group had crossed paths with, she suspected she'd have to punch him for suggesting it.

Before she could determine whether that was necessary, Aedyn hopped to his feet and tiptoed across the floor, careful not to wake Lydia or Black, who each took up one of the room's two beds. He pulled out one of two mismatched chairs from the table at the back of the room, opened the drawer, and pulled out some dice and a bundle of cards.

"This place has games," he whispered.

Elwyn shrugged and stretched to her feet, leaving Luatha curled up against the door. If Aedyn was not going to sleep anytime soon, she wouldn't be able to sleep either.

Aedyn grinned as she approached the table, looking infuriatingly awake despite the hour. "I knew you were more fun than you let on." He pushed out the chair opposite his with a bare foot.

"Don't push your luck," said Elwyn, taking the seat.

"Oh, but I have so much of it. It would be a pity to let it go to waste."

Elwyn sighed, feeling too exhausted to argue, and began to rifle quietly through the drawer. Some of the games were common, others were unfamiliar, and very few were complete. Eventually, she pulled a thin wooden board, riddled with painted divots, from the drawer. "Stand-off," she said, smiling reflexively. "I used to love this game."

"You don't come across as someone who used to love anything."

Elwyn's smile faded. "My mother used to play it with me," she said, fishing through the drawer for marbles. "But that was a long time ago. Can you help me with this?"

The two picked silently through the game pieces until they secured thirty of the tiny glass orbs.

"It's usually played with fifty," Elwyn said. "But we'll just have to make do."

Aedyn clasped his hands together, elbows on the table, and set his chin atop them. "Explain it."

"It's based loosely on the Rhysien Revolution." Elwyn turned the board so that the blue edge faced her, and the red edge faced Aedyn. "Not three decades back, Pondrelle ruled over Rhysia, but the island nation wanted independence. Being so much smaller, the Rhysiens couldn't hope to win an all-out war, but they're a clever and startlingly sacrificial folk. They took the resources for which Pondrelle had been using them—cotton, grain, potatoes, and the like—and they stashed away as much as they could in secret. Then, they set the entire nation's farmlands ablaze."

"They did *what?*"

"Set them ablaze." Elwyn dropped a few green marbles into divots of the same hue. "Pondrelle had no use for Rhysia without its resources, and their economy took a huge hit as a result of the rebellion. They searched hard for where the locals had stashed their goods, but they were unable to find enough to recover. After nearly half a decade, they decided it would be better to grant Rhysia its freedom on the condition that they had exclusive trade rights with the newly reestablished country."

"What about the Rhysiens?" Aedyn asked. "They needed those resources too, right? If the rebellion lasted a few years..."

Elwyn gave a solemn nod, dispersing yellow marbles throughout the board. "About a fourth of the population starved to death."

Aedyn scooped up the gray marbles and started dropping them into the matching spaces, silent for a moment longer. "I suppose every realm has its wars," he said, placing the final marble. "Faerie hasn't seen one for nearly two centuries, The War of Light and Shadow was the last. I'm too young to remember it. Actually, I was born in the middle of it, according to my father. I suppose my parents had little to do between skirmishes except each other."

"Gross. Also, there's no way you're *two centuries* old. You look maybe... twenty-three, tops."

Aedyn smirked. "I look good, right?"

Elwyn crossed her arms.

"You don't have to answer. I know I do. To be fair, we fae don't experience time the same way you do, so I am, for all intents and purposes, twenty-three. Not that it matters, given we can't exactly die of old age. War, on the other hand..." Aedyn's gaze dropped to the table, his smirk faltering.

"Did you lose someone?"

Aedyn painted a smile back on his face and gestured to the board. "How do you play?"

Elwyn placed three black marbles in her starting slots and instructed Aedyn to do the same with his six white ones. "It's pretty simple, honestly. I'm playing as Rhysia, and you're playing as Pondrelle. That's why there are more marbles, or 'resources,' on my side of the board. Following so far?"

Aedyn nodded.

"Good." She plucked up one of her black marbles. "As Rhysia, it is my job to horde the resources before 'The Hell Purge'—that's what they called it when they burned the fields. To do so, I need to move the resources all the way to this blue line." She tapped the painted edge of the board. "I can then remove them from the board, and they are safe for the rest of the game. My white marbles can move up to three spaces at a time in any direction." She demonstrated. "When I jump over a resource marble, like so, I can move it up to three spaces toward my side of the board." She returned everything to its starting position, then flicked a finger at Aedyn's white marbles.

"Finally," he said. "The part involving me."

"As Pondrelle, you are tasked with taking enough resources to sustain your economy by moving them to your red side of the board. You acquire them in the same manner as I do, but, as the country with the higher population and more advanced military, you get twice as many soldier marbles, and they can move up to four spaces at a time, rather than three. The same goes for resources they secure. Make sense?"

Aedyn nodded.

"Good. The game lasts five rounds. We each get one turn per round. If you have five of each of the three resources by the end of the game, you win. If you don't, I win. Ready?"

Round one.

Elwyn moved a white marble three spaces, hopping over a green and collecting it. The next one didn't collect a resource. The third hopped over a yellow.

"So, why can't you sleep?" she asked. When Aedyn looked up at her, she scooped an additional two resource marbles into her palm.

"I've never been any good at it," he said with a shrug. "Ever since I was a child, I would just lie there and think about all the things I would rather be doing. It eventually got so bad that the Sylphs prescribed a sleeping draught."

"What's that?"

"It's a kind of potion. It tastes okay, like honeyed wine, and it is honestly very helpful. Learo makes it for me every night."

"Who's Learo?"

"My attendant."

"An attendant? You really are a prince, aren't you?"

Aedyn blushed, pushing his hair out of his face. It fell back the second his fingers hit the table. "My turn?"

Elwyn nodded, and Aedyn picked up the first of his black marbles.

"What about you?" he asked, moving his pieces in the worst possible directions. "Why can't you sleep?"

"I'm sharing a room with a vulnerable child, a sadistic assassin, and a stranger of questionable morality."

"If you have questions about my morality, I'd be happy to answer them in lurid detail," Aedyn said, already moving the last of his white marbles.

Elwyn laughed. "No, thank you."

Round two.

"So, what's Faerie like?" Elwyn asked, hiding pilfered yellow and gray marbles in her lap with the others. "I've read about it in storybooks, but I somehow doubt they do it justice."

"Well, it's a big place, so I haven't been to all of it," Aedyn said. "The Shadow Realms are a mystery, though much has been written about the two largest, the Shifting Wilds and the Winter Wastes. The first is led by Mailair, an Augusky who claims to be chaos incarnate, and the second is ruled by Fuara, the Korrid Queen. Supposedly, she's the vilest creature to have ever lived, but I imagine that's an exaggeration.

"The Light Realms are more familiar. I'm from Talunasa, a textbook paradise—wealthy, florid, eternally sunny." His tone was unmistakably bored. "The Red Realm, Réimsdarg, is where my best friend, Amatha, lives. It lies directly beneath us, but don't tell them that. It's been the subject of debate since the kingdoms were made. We also have the Spring Isles and Chorial, but I've only ever visited those for parties. Suffice to say, I remember very little from those trips."

Elwyn shook her head, motioning for Aedyn to take his turn.

"What about this world?" he asked, eyes brightening. He picked up a white marble and jumped it over two yellow ones. "You've mentioned Pondrelle and Rhysia. Surely there's more to this place."

Elwyn watched Aedyn's fingers closely as they moved to the next marble. "Our lives are shorter than those of the fae, so we've not explored as far nor as thoroughly," she explained. "There's Muldrain, to the north, a harsh, unforgivingly cold environment by all accounts. There are lands to the far south as well, though few have ever traveled past Selea, and reports of that nation are pretty vague. Apparently, it's humid and feral, filled with all kinds of strange, dangerous creatures."

"Sounds like a Seelie ball," Aedyn said, laughing under his breath.

Round three.

Six marbles sat in Elwyn's lap, Aedyn none the wiser. She sat very still, lest they clatter to the floor and give her scheme away.

"You mentioned a best friend," Elwyn said, trying to distract Aedyn so that she could pilfer a seventh. He was dangerously close to obtaining five yellows. "Amatha, was it?"

Aedyn nodded. "We've known each other nearly as long as I can remember. Since I'm an only child, she's basically like a brother to me."

"*She's* like a *brother?*"

"It's not an insult," Aedyn said, moving a black marble over a yellow. *Dammit.* "It's more of an inside joke. The Daoine Sidhe don't really care about being considered ladylike or manly. Their culture is one of strength and courage, so they all come across as a bit of what we Daoine Maithe might call 'masculine.' The definition of that word changes with every culture, though, doesn't it? For instance, in my realm, I'm considered the height of masculinity, but your lover over there certainly doesn't seem to think so." Aedyn nodded toward where Black slept.

Elwyn glared, changing the subject. "So, what do you two do for fun?"

"Pretty much everything. We've played a lot of pranks, sparred in nearly every combat style, and squabbled over countless women. You know, the usual."

"You both fight over women?" There were plenty of mortal women with similar tastes, but they were expected to keep it hush. "Faerie sounds like a very accepting place."

"In some regards." Aedyn chuckled. "It isn't as though she's expected to breed an heir regent. Her father is the Sidhe Chieftain, but they obtain their throne through battle, rather than birth." He moved another marble. "Do you mortals truly police who others bed?"

"Kind of. The clergy sets the standards for morality, even for those who don't practice their faith. I suppose..." Elwyn shook her head, "*breeding*, as you so delicately put it, is a bit more of a priority for our kind, and even then, only within marriage. Unless you want your children to end up like myself or Black, that is. The standard is applied almost exclusively to women, of course. If it weren't for the brothels, the arrangement wouldn't be possible on a purely mathematical level."

"What's a brothel?"

"You, of all people, should know."

Aedyn blinked, befuddled.

"It's a place men can go to buy...companionship."

A few seconds passed, her meaning sank in. "You mortals are highly economical creatures, aren't you?" He grinned. "That sounds a lot more honest than court affairs. Where can I find one of these *brothels*?"

With how Elwyn's mother had been treated, she would never have called the brothel business an honest trade, but she was not about to go into those details with Aedyn of all people. "Next round," she said.

Round four.

Elwyn now had enough marbles in her lap to ensure her victory. She fought to keep from smiling at how oblivious Aedyn was to her tricks. All he had to do was count the marbles to know she'd been cheating, but he seemed far too distractible for that kind of a thing.

"What about you?" he asked, watching her take her turn. "Any best friends?"

"Luatha."

"The parasite does not count."

"First off, mortals cannot be trusted," Elwyn said. "Surely, you've figured that out by now. Granted, I've lived much of my life among the worst of them. Only one other girl has managed to survive the Greyscale very long, and she's become a bit unhinged in that time. The boys, as you can imagine, aren't particularly interested in making friends. Second, I'd appreciate it if you'd stop calling Luatha a parasite. Sure, she can be troublesome at times, but I care about her, and she doesn't like being called a parasite. So, you'll stop it if you want me to like you."

Aedyn's brow furrowed like he was solving a puzzle. He moved one of his marbles overtop a gray resource. "I think I do want you to like me, Slate," he said eventually. "But piskies *are* parasites."

"What do you mean?"

"I mean, they attach themselves to people, and they take...well, they take *something* from them. There are lots of different types, and they feed in different ways, or so I've been told. I've never actually met someone who's bonded with one before. It's a give-and-take sort of thing. They supposedly enhance the natural gifts of their host, whatever that means. I don't suppose you know what Luatha gives or takes, do you?"

Elwyn thought about it while Aedyn finished his turn. She had been very young when she met Luatha, and she had no idea what kind of skill set a ten-year-old could possibly have possessed for a piskie to enhance. All she'd ever been good at was hiding.

She shook her head. "No idea."

Round five.

Elwyn and Aedyn took their turns in silence, each focused on securing their victory. Oddly enough, she found herself wanting to prolong the conversation. She resisted the urge.

"And that's the game," she said as Aedyn moved his final marble. "Now, let's see who won."

"I did." Aedyn's smile was bright enough to hurt Elwyn's weary eyes. He gestured to the marbles on his side of the board. Five of each color.

"That's impossible," Elwyn said. "You cheated!"

Aedyn crossed his arms. "How dare you accuse me of such a thing."

"We only had thirty marbles to play with."

He shrugged. "There *are* thirty."

Elwyn's eyes swept from her horde to his. He was right. Despite the marbles she'd squirreled away, thirty remained. Aedyn had been paying closer attention than she'd thought.

"You're using your glamour!"

"You have no—"

Elwyn scooped the marbles from her lap onto the table, where they rolled about, bumping into her existing horde.

"—proof." Aedyn chuckled, clapping silently. "Well done. And here I was, thinking you and I had nothing in common." As he lowered his hands, seven marbles disappeared from his side of the board. "Play again?"

"No cheating?"

"Now where's the fun in that?" He folded his hands behind his head and leaned back in his chair. "How about this? We can cheat, but we can't cheat the same way twice. That way, it's like a game within a game."

Elwyn had to admit, it sounded like fun. "You're on."

"The fog of ignorance is a protective thing, it's true,
But what you don't know can hurt as much as what you do."

CHAPTER 21

BLISSFUL IGNORANCE

ELWYN

he fire crackled, flooding Elwyn's tired bones with comforting warmth as sparks danced around it like mischievous piskies. Her *actual* mischievous piskie had been quiet for the better part of the evening, which was unusual, but she suspected Luatha was merely relaxed. For the past few blessed days, nothing had gone awry. It felt almost eerie, considering all that had happened since the group had first met.

In fact, Elwyn had never felt so cozy in her entire life. Aedyn's coin trick had garnished enough supplies for the road and some more practical clothing. She'd happily traded Silva's ruined gown for wool tights, a dark tunic, and a new gray cloak to match the one she'd left in Amblewick. Aedyn had naturally mocked her tastes, but only briefly. He'd preoccupied himself by gathering information on Raths from the locals. Not surprisingly, his questions were aimed almost exclusively at pretty young women.

That said, the comfort extended beyond clothing and firelight. Elwyn's companions had become warmer, too—even Black, though "warmer," in his case, merely meant the temperature no longer dropped by twenty degrees in his immediate vicinity. Now, it only dropped by ten.

Elwyn kept her secrets close as ever, but often found herself chatting with the others about weather, weapons, and other safe topics to help pass the time. She could still only trust them as far as she could throw them, but she could likely throw Lydia a very long way. She could not throw Aedyn very far, by contrast, and she would never even attempt to throw Black.

"Food's done," the assassin said, pulling the skewered quail from the flames. Aedyn helped to steady the spit while he split the fowl apart with his working hand, passing them around the campfire.

"Not as awful as it looks," Aedyn said, struggling to chew through the dry skin.

"And just as good as it smells," Lydia added, attempting the same.

After days of sulking, the girl had finally begun to perk up again. Elwyn had trouble accepting that such a fragile child was some kind of magical vessel. Lydia still acted like the helpless little girl they'd discovered clinging to her mother's corpse. Only her peculiar pallor hinted at something more. Aedyn swore up and down he knew some beings, Undine, who could divine what was happening to her, but the thought of strangers pulling secrets from the child's soul made Elwyn bristle.

Then again, that quandary could wait another day or two. Why not enjoy the fire while it was bright, the food while it was warm, and the laughter while it was lilting?

Elwyn bit into a wing, grateful Black had thoroughly feathered the thing for once. It wasn't awful, though she'd begun to grow accustomed to the fancier meals Aedyn secured for them whenever they passed through a town. The further north they traveled, the wilder the land grew, and the rarer such feasts became.

"The boy not only burned the bird as dark as it could be,
He split it 'mongst the four of you, forgetting about me!"

"Pass another bite along," Elwyn said. "You forgot Luatha again."

Black scowled predictably, but pulled a bit of his own portion free and passed it down the line. "I'm still not convinced your invisible friend is real, but so be it."

"She's real," Lydia said, adding her leftovers to the offering before setting it down beside Luatha. "And she's nice, once you get to know her."

The piskie beamed.

"While I had grown accustomed to the mortal's spirit-blindness,

It's about time that somebody appreciates my kindness."

"Agree to disagree." Aedyn smirked.

Luatha stuck a tiny lavender tongue out at him, then returned to her meal without giving it another thought. She had grown used to Aedyn's barbs, like the rest of them had. It puzzled Elwyn that, once Black was made aware of Luatha's presence, the piskie still refused to reveal herself to him. Then again, if given the chance, Elwyn would have made herself invisible to the assassin, too.

Aedyn placed another log on the fire.

"Slow down if you want those to last through the night," Elwyn warned.

"The flames were getting low," he insisted, though they really hadn't been.

"The little Faerie prince is frightened of the dark," Black said with a hint of a smile.

Aedyn glared. "I'm just not used to it, is all."

Black scoffed and took another bite of braised bird.

Lydia played with a lock of her pale hair, as she did whenever she was trying to work up the courage to speak. "Does the sun really never set in Ta...in Tal—"

"No," Aedyn said, stretching his hands toward the fire. "Nothing ever changes in Talunasa."

"You don't seem too excited to return," Elwyn said.

Aedyn sighed deeply. "I've *consequences* to face when I get home, even if I manage to smuggle all of you in unnoticed. My father can be a bit of a...I believe the mortal term is *hard-ass*."

Black snorted. "He's the king, right? What's he going to do, lecture you to death?"

"I swear he's come close to it twice."

"My father was mean, too." Lydia pulled down a lapel of her frilly gray dress, revealing a patch of scorched skin beneath her collarbone. Elwyn wrapped her arm around the girl.

Aedyn's eyes widened, flashing gold in the firelight. "He harmed you?" he asked, as though such crimes were uncommon. "I'm so sorry, Lydia. I—"

"You thought for a moment that the struggles of a royal brat were comparable to the plights of us common folk?" Black snorted. "I'm sure it happens all the time."

Aedyn turned his pitying stare to the assassin. "Yours too?"

Black stared into the flames. "If you're talking about the bastard that sired me, yeah. He used to beat the shit out of me just for looking at him wrong. Not that I'm complaining. It made me who I am. Lucky for me, I found a Father who's ten times the man he was."

Elwyn let out a single, curt laugh.

"Something to say, Slate?" Black glared daggers in her direction.

She'd been hoping to avoid this conversation, but it was bound to happen eventually. "The 'Father' is a cruel, manipulative charlatan who uses urchins to carry out his dirty work," she said. "Surely, you realize he doesn't actually care for you?"

"He took us in." Black's fist balled at his side. "He gave us a chance and a purpose, things we'd never have secured on our own. It makes sense that you're ungrateful—you're an unremarkable agent who failed to live up to his standards. I, however, matter!"

"Really, Black? Why don't you return to him, then, withered arm and all? See how much you matter to him now?"

"I don't have to listen to this shit!" Black lurched to his feet and kicked at the fire, smattering it with dirt.

The outburst startled Lydia, who leaned into Elwyn, trembling. Aedyn tossed a log atop the flames before they could even dim. The assassin marched off to slump against a nearby tree, lost to another of his brooding sessions. Whenever he started to open up, someone would strike the wrong chord and send him flying into a rage.

It probably didn't help that Elwyn was so good at plucking his strings.

"It's alright," Elwyn whispered, squeezing Lydia's shoulder. With what the girl had just confessed, it made sense a man's wrath sent her into a panic. Elwyn had always wondered about her own father. Seeing how the others' had treated them, she wondered whether she was blessed to have never met him.

Luatha perched on Lydia's shoulder.

"Memories are magic with the power to scare or charm you,

They can teach you many things, but they can never harm you," she cooed.

It wasn't like the piskie to show such concern. At least, for someone other than Elwyn.

The girl loosened her grip on Elwyn's arm but didn't pull away. They sat in silence around the fire for some time, listening to the songs of crickets and frogs in the nearby fens. Staggered ticks from Brannon's pocket watch cut through the natural orchestra, throwing off the rhythm.

As usual, it was Aedyn who broke the silence. "Why did you leave?" he asked, looking to Elwyn. "The Greyscale, I mean. From what I gather, it was a tough life, but wasn't deserting the larger risk?"

Elwyn had to chew that one for a few seconds. "It wasn't safe," she said. "I know there are no truly safe places, but I at least *feel* safer when I'm making my own decisions."

"Relatable reasoning." Aedyn stoked the fire with a branch. "So, if that's the case, why did you wait nine years to run?"

Luatha straightened, crossing her little arms.

"I told her, the entire time, that we should slip away;
It took another voice with mine to prompt her to escape!"

Elwyn sighed, eyes lilting to Lydia. She may have looked exhausted, her eyelids drooping as she stared into the flames, but she was doubtless listening intently as ever. It's what Elwyn would have been doing, were the roles reversed.

"Truth told, I was content with the life of a thief," she said, choosing her words carefully. "It came easily to me, and dreadful as the Greyscale was, I'd seen equal terrors beyond the sanctuary walls. Then, one day, the Father decided it was time for me to branch out. He'd gotten it into his head that my skills would prove useful in other endeavors, so he sent me on a mission...better suited to someone like Black."

Aedyn nodded, catching her meaning. It was rare for him to focus for so long without becoming distracted by something else, but he motioned for her to continue. So, she did.

"Nine years." Elwyn still couldn't believe it. "After so long, you'd probably think it was something drastic that prompted me to flee, like an angel flitting down to personally tell me off, or the ground opening up and spitting me out on this island. It wasn't anything like that. The target's words helped—that look in her eyes, more compassion than terror—and so did Luatha's, but in the end, I simply couldn't..." Guilt gnawed at her stomach. She'd always been such a coward. "It's one thing to do what you must to survive, but to steal something so precious for profit? I didn't have the heart for it."

"You say that like it's a bad thing," Aedyn said. "To have a heart for something like that is a lot like not having of a heart at all, and that's certainly not you."

There was a sincerity in his voice Elwyn hadn't caught before, something entirely different from his usual, flippant charm. The warmth of it flooded her, putting the glow of the campfire to shame. It was mildly unsettling, really.

"And you?" she asked, eager to change subjects. "If leaving home was so risky, why go through with it?"

Aedyn shrugged, his smile fading. "It was...too safe."

Elwyn could not begin to relate.

Lydia stretched into a silent yawn, then rested her head on Elwyn's shoulder. Elwyn stifled a yawn of her own, having not slept soundly since Amblewick. Apparently, she did not hide her exhaustion well.

"You've kept watch for far too long," Aedyn said. "It's my turn."

Elwyn bristled at the thought of passing her duty off to another. But then, she was terribly tired, and they would not reach the Raths for another day or two. She could not stay awake forever.

"You're certain?"

"I have trouble sleeping outdoors, anyway." He winked. "I'm...*a little bit afraid* of the dark."

Elwyn smiled, resting her cheek against Lydia's hair, and Luatha curled up on her opposite shoulder. A dangerous, careless contentment seeped into her weary bones, and she was resigned to let it stay there, just for the night.

"Can you sing to us again?" Lydia mumbled. Aedyn had shared several of his peoples' songs throughout the journey, much to her delight. Elwyn found his voice strangely soothing as well, though she'd have never admitted as much aloud.

"You've heard all that I know," he replied. "The light singers are the ones who memorize our songs; I've just picked up a few things from one or two of them."

"Then repeat one," Lydia begged softly. "Pleeeeeeease."

Aedyn chuckled. "Alright, I give in. Do you want to hear Maggie McLee, The Song of the Sylphs, or Ballad of the Sea Queen?"

"Sea Queen," Lydia said with a final yawn.

"Good choice," Aedyn said, "I prefer the banned songs, too."

He whistled to find his pitch, and Elwyn allowed her eyes to close. She knew better than to let her guard down, and she refused to grow dependent on others. But for now...

"The Sea Queen sang on silver gales,
To bless the mortal sailors,
To make white billows of their sails,
And speed them to safe waters.

As time passed by, the queen did spy,
A brave, intrepid mortal,
His handsome visage caught her eye,
And there began her troubles."

...For now, she just needed...

"She bid him passage to her land,
Granted his lungs her glory,
Beneath the sea, he took her hand,
In blessed matrimony.

When curtains fell, her belly swelled,
The Queen would have a daughter,
The mortal King smiled happily,
To learn he'd be a father."

...to give her shoulders a break from the weight of it...

"When, to her bed, the Queen was stayed,
The King, he grew unhappy,
She bid him passage 'bove the waves,
To visit with his family,

Without a word for many days,
He stayed above the waters,
The girl was born a healthy babe,
But no sign of her father."

...For now...

"The Queen, distraught, then hurried off,
To search for her lost lover,
She found her King upon the sands,
Entangled with another.

With broken heart, she tore him free,
Took back the breath she'd given,
And dragged him deep into the sea,
Then, with her dagger, joined him."

...she just needed...

"So mind this tale, lest you should fail,
To keep your wild heart guarded,
Between the worlds, there hangs a veil,
And it should not be parted."

...to sleep.

BEAUS

"And so, dear children, it is important to remember what the scribes have written, that all have committed misdeeds in the sight of the Creator, but we may yet atone with humble spirits and acts of charity."

Beaus stood before his congregation, admiring the worshipful stares of his followers in the mosaic light of the stained-glass windows. Weekday services were typically quite small, but the pagan festivals of neighboring lands—like that which was currently underway in Rhysia—tended to spike an uptick in attendance. The pious believed their prayers could combat the ill-effects of misguided worship. Beaus had never shared their faith, but he would bask in it and all the coin it brought him.

He led the congregation in a closing prayer as Ghost passed around the collection box, then bid a choir of orphans to serenade their exit. The parishioners eagerly filtered from the sanctuary into the streets, where they would return to their sinful lives, confident their offerings would shield them from a Hell they'd doubtless earned.

Only one man lingered behind. Beaus had noticed him mid-sermon, his hands folded behind his head and his feet propped irreverently on the pew in front of him. His mottled red suit hinted at vagrancy, and the empty seats around him were omens of a foul odor.

Even if the stranger was not repulsive, Beaus had work to attend to. Not one, but two of his agents had vanished in a months' time, and he had not poured his life into building an empire only to watch it crumble at the whims of rebel children. He was on his way to the catacombs when Ghost appeared beside him, tugging on the hem of his robe.

"What is it, my child?" Beaus asked.

The boy pointed at the man in red, now waddling toward them.

"You think *that* is worth my time?"

Ghost nodded.

Beaus did not often heed the advice of his agents, but Ghost was an exception. Though the boy could not have been older than six, he had a keen eye and good instincts. It didn't hurt that he was mute, meaning Beaus could trust him with the syndicate's most dangerous secrets. This set him apart from the rest of the rabble, who he was learning not to trust at all.

"Hold up, Pa," the man in red said, breathing heavily as he finally caught up to them.

"It's *Father Beaus*." The priest scowled. "What is it you seek, child?"

The man laughed, assaulting Beaus with the most rancid breath he'd ever had the displeasure of smelling. "Been a while since anyone's confused me for a child," he said. "I'm at least a half-dozen centuries your senior."

Fascinating. A nebulous theory began forming in Beaus' mind.

"The name's Blithely Fox." He extended a hand that Beaus would not have shaken if his life depended on it. "As it happens, I'm in need of your services."

"My services for a wedding or a dedication, I'm sure," Beaus said, testing him.

Blithely grinned, his lips pressed tight. "Let's be candid, Pa. I know what kinda outfit you're runnin', and I have need of your agents. Lots of them."

"I see." Beaus scanned the sanctum for witnesses, finding none. "If you know what we are, then you must also know I don't negotiate without my enforcers present."

"Those burly lads by the gate?" Blithely chuckled. "They're a little tied up at the moment. Literally. I'm sure you'll make do without 'em."

Beaus blanched. Granite and Coal were not to be trifled with. This stranger, short and stout as he was, could not have subdued them through any earthly means.

His theory took on shape, color.

"Follow me," he said, continuing his march toward the catacombs.

Within moments, they arrived at the study. Blithely pressed past Beaus to take the chair on the far side of the desk. *Beaus'* chair. The Father's fingers tightened around his staff, but he restrained himself. If this stranger was what Beaus believed him to be, angering him would be unwise.

Sitting in the guest chair, Beaus bid Ghost to fetch two cups of tea. He wasn't thirsty, but he wanted to show Blithely that Saint Aldrich's Sanctuary, and everyone within its walls, belonged to *him*. Ghost returned in a blink, setting two ceramic cups between them.

Blithely accepted his eagerly, pinky out. "Business is best discussed over drinks."

"Indeed." Beaus folded his hands atop the table. "And I am always open to new ventures, provided the price is right, and it suits my vision. Tell me about this job."

"The details are simple." Blithely sniffed his tea, nose scrunching. "I need to hire some lads, no less than a dozen, to intercept a delivery."

"I see. And where will this delivery be happening."

"Rhysia."

Beaus straightened. He had lost too many agents to that damned island. "I'm afraid I don't accept foreign contracts anymore," he said. "They cause ... complications."

"Oh, I'm well aware." Blithely grinned. "Which is why you should accept. If your agents succeed in this mission, you can keep that little thief and your grumbly boy as a prize, alive or dead, your choice. Wait much longer, you'll lose your chance entirely."

"You know Slate and Black have gone?" Beaus asked, anger rushing through him at the mere mention of the missing agents.

"I know where they're headed." Blithely shrugged. "And I can get your agents there in a blink...provided you accept the job."

"I can spare a troop of initiates," Beaus said, eyes narrowed. "One agent may accompany them, but no more. Give me an hour, and I'll draft up the papers."

"No need." Blithely pulled a scroll from his pocket. He flicked his wrist, and the parchment unfurled, spilling across the desk and onto the floor. He snapped his fingers, and a quill appeared in his other hand, the nib needle-sharp. "I've got it covered. Oh, and we should discuss a contingency plan before signing, given your recent failures.

Beaus's jaw flexed. "The Greyscale does not fail."

Blithely shook his head. "It's always best to plan for any move your opponent *could* make, not just the one you think they will," he said. "I'm not saying the plan will go wrong, but if it does, you'll want a friend or two in low places. Trust me."

"What's in it for you?" Beaus asked. "Aside from the usual blood."

"I don't really owe you an explanation, but I suppose there's no harm in explaining anyway." Blithely leaned back in Beaus' chair and propped up his feet. Like most Leprechaun-kind, he was wearing very nice shoes. "You see, I'm a businessman, much like yourself. Except where you ransom souls for money, in a way, I do the opposite. Not always money, mind you, but power, prestige, acclaim, and so on. You know, things mortals value."

"Why souls?' Beaus's eyes roved the man's red suit. "The blood, I understand, but what use could you possibly have for spirits?"

"They keep me young and healthy!" Blithely smiled, all fangs. "Oh, I'd bounce back from death, but it would be as someone new. Thing is, I like me just the way I am. Not to mention, souls are right delicious. Provided you season 'em properly."

"Dare I ask?"

"Malice, madness, spite, suffering...The things that make a spirit zesty in life, make 'em zesty in death too. I've played with the recipe a bit, but I've found that about ten years is the perfect marinating time. Any shorter, and they're still a bit tough; any longer, and they fall to pieces. That's part of what's so irritating about this dilemma I'm facing: I've been patiently letting this particular spirit steep in her sins, and now she's gonna' go and ruin all my hard work."

"Bad for business, that."

"Right you are." Blithely winked. "Still, I'm starting to see the upside. To succeed, she'll need to change things in a way that's bound to be *good* for business."

"And you want to include me in that as well?" Beaus asked, more confused than ever.

"Think about it, Pa." Blithely's grin stretched wide. "A world in shambles, folks for whatever hope their grubby little fingers can reach. Imagine what they'd offer you—what they'd offer *us*—for our help."

"I'd keep the money?"

"And I'd keep the blood." Blithely nodded. "We can split the souls, if you'd like."

Beaus grabbed the quill.

ARYN

The Midsummer ball had finally ended, and the High Judges sat around an oraithvine table as round and golden as the sun itself. Though a legion of Maithe brigadiers, Undine guards, Sidhe warriors, and Sylph scouts waited beyond the doors, none were permitted entry. The rulers could not afford for their concerns to infect the general populace.

Aryn allowed Mearalas to relay the details of Fuara's message, hoping her characteristic cynicism would cast a fittingly somber tone over the meeting. As it turned out, Creagor had also received a new message mid-ball—one that supported the Korrid Queen's tale.

"Sluagh, hmm?" he asked, polishing his battle-axe with anticipatory fervor. A twist of his fingers, and it morphed into a spear. "Is fitting. One hobgoblin called her Ghost-Witch, and another, Yana. They say she hops between worlds, lately more than ever, and that her plans center around the mortal Midsummer."

"What could such a being possibly want?" Soen threaded slender fingers through silvery hair. "More importantly, why does Fuara feel so threatened by her?"

"That is what we must determine," Aryn said. "Despite my earlier reservations, I now motion to send Mearalas' scouts to gather intelligence."

"They are already posted on the White Shore, awaiting my orders."

Mearalas' smile had never been so smug. "Hopefully, we have not lost too much time to your wavering. Of course, I intend to have them do more than scout. If they obtain something, anything at all, with a strong link to the Sluagh, my seers should be able to divine her fate. I cannot think of another method for learning her plans before the window closes."

"That is not what we discussed." Aryn's jaw flexed. "And I had instructed you to hold off on your preparations."

Mearalas's smirk twitched. "You have no authority over me, Aryn. Have you already forgotten our—"

"It's wonderfully convenient that the scouts are ready to leave," Soen interrupted. "Perhaps we should excuse Mearalas to give them their orders?"

Aryn's anger ebbed, shame flooding in behind it. Leave it to Soen to point out the foolishness of a conflict without pointing it out at all. "So be it," he muttered.

Mearalas glided from the room with a high chin and jutting shoulders, arrogant as ever. Objectively, Honor and Law should have been harmonious. Why then, were the High Judges vowed to those ideals continually discordant?

Once the doors closed behind the Undine Queen, Aryn addressed his remaining peers. "I am hopeful this venture proves fruitful, but we must always prepare for the worst. Creagor, can you convince your stonemelders to double their production on weapons and armor without causing riots?"

"Is easy job." Creagor grinned, running a hand over his obsidian scalp shards. "The Sidhe have been lazing at ball all day. Nothing like a smithing contest to raise spirits."

Aryn looked to Soen. "As for distracting the people..."

"It is already taken care of," the Sylph said with a playful smirk. "When a brigadier told me of your meeting with that emissary, I idly mentioned to a group of young guards that you and Mearalas had been gone for an awfully long time. By now, rumors will have rippled out to the furthest reaches of the kingdoms. You are welcome."

Aryn was grateful for Mearalas's absence. She was much too proud to sacrifice her reputation for the good of the realms, but he was not. He'd sacrificed far dearer things than that already.

"I appreciate your efforts, my friends," he said. "It is important we maintain close communication. The moment any of us hears new information, we will reconvene at once. In the meantime, we must go about our business as though nothing at all has changed."

"The trials?" Soen asked.

"The trials," Aryn echoed, waving his dismissal.

Seelie Court proceedings were always put on hold during festivals, so the High Judges devoted the following days to the loftiest cases, and their subjects had come to view it as another celebration. It usually disgusted Aryn that so many were entertained by their neighbor's misfortune, but this time, the rite played to his favor. The people needed their little distractions, now more than ever. Wars were fought by the sword, but they were maintained through ignorance.

*"From certain angles, friends and foes look very much the same.
Though you may meet a friendly beast, don't ever think it tame,"*

CHAPTER 22

BETRAYAL

TAWNY

he scroll was tucked away at the very bottom of an elmwood chest. It had taken Tawny hours to locate, hidden beneath a stack of boxes in Mother's closet, and it had taken another to unbind the lock sigils. Tawny paid little heed to most of the chest's disturbing contents—the shadow tomes, the hearth-dried hearts, the tongues preserved in spell-scrawled jars. That little roll of ribbon-bound parchment, with its time-yellowed pall and tattered edges, was far more frightening.

When she finally worked up the courage to unfurl it, it stretched across the length of Mother's bedchamber, the excess parchment curling into a crescent against the wall. Tawny fully expected to find some archaic, inscrutable runes inked onto the paper. She was not sure how to feel when her eyes landed on common letters.

It was a contract—probably the one Daulle had heard mother mumbling about.

When she'd killed Flint.

The first few paragraphs read like standard legal fare, fraught with details about how the words were binding and the terms, once set, could not be renegotiated by either party. It set a timeline—ten mortal years, and not a minute more—and even specified that the signatory could use a touch of spirit, should they have no blood to scrawl with.

Further along, the handwriting changed, and the content became more chilling.

"I hereby promise my soul and that of my unborn child to one Blithely Fox upon the end of a single mortal decade. During this time, I will remain separate from the Sluagh to which I was destined, free to use both souls however I'd like, but I will share their curse of dual citizenship. On the final day of my contract, whether I dwell in the Mortal or Faerie Realm, Blithely Fox will be entitled—"

"What are you doing, dear?"

Tawny's breath caught. She turned slowly to find Mother hovering in the doorway, eyes flaring violet.

"Mother! I-I was just—"

"You were just prying into things that don't concern you!" Mother said, voice splitting. "Did I not raise you better?"

Tawny gulped, rising to her feet. It was not the first time Mother had been angry with her, but this was not some simple mistake, like confusing chickweed for doorweed and ruining a potion. Mother had never raised her voices at her before, and her eyes had never burned with such rage. As a sourceless wind swept around the woman, stirring her loose tresses and the gauzy layers of her gown, Tawny finally believed she was looking at a killer.

"I'm sorry!" she cried, blinking tears from her eyes. "I just...I had to know."

"Know what?" her mother's voices hissed over each other.

Tawny shied back until her shoulder hit the wall. "I had to know what you were doing. I had to know why you would..." She took a deep breath. "Why did you kill Flint?"

Mother's shadow stretched, splitting and breaking off into inky, yellow-eyed goblins. The minions crept forward alongside her. "What. Makes. You. Think. *That?*"

Tawny set her jaw, masking her fear. "Daulle saw you."

"That meddling boy!"

"He saw you drag our friend into the woods, to that altar. He heard you s—"

"Would you rather it was YOU?" Mother's voices swelled to a storm. "I chose the most pathetic mortal in these Shadow-forsaken Wilds for my purposes, but perhaps a more choice ingredient would have yielded better results!" She flexed her gaunt fingers and breathing through her nose. The violet light faded, and the squall died down. "I am very disappointed, dear."

Tawny clasped her fingers behind her back in an effort to stop their trembling. "I only want to know what's made you so frightened. This isn't like you. I know it isn't, no matter how many secrets you've kept." She tipped her head toward the scroll. "That contract spoke about a child. Who is—"

"I do not owe you any explanations," Mother snapped, light flashing in her eyes.

Tawny flinched, raising her palms in apology.

"Go to your chamber," Mother said softly. "Do not return until I call for you."

Tawny would never have disobeyed, but a legion of shadows followed her up the stairs to make sure of it, growling hungrily all the way.

BRANNON

As he crested what Aedyn had promised would be the final hill, Brannon spotted a cluster of circular buildings and let out an immense sigh of relief. The Raths. They had actually made it.

Just shy of two weeks had passed since he'd ambushed Slate at that ridiculous festival, but it felt like years. He'd suffered the others' company as best he could, so as not to arouse their suspicions, but he wasn't sure how much more comradery he could fake. These were not his friends. They were two tools and an obstacle.

The rest of the group burst into a cheer upon seeing their destination, all equally relieved. Brannon smiled genuinely at the thought of finally resting his feet. That dead arm of his was throwing off his balance, resulting in a bevy of aches and blisters, but he hadn't complained aloud even once. Best not to show weakness to those you'd later need to intimidate.

"What's the food like in the Faerie?" Lydia asked, skipping ahead of the others as they began their descent. "Are there cakes? Puddings? Pies? What about honeyed pheasant?"

Aedyn laughed. "All that and more."

"And the clothing?"

"The most beautiful you'll ever see, I swear it."

The child practically floated, she jumped so high. Brannon could not imagine getting so excited over snacks or stockings. Even the notion of traveling to another world—which would have either frightened or thrilled most others—felt like a mundane chore, just another box to tick on his way back home.

"Someone race me!" Lydia begged. "Please!"

"Oh, alright," Slate stooped beside the girl. "On your mark, get set—"

Lydia took off.

"Cheater!" Slate shouted, giving chase. "What do you think the fae-folk do with dishonest little girls?"

"We give them crowns," Aedyn shouted after them.

Surprisingly, the prince didn't join in the race. He was normally the most childish in the bunch, to the point of occasionally annoying the *actual* child. Now, he strolled along slowly, hands shoved in his pockets and face tilted earthward. Though curious, Brannon had bigger concern than some fae fop's fleeting discontentment. The girls were finally out of earshot, and he could ask some of the questions that had been burning in his brain.

"How will they know to heal me?"

"Excuse me?" Aedyn blinked over at him.

"The Sylphs," Brannon said. "I can imagine the plan's changed, now that we know the girl is the charm. You're too sentimental to offer her up as evidence, so smuggling us in is the only option. If we're meant to lie low, how will the Sylphs know to heal me?"

"This may come as a shock," Aedyn smiled, "but I've actually thought that one through."

"That *is* shocking. Are you sure you don't need a few more years?"

"Who knew you could be funny?"

"I assure you that it was a fluke."

Aedyn laughed anyway. "Seelie fae, like myself, aren't permitted to visit the Mortal Realm, but that rule doesn't go both ways. Mortals stumble in on occasion and are usually well-received. Sometimes they crash through the Parting Sea. Sometimes they stumble upon a potion. Sometimes they wander in through the Melding Caverns. Once, a little girl was playing 'Wish-I-May' in a toadstool ring, when she accidentally said the right thing while holding the right flowers and *poof!* She wound up right outside the gates of Samhria. We never did get her back home now that I think about it."

Brannon cleared his throat.

"All this to say that one of those buildings leads to the Melding Caverns," Aedyn explained, nodding toward the Raths. "If I send you through by yourself, no one will think anything of it. The Daoine Sidhe of the Red Realm are a burly bunch, but they are a kind and generous people. One look at your arm and they'll send you straight up to Talunasa. With the Midsummer Ball underway, the palace will be swarming with Sylphs. I'll simply slip through another tunnel and meet you there."

It was a decent plan, much to Brannon's surprise.

"Oh, and one more thing," Aedyn added. "Don't tell the Sidhe that you want to go 'up' to Talunasa. We have a bit of a difference of perspective there. They're wrong, of course, but we pretend not to notice."

"Understood," Brannon said, though it really wasn't.

The men caught up with Slate and Lydia just outside of the first Rath. Both girls were leaning against the wall, bickering over who'd won their stupid race despite a noticeable lack of breath.

"Save at least a little of your energy," Aedyn warned. "We still have quite a way to go."

"Fine." Slate straightened, taking Lydia's hand in hers. "What's next?"

Aedyn and Brannon explained the plan, and the girls agreed to it, though Lydia didn't look happy about it.

"I'll miss you," she said to Aedyn, who patted her on the head and assured her she would not have to miss him very long. She then turned to Brannon. "And you'll be off healing, so I'll miss you, too."

The words settled strangely on Brannon's shoulders. He shrugged them off.

Together, they marched to the first entrance, where Aedyn examined a blue rune that had been carved above the door, only to say "hmm" and move on to the next.

"You know where you're going, right?" Brannon asked. "I swear to fuck if you—"

"It's an ancient script, but you have no reason to worry." Aedyn waved the concern away. "The symbols are color-coded: blue for the Parting Sea, yellow for Talunasa, and red for the Melding Caverns."

"You're positive?"

Aedyn was already entering the Rath with the red marking. Brannon looked to Slate, who shrugged and followed after, before doing the same.

Though the Rath was weathered and gray on the outside, vivid patterns wove along the inner walls. They did not seem to have faded with time, though they must have been painted centuries prior. A round wooden door rested in the center of the floor. Aedyn flung it carelessly open, not bothering to check for traps. Luckily, all that waited beneath it were stone steps, descending into darkness.

Aedyn visibly shuddered. "Light?"

Slate pulled a matchbook and a few candles from her satchel. She lit a candle apiece for Aedyn, Lydia, and herself, ignoring Brannon altogether.

Fine by me. He didn't need some fickle little light, and he certainly didn't need her approval.

The tunnel snaked downward for at least a mile before splitting off into branches. Aedyn always kept to the centermost path, claiming to have learned to do so from a nursery rhyme as a child. The further they marched, the more Brannon's feet ached. The more his feet ached, the more he doubted Aedyn's sense of direction. The more he doubted Aedyn, the more seriously he considered killing him.

At last, Aedyn paused, casting candlelight over a rune on the wall. It was identical to that which had been etched above the door.

"We're getting close," he said, a smile in his voice. "Twenty more feet, thirty tops."

Footsteps scraped against stone. Brannon hadn't heard them until the others fell still, or if he had, he'd excused them as mere echoes. He bid the others to hush, then turned around slowly.

The soft sighs of languid breathing staggered through the stale air. Silhouettes crept through the darkness, smudges of charcoal against black. As the shapes drew closer, candlelight glistened in their eyes and yellow teeth.

"Who are you?" Brannon's left hand reached for a blade he no longer possessed. "And what do you want?"

Laughter echoed off the tunnel walls as a boy stepped into the undulating light. His matted brown hair and freckled face were familiar. Brannon had only ever regarded assassins like Wolf as paltry competition. From the scavenger smile the boy now wore, he'd viewed Brannon the same way.

"It's been a while, Black," Wolf said, eyes drifting to the others. "Sorry to intrude on whatever this is, but business is business. Father's been concerned, to say the least."

Sardonic though the claim was, Brannon couldn't help hoping there was truth to it. Sable had been only a petty thief, and Slate, a continual nuisance. But *he* had always been among the Father's favorites—a loyal soldier from the start. Surely, that counted for something.

A violet light burst to life in Brannon's periphery as Slate stepped forward, *icon* brandished. "Tell the Father he can go to Hell," she said.

"And if it isn't our favorite runaway," Wolf said as the shadows behind him inched forward. "You always did think you were better than the rest of us, didn't you?" He shook his head, pulling his *icon*—a battered hunting knife—from his belt. "It's a good thing the Father said we could bring you back *'dead or alive.'* After all the trouble you've caused, he didn't care much either way."

"Wait!" Brannon stepped away from the others, raising his good palm. "You can take me with you. I won't put up a fight."

Wolf snickered, and his initiates followed suit. "What good are you, with that shriveled husk of an arm?"

Brannon unconsciously grasped his dead arm. He'd thought those very words himself, but *hearing* them...

"It's not—"

"Don't kid yourself!" Wolf snickered. "You're a useless sack of shit now, not that you were much more before. Couldn't even retrieve a little runaway girl."

"Enough." Aedyn marched forward, unsheathing his rapier. "I'm going to give you a choice—go home now of your own volition, or I'll send you there in pieces."

Wolf did not look intimidated. "Looks like the wounded assassin found a suitor to protect his honor."

"Careful, Wolf," Brannon growled. "Even wounded and unarmed, I'm twice the fighter you are."

"Well, then you're still far outnumbered." Wolf leveled his *icon* at Brannon. "Get 'em, boys."

The shadows rushed forward.

Violet light gleamed off frenzy-wide eyes and sharpened steel, lending each agent a purple halo. A shadow slashed at Brannon's heart. He pivoted, and the blade lodged in his dead arm, painless. Brannon grabbed his assailant's face and slammed it into the wall. Something cracked. Something squelched. A body thudded against stone.

Brannon ripped the blade from his arm, wincing at a shock of phantom pain. He raked it across the throat of the next shadow to sprint past.

The glow of Slate's dagger had drifted deeper into the tunnel, but Brannon no longer needed it. At the simple feeling of cold steel against his palm, the fight flooded back into him like air to a shriveled lung. He sliced his way through the darkness with a feral, consuming hunger, and three more bodies fell at his feet. The thrill was dizzying, distractingly so.

A pommel slammed into his fingers. His weapon clattered to the ground. A weight crashed into him at an angle, slamming him into the wall. His dead shoulder popped on impact, loud enough to make his stomach flip.

"The Father always gets what he wants," Wolf said, knife pressed to Brannon's throat. The conviction in his voice was familiar—a near echo of the assassin's own sordid devotion.

Fool, Brannon thought, as much to himself as his foe.

The younger agent chuckled, sliding his knife up to the corner of Brannon's eye. "I was going to make this quick, but I think Father would like a trophy."

"Black, catch!" Slate shouted.

Brannon held out his hand just in time to catch the dagger by its handle. He recognized the heft of the hilt, the grooves worn into the leather wrapping. His *Aras Tosc*. Brannon had never missed anything quite so much.

Before Wolf knew what was happening, Brannon's dagger imbedded in his temple. Crimson sprayed through the air as the blade pulled free, and the agent crumbled to the floor.

Brannon took a moment, regaining both his breath and his bearings. At least a dozen agents had passed him by in favor of the others, but the thief and the prince were holding their own. Haunting violet arced through the darkness with Slate's every practiced slash. Whenever a strike landed, an agent wailed in agonized fear, and a phantom pain pulsed through Brannon's shoulder. Aedyn stood a bit further back, limned in the quivering light of Lydia's candle. Or so it seemed. When an agent slashed the prince's throat, he vanished, and the true Aedyn leapt out from the darkness, thrusting his rapier through his assailant's stomach.

Brannon was not about to let the others have all the fun. A blink, and he was battling alongside them. It was not easy, adjusting to one-armed combat, but Slate and Aedyn picked up his slack until he caught the rhythm. One at a time, the agents' dying wails filled the hollow in his chest. The violence was like supper to a starved man, and the aftertaste cloying—something rich and sweet and altogether inebriating.

Vengeance, valiance, vindication ...

Whatever it was, Brannon knew he'd be chasing it for the rest of his life.

"Take her alive!" a voice shouted as the remaining agents rushed them. Several fell, but a trio forged past, grabbing hold of Lydia. Her candle fell, guttering out.

Slate sprinted toward the child, trailing violet light. Brannon followed after. A blinding flash filled the tunnel, and he fell still, shielding his eyes. When he peered over his arm, squinting, Lydia's skin shone like moonlight. One agent released her, backing away. The other two froze in place, still gripping an arm apiece.

"*Aetri en Sca!*" the child shouted. The words slithered over themselves, and it was not merely the reflection of sound on stone. She opened eyes of violet flame as a wind raged suddenly around her, whipping through her hair. She lurched upward, ripping her captor's arms from their sockets.

Those agents fell, but the child continued rising. The wind grew stronger, louder, forcing Brannon to his knees. What remained of the Greyscale troop fled, their footfalls scraping as they clambered toward the exit. Lydia crashed to the floor, and her light sputtered out.

Slate continued her sprint, and Brannon followed her blade's dwindling light. Aedyn was waiting at the end of the tunnel, cradling the...what Brannon had *thought* was a little girl. She looked so peaceful again, her little eyes closed, her little arms limp.

Aedyn passed Lydia to Slate, who examined her by the fading glow of *Gelah's* runes. Perhaps it was the purple pall, but the girl looked paler than before. Her ivory skin and buttercream hair had been peculiar—sickly even —but her new, snowy cast was downright chilling.

It conjured images of a willow-thin woman and the shadowy beasts she willed into being.

"She's not breathing." Panic pinched Slate's voice. "W-what can we do?"

Brannon reached for her shoulder, but she instinctually flinched away. "We need to leave here." He looked to Aedyn, hoping he could think more clearly than the grieving thief. "The Fa—" He cut himself off, balling his fist. "The bastard who sent those agents might have thought to send reinforcements. If he did, they'll be here in no time."

Aedyn nodded, nudging Elwyn. "The Sylphs are her best hope, now," he said, helping her lift Lydia from the floor. "I'm going with you, no matter how it looks. I can get you to a healer faster than the Sidhe could."

Slate followed the prince, carrying Lydia, and Brannon walked backward behind them, knife raised. If any agents came after them, he was going to make their job difficult. Within seconds, Aedyn announced they'd reached the gateway, and Brannon whirled to find a yawning pit. The edges were visible the light of Slate's dagger, but only darkness stared back from its depths.

"Shall we jump?" Aedyn asked. It was more a suggestion, really.

Brannon blinked, frozen by the possibilities of what waited below. For all he knew, Faerie was a horrible place. Worse, even, than the nightmares he'd already lived through.

Aedyn elbowed his side. "Black?"

"It's Brannon," he replied.

He breathed deeply and dove.

The darkness splashed, and the weight of nineteen sorrowful years floated around Brannon, suspended in salty cold. He opened his eyes to murky green waters, stretching out in all directions. The shapes of his... colleagues—yes, that was it—drifted nearby, unmoving.

His pulse pounded as he searched for light, desperate to parse the heights from the depths. When he found none, he flailed, directionless. A burn like frostbite filled his lungs, clawing its way to his throat. His vision blurred, dimmed, then darkened.

After all of that...

How many minds had harbored those same last words?

A shadow drifted through the depths, lithe, lean, and envy-green. The next thing Brannon knew, cold lips pressed against his, forcing them open. Fresh air filled his lungs, briny as an ocean gale.

He washed up on glittering white sand, coughing despite his empty lungs, and squinted up at a world of violent color. Viridian forests sprawled over hills and spilled through winding valleys. Turquoise waterfalls sliced through the green, cascading from jagged amber cliffsides. Vivid lights, like fireflies, danced playfully in the distance, and gilded towers pierced the canopy, spiraling like seashells toward the cloudless, cerulean sky. In the distance stood a tree the size of a city, its massive branches, clad in gold and green, grasping toward a lemon-yellow sun.

Webbed hands grabbed hold of Brannon, yanking him to his feet. Several soldiers stood before him, clad in sleek cobalt armor. Their green skin glistened like viper scales, and thin, serrated ears that poked from their helms, reminiscent of gills.

"Who are you?" Brannon asked, his voice coarse.

The soldiers answered by leveling their spears at Brannon, and not him alone. Aedyn and Slate stood to either side of him, dripping wet and shivering. Lydia was draped over the thief's arms, limp as flayed flesh, and the bastard spawn of a butterfly and an imp clung to her shoulder—Luatha, he assumed.

He'd imagined piskies would look a little less...insectile.

One soldier stepped ahead of the formation, distinguished from her colleagues by a teal bandolier coated in barnacles. She leveled her spear at Aedyn, and he responded with that dopey smile he was always flashing.

"Trinstrina," he said, bowing as much as the spear allowed. "It's been a while."

No response.

"Or...is it Solelle?"

A grimace.

"Look, um, *you.* I know we have our history, but let's set that aside for the moment, and—"

The soldier whistled, pressing her spear to Aedyn's sternum, and two more guards stepped forward with weapons leveled at Slate and Brannon.

"Aedyn of the Daoine Maithe," the leader said. "You are hereby placed under arrest for violating the Treaty of Dusk."

Aedyn shrugged. "It's good to be home."

"The spoils of war determine what measures one might take,
So who can judge a person's heart, when it's among the stakes?"

CHAPTER 23
LOVE AND WAR
BRANNON

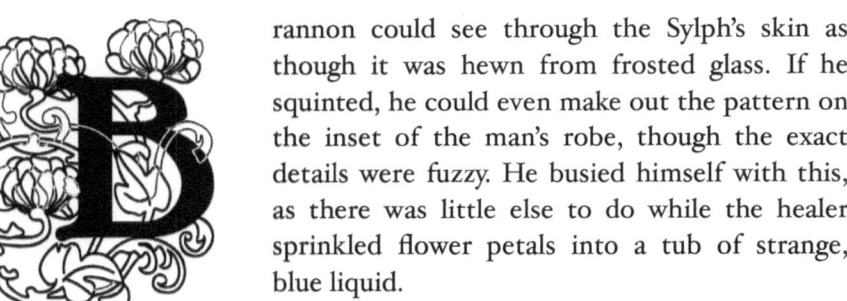 rannon could see through the Sylph's skin as though it was hewn from frosted glass. If he squinted, he could even make out the pattern on the inset of the man's robe, though the exact details were fuzzy. He busied himself with this, as there was little else to do while the healer sprinkled flower petals into a tub of strange, blue liquid.

"How long will this take?" Brannon asked, trying and failing to mask his impatience. "I'm beginning to doubt your skill."

The Sylph glanced over with knowing mint-green eyes, but he said nothing.

"N'e Alan has taken a vow of silence." The airy voice lilted in from the tent's entrance. "It helps him to hear the pulse of life, that he may better guide it."

A woman with the same translucent skin and silvery hair as the man flitted over on feathered wings, carrying a bundle of floral herbs that matched her periwinkle eyes. The moment her toes hit the floor, her wings vanished, and she dipped into a bow. "My name is Ferea."

"What is he even doing?" Brannon asked.

She tilted her head to the side, and one of many cherry blossoms fell from her hair. "He is preparing a tonic for you," she said, as though it should have been obvious. "The rot in your arms runs deep enough that our touch alone will not restore you. These Butterbreeze clusters," she handed the herbs to N'e Alan, "should help."

Brannon snorted. "Did N'e Alan tell you all that?"

"In a way," Ferea replied, missing the joke. "I have studied under N'e Alan for many decades and have learned to discern his instructions without need for words. You are, however, the first mortal I have seen him treat. Do you have a name?"

"Brannon," he replied, hating the taste of his own name. It was the second time he'd spoken it that day, after discarding it for nine pointless years. The thought sent fire through his veins, causing his every muscle to tense. *Nine years working for that bastard, and for what?*

"Anger interferes with the process," Ferea said, voice flat. "You mustn't feel rage here."

"Well, in that case, I'll just stop feeling it."

Her brow furrowed. "Irony?" she asked.

Brannon blinked, his anger ebbing. "Obviously."

"Our Speaker-Elect is skilled with irony." Ferea hung her head. "Regrettably, it is difficult for many Sylphs to grasp, myself included. We spend so much time in silence, it is difficult for us to hear the words behind the words."

"Oh." Brannon wondered what the Sylphs thought of Aedyn, who seldom spoke plainly. "I simply meant that it isn't as easy as you've implied, letting go of rage."

"Why not?" Ferea placed a hand on Brannon's good shoulder, and his skin tingled beneath her fingertips. "It takes discipline, yes, but emotions can be conjured, ebbed, and controlled like any other magic. Perhaps it would do you well to spend some time in our temples."

"*Temples?* Are you kidding...?" He breathed out, shaking his head. "Perhaps it would. Anything might help, at this point."

Simply talking to her had calmed him, he realized. There was something about her soft, slow speech and languid movements that put his mind at ease, grounding it in the present. Her mentor might have had the same effect, if his silence wasn't so infuriating.

N'e Alan nodded to Ferea, and she draped Brannon's dead arm over a wooden slab. The week of disuse had made it stiff as clay, but she managed to stretch it flat. She offered Brannon a parting bow before flitting away, vanishing through a gossamer curtain.

"Will this work quickly?" Brannon asked.

The Sylph looked at him like he was stupid, dipping a sponge into the tub. He held it there for a matter of seconds, then swiped it over Brannon's arm, wringing pastel potion over blackened flesh.

At first, Brannon felt nothing but disappointment. His jaw clenched at the possibility he'd hoped in vain, and his rage began to rise once more.

Then he felt something else.

It was subtle, at first, like the patter of raindrops on a dense leather cape. But it was a *feeling*. The sensation grew, spreading through his skin. It flared to a burn within seconds, but it was the most wonderful pain he had ever known.

N'e Alan dipped the sponge a second time, and Brannon watched in wonder as the darkness in his veins receded. By the third wash, the burn had faded to a tingle, much like that left by Ferea's touch.

Brannon focused on his fingertips, channeling every bit of strength he still harbored.

They twitched.

"It worked!" A laugh burst from his lips, unbidden. "It actually fucking worked!"

The Sylph's eyes widened at the profanity.

"I-I mean, thank...thank you." The words tripped over his lips, just as his name had. Years of disuse could do that.

N'e Alan smiled softly, then rose and bowed at the waist. He walked to the exit like any other man; no wings bursting from his shoulders, no feathers trailing behind him.

Now what? Brannon wondered. For the first time in ages, he had no mission to complete, no commands to follow, no mentors to impress.

Armor creaked, drawing Brannon's eyes to the entrance. Ferea had returned, this time flanked by two cobalt-clad soldiers. Brannon suppressed a sigh. He'd been so thrilled to have his arm back that he'd forgotten he was technically under arrest.

He glanced once more around the tent, admiring the colorful rugs and plush pillows. It was certainly a step up from the Greyscale dungeons. Hopefully, his next destination would be half as serene.

"Mortal Brannon?" Ferea asked, tapping again.

"You can come in, obviously."

The gossamer parted, and Ferea flitted in alone, alighting on a rug front of him. The bow she greeted him with somehow seemed more solemn than the last.

"The child came here with you, yes?" she asked.

Brannon had nearly forgotten about Lydia. Slate had said she wasn't breathing, but did something like her—whatever she was—even need air? Compelled by something like curiosity, only stronger, Brannon followed Ferea from the tent. The soldiers in cobalt fell into step beside them. After a short jaunt across a wildflower field, they came upon another tent, far darker than the first. Ferea parted the curtain, waving him forward.

A group of Sylphs were huddled at the center of the tent, heads bobbing and arms waving. Not a single word left their lips, but they were clearly deep in conversation. Static prickled Brannon's arms as he pushed past them.

Lydia lay bare atop a cot, covered by only a blanket. Her skin had taken on a gray tinge, and her lips were flushed lavender. A foul musk, like that of bread mold, hung in the air around her.

"Is she...?"

"She is dead," Ferea said.

Brannon hadn't experienced many emotions, so he was no good at identifying them. Whatever swelled in his chest at that moment was sharp and frigid, and it somehow made his ribcage feel even more hollow despite its heaviness. He hated it as much as he'd ever hated anything. Mere hours before, he'd watched that little girl transform into something luminous. Something powerful and fierce, meant to be admired. The closest thing to a god he could bring himself to believe in.

The transformation had been monstrous, but it was another memory that shook him. *She said she would miss me...*

He might just miss her too.

"It was a short life, wasn't it?" he asked.

"No," Ferea said. "She was never alive."

"What do you mean?"

"We Sylph know the flow of life as well as our own kin. We can feel its presence, speak to it, hear its whispers. What flowed ... No, what *flows* through that child's veins was never life. I believe it to be the *Shadows*."

She spoke with a gravity that made Brannon think that he should both know and cower at the word.

He wasn't one for cowering. "It is still there?" he asked. "The Shadows?"

Ferea flinched. "A trickle, like the water which pools in a leaf after the storm."

"Then heal her, just as you healed me."

Ferea hung her head. "This is not our domain."

Brannon gripped Lydia's frigid hand in both of his, looking down at her with mixed pity and wonder. "Surely there's something we can do..."

LYDIA

"Where do you think you're going?"

It was the last voice Lydia wanted to hear. For a moment, she was torn between running for the forest or climbing back up to the window she'd just escaped through. Then, her father ripped her from the ground and both options were lost.

The embrace was far from loving. He restrained both of her wrists with one hand, twisting her sideways so her kicks cut fecklessly through the air. The gardener watched them approach the kitchen entrance. He ignored Lydia's pleas for help, opening the door at her father's bidding.

Knowing no one else would help her, Lydia bit her father on the shoulder. He cursed, hurling her into the nearest wall. Her breath fled on impact, and her vision spun, shapes smearing.

Aetri en Sca...

The words were an ill wind—the jingling of wind chimes that warned of a looming storm. Lydia shouted overtop them, trying desperately to drown them out.

"Keep away from me!" she cried, but her father did not listen. He grabbed her by the hair so hard her scalp stung, wrenching her to her feet.

"I will not be disobeyed!" He slapped her hard across the face. "Least of all by the likes of you."

A flare of purple, a tug at her consciousness... Aetri en Sca...

Lydia spat and shrieked, clawing at her captor's hands as he dragged her to the foyer. She wished she were stronger. Worse—she feared she might be.

"Tallehan, stop!" her mother shouted from the top of the stairs. "You don't have to hurt her!"

"Stay out of this" he shouted back, starting up the steps.

Lydia dug her heels into the rug, fighting with all her might and hoping it was enough.

"Stop that, you little imp!" He kneed her in the gut, and a flash of light, blindingly beautiful, washed over the world.

"Aetri en Sca," she hissed.

Her eyes opened to a world of plum and indigo, shadow and flame, hope and dread. The whispers had grown to a thundering roar, calling to her, consuming her, and passing through her lips again and again.

A sepia skeleton gasped from its perch atop a crimson waterfall. Its sockets fixed on Lydia for a second before it ran away, shrieking. Lydia's father—now a twisted mass of fanged laughter, chitinous scales, and sunken eyes—retracted his sickle-claws, stumbling backward. Lydia flung herself at him, knowing her safety lay in his silence. She ripped the scales from his flesh one by one until the laughter stopped.

Crimson dripped from her fingers as she rose from the floor, held aloft by the dying breaths of those who'd passed beyond redemption. She released a soulful screech, a warning to any who might oppose her. But they did not flee. Or, if they did, they were not fast enough.

Lydia swept through room after room, finding and disposing of her foes. She loved watching them tremble, cowed by the majesty of one they once oppressed. Their fear lasted only seconds before she shredded their skin, snapped their bones, washed the walls with their blood. The whispers served as her guide—a magnetic force, tugging her onward. It led her up a snaking staircase and down a hall, to the room that had served as her prison for too long. What solace lay in wait for her, the vessel of the Shadows, beyond its painted door?

She flicked her finger, and the door burst open on the trembling skeleton of a woman, hunkered down beside a bed of leaves. The Shadows bid her to end the creature, to cut the final tie, but something inside her stuttered at the thought. Lydia fought the violent pull, and her toes touched soil... no, carpet. The violet light began to dim. The whispers faded slowly. Sinew and skin reknit over bones, fashioning together a familiar form.

"Mother?" Lydia whispered, her voice a nest of serpents. She reached out her hand; the creature shrunk back from her touch.

"Y-you are a monster," the mother-skeleton whispered.

She should not have said that...

The touch of a hand, warm against her icy skin, and a familiar, brooding voice pulled her back to the present.

"Surely, there's something we can do…"

Lydia's eyes blinked open.

ELWYN

Worry churned in Elwyn's stomach as she followed a pair of gilded guards through a tree that was also a palace.

The moment she'd washed up on the Talunasan shoreline, they'd taken Lydia away.

They'd also taken Luatha.

And *Gelah*.

Though her clothing was waterlogged and crusted with salt, she'd never felt so naked. *She wasn't breathing.* That thought echoed through her skull over and over, forcing tears to her eyes.

A warm hand touched her shoulder.

"She's going to be okay," Aedyn said, making Elwyn wonder whether she'd been mumbling aloud.

"Hands to yourself," a guard barked. There were four in total—two to their front, and two behind them. They shared Aedyn's burnished skin and aurous hair, but not, it seemed, his charming irreverence.

Aedyn obeyed, withdrawing his hand after shooting the soldier a biting glare. There was a darkness in his eyes that hadn't been there before. Elwyn wondered whether he was also fretting over Lydia, or if some other trouble had stolen his light.

Aware worrying wouldn't help matters, she let her gaze flit about her dazzling surroundings, allowing herself to become mesmerized by the sculpted windows, gilded wainscoting, and intricate tapestries. "This would be beautiful under any other circumstance," she muttered.

"This isn't the tour I was hoping to give you," Aedyn replied, though she hadn't been addressing him directly.

When the soldiers led them to an archway draped in a green velvet curtain, Aedyn tapped the back of Elwyn's hand, winking. She understood. The moment the fabric fluttered shut behind them, they slid in opposite directions, pressing their backs to the wall. The soldiers continued on their way, escorting a pair of illusions around the next corner. Elwyn covered her mouth to stifle a laugh.

"After a century of dealing with me, you think they'd catch on," Aedyn whispered, shaking his head.

"When they find us, won't this just make things worse?"

"It'll be worth it," he assured her. "Besides, they've been tasked with keeping me on the premises. So long as we don't leave the palace, we're technically not breaking any rules." He grabbed her hand and started toward a branching hallway. "Now, for that tour."

Together, they raced up a series of spiral staircases that led to a sprawling balcony railed in the same curious golden vine that wove throughout the entire palace and comprised Aedyn's own armor. He dropped Elwyn's hand, and she leaned over the edge, breathing in the rich, summer-grass air.

Now, *this* was a distraction.

Birds of every imaginable hue flitted over a rambling expanse of emerald foliage. Cliffsides cloaked in flowering vines jutted through the canopy, and grassy wildflower leas checkered the landscape like patches on a quilt. The tiny forms of people rushed to and fro near the palace roots. They gathered around crystal fountains, frolicked through gilded gardens, and wandered a market maze comprised of colorful, patterned tents.

"I've never seen anything like it," Elwyn said, breathless. "It's stunning. When I was little, I would climb a new rooftop every sunset in hopes of catching colors like these. Our world simply doesn't have them."

"I suppose it is something." Aedyn folded his arms on the railing. "I'd gotten so used to it all, I hardly noticed anymore." He grabbed her shoulder, flashing a smile that—even in a world like this—made everything else look dull. "This isn't the half of it."

He led her up another three more opulent stories, not pausing for a breath until they stepped out onto an enormous rooftop garden. The lawn was composed of clover, rather than grass, allowing for a clear view of a spiral path hedged in intricate topiaries. Each was carved from a different variety of flower or foliage, and all were wreathed with those mysterious golden vines.

"This is my favorite place in the whole palace," Aedyn explained, waving for Elwyn to follow as he started down the path. "Each of these is a ruler from Talunasan history." He looked at the statues with a kind of reverence Elwyn hadn't thought him capable of. "Most depict the Eternal King and Queen, which is why they look so much alike."

Elwyn hadn't noticed. But then, they were sculpted from plants. "Your parents?" she asked.

Aedyn nodded. "They're true fae—originals. They've been here since the Battle that Split the Sky in Two, and they've been reborn dozens of times since. In each life, they come a little closer to perfection. By the time the worlds end, they'll have become so righteous that the Creator will restore them to their place among the stars."

It was a very different story than the one taught by the Pondrellen Church. "Have you also been reborn before?" Elwyn asked.

Aedyn shook his head, chewing his lip. "I'm freshborn." He sounded nearly ashamed. "The population of Faerie is fixed, and it will stay that way until time dissolves. Whenever one of the originals ascends to Heaven or... takes a steep plunge, someone like me is born to take their place. I've never been through the cycle before, and I can't say I'm eager for the trip." He came to a stop before reaching the final statue, which was still a good mile from the end of the spiral pathway. "I hope I'm a better person, next time around."

Elwyn was taken aback. Aedyn had never given her the impression that he doubted himself before, and she certainly wouldn't have imagined that he didn't love himself—*disliked* himself, even. She followed his gaze to a topiary of an elegant woman, posed in a courtly curtsy. Her mossy gown flared like tall ship sails, and a delicate golden circlet sat atop her willow-whip tresses.

"My mother," Aedyn explained. "From this very lifetime. She died when I was young, too young to capture a single memory, but people say she was peerless—the most beautiful, brilliant, and brave she'd been in all of her many iterations."

"She sounds wonderful," Elwyn said. No one had ever said such things about her own mother, though she had also been beautiful, brilliant, and brave. On her good days, anyway. "Is that next one supposed to be you?"

Aedyn blushed, barely glancing at the slender statue that shared his stag-spike circlet. "As the freshborn child of the king and queen, I'm next in line to serve as regent," he said, kicking the sandstone. "I'm not appointed by the Creator or anything. It was just luck of the draw. When

I'm reborn, it probably won't even be to the same family. With the way I've lived, it might not even be..."

He allowed the sentence to trail off, giving the distinct impression he didn't like how it ended. Elwyn imagined she wouldn't like it either, so she changed the subject. "Is that your sister?" she asked, nodding toward the final statue—that of a pretty young woman in a gown of snowy white flowers.

Aedyn followed her eyes to the sculpture, then winced like he'd forgotten it. "I'm an only child, actually."

"Aedyn?" A man in flowing green and white robes shouted from the garden gate. "Is that you, sir?"

Elwyn tensed to run, but Aedyn grabbed her wrist. "I doubt Learo knows anything," he whispered. "Even if he does, he'll do little more than lecture me."

The man rushed over and grabbed Aedyn by the shoulders. "Thank the Creator you're alright, sir. Your father has been worried sick." His gaze slid to Elwyn and back. "Dare I ask?"

Elwyn shrunk. "I'm—"

"She's a mortal girl I rescued," Aedyn interrupted. "She wound up in the Parting Seas, but we both made it safely to shore."

Both of those statements were technically true, just not related.

"That sounds like quite an ordeal." Learo took a step back, eying them from wave-tangled tresses to salt-crusted soles. "I suppose I should see you both cleaned and fed, then. I'll fetch some help to see you to the seamstress, then have leftovers brought to your private dining room." He clapped his hands, calling some other attendants over.

"Private dining room?" Elwyn mouthed.

Aedyn smirked, shrugging. "My station may be droll, but it has its perks."

Elwyn had been stuffed into a sophisticated violet gown. Actually, she'd been shoved into a sophisticated lilac gown, but the dressing-room attendant—a grumpy, short woman with wild pumpkin curls—took one look at her, said, "No guest of the heir is going to walk around with that washed-out complexion, on my watch!" With a snap of her fingers, the garment changed hues.

The moment Elwyn was fully clothed, she was shoved out into the hall, where Learo was waiting to escort her to Aedyn's private wing. Unsure of what else to say, she whispered, "Thank you."

Learo arched an eyebrow, but the rest of his face remained rigid. As he led her through the winding palace corridors, Elwyn could feel the glares of everyone she passed. She blamed the attention on the gaudy gown and tried to wish it away. Thankfully, the walk didn't last long.

Aedyn's dining table could have seated twenty people, and it was topped with food enough for all of them. Candlelight rained down from a crystal chandelier worth more than all the gold in Saint Aldrich's Sanctuary, washing over bouquets of sugared fruit, platters of glazed meat, tiered cakes cascading with delicate blossoms, and a fountain flowing with something pale that smelled like wine mixed with perfume.

Her host leaned back in the very last chair, one boot propped against the table's edge. He'd changed into a royal blue suit, embroidered in gold and buttoned in silver.

To think, Elwyn had thought the green one garish.

"Thank you, Learo." He offered his attendant a genial smile and a flippant wave. "You're free to go."

"Be good, sir," Learo muttered on his way through the door. "For once."

Elwyn might have commented on the odd exchange, but her stomach keened at the sight of so much food. She hadn't realized how hungry she'd become. Hopefully, the gown's tight bodice would give a little. It didn't feel like it would.

"You look..." Aedyn shook his head, grinning. "Honestly, you look incredibly uncomfortable."

Elwyn laughed. "And you look nearly royal, Your Highness." Elwyn dipped into a mock curtsy. "Do I need to grovel before I can eat, or..."

"Creator forbid!" Aedyn tipped forward in his chair, using his ankle to push out the one to his right. "If I were you, I'd get straight to eating. Who knows when those guards will be back to haul us off."

Elwyn grabbed an empty plate and stacked as many treats as she could manage atop it—handfuls of ripe red berries, pastries slathered with jelly, some kind of meat that looked a lot like ham but didn't smell like it. She'd heard tales in which the Unseen enchanted mortals with their food, but Luatha had long ago proven those stories false. The moment she took her seat, she shoved a tiny, glazed cake into her mouth. Sharp flavors of honey and citrus clashed on her tongue, dissolving almost instantly and leaving her desperate for more.

"You like it?" Aedyn said, more a statement than a question.

Elwyn nodded, savoring a second cake.

"Citrinebread is my absolute favorite, and I'm not alone in that. It's a miracle Learo managed to nab some."

"It's the best dessert I've ever tasted! You weren't kidding when you told Lydia..." The words died on her lips, and she looked away, covering her eyes.

"Slate?" Aedyn sounded strangely panicked.

"I-I'm sorry," she managed.

A sunlit warmth hovered near her shoulder for a moment, then pulled away. Chair legs squealed against marble. He was leaving her to wallow in her worries. Elwyn couldn't blame him, and she'd expected nothing more, but it made her eyes burn that much brighter.

Something moist slammed into Elwyn's forehead, crumbling as it slid down the bridge of her nose.

"What the..." She startled straight, wiping her face. Her fingers came away purple. *Jelly?* She blinked over at Aedyn, who stood across the table with a berry tart in hand and a challenge in his smile. "Don't you da—"

The pastry hit Elwyn in the mouth, cutting her sentence short.

"You're not even going to put up a fight?" Aedyn shook his head. "Some fearsome rogue you are."

Elwyn swiped a cluster of grapes and slipped beneath the table. She popped up on the opposite corner, plucking one free to lobbing it. It bounced off the tip of Aedyn's nose, and he laughed, hurling a handful of noodles. Elwyn ducked, and they hit the wall behind her, sticking. She pelted him with a barrage of berries, but he deflected them until she was out of ammunition, then leapt atop the table, kicking the crockery aside. The fountain toppled over, drenching Elwyn in floral wine.

"I'm unarmed!" Elwyn flung a tomato, and it burst against his chest, staining his blouse red and his jacket dark. "That's not fair!"

"All's fair!" Aedyn grabbed a loaf from a breadbasket and gave it an artful flourish. "En garde!"

Elwyn joined him, grabbing her own baguette blade. She struck out, glancing his shoulder.

"Touché."

The loaves locked, and the two combatants circled each other like rival wolves. Elwyn was first to break away, lunging forward to slash at his side. He leapt back, parrying, then countering. Crusts crackled, crumbling to dust as the fight raged on. The two were matched for speed and grace, but Aedyn knew the battlefield better. When Elwyn tried backing him off the edge, he skirted to the side, kicking a melon her way. An ill-timed jump left her vulnerable, and his weapon slammed into her side, snapping down the center. She fell, smashing a platter of mushroom caps and sending a storm of soups and salads to the floor.

Aedyn placed a foot on her abdomen, gloating over her with that infuriating, cocky smirk plastered on his face. "Had enough?"

"I know when I'm beaten." Elwyn stretched her fingers, maintaining eye contact as she grasped the edge of a platter. The moment Aedyn removed his foot, she leapt to her feet and slammed a whole cake into his face. "But it's not now!"

She gave the platter a twist for good measure, then released it. It slid down Aedyn's chin and chest, trailing pink sludge and little golden crumbles. He blinked the frosting from his eyes, forcing a scowl before bursting into candlelit laughter that caught swiftly to Elwyn. For a moment —one single, blessed moment—her heart was so light it forgot to ache.

Aedyn hopped to the floor, extending a hand. Elwyn accepted his aid for fear she would trip on her skirt and faceplant on the marble floor. Their laughter faded to snickers as they sat on the table's edge, wiping the crumbs from their clothing as best they could.

As silence stretched between them, a touch of sorrow trickled back into Elwyn's spirit, guilt close on its heels. Lydia and Luatha might both have been in danger, yet there she and Aedyn were, playing like children.

"She's going to be alright," Aedyn said, sensing her gloom. "We're all going to get out of this just fine. With the exception of our outfits. Those are doomed."

A smile tugged on Elwyn's lips, though she didn't quite believe him. Clearly, this had all been an elaborate attempt to cheer her up. No one had ever done anything quite so kind for her.

"Something's still troubling you." He set his hand atop hers, and his warmth bled into her skin, spreading straight to her heart. It was an altogether bewildering sensation, though not entirely unwelcome.

"Many things, actually," she said.

"Mind sharing one or two of them?"

Elwyn forced herself to look his way. He nearly looked human, smeared in frosting with lettuce peeking from his hair, but the flecks of gold in his brazen eyes and the glow of his skin were anything but.

"You're a better person than I thought," she confessed. "It's kind of annoying."

Aedyn bit his lip, glancing down like he didn't agree. "Slate, I—"

"Elwyn." The name leapt from her lips, leaving a hollow in her chest where it had been hiding for nine long years.

"Elwyn," Aedyn echoed, tasting each letter.

A flock of butterflies burst to life in Elwyn's stomach, and she tried her best to smother them. Aedyn had said it himself: she wasn't the type to capture anyone's attention. Did she even *want* attention as feeble and fleeting as his?

When he reached out to brush some crumbs from her hair, the butterflies fluttered even more wildly. She hardly noticed him tucking a lock behind her ear until her scar was exposed. She nearly flinched away, remembering Davin's reaction, but Aedyn broke into one of his brilliant smiles, dispelling her worries in a blink.

"Now, why in the worlds would you hide something so interesting?" he asked, tracing the crescent with his thumb.

Speaking was suddenly quite difficult. "I...I don't like to be noticed," she managed. "It's easier that way."

"Easy isn't always best." Aedyn's smile stuttered, like he was talking more to himself than to her. "Elwyn, I—"

"Aedyn?" A flute of a voice swept into the room.

The prince's eyes widened, and he leapt to his feet. Whatever trance Elwyn had been in shattered, and she turned toward the doorway right as a woman burst through it. She was impossibly beautiful, with golden-brown skin and eyes the color of summer grass. Her hair cascaded to the floor in honey-hued ringlets, flecked with bits of topaz to match her powder blue gown. She looked strangely familiar.

The statue from the garden...

"I've been looking all over for you!" The woman darted around the table, throwing her arms around Aedyn, and Elwyn's heart dropped straight to her stomach. "Whyever would you vanish in the middle of a ball?"

Aedyn pried himself from the woman's arms, offering her an awkward pat on the shoulder. Noticing the frosting that smeared his—and now her —clothing, her smile faded, and she glanced to where Elwyn sat, frozen.

Her eyes turned from summer grass to venom. "Who are you?"

A fool, Elwyn thought.

Aedyn took introductions upon himself. "This is Elwyn, a mortal friend of mine," he said, painting on a charlatan's grin. "Elwyn, this is Eloana the Golden-Voiced. My Betrothed."

"Law to bind the words in place, Love that you might mean them, Justice sets the promised stakes, and Honor bids you keep them."

CHAPTER 24

THE PROCESSION OF THE JUDGES

ELWYN

lwyn stood on a balcony, overlooking Talunasa and hating the sun above her for its stubborn refusal to set. She had never wanted so badly to melt into darkness, and it had never been so impossible. This whole damned world was so colorful and bright, she stood out like a shadow on a snowdrift.

The balcony was empty, thank the Creator. No one to glare or gawk at her, no one to whisper or point. She gripped the golden railing with white knuckles, watching the crowds swarm like gnats miles below and cursing herself for being so monumentally stupid.

"Betrothed," she muttered bitterly, shaking her head. It was a good thing Eloana had shown up when she did. Nothing disgusted Elwyn more than the thought of becoming another forgotten name on Aedyn's list of barmaids and soldiers and Creator knows who else. Eloana had her work cut out for her if she wanted to keep hold of those reins.

She knew she wasn't being fair. Chances were, she'd misread the situation altogether. Even if she hadn't, it wasn't as though Aedyn had made an effort to hide his habits.

Her grief was to blame, really. Had she been in her right mind, she would never have let her guard down. There was only one reason she'd traveled to Faerie to begin with. *And she might be dead.*

The colors below began to blur.

Heavy footsteps climbed the staircase behind her, accompanied by the soft creak of metal amor. Elwyn wiped her cheeks dry. She would not allow anyone to see her in such a sorry state.

"Slate?"

The voice belonged to Black, or rather, *Brannon*. It felt strange to know his name, almost taboo, like she had walked in on him bathing. *Of all the cursed people in this shit world ...*

If he figured out why she was out there, moping, he'd never let her live it down.

She reluctantly turned to face the assassin and his Undine escorts—two of the soldiers that had hauled them to shore earlier that day. They had not resorted to shackles or chains, but they kept their cobalt spears at the ready. Brannon, for his part, didn't seem to care that he was captive. Perhaps he'd grown accustomed to it, as she once was.

"What the fuck happened to you?" He gestured to her ruined gown with a hand that had been dead hours before.

Elwyn could have asked the same. They'd shoved the assassin into a suit of burgundy brocade and slicked his hair back, making him look nearly civilized. It didn't fool her for a second.

"Were you...crying?" Brannon asked, disgusted.

Elwyn ignored him, instead approaching the nearest Undine. "I'll be taking my piskie back," she demanded. "And my dagger."

The soldier's nostrils flared. "You can have your things back after the trial," he said, webbed fingers clenching around his weapon. "Assuming they let you walk free, that is."

"Luatha is a *person*. Not a thing."

The guard circled around her, muttering something about symbiosis, then nudged her toward the staircase at spearpoint.

"We'll lead you to the Great Hall," said his colleague, a woman with beaded blue braids and a kind face. "There, you'll be reunited with your friends."

Friends, plural. Elwyn's hopes sputtered back to life.

Whispers followed the mortals as they were marched through the palace, growing louder with their every step. The halls were far more crowded than those Elwyn had already been through. Visitors idled around banquet tables, maids flitted about with feather-dusters in hand, emissaries rushed to and fro carrying packages and letter bags. Most shared Aedyn's brazen features, but there were many green-skinned Undine as well, plus several other, stranger sorts. Wispy figures with cloudy complexions flitted between the balconies, their pastel robes curling through the air behind them. Dusky giants loitered in the archways, sunlight slicking across their armor and catching in the crystals that crusted their skin. Two crimson-haired women with eyes to match paused mid-conversation to watch Brannon and Elwyn pass by.

From their expressions, they thought mortals were the strange ones.

Elwyn felt like an act in some perverse, legalistic circus. She had never wanted so badly to be unremarkable, to let those glares pass right through her like arrows through lace. Their derision weighed heavy on her shoulders, speeding her pulse and slowing her steps. She hadn't even been told what she was being tried for, and they'd already found her guilty.

As she climbed what the guards promised would be the final staircase, a heavy hand fell on her shoulder. "No touching!" barked the gruffer of the guards, but his warning was unnecessary. Elwyn had already shrunk away, fixing Brannon with a scowl.

He didn't look the least bit offended. "You are an infuriating person, you know that?" he asked, letting his hand drop to his side.

"Gee, thanks. That's just what I needed to hear."

"You've been that way since we were children—cowardly, ungrateful, obnoxiously self-deprecating—"

"Really helps."

"—but for all that, you are not an idiot." He shook his head. "Don't start being one now."

So that's what sympathy looks like on a sadist... Elwyn didn't want it, and she told him as much.

The staircase opened into a wide corridor, even more crowded than the others. The sheer size of the throng filtering into the gilded archway ahead made Elwyn's stomach clench, reminding her of Sundays at Saint Aldrich's. She put on a feckless façade and kept a steady pace, as she had when forced to attend a service. One key to blending in was pretending that wasn't the goal.

Learo was waiting beside the entry arch. One look at Elwyn's ruined gown, and he turned up his nose.

"That simply will not do." He grabbed Elwyn's arm, nodding to the guards. "Guide the young man to his seat. I'll see to it that this one is made presentable and return her to you shortly."

The Undine did as ordered, prodding Brannon through the archway as Learo guided Elwyn down an adjacent hall. The whispers that followed her might as well have been a windstorm.

"Keep your chin up, dear," he whispered, eyes fixed forward. "Never let a hungry trow know you've been wounded, never let a leprechaun know your soles are worn through, and never let a flock of gossips know you're a scandal-in-waiting."

Elwyn didn't think of herself as a scandal at all—past, present, or future. Scandals thrived on notoriety, and that was the last thing she wanted.

The fitting room Learo brought her to looked exactly like the one she'd changed in earlier, despite being located on a much higher floor, and the same squat redhead popped out from the overstuffed racks, greeting her with a scowl.

"What have you done to my precious baby?" she asked, scanning every inch of the food-stained gown.

"It is not our place to question the heir's guests, Marielle." Learo looked down his nose at her. "Fetch this one something a touch more durable, with a dark fabric, if you can manage it."

The woman grumbled something unintelligible, disappearing into a tangle of gossamer and lace, and Learo leaned over to whisper, "What *did* you do to her precious baby?"

Elwyn glanced at the feet, her face flushing.

"Ah." Learo straightened. "I've seen that look enough times. I will ask no further questions. A lady's liaisons are her own business."

"Liaisons?" Elwyn blushed even brighter. "You misunderstand. We didn't—"

"No need for excuses." Learo held up a hand. "I've had this conversation with many of Aedyn's guests, and I've grown weary of repeating myself."

Just when Elwyn thought she couldn't feel any worse.

The two stood in silence for an agonizing minute before Marielle returned, carrying two options—one, a voluminous navy dress, beaded with colorful crystals; the other, a sleek, black number that laced like a corset from cinched waist to feathered collar. Both looked like torture devices.

"Have a preference?" the seamstress asked.

"Which one will you miss less when she ruins it?" Learo replied.

Marielle tossed Elwyn the black gown.

Learo left the room, and Marielle set about her work, tucking, pinning, and lacing Elwyn into the clingy gown. Elwyn tried to apologize, but the seamstress *tsked* her through the entire process anyway, tugging a ribbon tight enough to pop something.

"Fitting this dress makes you look like a *Korrid*." Marielle spit the word like a swear. "You're obviously the trouble-making type."

"I try not to be," Elwyn wheezed, meaning it.

Marielle shoved her from the dressing room, and Learo guided her to the Great Hall, which was far larger and brighter than a mortal sanctum, though it shared the same reverent atmosphere. Sunlight filtered down from open windows to illuminate floral garlands, embroidered banners, and glossy marble tiles. Row after row of overcrowded pew—crafted from those strange, metallic vines so common to the palace—rippled out from a podium, upon which stood four pulpits: gold, bronze, silver, and cobalt.

Learo escorted Elwyn to the centermost pew right before the dais, which sat only Brannon and the two Undine guards. Elwyn sat midway between Brannon and the kinder of the Undine, and Learo departed with a brusque, "Don't let him down."

She was pondering what he'd meant when the soldier beside her extended a webbed hand. "Lapa," she said. "You must be a friend of the heir."

Elwyn wasn't so sure about that. She accepted the handshake anyway, fighting not to shudder at the soldier's cold, course touch. "I don't suppose you know what happened to the girl who arrived with us," she tried, a lump in her throat. "They took her away, and I don't know where. She was...she..."

Lapa shook her head, but Brannon scooted a smidge closer.

"She's awake, but it's complicated," he whispered. "We've got a lot to talk about, once this is all sorted out."

Elwyn had never been so relieved. That relief doubled a moment later, when the throng's rising murmurs prompted her to glance back. One of the slight, semi-translucent fae had fluttered into the hall, her hand clasping Lydia's. That poor girl looked even frailer than before, but her eyes were open, and she was moving. It was more than had Elwyn dared to hope for.

Heedless of the crowd's jeers and Lapa's warnings, Elwyn rushed out to meet Lydia, wrapping the child in her arms. "It's good to see you," she breathed, though Lydia's frigid skin and spoiled musk made her stomach churn.

"I'm...I'm so tired." Lydia buried her face in the crook of Elwyn's shoulder. "And cold."

"It's all going to work out," Elwyn whispered. "I promise."

"A broken promise is a dangerous thing," Lydia's escort interrupted. "Do not offer assurances in matters where you lack control."

There was no malice in the woman's voice, but Elwyn couldn't help scowling at her. She scooped Lydia into her arms and carried her to the front pew, setting her between Lapa and herself. To her chagrin, Lydia's escort followed, though her next advice was not aimed their way.

"Do not look so distraught, Mortal Brannon," she said, smiling at the assassin. "You have been called here as a witness, not a captive."

"It certainly looks that way." Brannon shot both of the Undine Guards a glare. "Never felt more free in my life."

"More irony?" The woman asked, smile stretching. "You are humorous, Mortal Brannon. It seems I, too, have much to learn."

She fluttered away without so much as a farewell, so Elwyn looked to Lapa for clarification.

"Has no one told you why you are here?" The Undine tipped back her cobalt helm, scanning Elwyn's face. "So long as your words are honest, you will not come to harm. You are here only as a witness to the deeds and character of the heir to the Summer Throne."

"The heir to the Summer Throne..."

"Aedyn of the Daoine Maithe."

As though Lydia's condition hadn't given her enough to fret over. While a small, spiteful part of Elwyn wanted Aedyn to suffer, another part of her pitied him. Sadly, even the pitying part of her had no clue how to paint him in a positive light.

She became so focused on her internal debate that she didn't notice Aedyn being escorted into the hall. At least, not until he took a seat beside her. He'd cleaned up since the food-fight, and his immaculate emerald suit and cape reminded her of those he'd been wearing when they first met. Their eyes met, and he flashed one of those stupid, gleaming smiles of his. Elwyn looked forward, inching away from him. He wilted in her periphery.

Good, thought the spiteful part of her.

The pitying part winced.

Trumpets sounded, and the crowd stood, all eyes turning toward the balcony, where a trio of heralds, clad in green and gold, stood poised above a row of velvet banners. The middlemost lowered his horn, stepping forward.

"Presenting the High Judges of the Seelie Court, equal in esteem and power," he shouted. "Today's procession begins with Queen Mearalas of the Undine, regent ruler of Chorial and High Judge of Law."

An emerald curtain parted around a beautiful woman with seafoam skin and midnight blue hair tucked behind a coral crown. A pair of Undine guards walked behind her, each carrying the hem of her teal gown in one hand and a blue banner, embellished with a cresting wave, in the other. She dismissed her retainers before reaching the dais, then strode proudly up the platform steps.

She rested one hand atop the cobalt pulpit, raising the other. "I swear to the Creator to preside over these trials in service of Law," she said, voice frigid. "That the Seelie may remain steadfast in their deeds and obedient to His will."

"Queen Mearalas isn't fond of mortals," Lapa whispered. "She's not too keen on Prince Aedyn either. Lucky for you, she's only a fourth of the vote."

Elwyn felt far from lucky.

"Soen, Sylph Speaker-Elect," the herald announced, drawing Elwyn's attention back to the curtain. "Regent ruler of the Spring Isles and High Judge of Love."

The woman who fluttered into the hall looked similar to the one who had escorted Lydia to the pew. Her pale locks flowed behind her like a river as she looped through the air, leaving her retainers—each bearing a silver flag featuring a falling feather—behind and below. Her spearmint robes pooled at her feet as she alit behind the silver pulpit, one dainty hand raised.

"I swear to the Creator to preside over these trials in service of Love," she cooed. "That the Seelie may always be known for our benevolence and grace."

"She's so pretty," Lydia whispered.

Lapa nodded. "Inside and out."

"Creagor, Chieftain of the Daoine Sidhe," the herald proclaimed. "Regent of the Red Realm and High Judge of Justice."

A hulking man burst through the curtain, his hands clasped above his head like he'd just won some kind of tournament. A loud cheer erupted behind Elwyn as countless fae who shared the man's dark skin and shoulder shards made the same celebratory gesture. Where the other judges were certainly respected, Creagor was clearly the most beloved. Two soldiers clad in heavy bronze marched to the dais behind him, each carrying a copper shield imprinted with scarlet flames. They fell back when he approached the bronze pulpit, slamming one gauntlet against it and thrusting the other skyward.

"I swear to the Creator to preside over trials in service of Justice!" A heavy accent clipped his voice, which boomed like thunder through the hall. "So it is known the Seelie repay deeds in kind—good for good, ill for ill!"

Another cheer rose from the pews, only to fade at the herald's next words.

"King Aryn of the Daoine Maithe," he announced. "Eternal Ruler of Talunasa and High Judge of Honor."

This time, the retainers came through the curtain before their charge, each holding one end of a long, emerald banner emblazoned with a filigree sun. The figure who stepped out behind them was nothing short of majestic, clad in gleaming armor and a flowing moss-green cape. His face could have been carved from sandstone, set with keen golden eyes to match his aurous mane. Though his features were fairer and more rigid than Aedyn's, the two shared the same arching eyebrows and squared shoulders. Even the king's crown—a heavy golden circlet that branched out into gleaming antlers—bore a resemblance to that of his son.

Aedyn straightened in his seat, bronze eyes following his father with the kind of reverence a monk might afford their god, should they happen to catch a glimpse. It certainly didn't match the way he'd spoken of the man.

"I swear to the Creator to preside over this court in service of Honor," the king proclaimed, upon reaching the golden pulpit and lifting a hand in oath. "That the legacy of the Unseelie be one of pure intentions and promises fulfilled."

His molten eyes swept across the crowd without even pausing on Aedyn, and he bid them to sit, directing their attention back to the herald, who had traded his trumpet for a scroll.

"Citizens of the Light Realms and Solitary guests," the herald said, unfurling the parchment with a flick of his wrist. "The Kingdom of Talunasa and the Seelie High Judges bid you welcome in honor of this esteemed occasion. We ask that you fix your hearts and minds on the Four Ideals as our rulers preside over all," he scanned the scroll, "twenty-seven of today's cases."

"Twenty-seven?" Brannon hissed.

"And you're last on the docket," Lapa replied, smirking.

It was going to be a very long day.

The trials had a simple cadence to them. The accused were permitted up to three witnesses, not counting themselves, and they would each answer a single question aligning with one of the four ideals. The judges had already tried a thief, a vandal, and an alleged murderer without doling a single guilty verdict, and Elwyn's outlook was creeping carefully toward optimism.

Then Elgard Springbristle took the stand.

The Maithe man was not much older than Aedyn, though his downcast eyes and wringing hands exuded a far more humble air. The judges called him to the dais the moment the herald announced him. No witnesses had come forward to testify on his behalf.

"That one's rumored to have courted a Korrid," Lapa whispered, nudging Elwyn with an armored elbow. "Consorting with a member of the Unseelie Court, outside of specified political ventures, is a violation of the Treaty of Dusk. Since the heir is facing similar charges, you'll want to pay close attention."

Elwyn did just that, fixing her eyes on the judges as they gathered in a brief huddle. They broke apart seconds later, having decided Mearalas would be questioning Elgard, given treaties fell most soundly under the Law.

"Being on your eighth cycle, you know well the edicts and ideals of our court," the queen said. "Weighing each equally, do you truly believe you can justify your actions?"

Elgard tried to lift his chin, but he was shivering too violently to feign confidence. "I know the virtues, I know the treaty, and I know when they do not align. The section you've cited was meant to prevent treason and insurrection, and I participated in none of those things." He squared his shoulders as best he could. "If the letter of the law now weighs more than its spirit, then the distinctions between Seelie and Unseelie have dissolved, and my supposed offense should not matter."

The crowd reacted, not with their usual whispers, but with a storm of curses and taunts. Mearalas pursed her midnight lips, narrowing eyes of the same deep hue. "Elgard Springbristle," She spoke his name with unfettered contempt. "Your account has been weighed against the Four Ideals and found wanting. You violated out most sacred treaty, and your example puts all of the Light Realms in peril." She looked over at her fellow judges. "Do we have consensus?"

One by one, they nodded.

Mearalas smiled at the defendant. "You are hereby sentenced to Descension and Exile."

The audience burst into shouts and wild applause. Aedyn sank against the pew. Elgard closed his eyes, a tear trickling down his cheek.

Elwyn looked to Lapa. "What's happening?"

"Oh, that?" The Undine glanced over her shoulder. "The sharks are being fed. Most people gorge themselves on the misfortune of others, and Descension and Exile is the harshest possible punishment the judges can dole."

"Not death?"

"Death is easier to bounce back from. For our kind anyway." Lapa nodded toward the aisle as a Sylph fluttered forward with a bottle of something black. "That's half the problem, actually. Elgard's crime was dangerous enough he's bound to be reborn as one of the Unseelie. The court intends to speed the process along, lest he drag his neighbors down with him."

"They're sentencing him to a fate worse than death," Elwyn gulped, "over a *fling?*"

If that was the case, Aedyn was as good as lost.

Lapa tipped her helm toward the dais, where two more Sylph had appeared. They held Elgard's arms in place while the first uncorked the bottle. "A travel potion," she explained. "Else this *would* be a death sentence."

The High Judges joined hands, chanting in unison. Elwyn couldn't understand the words, but they rang with unmistakable power. The color fled Elgard's skin, and his golden locks turned black as coal. A shimmer, like frost, swept over him, dulling his eyes to cloudy gray and dripping like talons from his fingertips. Almost instantly, he began to melt, steam rising from his skin as it sloughed away at the touch of sunlight. He wailed, and the Sylph tipped the potion against his lips. A heartbeat, and he vanished, leaving only a putrid puddle behind.

The fae behind Elwyn chittered excitedly; some even went so far as to laugh. *Sharks, indeed.*

She had long known—from Rhysien folklore as well as her life with Luatha—that the Unseen were not the sweet little creatures portrayed in Pondrellen nursery rhymes, but their cruelty was far worse than she'd imagined. She was stunned enough that she hardly noticed a Sylph whispering something in the Speaker-Elect's ear. At least, not until Soen addressed the throng directly.

"Due to unforeseen circumstances, we will be taking a short recess," she announced, sky blue eyes drifting over the crowd. "We will resume proceedings in forty minutes, beginning with the trial of Aedyn, Heir to the Summer Throne."

"An empty, burning passion that dies when it's contained,
There's a destructive nature at the heart of every flame."

CHAPTER 25

LITTLE FIRE

AEDYN

 oen's announcement stunned Aedyn, though he wasn't sure the change in the docket would make much of a difference. He'd kept his eyes on the king throughout the proceedings, watching his scowl deepen with every passing second. If that man had to wait for Aedyn's trial much longer, his lips were liable to slid right from his face.

Granted, all Aedyn's father had ever done was judge him. Only now he had a stage and an audience.

As the Grand Hall emptied, the Undine Guards bid Aedyn's friend to rise. "You are in luck," said the friendlier of the pair. "Regardless of your reasons for being here, you are guests in this palace. You may take your recess in the royal banquet hall, apart from the school of sharks. Or, rather, with a school of classier sharks."

Lydia and Brannon stepped swiftly forward, but Elwyn remained seated. "If possible, I'd prefer to wait here," she said. "I need time to think, and it will be easier apart from all the ruckus."

"If that is your desire." The soldier shrugged. "There are guards stationed at every door and window, so it's not as though you'll slip away." Her eyes slid over to Aedyn. "Joining us, heir?"

"In a moment," he mouthed.

The guard shook her head but started for the banquet hall, waving for Brannon and Lydia to follow. It would have been far easier for Aedyn to join them—to spend the recess drowning his worries in wine and witty repartee—but the easy option wasn't always the best one.

So, he waited until the Grand Hall was empty of all but soldiers, then took a seat beside the girl he hoped was still his friend. She didn't shy away this time, but she didn't acknowledge him, either.

He folded his hands in his lap, taking a moment to *think* before he spoke, for once. Though he'd developed an extensive log of lines for appeasing disgruntled women, none would fit this particular situation. He'd been bound to Eloana since before he even knew what a betrothal was, so he'd long avoided forming attachments, but this one had caught him unawares. It had felt much like his friendship with Amatha until just hours before the trail, when Elwyn sat on the edge of his dining table, dripping frosting and floral wine and filling the air with her rare, intoxicating laughter. Even then, he hadn't suspected she'd feel the same. She was much too smart for that.

"That's quite a dress," he tried, hoping to chip away at the ice. "I'm not certain whether I should be enchanted or terrified."

Elwyn frowned. "I may be unarmed, but I assure you, it's the latter."

Not the right path, then. Aedyn took a deep breath, running through his options. Being fae, he could not speak outright lies, but he'd never been particularly honest either. Perhaps it was time to give it a go.

"I'm sorry, Elwyn," he said. "Really, I am. I hadn't intended to give you the wrong impression..." *Was it the wrong impression?* "I only meant to cheer you up."

"Well, you've done a phenomenal job of it." She pulled her knees to her chest, perching her boots on the bench. Aedyn could practically see the walls rebuilding around her—one brick for every ounce of trust rescinded. "If you truly want to make me feel better, leave me be. Honestly, Aedyn, that's all I want from you."

It was the opposite of what Aedyn wanted, but his wants were not the point. Begrudgingly, he forced himself to his feet and toward the banquet hall. It took far more effort than it should have, being such a short walk. Guilt tugged on his heels with every mournful step.

It was all his fault—not just his and Elwyn's thwarted friendship—*all* of it. He'd failed to protect Lydia, and now she was falling apart before their eyes. He'd failed his father for the hundredth time, and now the man wouldn't even look at him. He'd failed to adhere to the most fundamental code of his kingdom, and now he was going to be condemned before the very pulpit he was destined to inherit.

If he had been content to tend his own business instead of meddling in that of another world, none of this would have happened. But he hadn't been content, and he had meddled, and everything he'd touched had burned to the ground. Like always.

An emerald curtain fluttered aside, and too many faces turned Aedyn's way. Brannon and Lydia weren't among them, but that was no surprise. They'd probably slipped out onto one of the many balconies, seeing the Seelie aristocracy for the hornet nest it was.

Post-holiday trials always drew a sizable crowd, but this was the densest Aedyn had ever seen. He was well aware they were there to watch him fall, but at least they knew how to celebrate in style. The buffet tables boasted more food and drink than many a humble woodland hamlet. Beautiful women and men flitted between them, dressed in stunning gowns, elaborate suits, and painted plaster smiles. Guests of less upstanding repute lurked in the corners and beyond the archways, hands shoved in their pockets as they waited for listless elites to inquire about shadowroot or essence.

Every petty distraction Aedyn could imagine hovered within arm's reach. The breadth of the bounty turned his head to a hurricane. He wanted all of it and he wanted none of it and he wanted something more though he knew it would leave him wanting, and he wanted, and he wanted, and he wanted, and he *needed* it to stop for one fucking heartbeat!

Furious at himself and everyone like him, he pressed gracelessly through the hall, ignoring the empty platitudes of false friends and a wealth of pitying glances tinged with mirth. He grabbed two glasses from a silver tray and ran them beneath a poppy-orange fountain.

"Aedyn?" Eloana placed a hand on his arm. As usual, he hadn't noticed her approaching. "Surely one of those is for me."

"If you'd like a drink, grab a flute," he replied, eying her from bejeweled slippers to braided updo. "I see you've dressed up for my demise, we might as well toast it, too."

Eloana's smile flickered. "I have an image to uphold," she hissed. "And you know well I would gain nothing from your downfall, only your ascent."

Aedyn fought a smirk. Eloana was not an illusionist, but he'd long suspected her of wearing a disguise. It was almost refreshing to see through it, for a change.

"Of course, they'll talk. It's all they ever do." He downed both drinks and marched into the throng, leaving her to seethe. Not a full minute passed before soft fingers slid down his arm and a gorgeous Glaistig slipped into view, all velvet-draped curves and wild crimson curls. Her name was...*fuck*, what did it matter? He'd known her in every sense of the word except the one that counted.

"Why so worried, darling?" She leaned in close, flashing a fanged smile. "I'm sure you'll emerge from this ordeal with your reputation unharmed. Shall we meet up after and soil it?"

For whatever reason, the offer brought bile to Aedyn's throat.

"Sounds fun." He tore his arm away. "But I've frankly had my fill of low-hanging fruit." He pressed toward the nearest staircase, desperate for distance.

There's not enough light in the room for the illusions these people are casting.

The staircase spilled onto a sandstone balcony set aglow by the eternal sunlight. He grasped the railing with trembling fingers, drinking in the green-apple air and trying to will the pressure from his veins.

It should have been midnight, by now. What he would have given to sit around a campfire with his friends, staring up at the stars.

By the time he forced his grip to soften, the marble had cut patterns into his palms. At this rate, he'd be in the throes of a full-on meltdown by the time he was called to testify. *What in light's name is wrong with me?*

"May I join you?" The voice belonged to Amatha.

Aedyn turned to face her, propping his elbows against the railing. "You're probably the only person in the worlds whose company I'd welcome right now."

"That is hard to believe." She broke into a brilliant smile. "But then, you did just reject Cela. I would not have done the same."

So that was her name, Aedyn thought, forgetting it before he formed his next sentence. "I'm sure she's feeling insecure right now, if you'd like a go at her."

Amatha crossed her burly arms. "You wound me."

"Sorry." His gaze dropped to his gilded boots. "I have no right to take this out on you. You've done absolutely nothing wrong."

"You are worried about what your father thinks."

Aedyn laughed coldly. "I *know* what my father thinks."

"I do not think you do." Amatha leaned against the railing beside him, attempting to imitate his posture. Her crystalline pauldrons threw off her balance, and she tipped awkwardly to one side. "This is not as easy or comfortable as you make it look."

"Nothing is ever as easy or comfortable as I make it look."

Amatha laughed, punching his arm. "There is the Aedyn I know and love."

Flippant as the words were, they raised his spirits. There were only a handful of people in the worlds who both knew and loved Aedyn, and that number was dwindling.

"I messed up, Amatha," he said, hanging his head. "Even more so than usual."

"By visiting the Mortal Realm?"

"That too." Aedyn sighed. "To be fair, I didn't know for certain where Deilin was sending me."

"Would it have made a difference?"

"No. I suppose not."

"That is just you, and it is no crime," Amatha replied, shrugging. "You live on wants and whims, bursting from passion to passion like a little fire. That is what Aedyn means in the old language—little fire. I have always thought it suited you."

Aedyn twisted over onto his elbows, looking out over the city below. The streets were nearly empty—unsurprising, given half the city had crammed into the palace, eager for entertainment. He wasn't any different, really. How many people had he exploited to quell his own boredom? How much damage had he wrought? If he was ever a little fire, the flames were steadily growing, and his every reckless act had been committed in service of feeding them.

"I spotted a tray of citrinecakes inside." Amatha patted him on the shoulder and started for the stairs. "I will retrieve them. Surely, you are hungry."

"That's all I ever am," Aedyn whispered.

ARYN

Aryn sat brooding in Talune's Heart, his eyes fixed on the circlet that graced the throne beside his. He shuddered at the thought of what Tearan might have said, where she truly seated there. She had loved their son, but that love would not have prevailed over her passion for her kingdom. She would have sacrificed everything for Talunasa and its denizens. In fact, she *had* sacrificed everything for them.

In the end, Aryn could hold no illusions on the matter. If forced to choose between her realm and her son—the only child they'd ever conceived in all their many lives—Tearan would have snapped the boy's neck at birth.

A familiar duet slipped beneath the throne room doors as the light singer sentries bid it open. Aryn bristled. He'd demanded solitude for the duration of the recess. His anger evaporated like a dewdrop in a sunbeam when Soen peeked into Talune's Heart, a half-moon smile on her lips.

"I do not mean to be a bother," she said as the throne room doors closed behind her. "I only thought that, before the trials resume, you might like to speak to someone who can yet speak back."

"Come in, friend," he said, rising to meet her midway down the emerald carpet. "You have never been a bother."

They spoke for some time, pacing the gilded marble tiles. Rather, Aryn paced and spoke, while Soen fluttered and listened. If the other judges had been present, he'd have kept still and quiet for fear of showing weakness. Soen had been a presence in many of his lives, in one form or another. She had always encouraged vulnerability—in this life, more than any before it. The Sylphs were healers by nature, and that gift was not confined to physical ailments.

"I cannot help but question your findings," he said, forcing the conversation toward loftier matters. "She is only a child, and from the Mortal Realm, no less. What connection could she possibly have to the Sluagh?"

"My mystics could not discern much beyond her nature," Soen answered. "It will be up to Mearalas' seers to divine the rest."

"Assuming she cooperates," Aryn growled. Mearalas was an adequate ruler for her own people, but she did not play well with others. "Why not call off these trials altogether and pour our resources into this investigation?"

Pity darkened Soen's ice-water eyes, and shame welled in Aryn's spirit. His reasoning could not have been more transparent.

"You know how proud Mearalas can be." Soen's toes touched marble, and she dismissed her wings. "If we want her to support this plan, she must think it was her idea."

Aryn nodded, tears burning behind his eyes. He would not allow them to fall.

Soen saw them anyway. "Do you want to talk about it?"

She knew he did. Soen always knew what people wanted, and she knew whether those wants aligned with their best interests. It made her a brilliant leader and an even better friend.

"I can't lose him, too." Aryn's voice nearly cracked, the words were so brittle. "I know my calling has its costs, but was Tearan not enough?"

Soen was silent as she mulled the words over, and Aryn cursed himself for speaking them at all. His peers were not aware of just how permanent Tearan's fate truly was. They did not know he would never see her again, not in this life or any other.

And they didn't need to know it, either.

Soen placed a hand on his shoulder, either missing Aryn's slip-up or pretending to. "Aedyn is not yet lost."

How Aryn wished that was the case. "There is no defending my son's actions this time," he said, shaking his head. "It's strange, really. I have long feared that boy would someday be reborn into darkness. It seems death no longer need factor into that fate."

"You speak as though his consequences are eternal," Soen said. "Aedyn will live many lives after this one. If the Seelie can descend to darkness, who can say the opposite is not also possible?"

"Would I even remember him?" Aryn asked, chest tight. "Will he remember me? We retain so little from our former lives, and those memories are little more than dreams—distant, hollow, cold. I cannot hope to be spared a thought for my fallen son, much less a warm one. Perhaps erasure would be for the best, but then..." He didn't believe his own words. Reminiscing about Tearan was agony, but he treasured every memory. His son would be no different. "What do you think will become of him, Soen?"

Soen wiped a solitary tear from his cheek, and he looked away, embarrassed one had escaped. His skin tingled where she'd brushed it—the residual spark of her healing aura. It did nothing to ease his pain.

"I am sorry, my friend," she said. "I do not know."

"That is quite alright," Aryn composed himself, hardening like clay. "Now is not the time for sentiment, but duty."

Soen granted him a final, pitying glance, which he returned with a gruff nod. She'd done the best she could, and he appreciated the effort.

Some wounds ran too deep for even a Sylph to heal.

"If you would pass a verdict, do so with reverent fear,
In judging someone's flaws, your own become glaringly clear."

CHAPTER 26
JUDGMENT
BRANNON

"e hereby resume proceedings with the trial of Aedyn, Heir of the Daoine Maithe!"

The herald's announcement made Brannon squirm in his seat, all too aware of the thousands of insipid eyes boring through the nape of his neck. One benefit of belonging to the Greyscale was that he'd never been forced to stand trial for his crimes. No agent ever had. Either they succeeded or died, or so the Father claimed.

Apparently, he and Slate were the exceptions.

He had been told he was expected to testify first, but that did nothing to stop his stomach from flipping when the Maithe King called him forward. The stakes felt, suddenly, horrendously high. When he'd first met Aedyn, he'd wanted little more than to skewer the pretentious fop with his own rapier. Through no conscious decision of his own, he'd come to regard Aedyn as an...ally. Those looked out for one another, or so he'd heard.

Brannon was unpracticed in that particular art.

He approached the golden pulpit, and the king regarded him with a somber nod. If the man cared at all for the outcome of his son's trial, it didn't show. That indifference reminded Brannon of his own uncaring fathers, and his palms ached for the daggers that had, once again, been stolen from him.

"Brannon, denizen of the Mortal Realm," King Aryn began. "Do you swear to the Creator your testimony will be honest and forthright?"

Something in those keen, golden eyes told Brannon the king would see straight through any lies he might conjure. "There's no good way to answer that question," he replied. "Forthright is doable, but I don't believe in a Creator, so swearing to one would be dishonest in its own right."

"Fair enough," the king said, impassive. "If not a Creator, what do you believe in?"

If only Brannon knew. In the past few weeks, he'd witnessed things he'd never thought possible, and the lines between reality and myth had all but vanished. "I suppose I'll have to swear by myself, just to be safe."

Surprisingly, no one objected to the change.

"You are new to this world and its customs," King Aryn said, "so I will reiterate how this works. I, the High Judge of Honor, have been tasked with examining you, so my question will relate to that ideal. You will answer honestly, to the best of your ability, or risk incriminating yourself. Is that clear?"

Brannon nodded. Simple enough.

"Very good," the king replied. "Would you call yourself a man of Honor?"

The question threw Brannon off. "Isn't this Aedyn's trial?'

"You can learn much of a person's character from the company they keep," King Aryn elaborated. "Apparently, you have been traveling with the defendant for two weeks, by mortal standards. More than long enough to qualify as company."

Brannon hadn't thought of that, having long avoided company of all kinds. "I'm not very familiar with honor," he said. "From what I gather, it relates to one's ability to stick to their word. If that is the case, I am far from honorable."

Murmurs swept through the hall.

Brannon whirled to glare at the gossips, jabbing a finger toward the frontmost pew. "See those girls right there?" he asked, prompting Slate and Lydia both to sink against the seat. "The pale one and the...the paler one? If I were a man of honor, they'd both be dead by now! I swore it a hundred times over, and I meant it." He turned back toward the Maithe monarch.

"I have become less honorable by your son's example, and I'm glad for it. Those girls are too, given they wouldn't be breathing, otherwise. Now, if you still want honesty, it shouldn't be criminal to break a rule if that rule is fucking ridiculous, and the law you're judging Aedyn against is *fucking ridiculous.*"

The mob's whispers swelled to jeers, the king's façade cracked, and Brannon realized he'd said the exact wrong things.

ELWYN

At Creagor's bidding, Elwyn swore to the Creator that her testimony would be honest and forthright, silently praying that, if such a god existed, He would prevent her temporary tiff with Aedyn from having eternal consequences.

"Very good," Creagor said, folding his hands on his bronze pulpit. "In your opinion, does Aedyn repay deeds in kind?"

That was the definition of justice, boiled down to the bones, but Elwyn still feared the question was a trap. The rapt attention of the throng behind her certainly didn't help matters. For the millionth time that day, she wished she was invisible.

"No," she said, eliciting a predictable storm of gasps and whispers. "Aedyn intervened on behalf of myself and Lydia, though we'd never met him, and we had done nothing to merit it. Then, when Brannon was injured in the skirmish, he worked tirelessly to find treatment for the wound. In the brief time I've known Aedyn, he's treated others with kindness whether they deserved it or not." With each syllable spoken, their squabble felt all the more petty. "Surely, that level of compassion is the furthest a person can get from Justice."

Though the audience expressed displeasure, the Sidhe Judge cracked a smile, and a touch of guilt fled Elwyn's shoulders. Now that she'd done what she could to save Aedyn's ass, she could go back to wanting to kick it.

AEDYN

Aedyn swore to his Creator upon taking the stage, meaning every word. Pity shone in Soen's eyes as she glanced down from her silver pulpit. It wouldn't help, but he appreciated it, all the same. When the judges rendered their verdict, he wouldn't hold it against her. She'd always been the most understanding of the four.

"Are you prepared to answer one question in testimony of yourself?" she asked.

He wasn't, really. He'd expected Lydia to take to the dais before him. Perhaps she'd opted out, intimidated by the pressure. Aedyn couldn't blame her.

"I'm as ready as I'll ever be," he answered.

Soen gave a somber nod. "Was your violation of the Treaty of Dusk motivated, in any way, by Love?"

She was going easy on him. Nearly anyone in the whole light-forsaken realm could connect any number of deeds to Love. It was the most erratic of ideals, the most difficult to define, let alone substantiate. Aedyn could easily have twisted his account, citing love of adventure or love of self, but that wouldn't have been forthright, even if it was honest. He'd sworn an oath to his Creator, and unlike most oaths, he took those seriously.

So, he burst into laughter.

"Are you well?" Soen whispered.

"This is incredibly inappropriate!" Mearalas snapped. "Compose yourself or relinquish your right to testify."

"Sorry." Aedyn tried to stifle his laughter, failing miserably. "It's just so utterly ridiculous. *Of course,* I didn't break the treaty out of Love. I'm not certain I've ever done anything with that particular ideal in mind. I think I'd like to," one startlingly sincere person came to mind, "but I'm simply not there, yet. Do you really want to know my motives?"

Soen did not answer, but the crowd did.

Aedyn turned to face them. "I was bored!" he shouted. "Are you really any different? If there's a soul among you who isn't here solely for entertainment, then by all means, stand here beside me and vow as much to your Creator!"

Though many scoffed and simmered, none came forward. Aedyn

smirked, abandoning the silver pulpit for the gold. If he was going to be condemned to exile, he might as well earn it.

"Judge me however you like," he growled, meeting his father's molten gold glare, "but know you've helped to build a kingdom of spoiled, selfish louts just like me. Sooner or later, we'll all answer for our arrogance. Even you."

He returned to his seat without waiting to be dismissed.

LYDIA

Lydia was grateful for the robe the Sylphs had leant her. It didn't warm her any, but it helped to hide her constant shivering. She didn't want Slate...*Elwyn* to worry. There were plenty of other things to worry about.

Aedyn's trial wasn't going particularly well, but she was confident her testimony could make up for the others. She had assumed she'd face the Judges before Aedyn, but then, fae customs were a mystery, so she kept her concerns to herself, waiting her turn like a good little whatever-she-was.

Her hopes guttered as the judges gathered in a huddle. That wasn't supposed to happen yet. She looked to her friends for answers, but they were too busy moping, slumped against the pew. Odd reactions. They should have been crying or hugging or breaking stuff. Lydia wanted to do all that and more.

When the judges returned to their pulpits, their faces were somber. With one exception.

"We have reached a verdict," Mearalas said, a smile twitching on her lips. "Having weighted the heir's indiscretions against the Four Ideals, we hereby find him g—"

"Wait!" Panic propelled Lydia from the pew and up the steps so swiftly she tripped on the hem of her robe. "He's supposed to get four testimonies! Please, I-I want to speak!"

Mearalas scowled. "We have discussed you, child," she said. "You are much too young to understand what's happening."

"I am not so sure..." Creagor tapped his fingers on his pulpit. "I beheaded many Unseelie before reaching her height. Perhaps we assumed wrong. If she wants to speak, I say we let her."

"I agree." Soen winked at Lydia. "Aedyn technically has the right to one more witness, and she's far more willing than I'd assumed."

"That settles it, then," King Aryn's voice was low—too low for the audience to hear. "She testifies."

Mearalas pursed her lips. "You are hardly impartial enough to make that call."

"Is what you said of my daughter." Creagor shrugged. "The girl testifies, or Amatha does. Take your pick."

"Fine!' Mearalas's webbed fingers flexed around the edges of her pulpit, and she turned narrowed eyes to Lydia. "It seems you've gotten your wish, child. I pray you do not blame yourself when it proves futile."

Lydia wasn't going to let that happen. Her legs trembled as she approached the cobalt pulpit, but she refused to let her frailty reach her face. The others had looked strong and brave, Elwyn especially. Lydia wanted, very badly, to be like Elwyn.

"Do you swear to the Creator that your testimony will be honest and forthright?" Mearalas rushed through the words as though they meant nothing.

"I do."

"Very well." She sighed. "Since your world does not adhere to our ideals, I doubt you understand their purpose. We exist solely to reclaim our place in the Heavens, and any who fall short of our values risk dragging their neighbors to Hell. In the end, it is a simple matter of good and evil." She leaned forward, scowling down at Lydia. "In light of all that, could you really call Aedyn a good man?"

The fae certainly loved their riddles. Luckily, Lydia had always loved riddles, too, and she'd answered this question once before.

"He's not a completely good person," she said, "but there's no such thing. You can't just separate people into good and bad, right and wrong, Seelie and Unseelie. It's more muddy than that." She glanced back at her friends—the cowardly thief who'd taught her to be cautious, the feral hound who'd taught her to be fierce, and the careless prince who'd taught her to care. The traits that seemed dreadful in certain lights shone like beacons in others. "We're all a little bit bad and a little bit good, but if we work together, we can help each other become a little bit better."

The crowd was quiet for a few nervous beats before breaking into thunderous applause. Lydia looked down at her feet, her face flushing.

Even if her words hadn't helped Aedyn, there was a chance they might help *someone*.

She wanted to make a difference, at least once, before...

"Wise words, girl," Mearalas arched a midnight brow. "But they are only words, and you are only a child. You cannot possibly grasp—"

"I'm not a child!" Lydia stomped a foot, a violet haze clouding her vision. "I'm just a stupid puppet tugged along by stupid magic, and when that magic's gone, I will be too!" The whispers coiled in her skull like serpents, begging to slip across her tongue, but she resisted. "I ought to let it all out, right here, right now! At least, then, Yana can't get to me!"

Mearalas's eyes flexed wide. "What do you know of Yana?"

The haze receded. The whispers faded. Lydia tugged on a lock of her hair, uncertain whether she'd just done a very good or a very bad thing.

"Fate is never absolute, it wavers at our whims,
In divining a future, you are putting it at risk."

CHAPTER 27
THE SEER'S MIRROR
ELWYN

"hat's a changeling?" Lydia asked, her icy fingers wrapped in Elwyn's.

"It's what you are," Aedyn said, voice grim.

"I thought you said I was a mortal."

Aedyn slumped forward, his gold-brown hair falling into his face. "I was wrong," he said. "That is often the case."

The four of them—Elwyn, Lydia, Aedyn, and Brannon—were sitting around a filigree table that a pair of robed Maithe had somehow *serenaded* from the floor. Were Elwyn and Aedyn on better terms, she would have asked him how that was even possible. There were more important matters to tend to, anyway.

Elwyn had no clue what a changeling was, but the word had been sitting like a stone in her stomach ever since she heard the guards whispering about it. She could only hope the High Judges gave a better explanation than Aedyn's.

The wait was not long. Roughly ten minutes after the group arrived in the throne room, a muddled troop of Maithe and Undine marched in, escorting their respective rulers. The monarchs stepped forward with little fanfare and delved straight to business.

"I am sure you have many questions," King Aryn said, his golden gaze flicking to Lydia. "You, most of all. Given our time constraints, I cannot promise to answer all of them, but we will do our best."

"Let us start with the girl's identity," Mearalas said, half sighing. "A soul must exit this world before re-entering, and we are not easily slain. Freshborn fae only come into existence when a spirit ascends to their eternal fate. Or descends, as the case may be. Suffice to say, we do not bear children often."

"What does that have to do with Lydia?" Brannon asked, a startling amount of concern in his voice. "Is she a freshborn fae?"

"Hardly." Mearalas scoffed, crossing her arms.

"We bring up the freshborn only to set precedent." Aryn looked everywhere but at his own freshborn son. "They are often sickly or withered, especially those born to Unseelie. It is not uncommon for their parents to make a trade."

"Mortal children can endure direct sunlight, unlike Unseelie," Mearalas said. "Hags and Korrids often use them to gather resources or send messages to the Light Realms. Yana likely stole the *real* Lydia for that exact reason, leaving you to rot in her stead."

"She's Unseelie?" Elwyn squeezed Lydia's frigid fingers. "That makes no sense. You just claimed she wasn't a freshborn, and the sunlight doesn't harm her."

"If she was born ill, you could cure her," Brannon added. "Like you cured me."

"She wasn't born ill," Mearalas said, voice flat. "She was stillborn. According to the Sylphs, Yana birthed the girl—if it can be called that— shortly after her own death, when she was meant to join the Sluagh."

"The Sluagh?" Elwyn asked, as though that was the most pressing question.

"I'll explain later," Aedyn whispered.

Elwyn didn't need to know that badly.

"Am I already dead?" Lydia asked, surprisingly calm. "Or am I on the way?"

"Both," King Aryn explained. "You did not survive your mother's death, but the magic she invested in you mimics life, though it would take a wiser soul than mine to discern what that says of your spirit. As for how much of that magic remains—"

"What does she want from me?" Lydia interrupted, either frightened of or uninterested in that detail. "She traded me off almost ten years ago. What use could she possibly have for me now?"

"That is what we hope to find out," Mearalas said. "There are seers of great skill among my subjects—powerful sages who can use your connection to Yana to gain insight into her schemes. Regrettably, it is unlawful to use a person—even the facsimile of one—in the ritual without their express permission. Do we have it?"

Elwyn released Lydia's hand to wrap a protective arm around her. "You will not harm her," she hissed.

"Do not impugn my honor, mortal." Mearalas' stormy eyes iced over. "It is not as though I intend to use the child for a scrying spell or soul tithe. Seeing rituals are harmless endeavors."

"I'll do it." Lydia said before Elwyn could get another word in. "On one condition. Dismiss Aedyn's charges."

The slightest smile tugged at King Aryn's cheek. Or perhaps it was a trick of light.

Mearalas's nostrils flared. "The heir must pay for his crimes, like any other," she hissed. "As High Judge of Law, I cannot simply allow him to walk free, and you are in no position to barter."

"Seems to me she's in the *ideal* position to barter," Aedyn interjected.

"That's right." Lydia crossed her arms, jutting out her little chin. "Let him go, or you'll have to find some *other* changeling to work with."

Elwyn fought a grin. When they'd met, Lydia was even meeker than herself, but she was fast becoming fierce. In ten years' time, she'd put them all to shame.

"Decide swiftly, Mearalas," King Aryn said, a hint of amusement in his voice. "The Mortal Midsummer will end by..." He glanced at a device above the entryway door—similar to a clock, though the symbols that marked the hours were inscrutable. "Tomorrow morning, Seelie time."

Mearalas gritted her teeth, webbed hands balled at her sides. "I accept the conditions," she hissed, turning to face the soldiers behind her. "Transport these four to Chorial. I will meet you there once we dismiss the trials."

The guards marched Elwyn and the others to an adjacent room, then set about returning their confiscated belongings. To Aedyn, they handed a gold rapier and five bands that could somehow turn into armor. To Brannon, they handed deadly daggers and a belt packed with smoke orbs and caltrops. To Elwyn, they handed a tiny blue birdcage dangling from a slender chain. Luatha fluttered about inside of it, chittering madly as she shook the cobalt bars.

"You'd better have treated her well." Elwyn snatched the cage with one hand, holding out the other. "The key?"

"These prejudicial merfolk don't plan on freeing me,
There's a reason we piskie-kind don't dwell beneath the sea."

"Your leech will taste free air again," the soldier said. "So long as you don't cause our queen any troubles."

Elwyn hadn't planned on causing any. But then, plans could change. "And *Gelah?*"

"Hm?"

"My dagger."

"Ah." The soldier pulled the blade from an oversized scabbard on his belt, hesitantly handing it over. "I don't know what you got here, and I'm willing to bet you don't either. Even so, you don't deserve it."

Lapa stepped out from the formation, hefting an overstuffed satchel that *clinked* with her every step. She pulled a bottle, brimming with bubbling liquid, from the sack and handed it to Elwyn. Something plump and pink wriggled at the bottom, flaring a mane of tiny tentacles.

"Do not chew the polyp," Lapa instructed, passing around the remaining bottles. "For the travel spell to take, it must be swallowed alive."

The thought brought bile to Elwyn's tongue, but she would rather swallow a polyp than be left behind at Samhria. "Will Luatha need a potion?" she asked.

Papa shook her head. "Keep her in hand, and your bond will transport her."

Bond? Elwyn added it to the list of things she'd ask about later.

When Lapa uncorked her potion and tipped it back, she followed suit, downing the contents in a single, nauseating gulp. The polyp slipped over her tongue and wriggled down her throat. A heartbeat later, gravity lost its grip. First, the world turned to a tumult of green and gold, and then a blur of blue and teal. Her soles landed on a slick floor, and the colors snapped into place.

Elwyn had landed in a tower of mosaic sea glass that ascended in a steep spiral of chambers and stairways. The floor was crafted of seamless stone, and phosphorescent algae smattered the walls in abstract patterns, casting an eerie, blue-green glow over driftwood furniture and sandstone fixtures. Outside, schools of silver perch wove through fields of emerald kelp and vivid anemones, visible only through the lightest patches of the piecemeal walls. A few Undine, dressed in flowing robes instead of armor, wandered idly about, but they paid their visitors no mind.

"Try not to touch the railing," Lapa said, ignoring her own advice as she started up a staircase. "Coral skeletons are pretty, but they rip thin-skins like you to pieces."

"Interesting choice in décor." Brannon tapped a finger against a baluster, and a red drop welled at its tip. "Do you skewer your guests often?"

"The spears are for skewering." Lapa tapped her weapon on the ground, grinning over her shoulder. "The coral is for gloating."

"You already get to breathe underwater," Lydia huffed. "Must you also brag about having scales?"

"What can I say." Lapa shrugged. "Undine are the most spectacular fae."

"Most spectacular?" Aedyn laughed. "Have you even looked at me?"

Lapa rolled topaz eyes. "Those who truly love themselves need not say it so loudly or so often."

Aedyn fell silent for the remainder of the trek.

The Archive was the tallest tower in Chorial, according to Lapa. Overstuffed bookshelves spiraled up the walls for at least twenty stories then opening to a pinprick of brilliant blue sky. Sunlight rained down on a bevy of statues, staves, and scroll racks, reflecting brightly on a glassy pool at the center of the floor. Three sigils ran along its stone border—red, yellow, and blue. They reminded Elwyn of those that had been painted above the doors of the Raths, back in Rhysia.

"The worlds have been divided, but they are still attached,
Several doors run between them, and that would be a latch," Luatha sang.

"The Seer's Mirror." Lapa nodded toward the pool. "It is among the oldest and most revered relics in Undine possession. Much of our history was lost during the Chorialan Cold Years." She glanced around at the artifacts as though she'd never glimpsed them before. "Perhaps that is why we are so skilled in looking ahead."

"How does the mirror work?" Elwyn asked.

"I would show you, if I could," Lapa said. "Only the most skilled of sages can access its powers. The changeling will allow them to divine Yana's fate."

"Call me Lydia, please." The girl wandered over to the pool, looking down at her reflection. "I know I'm not the real Lydia, but I don't like being called 'changeling.' Too close to 'Monster'."

"You are the *real* Lydia." Elwyn walked over and placed a hand on her shoulder. "I've never met anyone more real."

Lydia offered a feeble smile. She shook off a slipper, dipped a toe in the water, and jumped back, shivering. "It's freezing!"

Elwyn poked at the mirror's surface, surprised when it didn't ripple at her touch. It felt tepid to her, but she didn't share Lydia's condition. "Is there a way to warm it?" she asked.

"The temperature is fixed," Lapa replied. "That said, we Undine often travel through arctic waters, and have garments warded to keep out the chill. If I were to take the changel—*Lydia* to trade outfits, could I trust you three not to destroy anything?"

"Can we trust you with her?" Elwyn asked.

"It's not Lydia who needs protecting," Brannon reminded her. "Have you forgotten the tunnels already?"

Elwyn hadn't forgotten; that was the problem. Lydia may have torn those agents to bits, but the battle had left her a husk. If King Aryn was right, her magic was the only thing keeping her upright. Elwyn didn't want to know what would happen once that magic ran out.

"I'm coming with," she said.

"Me too!" Aedyn added, stepping up beside her.

"Unnecessary," Elwyn huffed.

"*I'll* accompany the brat and the fish." Brannon pushed between them, snatching Luatha's cage from Elwyn's hands. "Clearly, something is going on here that's none of my business, and I'd prefer to keep it that way. Either battle to the death before I return or come to some sort of arrangement that spares me all this moping and sighing!"

He marched from the room ahead of Lapa and Lydia, who swiftly caught up, leaving Aedyn and Elwyn in uncomfortable silence. That silence did not last long enough.

"Brannon's right for once, you know," Aedyn said.

"About one of us killing the other?"

"About us needing to fix things." He took a timid step closer. "I hate feeling this way, and I hate knowing you feel this way, and I recognize that I'm to blame for it. There is a reason I don't like to know much about those I...spend time with."

"The reason is that you're a complete cad." Elwyn wandered over to a bookshelf, pulling a random tome free. She couldn't read the title, but she flipped it open anyway. "To clarify, you were nowhere near *spending time* with me."

"I didn't mean to imply it." Aedyn's shadow stretched out beside hers. "Is there anything I can say to make things go back to normal?"

Things hadn't been normal to begin with.

"I haven't had many friends, Aedyn." Elwyn shoved the book back into place, frustrated by its cryptic letters. "I really thought you were one of them."

"Thought?" Panic pinched his voice. "Does it have to be *thought*, past tense? I know I can be a bit of a—"

"Cad?"

"Well, yes." He grabbed her hand. "But I'm still your friend."

Elwyn pulled her fingers free, shooting him a livid glare. It was a mistake. Those glittering bronze eyes betrayed no guile, only sorrow.

His pain was not a poultice for her own.

"Why don't you ever talk about Eloana?" she asked, sincerely curious.

"I was...you see, I...when the time was right, I'd ..." He sighed, slumping against the bookshelf. "I would never have brought it up. Truth told, she hadn't crossed my mind once throughout our travels, and she rarely crossed it before then. It's an arranged thing, so I naturally resent it, and..." He shook his head, shoulders drooping. "Excuses aside, it's as you said. I'm a cad. If I went around proclaiming that I'm promised in marriage, it would close a lot of doors that I'd rather like to enter."

"There has to be a less repulsive way to say that."

"I was going for a laugh." A smile flickered on Aedyn's lips, fading when Elwyn didn't return it, and he pushed himself upright. "Do you remember back in the dining room, when you said I was a better person than you first thought?"

"If I didn't, it would be a lot easier to look at you."

Aedyn winced. "Well, before we were interrupted, I was about to disagree. I am *exactly* the kind of person you first thought I was—arrogant, selfish, and utterly ungrateful. I have lived an exceptionally charmed life, but I'd gamble it all away in a heartbeat for the chance at something new, even if that something's worth less than half of what I had before."

"I wouldn't say all that." Elwyn was beginning to suspect that, frustrated though she was, she liked Aedyn far more than he liked himself.

"That's because you're nothing like me. You are easily the humblest, most sincere person I've ever met. You hold tightly to each blessing you eke out of life, and the few lucky people you allow close are better off for it, even cads like me." His smile returned in full. "In short, you are...well, you're remarkable."

Elwyn couldn't help blushing. "I wouldn't say all that, either."

"You should," he countered. "You are right to dole your friendship sparingly, but if you let me keep it, I swear I'll never gamble it away, not even for a chance at something more."

"So you understand that this..." she grimaced, unable to think up a better metaphor, "*door* is closed."

"Permanently? To everyone?"

"Cad!" She punched him in the arm, which he correctly took to mean their friendship was mended. His laugh made her happier than she wanted it to.

"One more thing," he said. "This temperance you're so crazy about has a certain appeal, but you could frankly stand to loosen up. How about I vow to teach you to be more impulsive, and you help me practice a touch more caution?" He extended his hand.

"You fae really love your deals, don't you?"

Aedyn shrugged. "It's a cultural thing."

They shook on it.

"It's practically a treaty now," Elwyn said with an uncharacteristic wink. "Break it, and I'll see you in court."

The others returned seconds later, and Elwyn immediately rushed forward to check on Lydia and Luatha. Already, the piskie's rhymes had become more colorful for Brannon's influence.

"I liked it better when I assumed she wasn't real," Brannon said, thrusting the cage into Elwyn's hands. "I had always imagined piskies to be likable creatures."

"You've always imagined piskies?" Aedyn appeared at Elwyn's side. "How surprisingly whimsical."

"Damn." Brannon's eyes shifted between them. "I thought for sure one of you would be dead by now."

"Elwyn, does this look as odd as it feels?" Lydia tugged on the sleeve of the clingy, scaled garment that stretched from her chin to her toes.

"I'm not much use in that regard," Elwyn replied, tipping her head toward Aedyn. "He's probably better for fashion advice."

Lydia eyed Aedyn's garish green suit, then shook her head. "Will we be starting soon?" she asked Lapa. "I'd like to get this over with."

"As soon as the queen and her seers arrive."

Mearalas strode through the doorway as though summoned, followed by a triad of Undine men. They were clad in flowing velvet robes, one yellow, one red, one blue.

"That's the Sluagh's changeling," the queen said, flicking a finger toward Lydia. "She's consented to the ritual and will give you no trouble."

The seers nodded in eerie unison, then drifted forward, each standing atop the rune that matched their robe. They began chanting in a deep, ominous tongue. The runes beneath them effused vibrant red light, and the pool did the same. Lydia strode dutifully toward the water, but Mearalas barred her path.

"Red is for going," the queen said. "Yellow, for dreaming. Green is for knowing. *Blue* is for seeing."

The runes and water shifted several hues until both gleamed a soft, surreal blue, then Mearalas dropped her arm, and Lydia stepped forward. When the girl arrived at the center of the pool, the seers' chanting shifted into a song, the harmonies woven like a rope. The waters rippled, building to a roil.

One moment, the Seer's Mirror reflected the cerulean sky above. The next, it showed a small, dusty room, cast in the glow of a dying lantern. Lydia's reflection had changed as well, having sprouted a foot and aged several years. She had emerald eyes, opposed to lavender, and buttercup yellow curls, but the round face and button nose were unmistakably hers. This new Lydia stared listlessly out an open window, gripping a tattered blanket to her chest.

After only a few heartbeats, the waters roiled again, a series of unsettling images flashing across the surface. Umbral creatures with phlegm-yellow eyes. A stone altar, stained with blood. A crooked dagger, gleaming in the moonlight. Then, the surface shattered, and the Archive filled with a light so searing Elwyn was forced to shield her eyes.

When she lowered her arm, the visions had vanished, and Lydia stood shivering amidst a still, summer sky.

TAWNY

Tawny clutched her favorite blanket to her chest, gazing out at the eternal sunset. The blanket brought little comfort, no matter how tightly she wrung it. Like nearly everything in the room, Mother...No, *Yana* had given it to her. That fact alone robbed it of value.

She had always known Yana was not her true mother, but she'd never felt like anything but her daughter. Now, she couldn't help wondering what her real parents were like. Somewhere in the mortal realm, a changeling was living her life for her. With the time disparity between worlds, she'd still be a child—an innocent, sheltered, lucky little child.

Tawny had never envied anyone so fiercely.

Claws scratched at her bedroom door, and several yellow eyes peered through the crack when she opened it. An onyx talon poked into the room, curling to beckon her out into the hall.

"Yaaa...naaa's...orrrr...derrrrs."

Tawny tried not to tremble as she followed the goblins down the staircase, through the kitchen, and into the reading parlor.

Mother sat beside the blazing hearth, sipping tea and thumbing through a tome. She looked harmless, draped in a modest ivory gown, her winter-white locks flowing freely over her shoulders. Nearly human.

"Ah, there you are, dear," she said, closing her book and setting it on the end table beside her. "Come join me, we have much to discuss."

Tawny tiptoed forward, leaving the goblins to chitter in the doorway. She came to rest beside the chair, fingers clasped behind her back to hide their quivering.

Mother arched an eyebrow. "Do you expect me to crane my neck for this entire conversation?"

Tawny gulped, reluctantly sidling in front of her. The coarse rug that bristled beneath her feet was unfamiliar, but the hearth fire at her back was the larger concern. One push, and this meeting would end in a most unpleasant manner.

"I'm sorry for snooping," Tawny said. "I should have asked directly about the contract instead of rooting through your things."

"It's quite alright, dear." Mother's voice was warm, almost amused. "If I were in your shoes, I'd be curious, too. That's why I've decided to tell you everything."

"R-really?"

"Really." Mother smiled softly, settling against the backrest. "It all started a decade ago. Well, a decade by mortal standards. Did you know you'd be only ten, had you lived there? The Wilds have sped your years, though your trips to the Light Realm stretched a few."

Tawny didn't know the exact count, but she'd figured something similar.

"I was with child, a daughter." Mother's smile melted away. "I'd never been the maternal type, but necessity demanded it. Unfortunately, before I could birth her, I was murdered by a mob of wicked men who deemed me even viler than themselves. Apparently, the Creator shared their opinion, as I was doomed to join the Sluagh. Do you know what the Sluagh are, dear?"

Tawny shook her head.

"You know that wind that blows through the Shadow Realm once every fortnight?"

"The Wailing Wind?"

"Those are the Sluagh, souls cursed to weave between the realms, tasked with tormenting each other for the rest of time. As you can imagine, I was not keen on joining their ranks."

Tawny shuddered to imagine it. "O-of course not."

"Oh, I just knew this story would frighten you, dear," Mother set her teacup atop her tome. "Why do you think I kept it from you, all these years? Alas, my secret has done more harm than good, it seems." She shook her head. "Suffice to say, when a creature offered me a deal—one that would keep me separate from that maddening horde for a decade more—I jumped at the opportunity."

"The contract," Tawny whispered. "Your time is running out, isn't it? I read something about a decade..."

"It ends in two mortal days," Mother said. "Four, by our clocks, but never fear—there is a loophole. You probably read it for yourself, glossing over it as I had countless times." She leaned forward, folding her hands in her lap. "Do you recall what that scroll said about my final moments, when the creature claims his due?"

"That he's entitled to your soul, and that of your child." Tawny gulped. "And that he'll come for what he's owed, no matter where you are at the time."

"Close. It says he will retrieve his due whether I am in the Mortal *or* Faerie Realm.

"Is there anywhere else to be?"

"Not anymore." Mother's eyes drifted past her, flickering with firelight. "And not yet. Did you know the realms were not always separate? It was only after the Battle that Split the Sky in Two that the Creator tore light from shadow. Before then, it was a seamless whole." Her gaze shifted back to Tawny, dagger sharp. "If something is broken, there is always a way to mend it."

Tawny's heart pounded in her throat. Her mother was speaking madness. The Light and Shadow realms were anathema to one another, and she didn't imagine the Mortal Realm shared many traits with either.

"How could you possibly hope to do that?" she asked. "You've never mentioned the Creator before, or anything about a battle. You've only ever spoken about—"

"The Shadows," Mother said. "The source of all Unseelie magic, ancient and mysterious. They grant requests, provided one knows how to ask. My wish is unfathomably large, mind you, but I understand the cost, and I'm willing to pay it."

Despite all she'd gone through, Tawny was relieved to hear it. Fear could drive the kindest people to unspeakable things. The Mother she knew was still in there, and she needed help.

"We'll do whatever it takes," she said, knees hitting the coarse rug. She grabbed her mother's frigid hands. "If there's something out there that could save you, I want to help you find it. I can't lose you!"

Mother blinked, her expression softening. "I...I hadn't expected you'd feel that way, dear." She looked away, blinking a shimmer from her violet eyes. "As it happens, I do have something to ask of you."

"Anything."

Mother took a deep breath, though she didn't need air. That was never a good sign. "Do you remember when I taught you how to make a cleansing potion?"

Of course Tawny remembered. "One of my very first lessons," she said, smiling feebly. "That was a good day."

"It...it was a very good day," Mother replied. "Only a swarm of rot-fae had gotten to the spriteberries—"

"We had to substitute elderberries instead." Tawny's nose wrinkled at the memory. "It smelled terrible."

"It took two weeks of burning incense to cover the odor." Mother paused, pursing her lips and squeezing Tawny's hands. "Well, dear, the spell I'm crafting requires some very specific ingredients, and there's one I've failed to gather. I'm afraid I need to make a substitution."

Tawny didn't understand. Not until Shadow Goblins crowded around her, latching onto her wrists, her legs, her hair.

"Mother?" Tawny struggled against them, the grim reality setting in. "Mother, please! Don't do this!"

Yana looked away.

Even as the Shadow Goblins dragged her up the stairs, Tawny pleaded and groveled, believing Yana would come to her senses. That an ounce of the love she'd always shown had been sincere, that this was only an act of desperation, ill-conceived and easily reversed.

Then, the hearth fire flared, its golden light catching on the pair of nubby horns that poked from Mother's new throw rug.

Daulle.

"Fear is a common factor in every valiant myth,
No one has ever saved the day without taking a risk."

CHAPTER 28
COWARDS AND HEROES
AEDYN

pparently, the High Judges were meeting in Chorial, the exception being Aedyn's father. The king had opted to remain in Talunasa to oversee what remained of the Midsummer festivities. Usually, Aedyn hated filling in for him, but Mearalas had shown such disapproval on this occasion that he found himself looking forward to it.

"Absolutely not!" The Undine Queen hissed from beside the meeting hall, her eyes darting between Aedyn's friends. "Mortals have never been permitted to attend Seelie Councils, and the information we are about to discuss is meant for royal ears only."

"And those of your guards," Aedyn said, nodding toward the legion of cobalt-clad troops beyond the archway. "Unless you're planning to shoo them from the hall..."

Mearalas's eyes narrowed.

"As I thought." Aedyn placed a hand apiece on Elwyn and Brannon's shoulders, and they both shrugged him away. "I've chosen these two as my retainers for the evening, as is my right. As for Lydia..." he nodded toward the girl. "Well, this meeting is more or less *about* her, isn't it?"

Mearalas's scowl reached record depths, but she turned without a retort, beckoning them to follow. Aedyn flashed Elwyn a swift smirk and was relieved when she returned it. Perhaps things were truly back to normal between them.

They followed the Undine Queen into the hall, then down a series of stone steps that descended in concentric circles toward a sheer glass floor. The sea below was dark as pitch, but jellyfish and eels drifted about it, sparking bright against the black. Aedyn fought a shiver, remembering how it had felt to drift about the depths, certain he'd led his companions to their doom. All because he'd been too proud to admit he'd gotten a little lost. They were lucky the Seaglass Guard had been passing through at the time. That was usually how things worked out for Aedyn—sheer luck. Eventually, it was going to run out.

Creagor and Soen were waiting on the bottommost bench, strangely silent. Their serious expressions made Aedyn's spirit sink. Soen had always been excellent at concealing her thoughts, and Creagor was the most jovial judge, despite his sudden outbursts, Once, while drunk at a Beltane festival, he'd demolished an entire temple for "blocking his favorite cloud," then returned to the feast as though nothing was amiss. If he was visibly somber, circumstances were grave, indeed.

Aedyn kept his smile fixed as he took his seat, patting the stone benches beside him. Elwyn's arm brushed his, and her touch tingled like that of a Sylph. He tried his best to ignore it, determined to keep his word. He'd promised her his friendship, *only* his friendship, and he never wanted to break her trust again.

"Hours have passed since Lydia looked into the Seer's Mirror," he said as Mearalas took her seat. "Surely, your seers have deciphered the visions."

"Patience, heir." Mearalas grimaced, crossing her slender seafoam legs. "You and your...*pets* are guests at this Council, and you are not above tradition."

"We always begin with vows," Soen reminded him, raising her palm.

Aedyn sighed, following suit.

"For Honor, Justice, Love, and Law," he said in unison with the Judges.

"You too." Mearalas glared at Aedyn's guests, who hadn't known to chant along.

They did as told, though Brannon spoke with the kind of searing sarcasm that might have caught any other kingdom on fire.

"Well?" Creagor nudged Mearalas with his elbow. "There was much rush in getting here. Are we not crushed for time?"

"Pressed," Soen corrected.

"Is what I said. Time intends to squish us."

"Actually, time is on our side." Mearalas smiled for the first time since the trial. "Yana intends to destroy the world as we know it, but her plans are flawed, and her time is short. The best thing we can do is wait out the Mortal Midsummer here in Chorial."

"What are you talking about?" Brannon asked. "Earlier, you said Yana intended to destroy the world."

Mearalas refused to look his way. "I am under no obligation to answer your questions, mortal."

"Allow me," Aedyn whispered to Brannon before clearing his throat, smirking at Mearalas. "What are you talking about? Earlier, you said Yana intended to destroy the world."

Mearalas grimaced, nostrils flaring. "I actually said she is trying to destroy the world *as we know it*. There is a difference."

"Perhaps you could elaborate," Soen suggested, eyelashes fluttering. "For the mortals' sake."

Mearalas huffed, snapping her webbed fingers, and a cobalt-clad retainer rushed down the steps to hand her a scroll. She tugged the topaz ribbon that bound it, and it unfurled swiftly, brushing the glass floor between her sandaled feet.

"The findings?" Aedyn asked, scanning the full length of the scroll. "I don't suppose you'd care to summarize..."

"I do nothing in part, heir of Aryn." Mearalas fixed her eyes on the parchment. "It should be noted that this prophecy, like all prophecies, is subject to error," she said. "Futures are fickle things, shifting with the whims of anyone involved. That said, the longer a scheme simmers, the more rigid it becomes, and Yana's scheme has been in motion for a decade, ever since she made a deal with one of the Far Darrag."

"Blithely," Aedyn whispered.

His mortal friends paled at the name.

Mearalas ignored the interjection, eyes sliding over the scroll as she recited the seer's visions word for word. Yana was one of the Sluagh, but her dealings had helped to delay her torment. To buy more time, she intended to invoke the Shadows on the final night of Midsummer, when the Veil was at its thinnest, and to beg their intervention with a soul tithe.

"What's a soul tithe?" Lydia asked.

"And what are the Shadows?" Elwyn asked.

Aedyn repeated the questions, much to Mearalas' annoyance.

"You already know the answers, heir..."

"Humor me."

Mearalas grimaced. "The Shadows are the force from which the Unseelie draw their powers, either consciously or innately. They are evil beyond measure, and they seek the ruin of all, but they will bend to the will of a skilled enough spell-caster, provided the price is right. Hence, the soul tithe, which is exactly what it sounds like."

"What does Yana mean to request?" Soen twirled a silvery lock around her finger, playing ignorant for the sake of those who truly were. "How could the Shadows possibly save her?"

Mearalas's eyes leapt back to the scroll. "Her contract with the Far Darrag specifies that he will lay claim to her soul whether she is present in the Faerie or Mortal Realm when her debt comes due. She intends to meld the worlds so that neither technically exists."

Aedyn should have had a million questions, but his mind was utterly blank. He could not have fathomed a plan as brash as Yana's, and that was saying something.

"The worlds were created as one," Soen mused, staring into the distance. "But no record remains from before the Battle that Split the Sky in Two, and even Aryn's memories of that time are hazy. It is impossible to fathom what a melded world might look like."

"Many will die." Creagor's proud shoulders dropped. "Whole kingdoms will be leveled over one foolish soul."

Aedyn's eyes lilted toward the sea glass ceiling. He did not want to be stuck in Chorial when the worlds collided. "What can we do?" he whispered.

"The wreckage is only the first concern of many," Soen said, oblivious to his query. "Our alliance with the Unseelie was forged along specific boundaries, and those boundaries are soon to be eradicated. I cannot imagine a scenario where that doesn't lead to war."

"What can we do?" Aedyn repeated, louder.

"Not only war, but chaos," Mearalas added. "There is no telling how the continents will rearrange, how the magical will mingle with the natural, how time itself might bend, might buckle, might break. Can you imagine the sun rising over Unseelie lands." She shuddered—a first for her. "Or worse, night falling on our own?"

"So, what can we *do*?" Aedyn shouted.

The High Judges paused their conversation, blinking his way.

Mearalas straightened. "Absolutely nothing," she said. "A request of this magnitude requires the sacrifice of one's firstborn child. The Shadows will see anything less as a slight" She glanced at Lydia. "We have the one thing Yana needs to complete her spell."

That was a profound relief, at least to Aedyn. Given how Lydia squirmed, she didn't feel the same.

"The girl from the Seer's Mirror," she whispered. "The one who looked just like me. She's the substitution, isn't she? Yana's going to kill her for no reason."

"Is regrettable." Creagor shook his head. "But it is best possible outcome."

No, it wasn't. "The best possible outcome is one where no one dies," Aedyn said. "Maybe, if we hurry—"

"Do not dare finish that sentence, heir!" Mearalas snapped. "Yana's plan may be foolish, but *she* is not. She might well have guarded herself against prophecy, hiding bits of her plot from prying eyes. We cannot assume she isn't planning to come after the changeling one more time, and we cannot allow her an opportunity to succeed."

She nodded to the retainer who handed her the scroll, and he tapped his spear against stone. The sound rang through the meeting hall, and a storm of cobalt grieves answered, marching closer. Aedyn did not need to look to know an army of Undine waited at the top of the steps.

"You will be guests in Chorial for the night." Mearalas stood, glaring down at Aedyn. "In the morning, my soldiers will see you home safely— each to your respective realms."

LYDIA

Lydia walked hand-in-hand with Elwyn as Lapa led them down branching halls of mosaic glass, a million anxious thoughts whirling about her brain. That meeting with the judges had been more confusing than enlightening, but she knew enough to understand that Mearalas was being selfish.

"Our guest wing boasts over six hundred chambers," Lapa said, as though they were actual guests, not prisoners, "The queen was only willing to spare two, so you will have to share. Men in one, and ladies in the other, of course."

Lydia had once thought that a common rule, but she'd been sleeping close to the other three for weeks now, and they'd not once been struck by lightning. It seemed cruel that they should have to be apart for even a minute of their last night together. Lydia wasn't even certain which realm she'd be returned to, come morning. Given Mearalas' cruelty, she might easily command Lydia to live amongst the Unseelie she'd never met.

She tapped Lapa's armored elbow. "Are two rooms truly necessary?"

"Cramped, I know," Lapa said, misunderstanding. "It is a miracle the Queen is allowing you to stay in rooms at all, rather than the dungeons. No mortal has set foot in Chorial since..." She shook her head. "It has been ages. That is all you need to know." She paused in the middle of a corridor lined by countless guards. "Gentlemen on the left." She pointed toward an open door. "Ladies further down, on the right. I will be posted at the end of the hall just in case you have any questions."

"In case we try to escape, you mean?' Aedyn smiled, though he wasn't joking. He did that a lot.

Lapa departed with a terse wave. It wasn't a 'no.'

Elwyn started toward the rightmost room, tugging Lydia along. Lydia slipped free, running up to Aedyn for a final goodnight hug. He scooped her up and spun her around like her father used to, when he'd thought her a child, and his warmth nearly made up for her utter lack of it. It was nearly painful, letting go.

"Sleep well, Lydia." He offered a gentle smile. "Don't you worry about tomorrow until we get there."

Lydia nodded, though she had little control over her worries. Even Brannon looked worried, and he rarely looked anything but grumpy.

Already, he was marching toward the door that would doubtless slam behind him a moment later.

Frantic, Lydia dashed over and wrapped her arms around his waist. He froze from head to toe, his brow furrowed and his lips agape. Lydia thought, for a moment, he might shove her away. Instead, he patted her awkwardly atop her head.

"You're...something else, Lydia."

"And *you're* a little bit of a good person," she replied, releasing him. "No matter what you think."

The group parted ways without another word, and Lydia followed Elwyn to their room. It was cramped and dim, compared to the rest of the palace, lit by a scattered starscape of glowing green specks. Shadows of fish and other slippery things drifted beyond the walls, hemlock green against a sea of sage. A sleek sleep robe had been laid out on each of the beds, and a bowl of dried leaves sat on driftwood table between them. Lydia couldn't tell whether it was meant as a snack or potpourri.

Elwyn set Luatha's cage on the table before sitting on the edge of a bed, her shoulders drooping and her eyes miles away.

"You've looked sad all day," Lydia said, plucking the robe from the opposite bed. "Moreso than usual."

"It's been a lot," Elwyn replied. "But it's over now. Nothing to fret about."

Lydia hated being lied to.

"So, it's not about Aedyn, then?" Lydia slipped the robe on over her clingy outfit before wriggling free of it. "You two usually talk a lot, but you've barely said a word since the trial, even after Brannon told you to work things out."

Elwyn's flushed face was hardly visible in the dim lighting, but it still made Lydia smile. She couldn't think of two people she liked more than Elwyn and Aedyn. It was pleasant to think they might like each other, too.

"You're too observant for your own good, you know that?" Elwyn donned her robe overtop her dress. "If you must know, we had a misunderstanding, but we worked it out. Nothing to concern yourself with."

"But, what about—"

"You ask too many questions! I think it would be best,
To leave them for tomorrow and let me get some rest!" Luatha squeaked.

"Sorry," Lydia whispered, watching the piskie furl against the side of her cage. She must have had a hard day too, trapped as she was.

Elwyn pulled her pretty dagger from its sheath and tucked it beneath her pillow, ever ready for a fight. Lydia knew she should let her rest, but it seemed a pity, wasting time on slumber when so little remained.

"Today is my birthday," she whispered, crawling beneath her covers. "In a few hours, I'll finally be ten."

"I…I've never celebrated a birthday," Elwyn said. "I think I'll be turning twenty soon, but it's hard to say for certain."

"So, you don't have any birthday traditions?"

Elwyn shook her head. "You?"

"Yellow cake for breakfast," Lydia said, practically tasting buttercream. "A walk in the afternoon, and honeyed pheasant for supper. My mother would sing a silly song about a little girl who never grew up. The words were happy, but her voice was sad, like she wished it would come true."

"Perhaps we can find some cake in the morning," Elwyn suggested. "You wouldn't want to hear me sing, though. My voice isn't half as pretty as Aedyn's."

"What about a story instead?" Lydia asked.

"I haven't memorized any, but I could make one up, if you'd really like."

"I'd really like."

Elwyn chuckled. "Once upon a time, there was a coward," she began, perching on the edge of Lydia's bed. "She had ample opportunities to help other people, but she focused only on protecting herself. It was a sad life, and a lonely one. She truly believed everyone would eventually abandon her, just as she would abandon them."

"Was she right?"

"Not at all." Elwyn smiled softly. "One day, the coward was captured by a monster. Only, maybe he was not quite as monstrous as she thought, but I suppose that's beside the point." She shook her head. "I'm afraid I've had no practice telling stories."

"That's alright." Lydia rested her head against Elwyn's shoulder. "I want to hear the rest."

"If you insist." Elwyn chuckled. "The coward and the monster soon came across a little princess in trouble. The monster wanted to leave her behind, and the coward nearly went along with it. At the very last second, she ran back to rescue the princess, and the princess wound up saving *her* instead."

"How?" Lydia asked. "Did she have magic?"

"In a way. Cowardice is a kind of curse. It eats away at a person so slowly they don't even realize something's wrong. In saving the princess, she committed her very first act of courage, and the curse was broken. She just didn't realize it until later."

"If that's the case, she shouldn't be called a coward anymore," Lydia mused aloud. "What is she now?"

"That part of the story is yet to be written."

Lydia grimaced. "You really need to work on your endings."

"And *you* need to get some sleep." Elwyn laughed, rising to her feet. She brushed Lydia's bangs aside and kissed her forehead. "I promise, I will do all I can to give you the childhood that was robbed from me."

Lydia rolled over so Elwyn wouldn't see her crying. The story had answered more than its author intended. Princess or not, Lydia had always been a coward, and nothing frightened her more than what she needed to do next.

It was time to break the curse.

*"In waking hours, it's seldom clear which choice is wrong or right,
But both become so obvious when you can't sleep at night."*

CHAPTER 29
INSOMNIA
AEDYN

edyn had always struggled to fall asleep, and this night was no different. He wanted to blame it on the briny air, the slippery blankets, or the itchy Undine robe, but the truth of the matter was that he felt guilty.

Lydia had been right. Yana intended to kill an innocent girl soon, and they'd chosen to sit back and let it happen. Sure, the High Judges had made a decent point—the death of one person was preferable to that of thousands, maybe more—but the lesser of two evils was still evil.

My friends would get hurt, he told himself. It was the only reason he'd crawled into bed, determined to heed Mearalas' orders. Still, he couldn't stop tossing and turning, his every other thought flickering to noble battles and valiant rescues. If he really wanted to wait out the morning, he needed a distraction.

"Brannon," he whispered.

No reply.

"Brannon," he said again, louder.

The assassin jolted upright, ripping his daggers out from beneath his pillow. "What the fuck, Aedyn?" he growled.

"How bad do you think it would be if Yana got her wish?"

Brannon groaned, falling back to his pillow. "Bad, Aedyn. Why else would the Sea Bitch have gone through all the trouble of trapping us here?"

"Fair enough," Aedyn said. "Sorry for waking you."

He folded his arms behind his head to keep from fidgeting, bit his lips to trap his questions, and turned his mind toward thoughts that wouldn't depress him.

It lasted all of a minute.

"Brannon?"

"Do you think I'm suddenly beyond killing you?"

"Why do you hate Elwyn so much?"

It was not the most pressing question he had about Elwyn, but it was the most relevant. If Mearalas had her way, the mortals would soon head back to their own realm. He needed to know they wouldn't return to the same mess he'd found them in. That they wouldn't be alone.

"I don't hate her so much," Brannon replied. "Not lately, anyway."

A mild comfort. "Then, why *did* you hate her so much?"

"If I tell you, will you let me sleep?"

"I'm not in control of that," Aedyn said, "but, if you tell me, I'll try very, very hard to stop talking."

Brannon furled forward, extending a dagger.

"I thought you weren't going to kill me," Aedyn said.

"Don't be too sure." Brannon chuckled. "At the moment, I'm only trying to show you something. I call these daggers, *Aras Tosc*, my Greyscale *icons*. They were military dirks when I first obtained them, but I've since honed them into something sharper, more lethal. Even back then, I knew what I wanted to become, and it involved no dull edges."

"Does it have magic, like *Gelah?*"

"No." Brannon's brow furrowed. "Slate's...*Elwyn's* weapon is unique."

Aedyn had figured as much. He had a theory as to why, but he wanted to learn more before talking about it. "What makes an *icon* so special then?"

Brannon leaned back against the headboard, twirling the dagger. "They're hard-won weapons," he explained. "Greyscale initiates obtain them during something called the Rite."

"Sounds important and enigmatic."

"Oh, it is." Brannon grinned. "It is also what some people, *weak* people, might call cruel. Not counting a bit of pointless pomp at the end, it's comprised of two missions. In the first, initiates are tasked with finding a weapon that suits their tastes. The manner in which they secure it determines their role within the syndicate. Thieves steal their *icons*, enforcers obtain theirs through muggings, spies and charlatans talk them right out of the hands of merchants. I had my mind set on becoming an assassin—*the* assassin, really—so, I tore these daggers from the hands of a guard and used them to slit his throat."

Aedyn sat up, twisting toward Brannon. The assassin recounted the murder almost wistfully, without a hint of regret. Something inside the mortal was clearly broken. He'd have been a better friend to have noticed it sooner.

"What is the second part of the Rite?" he asked.

"Ah, that's where it gets grisly."

"Because it was such a nursery rhyme up to this point."

Brannon leaned back against the headboard. "The Father paired us up, two-by-two, and pitted us against each other. Whoever survived would become an agent. That day, there were odd numbers of both thieves and assassins in the mix. So, I was matched against Sl—Elwyn."

"But she's still alive."

"Don't I know it." Brannon struck his daggers together. "I was poised to win—really, I was. I had her pinned, my dagger pressed to her little throat. A simple slice would have done her in, but I wanted to savor my victory. I ran my dagger down her cheek just to hear her whimper. The blood dripped onto that blade of hers, and the damned thing started glowing. When I startled back, she slipped free."

Aedyn's fingers had balled into fists. He willed them to relax. The damage was already done, but he hated the thought of any harm befalling Elwyn.

"Why didn't she kill you?" he asked.

"Fuck if I know." Brannon shook his head. "If she'd freed my guts at that moment, I'd have died respecting her. But she ran, as she's prone to doing. I spent the rest of the evening searching for her, but she's always been a slippery little eel. In the end, it was the Father that found her. I thought for sure he would demand a rematch, but he inducted us both instead, citing that we'd 'benefit the syndicate equally.' That decision played to Elwyn's favor, but not mine."

"Because you hate sharing."

"I really do," Brannon said with a curt laugh. "Moreover, it set my career off at a disadvantage. In the eyes of the other agents, I was not a peer, but a fluke. It took several years of blood and backstabbing to finally gain their respect, and a few more to gain their fear."

Aedyn had hoped the story would bring out some kind of emotion, but no. Brannon was being so very *Brannon* about all of it. "How old were you?" he asked, dreading the answer.

"Ten." Finally, a hint of sorrow crept through. "We were both about ten."

Aedyn dropped to his pillow. The conversation hadn't been the most helpful distraction, and furthering it would only heighten his unease. "Goodnight, Brannon," he muttered.

There was a long pause, then a grumpy, muffled, "Night."

Three heartbeats.

"Hey, Brannon?"

"Hm?"

"Thanks for sharing."

"Don't push me, Aedyn."

Aedyn forced his eyes closed, praying sleep would take him. The strangest scenarios played out behind his eyelids—memories, but not his own. He imagined himself as a young boy, forced to prove his worth through violence. He imagined himself as a little thief, struggling to survive the cruel games of her mentors. He imagined himself as a beloved child who woke up one morning to find no one truly loved him.

He imagined what it might take, in any of those situations, to begin to heal.

LYDIA

Lydia could tell from the slow cadence of Elwyn's breathing that she'd finally fallen asleep. The soft purr lilting from the cobalt cage meant the piskie was out, too.

It was time.

She slipped silently from beneath the covers and tiptoed to the door, not bothering to change into her day-clothes. She wouldn't be needing them, where she was headed. The moment she stepped into the hall, two spears crossed to block her path.

"*I need to use the washroom,*" Lydia mouthed.

The guards exchanged suspicious glances.

"End of the hall," one whispered, tipping his head toward his colleague. "She'll be escorting you, so don't get any ideas."

It was a little late for that.

Lydia ignored the stares of the sentries as she was shepherded down the hallway by her shoulder. Some looked a little bored, but the bulk were as alert as they'd been upon arrival. Lapa stood rigid at branching hallways with her spear raised at the ready. She nodded at Lydia as she passed by. Lydia returned the nod, silently wishing the soldier well, then slipped from her escort's grasp and bolted toward the Archive.

A shrill whistle pierced the air, and a storm of shifting armor *clanged* and *clattered* to life. Lydia sprinted that much faster. Mentally, she'd been prepared for a pursuit, but the magic beneath her skin sparked instinctually. A violet haze filled the glittering corridor, and whispers drowned the ruckus behind her.

Aetri en Sca...

Not yet, Lydia begged. She needed the power the Shadows would lend her, but she could not afford to lose control. Not in a kingdom sculpted from sea-glass. Not in the presence of so many innocents. Not with her friends soundly sleeping nearby.

A few more twists and sudden turns, and the Archives appeared at the bottom of a spiral staircase. The sentries beside it startled upon seeing her, rushing forward to bar her path. Lydia scrambled down the steps regardless, preferring the few to the horde behind her. Fingers brushed her back, nearly latching. She leapt down the final steps and slid across the floor, stooping to duck a pair of lowered spears.

She was almost through the doorway when webbed hands gripped her shoulders, lifting her from the ground. Armored arms wrapped around her, and for a moment, she was back at her family home, begging her father for mercy.

The haze grew brighter.

Aetri en Sca...

Lydia writhed and wriggled, kicked and clawed, screamed and pleaded, but her captor's grip only tightened. "Be still, child!" The panicked voice belonged to Lapa. "You have no clue what you're doing!"

"Neither do you!" Lydia screamed above the voices in her mind. "Let me go!"

Lapa started toward the steps—away from the Seer's Mirror and the destiny beyond it. She would not listen to Lydia, so the whispers took control.

"Aetri en Sca!"

The mosaic landscape began to churn, oozing like puss from a fetid wound. Chitinous limbs burst from the seashell sconces, and tentacles writhed out from between the stairs. The stately guards morphed into monsters of slime and sea glass. Lydia fought to remember their true faces, lest she claw at the false ones in a fit of terror.

"Let. Me. GO!" Her voice split into many. The soldiers flew back, Lapa included. Lydia braced herself for a *thud* that never came.

She was floating feet above the ground, suspended amidst a mob of cowering creatures. One of those creatures rushed her, and she held out her hand—pure reflex. A force like lightning crackled across her palm. It leapt to her attacker, forcing him and several others to the ground. Lydia repeated the process with the same results, and again with the same. Soon, the whole troop lay in a tangle, broken and bleeding. But breathing.

A sourceless wind whipped around Lydia as she drifted into the Archive. Sunlight gleamed off the Seer's Mirror, but the Shadows' glow turned it a vivid violet. She rushed toward the waters, heedless of the voices that called out from all around her—spirits trapped in treasures and spell-sealed scrolls. They had earned their prisons, and she had no desire to free them.

She landed in the waters, and the Shadows did the rest. Their glow spread like poison through the pool and leeched into the sigils surrounding it. Soon the light burned such a violent crimson that even the lilac pall could not mute it.

Red is for going...

"The summer fades to autumn and winter melts to spring,
If dark denotes the sunrise, then what does brilliance bring?"

CHAPTER 30
SEARING LIGHT
AEDYN

edyn had finally drifted off when a thunderous din rose in the hallway. Creaking armor and fearful shouts rang out for just a moment before fading. It could not have been a good sign.

He scrambled from his bed right as Brannon began to stir.

"What the—"

"I don't know." Aedyn pulled his trousers on beneath his robe, grabbing the gilded bands from his pockets and slipping them onto his wrists, neck, and ankles. He was reaching for the door when it flew open. Elwyn burst into the room, barefoot and frantic. Aedyn grabbed her by the arms, meeting her fear-wide eyes.

"L-Lydia's gone," she managed.

A chill cut right to Aedyn's marrow. There was only one place Lydia would have gone. "Brannon..."

"I heard it! I'm up!" Brannon threw his cape over his robe, daggers flashing in his hands.

"Run ahead of us," Aedyn ordered. "Tell the seers what happened, then meet us in the Archive."

Brannon grunted but did as told. Elwyn followed after, dragging Aedyn by the wrist. The guards had vanished from the hall. All of them.

"Get your dagger," Aedyn said, steering Elwyn toward her room. "And the piskie."

"I have *Gelah* right here." She pulled the blade from her thigh. "And—"

Footsteps echoed from around the corner. A guard shouted orders, only yards away. Reinforcements had arrived.

"We'll need to come back for her." Elwyn winced as she said it.

Aedyn blinked, and she was a speck in the distance. He cursed under his breath. Elwyn was heading into battle at half-strength, and she didn't even know it.

"Fás," he muttered, and armor grew like vines from his cuffs as he sprinted toward the Archive.

TAWNY

The world was churning, but not as fast as Tawny's stomach. The autumnal eddy melted into a starscape as the acrid taste of the travel potion faded. Days of isolation had frayed her thoughts to ribbon and turned her belly to a cavern. Empty acid rose in her throat as the Shadow Goblins jostled her along, their claws piercing her skin and tugging her hair, but nothing was more nauseating than knowing she used to think of their leader as her mother.

Despite the tumult, there was a tranquility to this new world—a sweetness in the summer breeze that felt nearly like a welcome...or perhaps a "welcome back." The starscape above glittered bright as will-o'-the-wisps, so much starker than the pale constellations that hung over the Wilds.

They would make for a beautiful last sight.

Eventually, the starscape stopped spinning, and Tawny's captors tossed her atop something hard and cold. Yana loomed above her, violet eyes aglow. It took all of Tawny's scant strength to look away, unwilling to hold that traitorous gaze.

The greedy yellow eyes crowding around her were not much better. When this was all over, those goblins would probably pick her bones clean.

"I raised you better than to cower, dear." Yana's voices hissed. "This will be over before you know it."

A red-hot rage swelled in Tawny's chest. A whole lifetime of lullabies, spellwork, and suppers, and that woman had only ever thought of her as a component, no different than the herb garden she kept on the kitchen windowsill.

Words did not come easily to lungs so weak, throats so sore, or lips so dry, but Tawny managed to force one out. "Why?"

"You must understand, there is no other way," Yana replied, too calm. "Fear not, dear girl, the bones have spoken. You are the key to getting exactly what I need."

"I ... I already know w-why you're killing me." Talking hurt, but Tawny fought through the ache. "I'm asking why...why you ever treated me like your child. Why go through the trouble of making me think...making me think..."

Making me think you cared.

Be it owed to sorrow or frailty, she couldn't bring herself to finish the sentence.

"It must be difficult to see, in these circumstances." Yana caressed Tawny's cheek with a skeletal finger. "But I really do love you."

Tawny would have laughed if she had the breath for it. "Just...not as much as yourself."

A sinister dagger appeared in Yana's hand, its hilt formed of silver serpents. Tawny looked past the twisted blade, to the shimmering stars above. Perhaps it was a symptom of delirium, but they seemed to be moving.

Yana hoisted the dagger high in both hands. "*Aetri en Sca.*"

Tawny clenched her eyes shut, bracing for the bite of the blade. A voice cut through the night, softer than Yana's, though woven from the same, sinister whispers.

"Wait!"

LYDIA

"Wait!" Lydia shouted, floating into a circle of stones.

Yana froze, her dagger poised above the yellow-haired girl from the Seer's Mirror.

"It's me the Shadows want," Lydia said, drifting closer. "Not her."

A smile slithered across Yana's face as her violet eyes flitted to Lydia. "I was beginning to doubt the bones' prediction," she said. "I ought to have known better. Fate has a way of twisting at the last second, does it not?"

Only when someone intentionally twists it. "You've been expecting me."

"More or less." Yana lowered her dagger. "Futures are fickle things, as I'm sure you've learned, but I had a measure of faith. Once I divined that Mearalas' seers would be spying on me, I knew what I needed to show them. More importantly, I knew what I needed to show *you.*"

"Don't give yourself too much credit," Lydia said, wind whipping around her. "You didn't make me come here. I chose it for myself."

She let her gaze slide to the altar and the girl atop it—the *true* Lydia Devlin. Those emerald eyes and golden curls looked just like her mother's. It warmed Lydia to know she would have grown into someone beautiful.

No, the voices reminded her. She'd never had green eyes or yellow hair, and she'd never been meant to grow up. She looked more like herself than ever now. Even the goblins knew it, and they cowered at the fact, shrinking back beyond the stone circle. How silly, that Lydia had once been frightened of them. What were such pitiful creatures to something like her?

"You like making deals," she said, meeting Yana's glare. "Make one with me."

Yana beamed like a gambler with cards up her sleeve. "You wish to trade your life for hers?"

It wasn't really a question.

Lydia had been telling herself she wouldn't be afraid. Yet, there she was, offering her life to the monster who had made her, and she'd never been more terrified. Surely, Elwyn had felt the same when she'd charged a horde of goblins, not knowing the sunlight would dispel them. She had offered her life for a stranger, and it was time for Lydia to do the same.

"I wasn't supposed to live at all," she said, as much to herself as to Yana. "It may not have been a very happy life, but I'm grateful for it. There were moments, many of them recent, that made all the worst parts worthwhile. No matter your intentions, I have you to thank for that. Think of this as my way of repaying the debt."

ELWYN

The Seer's Mirror and the runes around it glowed ruby red when Elwyn arrived, and a starscape shimmered just below the surface. Elwyn held her breath, made a wish, and jumped. A tepid splash, and she was falling through a sapphire sky, comets blazing past in all directions.

Her bare feet landed soundlessly on a grassy hill overlooking a circle of stones. Lydia lay upon the altar at their center, Yana standing poised beside her. Both figures shone with the milky light of a full moon—a stunning contrast to the inky creatures surrounding them—but it was the knife in Yana's hand that captured Elwyn's attention.

Her feet started down the hillside before her thoughts could catch them. Lydia's name leapt from her lips. Countless sallow eyes snapped her way, and one by one, the Shadow Goblins broke off from their horde. They stalked toward her, their collective rumble shaking the earth, but Elwyn hardly heard them.

The darkness leapt forward with talons splayed. Elwyn ducked, but a claw caught her collar, dragging her to the ground. Before she could rise, another goblin latched to her. Then another. And another.

Soon, she saw only pitch black and flashes of phlegm-yellow. Fangs sank into her shoulder. Talons tore at her shins. Fear seeped in behind the sting, numbing mind and body both, but her spirit was not so easily broken.

She'd made Lydia a promise, and she intended to keep it. That thought lent her strength enough to shake the goblins loose, stumbling back to gain high ground. Desperate, she pressed *Gelah* to her tattered skin, bathing the runes in warm blood.

The dagger did not glow.

BRANNON

Brannon did not care about saving the worlds—not a single, damned one of them—but purpose swept through him as he landed on that hilltop, daggers in hand. He had arrived just in time.

Lydia lay on an altar, Yana gloating at her side. Elwyn was rushing toward them—fighting, falling, failing. But it was the eyes that caught his attention. Hundreds of them, blinking out from a writhing mass of shadow. The sight brought a feral smile to his lips, the promise of foes worth slaying. Though he'd once found them frightening, they now looked so feeble, so foolish. Brash little rats who fancied themselves monsters.

He would show how a true predator hunted.

"Get to Lydia," Aedyn shouted, barreling past in gilt armor. "I'll help Elwyn."

Brannon sprinted after the prince, his *Aras Tosc* glinting with each stride. He was not about to let some pretentious fop have all the fun. A goblin leapt toward him at the bottom of the hill. His daggers pierced its belly, ripping outward. Another latched on to his arm, slicing through the Undine robe. Brannon flung the creature off with ease, dragging a blade across its throat. He lodged his other knife in the next assailant's eye. Yellow dripped like egg-yolk from the blade.

Over and over, the shadows attacked. Over and over, they fell. Each dying hiss fed Brannon's thrill, and each left him that much more hungry. He nearly forgot why he was fighting.

Get to the girl, you idiot! He chided himself, forcing his way through the swarm. If Yana noticed his approach, she gave no sign. She closed her eyes, chanting something over and over as she raised her dagger high. Lydia trembled beneath her, neither broken nor bound. If she wasn't going to save herself, Brannon would have to do it for her.

He gritted his teeth, fending off a flurry of claws and teeth as he waded toward his goal. Blood matted his tattered robe to his skin, much of it his own, but he refused to slow or turn around. He'd been through too damned much to give up now. They *all* had.

Like hell was Yana going to win this.

ELWYN

The darkness enveloped Elwyn. A pair of yellow eyes seared into her own, and a string of dark drool dripped down her cheek. She could not breathe. She could not scream. She couldn't even lift her dagger to fight. Staring death in its putrid face filled her, not with fear or anger, but sorrow.

She had failed, and Lydia would pay the price.

A flash of gold burst through the black. The goblin reared back, pierced through by a slender blade. One by one, the shadows fell, until the weight was gone and air returned to Elwyn's weary lungs.

Her eyes landed, first, on Brannon as he sliced his way through the horde. A wildcat grin stretched his lips despite the crimson dripping from his skin. Next, she saw Aedyn. *Lots* of Aedyns. At least ten gilded figures formed an arch around her, each poised to skewer the circling beasts. When a monster clawed at one of the illusions, it vanished in a cloud of shimmering smoke, and the real Aedyn leapt forward to attack.

Using the chaos to her advantage, Elwyn clawed her way toward a too-distant altar.

More than once, a creature leapt toward her only to meet the end of a gilded blade. Aedyn called for her to stop, but the altar's call was stronger. Yana's dagger raised high above it, poised over Lydia's innocent heart.

"*Aetri en Sca!*"

Warm arms wrapped around Elwyn's waist, ripping her from the soil.

"You have to stop!" Aedyn begged, tears falling as he pressed his forehead to hers. "We're too late."

Elwyn fought against him, turning just in time to watch the dagger fall. A searing light erupted from the altar, drowning the world in blinding white.

When that light finally faded, everything had changed.

"There's little that evolves more swiftly than a spirit torn,
Such sorrow can coax blossoms forth in equal breadth as thorns."

CHAPTER 31
MOVING FORWARD
ELWYN

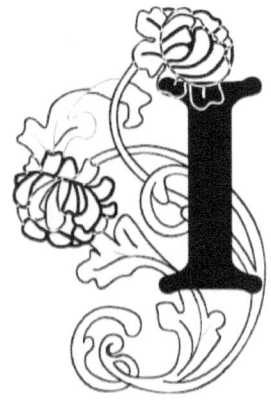t wasn't Lydia. Not really.

It was small, like her. It shared her snowy hair and pallor. It even wore her timid smile, but it wasn't her. People were so much more than the skin that housed them.

Elwyn sprinkled dirt into the grave. It was much too shallow, but it was the best they could do, for lack of a shovel. There were so many things she wanted to say. She wanted to tell Lydia one last bedtime story, to attempt to sing her a song, to thank her for breaking the curse she'd long suffered. Elwyn wished, with all her broken heart, she could have returned the favor.

"I'm so sorry," was the best she could manage before a sob strangled her voice.

"You deserved better," Aedyn said, staring down into the pit. "You deserved a better life. You deserved a better death. You..." His voice hitched, and he wiped his eyes with his sleeve. "...you deserved better saviors than us. Wherever you are now, I hope you've found all you deserve.

Soil sifted through his fingers, twisting in the breeze. It morphed into a flock of butterflies before alighting on the body, their pastel wings splayed. A smile found Elwyn's lips. Lydia would have loved that.

A moment of somber silence passed before Elwyn lifted her eyes to Brannon. He stood opposite them, arms crossed and face blank. "What?" he asked, catching Elwyn's stare. "If you're waiting for me to mourn, it isn't going to happen. I see no point in conversing with carrion."

Elwyn tore *Gelah* from its sheath. The blade's magic may have fled, but it could still slice well enough. Aedyn grabbed her shoulder before she could attack, and she slipped away, scowling. He had no right to touch her.

She could not forget how he'd held her when the world crumbled. The warmth of that embrace haunted her, churning her stomach. Some small, sick part of her had relished the moment, though it had changed nothing at all. Yana's dagger had found its mark, and the Shadows accepted her offering.

If this was affection, it felt a lot like guilt.

Elwyn meant to storm away—really, she did—but the weight of her grief dragged her to her knees beside the grave, and she buried her face in her hands.

The others filled the pit without her help, and they finished long before she regained her composure. When she blinked the last of the tears from her eyes, a shadow still stretched beside her own. Just the one.

Brannon must have wandered off to look after the stranger who had ambled forward shortly after Yana vanished, palms raised and frail legs trembling. Whoever she was, Elwyn hoped she wouldn't stick around long. She couldn't stand looking at her face. It looked too much like Lydia's.

"We should head out," Aedyn said, his voice wavering. "None of us know the dangers of this new world, but it would be best to find shelter before dark."

Elwyn wiped her eyes, glancing over her shoulder. Disheveled and downcast, Aedyn hardly looked like a royal anymore. The façade he'd once worn had shattered to splinters, so that his every muddled emotion could be read on his face. Sorrow, confusion, fear...perhaps a touch of longing.

What a pair they might have been—the remarkably unremarkable thief and the selflessly selfish prince.

"Elwyn?"

"I'm not ready," Elwyn replied. The words meant a lot of things.

"Then I'll wait," Aedyn said.

Perhaps those words meant a lot of things, too. Not that it mattered. If the past few weeks had proved anything, Elwyn was better off with her walls fixed firmly in place. She'd let Lydia slip past her defenses, and now she would forever feel the lack of her.

She couldn't put herself through this ever again.

Once Aedyn left to check on the others, she finally forced herself to stand and take in her new surroundings. The stone circle and everything inside it remained unchanged, but the woods beyond were entirely unfamiliar. Twisted emerald trees, their branches dripping with crystalline fruits, had entangled with common firs and elms, uprooting and displacing them. Whole cliffsides had crumbled away, towers and pillars bursting from the rubble. Something growled in the undergrowth, hidden by strange, floral foliage.

In the distance, Talune stood tall and proud as before, a gilded palace winding through its branches. Elwyn didn't want to think about the Rhysien towns now crushed beneath its roots. She didn't want to think about the souls lost when the worlds collided. She didn't want to think about Luatha, trapped in a sea glass kingdom when the force of two oceans came crashing down.

So she wouldn't think about it.

Not until she absolutely had to.

Forcing her thoughts to the present, Elwyn marched to the edge of the stone circle. Brannon had, indeed, decided to watch over the strange girl. He didn't look particularly happy about it, but he wasn't tensed to fight her, either. He'd changed, perhaps as much as Aedyn had. Though not enough that he wouldn't stab Elwyn for bringing it up.

Without a word, the group gathered their scant belongings and started off toward Talune. Elwyn kept pace despite the heaviness in her feet. She was not ready for whatever challenges lay ahead, but that didn't really matter. There was no choice left but to move forward. Perhaps it would not be as difficult as she imagined.

If Brannon could change…if Aedyn could change…

If the whole *world* could change…

Elwyn could change too.

"The first notes of a faerie reel are chaos, unrehearsed,
But don't assume this fate is sealed, for comes the second verse..."

Thank you for reading! Did you enjoy? Please add your review because nothing helps an author more and encourages readers to take a chance on a book than a review.

And don't miss the next book of the *The Reel of Rhysia* series, THE UNFAMILIAR, for pre-order now! Turn the page for a sneak peek!

You can also sign up for the City Owl Press newsletter to receive notice of all book releases!

SNEAK PEEK OF THE UNFAMILIAR

The darkness reeked of blood and fetid flesh. Kaster inhaled it like rosemary perfume, desperate to remind himself he was not yet among the rotting. He no longer trusted the grit of the bars or the cruel laughter that keened beyond them. He doubted the drum of his pulse and the weight of his limbs.

Death was the one true reminder of life. It could not mock what it had already claimed.

Judging from his hollow stomach and the splintered remains of his fingernails, he'd been steeping in shadows for no less than three days, lulled to a stupor by revels of his captors and the soft scrape of the vines that writhed around his cage. Enough rainwater had trickled through the tendrils to keep him breathing, but not enough to soothe his sandpaper tongue. The fruit the monsters left him had moldered untouched.

Others had been fed to the living walls in that time. Kaster had flinched at their screams, grieved at their prayers, commiserated with their curses. It had been a while since he'd heard so much as a cough, but they were surely still out there, tongues pinched between their teeth as they strained their ears for the cries of imprisoned loved ones.

Creator knows what Kaster would have given to hear Nella's voice again, no matter the context. Sorrow was selfish in that respect.

Not for the first time, he considered shoving an arm through the bars and rooting around until a thorn found an artery. A terse slice in the right direction would bring his misery to an end. Before he could muster the will, a vine shifted, allowing a sliver of light into the darkness. Though sickly green and faint as an afterthought, it served as a vague reminder of the world beyond the wall. Echoes of summer strolls and moonlit dances lent him strength enough to swear. If there existed a concept crueler than hope, he'd yet to make its acquaintance.

Kaster braced for the vines to swallow the glow as they had countless times before. To his astonishment, the sliver grew to a gash, spilling sallow light and laughter. A legion of spidery hands stretched forward, grasped the bars, and jarred his cage from the shadows.

Incandescent lichens spattered the bramble hallway, limning the caprine horns and tapered ears of his captors with a ghastly pall. They were not the fair and noble fae-folk of Rhysien lore, but a feral mockery of the myths, nearly human from the waist up with coarse fur covering them from haunches to hooves. Scarlet sigils painted their bare skin—some glistening wet, others dry and flaking—and bits of bone, still flecked with flesh, had been braided into their hair.

More disturbing than the hunters were their trophies. The captives that hadn't been caged now dangled from the walls like cattle carcasses, pierced through by sickle-sharp thorns. Some had been picked nearly to the bone; others, stripped of clothing and in many cases skin. A few still twitched and trembled, lips gaping around silent screams.

Bile burned Kaster's throat as he scanned the bodies for a swatch of floral linen, a lock of sandy brown hair. A few familiar faces numbered among the broken, but Nella's wasn't one of them. Not that it mattered. If the creatures hadn't yet killed her, it meant only that she was buried in a wall somewhere, waiting for her captors to return and...and...

Just what did they have planned for them, anyway?

Kaster probed the gloom as the monsters jostled him through the halls of their writhing fortress, finding only stray bones and heaps of offal. The corridor wound on for some time before a golden glow drowned the green, and the creatures hefted him into a massive hollow churning with their horrid kin. The throng parted to let them through, and several onlookers jabbed wooden pikes through the bars, cackling madly when Kaster danced to dodge them. The rest followed him with unsettling oval eyes.

A wide patch of earth had been left open at the crowd's center, its russet clay marbled with a red far deeper, more damning. After dropping the cage unceremoniously to the mire, three pairs of hooves trotted off to join their peers. One creature lingered behind, its fingers and teeth stained crimson. "You should feel honored," it said, sliding a key into the cage door. "Not many are afforded this opportunity."

Kaster would take any opportunity offered him. The moment the lock clicked, he rammed the bars with his shoulder, knocking the bastard off balance. Rage propelled him from his confines, but days of disuse stiffened his limbs. He landed only a few strikes before several monsters rushed to intervene. In subduing Kaster, they nearly tore his arms from their sockets.

"Now, now. None of that."

The voice was neither rich nor commanding, but it brought the brutes to heel. They shoved Kaster behind them and melted into the press, ears twitching toward a throne of thorns on the far side of the hollow. Upon it lounged another beast, elbow perched on a bramble armrest and a sharp cheekbone resting between their thumb and forefinger. The creature was neither male nor female, but a bizarrely beautiful blend of both, with burnished bronze horns that curled outward in chaotic spirals and a collar of autumn leaves draped over their torso. A long ebony spear rested across their lap, topped with a horned skull that matched their face for size and shape.

Kaster could only assume this was the beasts' ruler. The fae monarchs of folklore were twice as regal if not half as entrancing, but thrones and scepters—however sylvan—spoke with a certain auspicious tone. Strange, how a legend could prove so false and so true in the same stroke.

"It's poor manners to damage a prop before the play begins." The ruler clucked their tongue. "There are toys aplenty for you to break, and our trove grows greater with every moonrise. Let us not act as scavengers when the hunt has never been more blessed. And as for you..." Their keen ochre eyes flicked to Kaster, and a smile strained their rot-black lips. "Right idea. Wrong target."

The crowd's attention shifted as a second copper cage was carried into the hollow. Shadows rendered the captive a huddled silhouette until a monster jarred the door open and flung them into the clearing. Firelight spilled over sandy tresses, glinting off strands of copper and gold. Kaster's heart plunged to his stomach.

Her cornflower dress was torn and tattered, the skin beneath it mottled plum, but when her sapphire eyes met his, all other hues faded. The same spark that had consumed him when they'd first locked eyes from across a Beltane bonfire sent Kaster sprinting forward, heels slipping on the mire. Nella met him halfway and twined her arms around his waist, burying her face in the crook of his shoulder. He breathed in what little rosemary still clung to her skin, and for one second—one blissful, ignorant second—he was overcome with joy.

Then, he heard the laughter.

It started as snickers, soft and serpentine, then spread through the hollow, swelling to a storm. Kaster went cold. Nella stumbled back. A pair of blackwood short-spears landed in the clay between them.

"Life is a resource reserved for only the strongest of a species." The ruler's voice carried over the clamor. "It is hoarded by violent hands, bought with the blood of the weak, short on supply, and ever in demand." They leaned forward, fingers steepled beneath a wisp of a beard. "You both want it, and I am willing to offer it. To whichever of you proves most worthy."

A stone formed in Kaster's empty gut as they glanced down at the spears. Nella hesitated. Kaster did not.

The moment his fingers wrapped around blackwood, he barreled toward the crowd. He stood no chance of fighting his way to safety, but he could drag a few fae bastards to the grave with him.

The monsters scrambled back from his strikes before pressing in, sneering and shouting. A set of square teeth found his wrist. The spear tore free. Horns rammed his torso, sending him sprawling. Pain branched through his ribcage like lightning, and the landing stole what remained of his breath.

Each cough tasted of copper. Each gasp felt like shattered glass.

"Kaster!" A pair of trembling hands clasped one of his own. When he opened his eyes, Nella's face danced above him in triplicate. "Can you sit up?"

It hurt like hell, but he managed it. The moment her faces melted back into one, he cupped it with his palm, forcing the bitter truth to his lips. "The fae can't lie, right?" Each syllable sparked pain in his side. "If we play by their rules, then one of us...one of us can..."

Nella squared her shoulders. Her eyes were bloodshot from weeping, but there were no tears in them now. Tender though she could be, no one had ever mistaken her for weak. "They want a show," she whispered. "Don't you dare go easy on me."

She tore away without another word. By the time Kaster rose and reclaimed his spear, she was armed and standing at the ready. She could easily have struck while he was down, but it wasn't in her nature. This would be a fair fight. They owed each other that much.

Seconds ticked past in silence as Kaster bolstered his resolve, attempting to reimagine his closest friend as a foe. Nella's trembling jaw set, a sure sign she was doing the same. Their reticence was met with impatient murmurs. Several monsters hurled taunts and curses into the makeshift arena. A few lobbed actual stones. If the horde didn't get a spectacle, and soon, they would claim both combatants' hearts as consolation.

Kaster gave a curt nod. Nella returned it, and they both rushed forward.

Their spears clashed like swords, sending tremors to Kaster's elbows. He twisted his weapon but failed to disarm her. Her strike missed his neck by a hair's breadth. Their every move was cautious and halting—a little too slow, a little too soft—and the result was more a dance than a battle, like the one they'd shared at their wedding feast. Nervous and giddy, they'd both tried to follow the other's lead only to wind up tumbling to the grass. What a vision she'd been, all giggles and lace and white satin ribbons.

Kaster clung to that memory as his spear sliced across her shoulder. Blood wept from the wound, staining her sleeve an unforgiving crimson. The ache that blossomed in his chest was brighter than that of his broken rib. Nella's startled cry set the rabble to cheering. She recovered quickly, flipped her spear, and rammed the butt into Kaster's side. His vision burst with violent sparks that guttered into shadow.

The impact of this head against the ground startled him lucid as Nella crawled atop him, pinning him in place with her knee. For a disoriented moment, he thought she meant to kiss him. How many times had they tangled like this, clothed only in candlelight?

The crowd's cruel heckles jarred him back to the present. He'd lost his weapon in the fall, but Nella's was still clutched close to her chest. The victory was hers, if she'd only take it.

"I...I can't," she whispered, tears streaming down her cheeks. The pink swell beneath her lashes made her eyes shine that much brighter.

"It's alright, love." Kaster forced a feeble smile even as terror spread through his veins. "I've had two years more than you already, and you've made these last four the best they could be. Just make it quick. Please."

Nella drew a shaky breath, whispering an apology as she raised her spear overhead. Kaster closed his eyes, picturing the life they might have built in a kinder world, the life they'd been planning over their morning porridge for years. Children, gardens, a little stucco cottage by the seaside. Resigning it all to dream, he let himself go lax.

He didn't feel himself prying the stone from the clay. Didn't fight its weight as his arm struck forward. But he felt her skull cave. Heard it crack like porcelain.

How heavy he became, as her weight rolled away. How empty. He should have been crying, cursing, condemning himself as another in a world of demons, but he lacked the strength for sorrow and the clarity for contrition. Cluttered as his mind was, it held room for only one coherent thought...

I won.

Promises of fresh air and sunlight drew him to his feet. He was careful not to look Nella's way as he wiped her blood from his fingers, lest a twitch ruin the moment. He needed to believe it had been quick and painless. That she'd died believing he loved her more than himself.

The roar of the throng was distant, dull. An ashen pall had fallen over the hollow, but with every blink, a color returned. Warmth oozed from flickering torches. Clay squelched beneath his soles. Soon, he was lucid enough to catch the musings of the monsters.

"A spear to the gut would do the trick!"

"I say we stick him on the wall and watch him wriggle!"

"How many bones do you suppose we can snap before the screams stop?"

Panic hit Kaster like a flash flood, scouring away what remained of his daze. He turned pleading eyes to the bramble throne, where the ruler welcomed suggestions with enthusiastic waves. "B-but...but you have to let me go!" he shouted, rousing fire in his ribcage. "Your kind can't lie! Y-you said I could live if...if I—"

"I *never* lie." The ruler jabbed a finger his direction. "You're breathing aren't you? Blinking like a halfwit? I know for a fact your heart's still pumping; I can hear its pathetic stutter from here. Just what do you believe you are owed, mortal?" They cocked their head, a smug grin slithering across their face. "I said I'd let you live. I never said how long."

One by one, the creatures turned to face him, hunger gleaming in their oval eyes. At the snap of their ruler's fingers, they rushed forward.

Don't stop now. Pre-order your copy of THE UNFAMILIAR now! And find more from Lilla Glass at www.lillaglass.com

Don't miss the next *The Reel of Rhysia* book, THE UNFAMILIAR, pre-order now, and find more from Lilla Glass at www.lillaglass.com

Months have passed since the old worlds ended, and Elwyn has yet to find her place in the new one. Her fortunes turn when she's presented with the opportunity she didn't know she'd been waiting for: a shot at revenge against the spectral menace whose meddling doomed her closest companions.

Brannon has traded a life of bloodshed for one of incense and mantras, and he regrets the decision. When forced to confront the brutes who shaped him, he becomes more volatile than ever before and seeks out a worthy target for his rage. In setting fire to his past, he might just burn down every bridge he's built since.

Plagued by guilt for failing his friends and kingdom, Aedyn is desperate for redemption but would settle for distraction. A chance for both arises when he's recruited for a dangerous mission involving monsters who could crush his heart with their bare hands and a woman who could do the same with a smile.

Together with a friend they'd thought lost forever, a courageous fae warrior, and the embittered ward of their greatest foe, this ragtag group of ruffians ventures to an uncharted land filled with magic and mayhem. If they can uncover evidence of Unseelie plots, they could turn the tides of an inevitable war. If they fail, they might lose everything they cherish.

Please sign up for the City Owl Press newsletter for chances to win special subscriber-only contests and giveaways as well as receiving information on upcoming releases and special excerpts.

All reviews are **welcome** and **appreciated**. Please consider leaving one on your favorite social media and book buying sites.

Escape Your World. Get Lost in Ours! City Owl Press at www.cityowlpress.com.

GLOSSARY OF FAE

The world of The Unseen is rife with strange and spectacular beings, any one of whom will resent (and possibly maim) you for confusing them with another. For your safety, I've enlisted the help of a certain plucky piskie in comprising this compendium. May it serve you well.

Augusky (ä-güs-kē):

> *"The Shifting Wilds are chaos—the dwelling place of fools,*
> *But these fickle, half-goat shifters despise structure as a rule.*
> *While not expressly evil, they've no respect for life,*
> *To hear their racing hoof-steps is an omen of pure strife."*

Daoine Maithe (dī-nuh mä-hä):

> *"If you run across the light-fae, you are guaranteed to stare,*
> *They're as stunning as a sunrise, and they're very much aware.*
> *These Talunasan denizens dwell 'neath a ceaseless sun,*
> *And bend its brilliance to their will, becoming anyone."*

Daoine Sidhe (dī-nuh shē)-

> *"The residents of Réimsdarg are the meat of many tales,*
> *These giants fight for Justice, Light, and (on occasion) ale.*
> *With magic made for shaping stone, and tactical renown,*
> *They can craft cities in an eve... or smash them to the ground."*

Glaistig (glī-stig)-

"They dance beneath the moonlight and sing a pretty song,
And though you'll try resisting, you're bound to dance along.
It takes less than a measure for your heart to be beguiled,
But in the end, they'll leave your veins as empty as their smiles."

Goblin-

"Some goblin-kind are summoned by a dark and spiteful curse,
Others are shaped by accident when mindless magics merge.
Entropic aberrations in a world with fickle laws,
Be they made of mire or shadows, they are born with eager claws."

Hobgoblin-

"They toil beneath a blood-red sun, mining for gemstone veins,
It's more a hobby than a job, so they seldom complain.
These neighbors of the Daoine Sidhe are generally polite,
They share the goblins' pointed teeth, but do not share their bite."

Korrid Sidhe (kōr-id shē)-

"These ambitious Unseelie truly see their cause as right,
But the wily winter wanderers cannot withstand the light.
They dwell in frigid darkness 'round a palace called Gembread,
And craft a headless army to extend the Shadows' reach."

Leprechaun-

"A leprechaun attired in green might meddle with your luck,
If wearing white, it's on a break and more than likely drunk.
If clothed in red, you'd better run before the chance is gone,
Or better yet, despite their dress, avoid the leprechauns!"

Piskie (pis-kē)-

"A streak of iridescence, giggling as it zips by,
You might think it a dragonfly, if insects spoke in rhyme.

These pert, precocious, wing-ed things can make for decent friends,
But if you dare offend them, they will get swift revenge."

Rot Fae-

"A bit smaller than piskies with brittle leaves for wings,
These pests fly through the Shifting Wilds in search of florid things.
Their fangs produce a venom that can cause instant decay,
So if you chance upon them, you'd do best to walk away."

Sluagh (slü-uh)-

"These souls fell short of Heaven; vast evils weighed them down,
And, either doomed by deeds or deals, Hell swiftly spat them out.
So, now, they weave between the worlds—the vilest of all fae,
And spread their anguish far and wide, awaiting Judgement Day."

Sprite-

"They drift around like pollen, shimmering in the dark,
Like elemental spirits, or maybe simple sparks.
None know whether they think or feel, or if they just react,
But sometimes, if you smile at them, you'll catch them smiling back."

Sylph (silf)-

"The stoic, Spring Isles wind-fae are healers of great skill,
They have a touch like static and white wings that sprout at will.
Many are vowed to silence; the rest are careful with their words,
So, even if they don't reply, have faith that you've been heard."

Undine (uhn-dēn)-

"Some sailors call them sirens although they seldom sing,
And few engage in wrecking ships, despite the mirth it brings.
They breathe both air and water and can grant that gift to you,
But be certain of their motives before they drag you 'neath the blue."

ACKNOWLEDGMENTS

When I first started crafting this story, I did not yet think myself a writer. Thankfully, there were plenty of other people in my life who knew better, and that list began to grow as the tale took shape. I am eternally grateful for each and every one of you.

First and foremost, I owe a huge thanks to the team at City Owl Press —especially my editor, Tee Tate—for giving this strange little story a home, and for being some of the most encouraging, supportive, talented individuals I've ever met. It is an honor and a blessing to be a part of this community!

I am also eternally grateful for my husband and best friend, Justin Glass —a constant source of warmth, encouragement, and, perhaps most importantly, cheesy puns. I have heard rumors that writing is a lonely art. Thanks to you, I don't believe them.

This story would be an unreadable mess without my many critique partners and beta readers: Allie Clause, B.M. Valdez, Patricia Sabensgy, and the Gracewriters, to name a few. A special shout-out to Melissa Bodenhamer and Chani Lupo for trudging through the earliest, ugliest drafts and finding seeing something in them worth sharing, and to Jay Allchin, for claiming he would eat his hat if the book didn't get published. This made querying a win/win situation for me, as I very much wanted to get published, but I also wanted to see someone eat a hat!

This book is, at its core, about family, so I'd be foolish not to acknowledge my own, both those I was born with, and those I stumbled into. Special thanks to my siblings (Angie, Jason, and Eli), my foster family (the Miesses), the families who grafted me into their own at one point or another (Lupos, Ericksons), and my own misfit fellowship of tricksters and ne're-do-wells (You know who you are!) I would like to thank my parents as well. You're no longer with me, but you always encouraged me to be curious and creative. I like to think this would have made you proud.

Last, but certainly not least, I want to thank anyone who picks up this book. I sincerely hope reading it brings you a bit of the joy and whimsy I felt while writing it, and that you will continue to follow my misfit fellowship as their journey continues.

ABOUT THE AUTHOR

LILLA GLASS is an author from Olympia, WA. While fantasy is her first love, she dabbles in horror, sci-fi, and the occasional (gasp) non-speculative work. Her short stories have been published in anthologies by Mystic Owl Press, Papillon du Pere, and Madhouse Books.

In the rare event that she isn't writing, Lilla works one of those pesky day-job thingies, reads stories and poetry she wishes she wrote, hangs out with her husband and bunny, and plays the occasional tabletop RPG.

www.lillaglass.com

instagram.com/lilla.glass.author
tiktok.com/@lilla_glass

ABOUT THE PUBLISHER

City Owl Press is a cutting edge indie publishing company, bringing the world of romance and speculative fiction to discerning readers.

Escape Your World. Get Lost in Ours!

www.cityowlpress.com

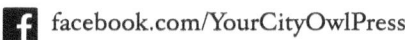 facebook.com/YourCityOwlPress
X x.com/cityowlpress
instagram.com/cityowlbooks
pinterest.com/cityowlpress